HAMMOND INNES

Hammond Innes was born in Sussex in 1913. He has previously written twenty-nine international best-sellers, all of which are now being reissued by Pan. He has also written a superb history of the Conquistadors, two books of his world travels and sailing, and an evocative illustrated book on East Anglia. It was in the early fifties, with books like *The Lonely Skier*, *Campbell's Kingdom*, *The White South* and *The Wreck of the Mary Deare*, all of them filmed, that he achieved international fame.

Also by Hammond Innes

FICTION

Wreckers Must Breathe
The Trojan Horse
Attack Alarm
Dead and Alive
The Lonely Skier
Maddon's Rock
Killer Mine
The Blue Ice
The White South
The Angry Mountain
Air Bridge
Campbell's Kingdom
The Strange Land
The Wreck of the Mary Deare
The Land God Gave to Cain

The Doomed Oasis
Atlantic Fury
The Strode Venturer
Levkas Man
Golden Soak
North Star
The Big Footprints
The Last Voyage
Solomon's Seal
The Black Tide
High Stand
Medusa
Isvik
Target Antarctica

TRAVEL
Harvest of Journeys
Sea and Islands

HISTORY
The Conquistadors

HAMMOND INNES

DELTA CONNECTION

PAN BOOKS

First published 1996 by Macmillan

This edition published 1997 by Pan Books
an imprint of Macmillan Publishers Ltd
25 Eccleston Place, London, SW1W 9NF
and Basingstoke

Associated companies throughout the world

ISBN 0 330 35027 7

Copyright © Hammond Innes 1996

1 3 5 7 9 8 6 4 2

A CIP catalogue record for this book is available from
the British Library

Phototypeset by Intype London Ltd
Printed by Mackays of Chatham PLC, Chatham, Kent

To
KEN and MARY
real friends are beyond price

CONTENTS

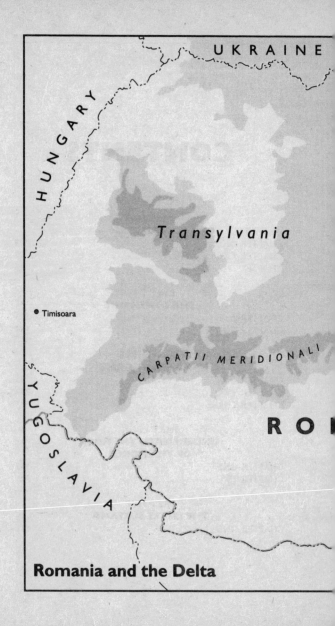

Romania and the Delta

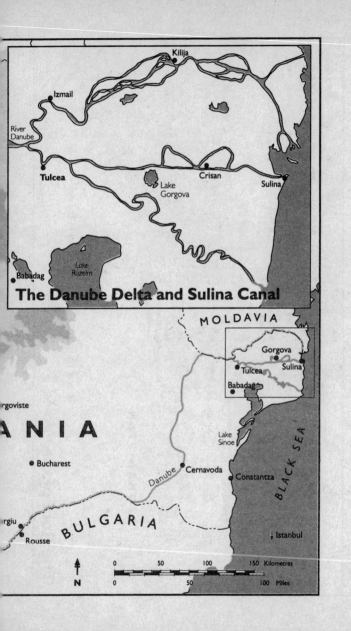

The Danube Delta and Sulina Canal

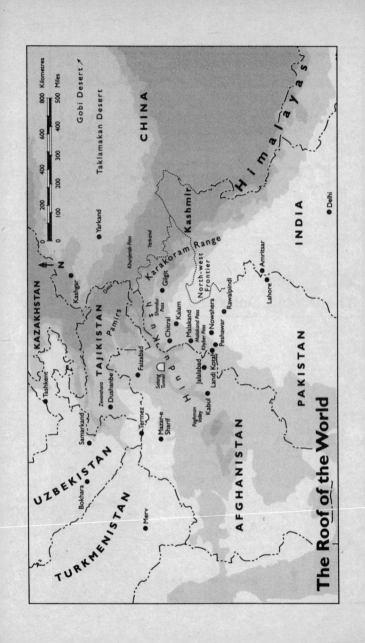

The Roof of the World

PART ONE

RUST

CHAPTER ONE

I said my name and there was a long pause. Then the rattle of a chain and the door was opened by a man I barely recognized. 'I was expecting—' He stared at me. The chainsaw had started up again in the street below, the sound of it quite loud here in this high-ceilinged room with the tall windows facing north and east. It was snowing again, a light drifting, and the room was cold. 'Of course. Your letter. Last week, I think. I got your letter last week.' He nodded, grasping my hand and smiled suddenly, a grimace full of metal teeth. 'They let you in, then.' He was wearing a tattered cardigan under what looked like an old army greatcoat.

I shut the door for him, turning my back, giving myself time to compose my features, I was so shocked. 'I didn't know,' I murmured.

'Of course not. It has been a long time since we last saw each other, and not communicating...' His hair had turned white and he walked with the aid of two sticks, his body bent forward. 'The *Securitate* hold me for almost two years.'

It did not surprise me, remembering some of the talk overheard between him and my Uncle Jamie. 'What had you done?' I asked him.

'I am a writer. You know that. And I try to write the truth. That is all.' His shoulders lifted in a quick, impatient shrug and he resumed his seat by the window. 'But then they want names. They want the names of my friends, my associates.' He waved me to a chair. 'Bring it over here, beside me. I am a little deaf now. And that saw – he has been logging up for two whole days. He does it for several of the people in this street, and the sound of it going on and on . . .'

But at that moment it stopped. 'Soon we have heat,' he said, rubbing his mittened hands together and smiling that metal grimace. A long silence followed, and sitting there in the stillness of that bare, bleak room, I was overcome by a feeling of sadness. Once, he and his wife had owned the whole building. I remembered her as a tall, full-bosomed, stately woman, dark, with a quiet beauty. Her name was Ana and she was half Scots, half Romany, her father the chief engineer of a small tanker that had been lost in a storm off the Turkish coast when bound for Istanbul.

I asked after her, but he didn't answer, talking instead about the house and the way things had changed for him. He had just the one room now and the few pieces of furniture in it. The desk I remembered. And the chair he was sitting on, a high-backed antique chair with crude tapestry that had a Turkish

4

look to it. Bought in the bazaars of Istanbul, probably; the Bosporus was only a short voyage south by ship along the Bulgarian Black Sea coast. The same tall, ornate cast-iron stove thrust its flue in a long curve up the chimney of what had once been an open grate.

'And Vikki?' I asked. 'Is she all right?' It was four years since I had last seen her. I had written twice, but she hadn't replied. 'Did she get my letters, do you know?'

'Oh, yes. Ana tell me. That was just before . . .' He fell suddenly silent then, a frozen look on his face and the fingers of his right hand beating out an agitated tattoo on the arm of his chair.

'Why didn't she write, then?' You would think the daughter of a journalist . . . 'Is she all right?' I asked again.

The fingers were suddenly still, the grey eyes staring at me, the mouth a tight-shut line. 'Yes, she is all right. I think so.'

'And your wife?'

There was a pause, and then he said, 'Ana . . .' The sound of his wife's name hung on the air between us. 'They cannot hurt her now, not any more. I am sure of that. And Vikki,' he went on quickly, 'she is all right, I am quite sure. She never writes, but – yes, I am sure.'

'Still dancing?' I was remembering that first time we had met, a sudden mental picture of those startling, almost emerald-green eyes of hers half closed, the face set as though in a trance and her body, taut and hard, against mine.

'How do I know what she is doing now?' He said it almost angrily, then added, 'She is a very strange young woman.'

'Where is she, do you know?'

He did not answer for a moment, his face turned to the window, lost in his own thoughts. Finally he said, 'The one time I hear from her she is in Kazakhstan. She is safe there I think. I hope so.' And he went on, speaking quickly now, 'If she had been an acrobat the State would have sent her all over the world. But she is a dancer. That is not the same. So in the end she smuggle herself out of this port here in an old Greek freighter bound for Odessa. After that I hear nothing until a man who look like a Jewish rabbi, but is American I think, come to see me—' He shook his head. 'I don't know. Dancing is a strange world. This man tell me she is taken up by a member of one of the ancient khan families. He don't give me his name or say which of the khanates it is he belongs to. But she is well and she send me messages, and to Ana of course. She don't know about Ana . . .' He stopped there, and I didn't say anything, the look on his face shutting me out.

The silence that followed was almost overpowering. It filled the room. Then the chainsaw started up again, and the noise of it was almost a relief. I got up and went across to the window. The truck standing parked against the wire at the top of the escarpment had delivered five large-diameter tree trunks, but only one had so far been logged up. The logger seemed to be having some difficulty with his saw, a strange contraption, something like a mechanized bowsaw.

'You have a fine view from here,' I murmured, staring out at the vast expanse of Constantza port, watching the drifting powder of the snow.

'*Da*. It is a good view, full of interest. But it does not change and I never go out.' Then, quite abruptly, he seemed to pull himself together, turning to me with a sudden smile. 'I remember now. When you first met. She was just five. And you—?' His tufted eyebrows lifted as he frowned in concentration. 'You were about seven, I believe your uncle said.'

That had been at the Dunărea, a restaurant overlooking the old harbour and the Romanian Naval Headquarters. I nodded, my mind switching with relief to my Uncle Jamie, who had lived a relatively normal life and had died in his sleep. James Henry Long had been a marine surveyor and shortly after he retired he had agreed to check the costings of a small bulk carrier that was in for repairs at one of the three Constantza shipyards. She had been in collision with a Turkish freighter at the Marmara end of the Dardanelles.

I remembered that very clearly because it was all mixed up in my mind with my first visit to a foreign land, my first flight in an aircraft, and of course my first meeting with Vikki. He never told me why he suddenly decided to take me with him to Romania, but looking back on it, I think he felt it would help me to forget how bad things had been at home since my mother had remarried.

We had stayed with some people he knew, a B. & B. arrangement in an apartment just off the road leading up to the Archaeology and Natural History Museum.

A big motherly soul, with a fat, round face and very straight, coarse hair and eyebrows, kept an eye on me during the daytime, and in the evenings my uncle would take me for a walk round the town – 'to get the rust and the smell of oil and bilge water out of my lungs'. I always remember that, rust, oil and the smell of the ships' bilges. Somehow it had filled me with excitement. I can't think why, when there was so much that was new to see as we explored the Tomi district, which is the oldest part of Constantza, and walked out to the end of the original harbour wall. From there one could see what a natural defensive position the Tomi headland must have been. Now it was dominated by the elegant white building of the Naval Head-quarters, and below it was the esplanade circling the massively ornate casino building.

Sometimes we would sit and have coffee looking out across the Black Sea, which was nearly always uninviting and restless. Occasionally a navy helicopter would land on the hardstanding below the navy build-ing. Finally, about eight o'clock, we would go either to the Casa en Lei or to the Dunărea for our evening meal. The food was always much the same, and never exciting, but my uncle said the wine was good. He thought it too strong for me so I had it diluted with water and didn't like it much.

What I did like was the Dunărea itself, and that because of Vikki. There was a dance band and leader with a big moustache and a microphone, and that first time I saw her, as soon as he had started to sing and the band had struck up, she came trotting out on to the

floor, her expression one of total absorption. The floor
was a few square metres of polished wood set against
the platform on which the bandleader and his four
players were grouped, the tables huddled round three
sides of it. I remember my uncle saying afterwards
how surprised he had been, for this was about twenty
years ago and they were playing North American rock.

After all this time the scene was still vivid in my
mind, that little figure, alone on the floor, the pink of
her cotton frock bobbing up and down, her ribbon
tied in a bow flapping against her flaxen head of hair,
and her dancing so wild, her little face so trembling
with concentration, that the whole restaurant watched
spellbound.

All except me. I was already jazz mad and the
percussion beat had my feet tapping, my body swaying, so that in an instant I had joined her. It just seemed
I couldn't help myself, and she had paused in her
dancing, staring at me, her mouth puckered as though
she were about to burst into tears, her eyes narrowed
to slits of hostility. Then, suddenly, she grabbed hold
of my hands, pulled me to her, and I found her hard,
compact little body pressed against mine, her eyes
gradually becoming glazed as though lost in a trance
– and we had danced, and danced, and danced, making
up the steps as we whirled around.

That had been the beginning of a childhood
relationship. I don't think one could call it friendship,
or even anything more personal. I was the right age
and I could dance. That was all that mattered to her.
She and her parents were at the Dunărea almost every

night the band was playing, and because my uncle was a kind man and probably felt it would help to keep my mind off how bad things had been back home in Fremantle before my mother shipped me off to live with him in England, we often ended up eating at their table. This went on for several months, for he was engaged to survey other ships for Lloyd's as they came out of the yards.

I asked Vikki's mother once whom she danced with when I was not there. 'Nobody,' she replied stiffly. 'She dance on her own – always. Give her music and . . .' She smiled, then gave a little shrug. 'She make up her own dance. She does not need anyone else. Except you, of course,' she had added quickly, smiling at me, the dark, heavy features lighting up as she stared into my face. I think now there may have been a speculative look in her eyes, but that could be imagination. To me, at that age, Vikki was just a little girl who could dance me to a standstill. In any case, by the end of the year ship surveys had become fewer, until my uncle had no more work in Romania and we returned to his little house in the dockland area of London.

Two more visits in succeeding years, 1970 and 1971, and after that I was at school and didn't see Vikki again for almost ten years. It was in 1980 that I was next in Constantza, staying with my uncle at the Intim Hotel on the Tomi Peninsula with its view over the port. By then Ceauşescu was in power and conditions had worsened. I had written to Vikki several times, of course, but she never replied and her father sent word that it was not advisable for us to communicate. That fourth visit was much shorter than the others, but it seemed in fact longer. So many impressions – Vikki in the full flush of sexual awareness, the things people told me, talk I overheard. I had learned the language by then, and it shook me, the terrifying, heart-rending stories.

And now, here I was back again, and Vikki, she would be in her middle twenties. She had a 'protector' and had been smuggled out of the country. I asked him for an address where I could contact her in Kazakhstan, but he shook his head. I thought perhaps he was putting me off for political reasons, but it wasn't that. 'I do not know,' he admitted reluctantly. He looked suddenly sad, almost bewildered. 'I just do not know.' The words seemed drawn out of him.

What could I say to this ghost of a man whom I had last seen when he was full of vigour, his brain alive with thoughts about all the fundamental issues of the day that affected his country, Europe, the world? I knew he loved her dearly and to have to admit he didn't know where she was – I could see it hurt him.

He had been the senior editor on one of the leading newspapers when we first met him, dealing with the art and book pages, theatre, also travel, in the Soviet Union mainly, and in his spare time he wrote as a freelance, chiefly for *Zig-zag*.

'I thought I heard something,' he said. He was leaning forward now, craning his neck to peer over the narrow balcony to the street below. 'A motor bicycle, was it?'

'Sounded more like a car. Are you expecting someone?'

He hesitated, his fingers drumming once more against the smooth-polished wood. 'Yes,' he said finally. 'Once I know what has happened today I can finish the piece I have written and it can go to the printers.' Then to himself he muttered, 'He would be on his motor bicycle, I am sure of that. A car would be too big, too slow in the mountains.'

I didn't say anything, sitting there, staring out of the window at the first glimmers of light appearing across the vast expanse of the port. There was a strange air of expectancy in the room, of tension almost. Then, finally, he muttered, 'We are near the end now. I really do believe Laszlo Toekes started a fire Ceauşescu will not be able to put out.'

I realized he was talking about Timisoara. Laszlo Toekes was a Hungarian pastor of the Calvinist Reformed Church. He had ignored the Government order to leave Timisoara, and the population, Romanian as well as Hungarian, had taken to the streets. There had been several journalists on the flight from Stansted to Bucharest's Otopeni Airport. That was how I knew about it.

'Not long now,' he said again in a much more positive tone of voice, as though trying to convince himself. 'Today – or is it tomorrow? No, I think it is today Ceauşescu return from Tehran. He is gone there to clinch a deal with the Iranians for some important defence contracts. His wife, Elena, has been left to govern in his absence. With the help of Manescu, that henchman of theirs. It is they who are having to deal with this situation. Either he has misjudged it . . .' He looked round at me quickly. 'What do you think? I only hear what the radio say.' But he did not wait for a reply. 'It will be tomorrow, then. It will be decided tomorrow. It has to be. And tomorrow is Thursday?'

I nodded. 'Thursday, December the twenty-first.'

'Good. Thursday is my lucky day.' Then he asked me what I thought the outcome would be. 'All Ceauşescu can talk about is that it is one great international conspiracy. He does not seem to realize that in Hungary, Poland, Czechoslovakia, Yugoslavia, all the countries across our borders, and in Russia too, Communism is crumbling. It is like when you set dominoes up – no, those edifices they build with cards, or matches – *pouff*. And one by one they fall till the whole structure is in ruins. Already only Romania and Albania appear untouched by the new revolution.'

He had switched to his own language, his voice gathering strength, his mind honing the phrases. It was as though he was regurgitating something he had already written, or something he planned to write. He was speaking very fast, the words tumbling out of his mouth, those dreadful teeth seeming to get in the way.

And then he switched back into English. 'The militia could not handle it once the students from the Polytechnic and the University were out in the streets, raiding the bookshops, burning the books. No, not real books, but those swollen, repetitive pamphlets of Ceauşescu's. The President's own writings publicly burnt!'

Suddenly he leaned forward, gripping my arm, the moisture of his intensity catching the light, spittle gleaming on those teeth. 'I tell you, Paul, it is very close to the end now. Milea send the army in, and the *Securitate*, the whole big column given tank support – and all they do is roll across the city to the western suburbs, the area nearest to Hungary, and settle in to the barracks there. No shots fired. A few baton charges. That is all.'

A pause, and then he went on, 'That was last night. Some arrests were made, that is all. The Defence Minister, Vasile Milea, is afraid if he crack down too hard it will infuriate the crowds. But today – today is Wednesday. Today may be different. The telephone no longer works. The radio is jammed with martial music . . .' His voice trailed away.

'I have done what I can,' he went on, but slowly now, a reflective tone as though he was speaking to himself. 'I write a long article for *Ellenpontock*. I don't know if they publish it yet. And a pamphlet. A dissident press at some concealment they have in a basement in Rimnicu Vilcu, which is a town at the entrance to one of the passes through the south Carpathian mountains. They print a hundred thousand copies. That is more than my book.' He nodded. 'Yes, I wrote a book. It was much talked about.'

Another pause, a longer one this time, his mind seemingly far away. My mind, too, for I was wondering what it was that drove a man like Mihai Kikinda. A lovely wife, a daughter whose feet were forever dancing, a secure position as arts editor on the best paper in Bucharest, and this house looking out across the port to the concrete robots that kept the restlessness of the Black Sea at bay. In a dangerous country few men had been better placed. And then to throw it all away, to attack the system, deliberately, knowing what the end must be. Why? What compulsion drove him? Was it idealism, or the need to satisfy his ego, to prove he was more than just a journalist? Why do men – some men . . . ?

He was talking again, about the book he had written. He had a lonely man's urge to talk. 'I was not very kind to the Government and they don't like that. It sold well, and they don't like that either. But it is lei the publisher pay me and that is nothing. Every day, every month, it devalues itself. It is really only worth what you can get for it in the shops, and the shops are empty. So all it bring me is trouble. Like any good writer, my thoughts are in advance of events. But now . . .' He shook his head.

A suppressed sigh and his mood changing, he suddenly asked again why I was here. 'If it is not Timisoara, then what? I am surprised you are allowed in. I was told last night that today, or per'aps tomorrow, all the customs posts will be closed, no aircraft, no transport, no communications, the whole country sealed off from the outside world. You must have known it was dangerous. Only Romania and Albania still adhere to the old, hard Brezhnev line. So why do you come if you are not a journalist?'

I nodded towards the window. 'Because of that,' I said. The house was perched high up on the very tip of the Tomi Peninsula, the whole port spread out before us. It was nightfall now and the lights were coming on. Directly below us was the railway line. No trains moving. And beyond the railway line was a cruise liner. No activity on it. Five kilometres of docks stretching as far as the eye could see, the largest port on the Black Sea and the largest in Europe after Rotterdam. A whole enormous area full of ships encased in a sea wall composed of monstrous club-headed, star-shaped blocks of concrete so that it looked as though it was perpetually being stormed by a besieging army of petrified robots.

I mentioned the plan to extend it another two kilometres to the south, out by Agigea, and he said, with a glimmer of his old enthusiasm, 'Agigea will be a free port, like Sulina at the entrance to the Danube delta. Per'aps.' And he added, with that ghastly smile, 'There is nothing free in Romania now, except death.'

Silence then, and I stared out at the port. It was one of the best views to be had of it, the cruise ship right below us, painted white with yellow trimmings, and, out along the northern breakwater, the navy ships, all grey camouflage, and a tanker moving slowly with a Panamanian flag at the mast. Apart from these vessels, the whole port reeked of neglect and disrepair. The ships lying alongside, the sheds, everything patched with rust, the red dust of it drifting in clouds from the wheels of trucks moving along the quays. I had managed to walk part of the quay that morning, explaining at the gate that I was looking for the captain of the *Suleiman* C, an old Turkish cargo vessel I had once taken passage on from Alexandria to Ródhos. The fact that I was staying at the Intim Hotel, which was reserved for ships' captains and those with port business, was what got me through the gate without a work pass.

I stood up and asked if I could open the French window. Leaning out against the balustrade, I could see the main gate to the port some two hundred feet below me away to the left, and opposite it the Port Office. And beyond that . . . I had never seen such a concentration of rusting ships, and more waiting off for a vacant berth. Feeling in my pocket, I turned and handed Mihai Kikinda the letter I had brought with me from London. 'If you care to read this, sir,' I said, 'it may help to explain both what my job is and why I am here asking you for an introduction.'

He got up and hobbled across to the desk, fumbling for his reading glasses. They were thick-lensed and steel-rimmed, so that his appearance became even more ghostlike as he stood there, balancing himself against the desk and going slowly through the letter. 'So you have both legal and merchant banking experience?' He folded it up and handed it back to me. 'And you are here to carry out what amounts to a feasibility study of this scrap project?' He resumed his seat. 'Well, you have only to look out of that window, or go to Sulina, to see that there is no shortage of the raw material. There is scrap everywhere. And not only in the ships laid up. There is scrap in the factories, machinery abandoned and disintegrating, and on the land—' He checked, his head on one side, listening. A vehicle was bumping along the potholed track that ran along the lip of the escarpment, the sound of it fading away as it turned into the next street, leading up towards the mosque and the main square.

'That was definitely a car,' I said.

He nodded. 'So that is not from Timisoara and I must be patient. We must wait.'

'For news?' I asked him.

'Yes. News of what has happened there today. News that may mean the beginning of the end . . .' He shook his head. 'That, I think, is too much to hope. It is so easy, when you are alone like I am, to fantasize.' And he went on to talk about the newspaper article he had already written. It was there in a secret drawer of his desk, something much more outspoken than he had been able to publish so far, except in the underground press, the samizdat. 'The Hungarian minority in Timisoara is very strong. They are well organized. Laszlo Toekes himself is Hungarian, which gives some substance to Nicolae Ceauşescu's constant cry of an 'international conspiracy'. For him that explains everything, the collapse of Communism in all the surrounding countries – everything. In that he includes Russia. Nobody loves the Russians. He knows that, and he plays on it. He is a peasant, with a peasant's cunning. Political sagacity, even. But Ceauşescu is gone to Iran and today everything depends on the army. If they have been given the order to shoot—' He paused, his eyes half closed. 'Will they obey? That is the question. Will they massacre their own people? If they fire on the people, then it is no longer the People's Army. That could be the torch that sets the whole country alight, and the demonstrations may spread beyond Timisoara. Then I must rewrite what I have already written.' Again he paused, listening. 'When he comes I think it best you go behind that curtain there.' He gestured over his shoulder. 'The toilet is there. It is a bucket. That is all. When it is full, or it begins to smell, then Vanya empties it for me. But it is all right for the moment.'

I asked him why I should hide from his visitor. He just sat there, frowning, the fingers of his right hand fidgeting again. At length he said, 'Because I don't know who it will be. If things have gone badly —' He stopped there, suddenly staring at me almost angrily. 'I don't think you realize . . . No, why should you? I have a position in my country. The books I have written. Not published, I know. But privately circulated. They have had a large readership, so that, with my articles, and also what has happened to me – what they have done to me – and to Ana . . .' His fingers increased their drumming, and as he turned his head away I saw there were tears in his eyes. 'You know about that, do you – what has happened to her?'

I shook my head.

'Don't you read about it? In your papers?' He laughed. At least I think it was a laugh. 'No, of course not. It was kept very quiet. But a Russian diplomat was there, and later he talked.'

'What happened to her?' I asked, for he had fallen suddenly silent, and the look on his face . . . 'What happened, for God's sake?'

'Listen!' He held up his hand, turning to the window and pushing it open again. The car was back. The same car, I was certain of that. And then it stopped.

I jumped up, thrusting past him and peering over the balcony rail. It was a black saloon spattered with mud, a Dacia by the look of it, and parked right below me. A man got out of the driving seat, looked up quickly, then hurried inside.

'Quick!' Mihai had joined me on the balcony. 'In the toilet.'

'Why?'

The metal teeth gleamed in the light from a nearby street lamp. 'Something has happened. It is not the man I am expecting.'

'Who then?'

'*Securitate*, most like. Quick!' His hand was on my arm, thrusting me towards the alcove. I could feel his trembling. 'Please. They do not permit me to see foreigners.'

'The stairs,' I said. 'I'll go down the stairs.' But I hesitated, unwilling to leave him, and by the time I got to the door I could hear the man's footsteps on the landing below.

'Please,' he said again, and I was so appalled at the sick, scared look in his eyes that I did as he asked. With the heavy curtain pulled across, the interior of the alcove was very dark, the chemical-toilet smell much stronger. I felt for the seat and sat down just as the door of his room was burst open. 'Mihai?' The voice was almost musical, like that of an Italian tenor.

And then, quite clearly, I heard Mihai cry out, 'Oh, my God!' in English and in a voice that was full of hatred and despair. '*Tu!* Why you? What do you want?' There was a rustle of papers and through a chink in the curtain I saw him retreating back to his chair, his eyes wide and appalled. 'Miron!'

'*Da. E mie.*'

The man moved quickly into my line of vision, leaning down and bending over Mihai, a thickset man in a raincoat. That was all I could see of him, and the two of them speaking very rapidly. They were speaking in Romanian, of course, and too fast for me to understand, but the impression I got was that they knew each other. The power saw started up again and after that I couldn't hear them at all. Miron! Miron who? Was this the man who had arrested Mihai's wife years ago, the man who had had her beaten up, then sent to a clinic to be operated on so that she would never be able to bear children? Uncle Jamie had told me about that. Not the first time we came over. He would have thought me too young then, but later, on the aircraft, flying in to Otopeni the second time. Miron? But I couldn't be certain after all this time if that was the name he had said. A monster! I remembered he had described the man as a monster, but he hadn't said why exactly. It was Vikki who, with no inhibitions whatsoever, had filled in the details for me.

'*Unde? Unde?* Where? Where?' The voice was suddenly raised, no longer musical, but harsh and demanding, so that it got through to me above the noise of the chainsaw, and the vibrancy of it made me think it safe to pull the curtain further from the wall. 'Where? Damn you, where?' The sound of the logger's saw ceased abruptly and in the silence I heard the words quite clearly. 'You tell me. If you don't—' His hands had clamped themselves round Mihai's neck, closing over his windpipe. 'You tell me. Now!' I can still see those hands. They were thick and stubby like his body, with black hair on the backs and on the knuckles.

'You know what this is, don't you?' He let go of Mihai's neck, thrusting a muddy, crumpled notebook into his face, thrusting it so violently he might have been trying to ram it down Mihai's throat. 'You don't answer. But you know what it is. Lies. Lies written by your friends in Timisoara. All lies. And you – you are going to publish it. Where? Who is the printer?'

Silence then, the two of them face to face, staring at each other, Mihai's eyes very wide, his lips trembling. And then, in a sudden determined effort to assert himself, he demanded to know how Miron had got hold of the notebook.

To my surprise the man told him, in detail. They had stretched a wire across the road. In the mountains, he said, between Slatina-Tinis and Armenis. There was something else I couldn't catch, but then he added on a rising note of excitement that it had caught the motorcyclist across the throat so that his head had been practically severed from his body. 'It is Adrian Brasov. We have fix that wire very good, eh? Is perfect.' There was a note of satisfaction in his voice. 'The neck is broken, very neatly where it join the backbone.' He

22

said it quietly with a chop of his hand across his throat, a clinical report as though it was all in a day's work and a job well done. Then he was leaning down, reaching for Mihai's windpipe again, tightening his grip as he repeated his demand for the name of the printer.

And there was that obstinate look on Mihai's face. He had made up his mind. He wasn't going to tell him.

The man would kill him. I could see it in his face and as he reached for his scarf the thought was in my mind that they were related in some way. Miron! But I couldn't remember the name Miron ever being mentioned, not even by Vikki. Had *she* known who had had her mother's reproductive organs removed? That was when the thought entered my head. Vikki had been seventeen then, and she had been telling me about something that had happened to her mother at least twenty years before. Before she was born.

The saw had started up again and Miron was shouting, the two of them struggling and Mihai's face becoming congested as he gasped for air. I suppose that was what did it, the sight of his face as the scarf was twisted and tightened, the whistling gasp as he struggled to breathe, the blood in his cheeks congesting, turning blue. My muscles became suddenly tense, my whole body nerve-taut, poised for the leap, the same feeling inside me I had had when my mother's lover had accused me of being a coward, taunting me, up there in the bows of *Waltzing Matilda* with the seas breaking over us, surf up to our waists and the weight of the water wrenching at my handhold on the stainless steel of the pulpit. 'You wouldn't dare,' he had taunted, reading my mind with the red lips smiling through that little black beard.

I parted the curtain gently. No sound, only the two of them struggling, the man called Miron with his legs straddled and his shoulders heaving as he braced himself to hold Vikki's father – yes, I was still thinking of him then as Vikki's father – and the man's legs wide apart, his testicles there to receive the toe of my shoe.

It was an open invitation, and what happened then happened in a flash. I was suddenly out there, and my leg swinging for the kick. I put everything I had into it. I couldn't bear the thought of Vikki's poor wretch of a father being imprisoned again and subjected to more torture.

Crazy? Of course it was crazy. And he wasn't her father. He couldn't be. It was done on the spur of the moment, without thinking of the consequences, of what might happen later – to Mihai, to myself. This was a police state, and I was attacking a member of the police, the *Securitate*.

I felt my instep connect, the softness of his vulnerable parts, the sense of flesh and gristle yielding, the man jerking and sagging, Mihai's arm jabbing up at him, clutching for support. There was a pause, a moment of stillness as I reached down to grab hold of the man's throat. The scream came just as I caught hold of his raincoat collar, a high-pitched scream. It lasted only a second, then disintegrated into a clotted gurgle, the body suddenly jerking in spasm, then sagging, a dead weight collapsing over Mihai, the arms draped round his neck.

I was off balance and I half collapsed, my nerves numb and my body limp. There was a long silence. At least it seemed like that. And then I heard Mihai say, 'Thank you, Paul.' A tight little nervous laugh and he added quietly, 'It seems we both had the same idea.'

That was when I saw the knife. I was lying virtually face down across the *Securitate* man's body and Mihai was gripping the black plastic haft of one of those cheap little kitchen paring knives. I watched him pull it out from below the ribcage, blood on the blade and blood dripping on his cardigan, the knife so close I could have licked the red gore off the blade. For a moment that primitive, ugly thought was there in my mind, but then it was overlaid by the realization that the man might be dead. What the hell had I got myself into?

I levered myself up, at the same time turning the body over. A nerve was still twitching in the tight-curled fingers of his right hand. His eyes, wide open in shock, stared up at me, dark and glazing. Dead!

'He's dead,' I said.

Mihai nodded.

I was on the edge of panic then. 'What do we do now?'

'You go,' he said, thrusting upwards with his hands and rolling himself clear of the body. 'Did anybody see you when you arrived? Who let you in?'

'A woman,' I said. 'A dark, thickset woman in a shapeless woollen jacket.'

'Lydia.' With the aid of a chair he forced himself to his feet. 'You must go.' His body was trembling uncontrollably, but it is the face that sticks in my mind, the look of utter despair. 'Check out of the Intim Hotel. Say you have been called away – to Bucharest, anywhere. You can lose yourself in Bucharest. The police, even more the *Securitate*, will have bigger problems to deal with than this.' He indicated the inert figure sprawled at his feet, pausing for breath.

And then in a sudden rush of words: 'There were almost a hundred thousand people crammed into the centre of Timisoara today. That's what Adrian had written in that notebook of his. A third of the city's population. And, as always when things are bad for the Party, trainloads of workers were brought in to support the regime. But when they saw the crowds and discovered what was happening they joined the demonstrators. It's all there in Adrian's notes. Members of the *Securitate* were defecting and some of the military, returning to their barracks, flew white flags over their tanks. Everything in a state of confusion.'

He paused, his hands still trembling. But he had taken a grip of himself now, and after a moment he went on, speaking more slowly. 'There is also trouble in Cluj and Tirgu Mures, and that' – he pointed to the body – 'that man accuse me of being partly to blame, particularly here in Constantza where there are all sorts of rumours and people gathering in some of the streets. That is why he was sent, to stop me writing more of the truth.' He paused again, swallowing hard and rubbing his neck. 'Everything depend now upon the army and Ceauşescu. If Nicolae is decisive – if he act with firmness – and if Milea, the Minister of Defence, support him . . .' The little shrug and the wry smile said it all. 'I must do what I have to do, what Ana would have wished, God rest her soul –' this last said almost in a whisper.

He bent and picked up the cheap little red-covered book with its muddied, crumpled pages, lined as though it was a school exercise book. 'It is all here,' he said again. 'I have only to write the details into my letter to the people.' He nodded, still running his hand over the back of his neck, massaging the muscles. 'Yes, I am writing it in the form of a letter. It is more direct. More personal, eh?'

His eyes were bright now, an almost fanatical gleam, and he was looking directly at me. 'Can you deliver it?'

I didn't know what to say. Between us we had just killed a member of the *Securitate* and now he was asking me to involve myself politically by acting as courier for what sounded like a highly inflammatory document. 'I've only just arrived here,' I reminded him. I had no idea what checkposts there were or whether there were army or police patrols out in the streets of Constantza. I didn't even know whether there was a curfew in force, and when I asked him he didn't know either.

'Take his raincoat and hat. You drive that Dacia of his. Nobody will stop you. Not tonight. And you take it to this address.' He hobbled across to the desk, slumped down and picked up a pen. 'But first you check out of your hotel.' He scribbled down an address on a slip of paper and handed it to me. 'The man's name is Dumitru. It is a little food shop in Basahabi, which is just outside Constantza on the road to Bucharest. His name is on the front of the shop.'

The whole thing was absurd, quite impossible. I looked down at the body sprawled at my feet, wondering what to do with it. I couldn't leave it here. If they found it in his room . . . I started to explain, but he waved me to silence. He was sitting hunched over a wad of handwritten pages, his pen moving fast over a blank page. 'I'll see if I can carry him downstairs.'

'Don't interrupt. I'm writing.'

'If I can get him out without anybody seeing me . . .'

'Later, later.' He shushed me with a wave of his hand.

And after that I couldn't get anything out of him. He was completely engrossed in the words he was scribbling down. And when I opened the door to the stairs I heard the sound of voices, two people, a man and a woman, on the first-floor landing.

I gave up then, sitting there, waiting in the still, silent room, realizing it was up to me to get rid of the body, and wondering how I could get it down the stairs and into the vehicle without being seen. It was snowing again, a festive fluttering of large flakes like white butterflies.

Mihai had the answer to my first problem, and it was brutally simple. 'You push his body over the balcony here. But for that you must wait until the street lights are out.'

He had finished his writing by then, and when I said it hadn't taken him long, he smiled, a touch of pleasure and pride. 'Most of it was already written. The little extra I have now written is done at speed, in the great heat of passion, and it is good.' He nodded. 'Yes, I think so.' He sat back, his eyes half closed. 'I wish Ana were here to read it. I think she would approve.' He went back to his chair by the window. 'I miss her,' he went on, speaking slowly, almost dreamily. 'Now there is nobody to criticize what I write. Nobody whose judgement I respect. And nobody to praise me when it is good.' His lips spread in a little secret smile. 'She made my writing so much more—' He hesitated for the word, and then added, 'So much more fun.'

'Who is he?' I asked, my mind still on the disposal of the body. If I pushed it over the balcony rail ... Then if they eventually caught up with me my story would have to be a good one. Tipping it over into the street, it would certainly make a noise as it hit the tarmac. It would be messy, too. And then I had to get down the stairs unobserved, get the battered wretch into the Dacia, drive it to some spot where nobody would find it, at least for several days.

Where?

The chainsaw, which had been silent for some time, started up again, the sound of it tearing at my brain, confusing me. Suppose somebody saw him fall ... However badly he was injured there was still the knife wound. I couldn't see any possible way of explaining that.

But Mihai's thoughts had leapt ahead of me. 'After you have handed Dumetru the pages to print, you go out of Bucharest to the west, Route 70. You find Adrian, the courier they kill. You leave his body there and they will think there is a fight between him and Adrian and that is how he is killed. It will explain everything, eh?'

I shook my head. Of all the crazy ideas! 'It will be snowing up there in the mountains. Suppose I can't find your friend's body. And where do I get petrol?'

'A shop. You ask at a shop. You have dollars?'

I nodded.

'Then no problem. There is a black market. They are all in it, the shopkeepers, and the taxi drivers, most of them anyway. And dollars is what they like. Dollars will buy you anything. It is the black-market currency.'

'And you expect me—' I shook my head. 'Impossible!' He hadn't thought it through properly. The Dacia would already have covered well over 800 kilometres. Unless he had just filled the tank— I looked down at the body again. The eyes were fully glazed now, a dark, almost gypsy brown, and the skin of his face matched the eyes despite the loss of blood. 'Who is he?' I asked.

'*Securitate*.'

'Yes, but his name?'

'It is not important.' He dismissed it with a wave of the hand. 'Once he is disposed of, you either go back to Bucharest, to the security of your Embassy there, or you take to the street, mix with the crowds and watch what happens.' He leaned towards me. 'Go home to England as soon as you feel it is safe to pass through Immigration, and of course when you have your flight booking.'

'Before I do all those things—' My mind was still on the blanket-wrapped bundle at my feet. 'You knew him, didn't you? As soon as he came in . . .' I hesitated, seeing the closed look on his face. But I had to know. 'There is a connection between you. Right?' That had been the implication. 'Is he a journalist, somebody you worked with? What's his other name? You called him Miron. Miron who?'

He stared at me, obstinately silent, the fingers of his right hand becoming agitated. And I sat there, waiting, until at last he said, 'Dinca. His name is Miron Dinca. We were at school together. Then afterwards . . . we went different ways.'

'He turned to Communism?'

'*Da.*'

'But before you went your different ways you were friends. Is that what you're saying?'

'No. Never!' The explosiveness of his denial was absolute. 'We were never friends. Never!'

I could get nothing more out of him after that. He just sat there with that shut look on his face. But it didn't matter. The man was dead, and I became engrossed in my reaction to that fact, the sense of elation. I hadn't killed him. Neither the kick I had given him nor my hands gripping at his throat had been the cause of death. His fingers had been forcing mine apart, their strength powered by desperation and a determination to continue breathing. It was the knife that had killed him.

I knew that. Yet I was full of a sense of elation. It frightened me. It frightened me, not only because of the violence of my emotive reaction to the man's death, but because it was the same feeling I had had up there on the pitching foredeck of the *Waltzing Matilda* when I had looked back and seen Kas's disembodied head, the eyes wide and staring straight at me, his mouth agape. He was calling to me, pleading, and I had done nothing. I had just stood there, clutching the forestay as the waves swept over him, the relief I felt overlaid by that quite uncontrollable sense of elation.

Mihai was talking, but the chainsaw had started up again and I didn't take it in, my mind still on that moment out by Rottnest Island off Fremantle when I had stood and watched Kasim drown, the sails flapping as the boat veered off course till it was lying broadside to the waves and rolling, rolling with sickening plunges and drifting down on the floundering man. At one point he was so close alongside that I was sure I could have reached out my hand and caught hold of him.

But I hadn't. I had done nothing. Nothing. Just standing there, crouching down as a wave broke over me. And all the time that extraordinary sense of elation as I watched my mother's lover drown. How I hated that man. The bruises she tried to cover up, the way she cringed when he lost his temper. He had killed her. That was my excuse for crouching there and doing nothing to save him. He had killed her by being the sort of man he was. He had a lot of charm, I admit that. Virility stamped all over his hairy body, the way he walked, his whole manner, and the look on his face. Always that contemptuous look as he worked to undermine my confidence, destroying my morale whenever I visited her and he happened to be there. On these occasions, visits that should have been happy and full of affection were made a hell for both of us.

It was hard now to recall her beauty when I was just a child and my father had been alive. That poor, sad face, the nervousness, the fear bordering on terror at times. That was the picture of her in my mind as I stood there and watched the waves obliterate him. God! How I revelled for that moment in the knowledge that I had finished with him.

I looked across at Mihai. Something he had said . . . Was that how he had felt? Had he felt the same elation, looking down at the dead man on the floor between us?

'Get the blanket from my bed, please, and cover him up.' His face was full of sadness, no elation there at all.

I did as he requested, appalled at the thinness of it and the fact that its removal left only two of the same thin, nondescript coverings on the bed. But he had been talking about his wife. He must have been. I was sure I had heard him mumble her name. Ana. I asked him what he had said, and he stared at me, frowning. 'You did not hear? You took in nothing of what I was telling you?' A pause, and then he went on, 'I was talking about Miron. Miron and Ana. He was Ana's brother. No, not her brother. I do not remember how you say it. But they had different fathers.'

'Half-brother,' I said, and he nodded.

'*Da*. Half-brother. He fell in love with her, you see. No, not in love. Obsessed. From the time they were children.' And he added, his voice a whisper, 'He was a monster.'

After that he sat there, silent, as though that explained everything.

I should have persisted. If I had known then what I know now I would have been prepared for what I was to walk into only just over a month later. I should have asked him for all the intimate details that had culminated in the hard, vitally energetic little figure I had first seen tripping so daintily, so determinedly on to the wooden square of the Dunărea dance floor.

I had the opportunity then. We had time to kill, but he seemed locked in on himself and his use of that word 'monster' . . . Something terrible had happened to his wife. I was certain of that now. But I couldn't ask him about that. It was obviously too raw a subject. But I felt the need to break the silence somehow, and in the end I fell back on the only point of common interest we had, which was Vikki. But when I asked him how and when she had managed to slip away to Kazakhstan, he gave a little shrug. 'I cannot remember now.' He passed his left hand across his forehead and I saw that the first joint of the little finger was missing, a pale stump slightly bent by what I suspected was arthritis.

'Was it before they arrested you? Were you here when she left?'

He did not answer that for a long time, and then, when I had almost forgotten I had asked him the question, he said, 'Yes, I was here.' And after a moment he added, 'She was twenty-three then, coming up to twenty-four.' He sounded a little vague about it, but then he nodded. 'I remember now – she had just had her birthday. She was twenty-three.' He shook his head slowly. 'A strange young woman.' He fell silent again, and thinking perhaps he was about to add something that would explain her decision to leave Romania, I too remained silent, the clock ticking away the minutes the only sound.

Looking at him, sitting there, crouched in his chair, so still, and with tears glistening at the corners of his eyes, I wondered whether his feelings for her were only paternal. If they had adopted her, it fitted into the pattern of a wife with an urgent desire for a child she could no longer bear. It would account for the difference in their temperaments, for Vikki's fair complexion, the ash-blonde hair, those emerald eyes, so secret, so withdrawn – perhaps also for her lonely involvement with solo dancing and the equally solitary occupation of computer hacking. Hell! It would account for so many things that had puzzled me. 'So what is she doing now?' I asked him.

He did not reply; a slight shake of the head, a small shrug, that was all, and I did not pursue the matter.

He was crouched down in his chair, his eyes almost blank as he stared towards the window. And then, after several minutes, he repeated what he had said before, nodding his head and adding, '*Da*. She is strange in so very many ways. I confess I do not understand her. I have never understood her. But Ana – yes, they were very close. She knew, of course. She must have known. But she never told me. She was a very secretive woman in some ways.' Silence again, a withdrawn silence as though he was considering their relationship.

And then, suddenly, he was talking. Slowly at first, but gradually the words coming faster as he built up a picture of her personality. Much of it merely corroborated my own impression of her, but now he was showing me what it was like to be responsible for such an independent, wilful child, and I realized how accurate his description of her had been. She *was* a very strange young lady, the square features, the straight nose, the blondeness of her. Not Romany, of that I was certain. Remembering what I had pieced together of Ana Kikinda's sad history, my mind went chasing all sorts of possibilities as to the stock from which Vikki was sprung. She was so different from the 'parents' in her physical appearance. And so very different in her behaviour.

Dacian? That was all I could think of. A throwback to Alexander's invading army. That would account for the features, and the fairness. The seed of that army was scattered all along Alexander's great sweep of conquest, and nowhere more noticeably than in Dacia, that province to the north-east of Romania.

From what the Kikindas had told me I was left with the impression that she was their only child, and with the father in prison and the mother in a permanent state of shock it was not surprising that she had grown up a very solitary person, an individual turned in on herself, with only two outlets – her dancing and her computer.

'It was after they released me, after Ana had been taken away from Ceauşescu's presence and caused to disappear.' He was speaking slowly, a hesitant emphasis on every word. 'I was here in this room, in this very chair, and she rushed in, her face flushed, her eyes alight with excitement, so that their bright green had a strange translucence. How can I describe it? They were positively electric, her whole body incandescent with excitement. "Dada!" – that is what she called me. "Dada, I am through. I have broken through." '

He had tried to get some sense out of her, but she was bubbling over 'like a cauldron', her words coming in such a rush they were almost unintelligible. 'It seems incredible,' he said, 'but what she had done was to break into the Romanian military computer.' He leaned forward, staring at me earnestly. 'I am telling you this because I think you should know what sort of a person Vikki is. She is . . .' He hesitated. 'A very one-off sort of person. Very concentrated on what she is doing. Almost demonic in her concentration. I have already tell you that she is numerate. Her dancing had gradually become a matter of numbers. Her steps were so complex it was the only way she could keep track of her movements. And it was numbers again as she played with the little computer she had brought back from Moscow . . .'

What she had done apparently was to break into the military computer at Army Headquarters, and through that, she had reached into the Ukraine. 'They had a big armaments deal with Russia in preparation. Apparently all they needed to complete it was a bank guarantee.' He had questioned her, very sharply he said, and she had admitted that she had got as far as trying to pose as one of the banks involved. He shook his head. 'I was appalled, of course.'

At first he hadn't believed her, but when she had convinced him he had tried to explain to her how dangerous it was. But she had gone off at a tangent then, talking about a Russian scientist who had been trying to get the military bureaucrats to understand that their desperate race to keep up with the Western world had loaded the land with toxic waste. 'And there are stockpiles of chemical weapons hidden away underground. Well, of course, we know that. But where? The man was trying to find out. All this flashing from the screen of her little computer. But then, suddenly, she had found herself jammed, the digital window she had opened abruptly shut down.' His head jerked round on me. 'Do you know anything about computers?'

'A little,' I said. 'Not much.'

He nodded. 'I know nothing. They are a complete mystery to me. I am too old, that is the trouble. She is playing first with a cheap one I got her from a newspaper I work for when she is quite small. But to break into the computers that carry military secrets, that is crazy. But when I tell her that she just laugh. Somebody, she said to me, must try to save this country. And she quoted a figure of – I think it was forty per cent of all illness directly attributable to the toxification and pollution of the environment, fifteen per cent of all Soviet territory uninhabitable through the dumping of toxic waste. Is she right?' He raised an eyebrow at me, but did not wait for a reply. 'I fear so. Yes. They do not care. Have another vodka and damn the future! They dare not stop or they lose their employment.' He muttered something about Chernobyl. 'There will be another soon, and then another. I tell you, they don't care.'

A pause and then, 'The stupidity of it all!' His fist came down on the arm of the chair. 'I have been warning. Others have been warning also. But what can we do, except write about it, try to make the world understand? And Vikki,' he added. 'What can she do? She says she has read warnings made by a nuclear scientist – I think nuclear, a physicist anyway – and she is angry. Vikki can get very excited, emotionally you understand, and if she start to make an input of her views . . . She just does not realize the danger. I do not care for myself now, but she is young with all her life before her.'

He leaned forward, his voice urgent now as he said, 'Find her, Paul. Find her if you can. Perhaps she listen to you, a young man of her own age.' And he added, 'As I tell you before, I do not understand her. She has sudden enthusiasms, and then nothing seems to stop her, no sense of fear, none at all.' He stopped there, dabbing at his eyes. 'Perhaps if Ana had been here, but Miron had come for her only two or three nights before and there was only me. Do you think she will be playing around with that damn computer in Kazakhstan or wherever she is now, or will she have become bored with it? Maybe she get some sense—' He stopped abruptly. The sound of the chainsaw had ceased, the room suddenly silent, as he sat listening for a moment, his head slightly cocked. 'Not long now.' The saw started up again and he said, 'She is very obstinate, very headstrong.' He shook his head again, and then very slowly he repeated the words he had said before – 'I just do not understand her. I think she live in a fantasy world. She should have boyfriends—' He stared at me very hard with his watery grey eyes. 'She should not be dancing always alone, even though when she left here she was beginning to get engagements in the entertainment world.'

It was strange. He had been so silent after we had killed Miron Dinca, but now I could not stop him talking. He went on and on, but not about his wife, or about Vikki. Now he was talking about his life as a journalist, how he had become involved in politics, his writing becoming increasingly slanted against the ideology of Communism until he was openly critical of the Ceauşescu regime. 'That is when I begin to fall' – he hesitated – 'to fall foul of the authorities.' There were visits from the *Securitate*, always unexpected, or phone calls, watchers across the street, men who followed him wherever he went, others in the house, Vanya in particular, spying on him, his telephone tapped, his correspondence opened, and then sudden raids in the middle of the night, fists banging on the door, men with the blank faces of those who enjoy frightening people, turning everything upside-down, making as much mess as they could. It was harassment. And yet, with an extraordinary courage I could barely understand, instead of accepting the situation and toning down his criticism of the regime, he had fought back with the only weapon he had, his pen. 'That was when Miron start in on us. One night, he came with the hard boys, men with blank faces. But it was not me he wanted. It was Ana.'

He fell suddenly silent again, and it was at that moment the buzz of the chainsaw finally stopped. He glanced at the clock on the desk. 'We have peace now, I think. He usually stop just before eleven.' It was now twelve minutes to. 'The house he is cutting a tree trunk for gives him tea, or vodka perhaps – some sort of refreshment. Then he will go and there will be nobody to see you slipping away from this place. Also the lights go out about this time.'

I bent down, took hold of the dead man's arms and dragged the body closer to the window. This had the effect of switching my thoughts from the journey that lay ahead of me to the man who was the cause of it. Mihai was looking directly at me. 'It's odd, isn't it?' I said as I straightened up. 'Both of us seem to have family relationships that have gone wrong.'

He didn't say anything, his eyes on the windows as though engrossed in watching the snowflakes drifting down. I opened one of them and slipped out on to the balcony, looking down the street to where the truck was parked close against the house with its pile of cut logs. They already had a coating of snow a centimetre or two thick. It looked rather deeper in the back of the truck where it had drifted. There was no pavement, the rough, potholed road running right up against the house walls, the street too narrow for the truck to turn. I leaned over the balcony rail, looking straight down. It was a gamble, but it might work. The Dacia was parked opposite so that the side of the truck would be right below me and the sound of his fall would be cushioned by the snow.

I turned quickly, my mind made up. He was a heavy man and it took all my strength to haul his body out on to the narrow platform of the balcony and drape the arms over the rail so that he was supported there, sagging like a vomiting drunk.

'You asked me for an introduction.' Mihai was back at his desk. 'I do not know any person who is an expert on scrap metal. But this man will know somebody. And it is possible he can organize your departure to England – per'aps. He lives in Bucharest.' He tore the sheet he had been writing on from his notebook. 'This is his address and telephone number. His name is Luca. He is Jewish and a dealer in all sorts of things. He knows everybody. But please, you must memorize what I have written on that piece of paper, then destroy it. You promise.'

'Yes, of course. I promise.'

'Good. Then you will deliver these writings to Dumitru at Basahabi village.' He reached for a bundle of papers lying ready on the table beside him and handed it to me. There was no wrapping, just an elastic band holding the sheets together. 'You will not fail me, please. It is very important that people know what I am thinking. You understand?'

'I'll get it to him somehow.'

He hesitated. His eyes were fixed on mine. 'It is much to ask, but . . .' He reached out his hand, gripping hold of my shoulder. 'I am happy you came – so very happy. Thank you, Paul.' And he nodded towards the figure draped over the balcony rail. 'What you are able to do with that is of no importance compared with the delivery of that packet. It don't matter what happen to me. It is my writings that are important. That is what Ana always said, and that is what I believe.'

At that moment the lights at the end of the street and at the intersection by the Catholic church went out, the tall French windows suddenly dark. 'You go now,' he said. 'As soon as he drive that truck away.'

I nodded. And then I said, 'Your wife – a little while back you were telling me about your wife.' I couldn't very well ask him whether it was true that the dead man had arranged it so that she couldn't have children of her own. But I could ask him what he had been trying to tell me. And then, remembering how he had reacted each time he had mentioned her name, I asked him point-blank whether she was still alive.

He didn't answer for a moment. Then he said, 'I fear I cannot answer that.' Adding almost in the same breath, 'I hope to God not.' And then suddenly the whole tragic story began to pour out of him. Apparently she had arranged to get herself included in a delegation of workers called to express admiration for and solidarity with the regime. 'TV cameras, reporters, most of the ruling hierarchy, and the Great Communicator himself. You know how mystical the peasants are, and this country is seventy per cent or more peasant – they must have a god figure to lead them, and Ceauşescu is God. That is what I have been attacking. A politician should not have that sort of aura. Something you British find it difficult to understand. Your Prime Minister is not even the head of your armed forces. He or she has political power, but it is the monarch who has all the pomp, and the sworn allegiance, too.'

Silence then, and I had the feeling his mind had switched on to something else, as though involved in the composition of some future piece of writing, the phrases beginning to form, his eyes half shut. But then he went on as though there had been no break in the flow of his words, telling me how Ana had somehow pushed her way to the front of the delegation, and when the leader came to the end of his speech, and before Nicolae Ceauşescu could begin a doubtless interminable reply, she suddenly stepped forward. 'This is only what I hear, you understand, at second or third hand. I was in prison. I had been in prison already one year, forty-three days, and she had only once been allowed to see me – what they had done to me. For her benefit I was beaten up again, then dragged into an office, some sort of interview room. I was all covered in blood, my teeth smashed in, half my lower jaw hanging loose and my right eye forced out of its socket.' His voice trailed off.

'You don't have to tell me all this,' I murmured.

'No, no. But I want you to know. If in your travels you come across Vikki . . .' He hesitated. 'Ana and I, we sometimes thought that you two—' He smiled. It was a smile that illuminated his whole face. 'Well, never mind. Dreams. I am dreaming, you see, particularly when in prison. It is all you have to keep you alive then – dreams.'

He was silent for a time, shut in with his thoughts, and then he said, speaking so softly I could hardly hear him, 'She pleaded with the bastard. On humanitarian grounds. On cultural grounds, referring to me as a poet of genius, which God knows I am not. She even knelt before him and kissed his boots.' He shook his head and sighed. 'Perhaps that is a mistake. Ana was a very proud woman. But instead of kindness or a gleam of pity, Nicolae went into one of his interminable speeches. Do you know this? Just before he leave for Iran he deliver a speech to the Party Congress after they had unanimously re-elected him Leader of the Party, and it lasted six hours. Six interminable hours.'

His lips spread in a thin smile. 'I have no doubt the words he flung at Ana were similarly long-winded and platitudinous, full of unfounded accusations, about Russia and the West and conspiracies, all the world attempting to undermine the glorious regime of pure Communism that he had erected, he and that woman Elena Lupescu, his wife, the two of them together.

'I am told it was when he referred to me as a coward, a creeping insect poisoning the nation's prowess with the vitriol of thoughtless words, that it was then that she rose to her feet, calling him all sorts of names that we use in Romania for people who are cruel and senseless . . . Oh, I don't know, a whole string of words. The Romany blood in her, I suppose. She could be very basic when she was angry. And he just stared at her with that cold, blank look on his face. It was then that she stepped forward and hit him. Across the face. She hit him twice, with the flat of her hand, her wedding ring cutting into his cheek, and he just stood there, too shocked and dazed to move or even to say anything more. If there had not been so many people in that audience chamber she would have been gunned down instantly. Instead, his bodyguard seized hold of her, two of them wrenching at her arms, two more at her legs, and they rushed her out.'

That dreadful little scene must have happened several years ago, but like most Romanians Mihai was highly emotional. He muttered the beginnings of a prayer – but whether for her tortured body or for her soul I do not know. He was crying and I could not hear the words he spoke so softly and so fast. I think he mentioned the Virgin Mary, but he was not a

Catholic. He was not Greek Orthodox either, or Russian Orthodox. I don't think he knew what he was. But not an atheist.

He stayed like that for some little time, his head bent and his hands over his face. Finally he straightened up, his face turned to the window, not to me, and he whispered, 'That was the last anybody saw of her.' And then, even more softly, he added, 'So brave. So full of emotional impetuosity. And all my fault. I have prayed to God – that they have kill her quickly.' He looked at me. 'Yes, I have prayed for her death. And she is dead. I know it. I feel it, here in my heart.'

He was on his feet now and he seized hold of my arm. 'There is something more I have to tell you. It is so that you do not feel any guilt about that man's death.'

He didn't say anything for a long time after that, and I sat there thinking back to that first meeting. It had been here in Constantza. But at that moment the truck's engine started up and I jumped to my feet, flinging open the french windows and seizing hold of the sagging body. My eyes were on the truck itself then, waiting for it to move. The driver leaned out of the cab and called to someone in the door of the house – 'See you tomorrow.' Then he slammed the truck into gear.

It was an old vehicle, tired and overworked, the springs on my side almost at the point of giving up, so that the whole vehicle had a drunken tilt to it as it ground its way towards me.

Bending down to grip hold of the legs of the

stiffening corpse, even the driver's cab was below my line of sight, so that all I could do was gauge my moment by ear.

'Do you need help?' Mihai was out of his chair and leaning over me.

The sound of the engine was already much louder, the thump of the old diesel smoothing out. A quick glance over the balustrade and I saw the truck was picking up speed. 'Just tell me when,' he said, bending down again, gripping hold of the man's legs and lifting them off the stone base of the balcony so that the body was almost horizontal, the weight of it resting on the brick parapet. I was half standing then and for an instant I could just see the roof of the cab, a blur of white in the snow. Then the brickwork hid it.

'Now!' I felt Mihai's muscles tense. 'Now!' he repeated urgently, and I suddenly realized he had not understood my intention. It was too soon. I knew that. We couldn't just drop the body. It had to be flung.

With the two of us we were able to thrust it well clear of the balcony, out into the street below. I almost followed it, I put so much effort into that thrust. I finished up leaning over the side, looking straight down as the body hit the roof of the cab with a dull thud. 'Too late,' Mihai muttered.

The driver braked and I watched as the body slithered very slowly over the back end of the cab, a cascade of snow following it, so that the corpse finished up half buried under it and lying on a tarpaulin amongst a lot of ropes, saws and other forestry equipment. I could just see the head poking out of the snow so that he looked as though he was drowning in it, the rest of him enveloped in a white surflike shroud.

The truck stopped, but fortunately the driver did not get out. He just pushed open his door, leaning his body out and twisting round so that he could see there was nothing lodged on the cab top.

Mihai touched my arm. 'You must go quickly, before he decides which house drop something.'

We were both of us crouched down so that he couldn't see us. I heard the cab door slam shut, the engine pick up speed. Cautiously lifting my head, I watched as the truck turned the corner at the far end of the street and disappeared. 'Where does he live?' I asked.

But Mihai did not seem to understand that I had achieved exactly what I had hoped. 'Go quickly. Now.' His voice was urgent. 'When he finds Miron's body . . .' He hesitated. I asked him if he thought the man would go straight to the police, but he said no, he had had a long day and would surely drive straight home. Unfortunately, he had no idea where that was. He'd had only had one brief conversation with him, and that was from the balcony when the logger was working for the house opposite.

He was trembling as he turned back to his chair. I shut the windows. I, too, was trembling. For all I knew the man might live in the neighbourhood, and if he climbed into the back of his truck before going to bed . . . 'If he doesn't go to the police,' I said, 'what will he do with it?'

Mihai shrugged. 'Does it matter? Is not your

problem now. Not mine either.' He was suddenly smiling. 'We are very fortunate. Or per'aps that is what you intend, eh?' He thought we had nothing to fear now. When the truck driver discovered the body he would be too scared to go to the police. 'He will do what I asked you to do. He will take it into the forest somewhere and nobody will ever know.' He nodded to himself, still smiling. 'Very clever of you.'

He reached for the wodge of papers and began writing on the back with the stub of a pencil. 'When you reach Bucharest you go to this address, ask for Luca. He is Adrian's brother, so give him the news gently that Adrian is dead. You can tell him also that the man who killed him is dead.' He handed me the bundle, impressing on me again the importance of first checking out of my hotel. 'You must show no nervousness then. Try to think of something else.' And he added, 'Luca and his wife will look after you till you can leave the country in safety. But be careful. He is a powerful man. Very political. Give him some respect. Okay?'

I thanked him and he rose from his chair, gripping hold of both my shoulders and hugging me, his stubbled cheek hard against mine. It was almost a passionate embrace and there were tears in his eyes as he released me. 'Someday – maybe . . .' He suddenly bent down, seizing hold of my hands and kissing them. 'If you ever come across her remember what happened to her mother.'

His gesture, and those words, made a deep impression on me. But I didn't understand what he was trying to tell me. I thought he was referring to the scene in the audience chamber of the Central Committee Building.

'Does Vikki know?' I asked him.

'Oh, yes.'

And that seemed odd. 'You said somebody had smuggled her on to a Greek ship bound north-east across the Black Sea to Odessa three years back.' I thought perhaps his memory was playing him up. 'She couldn't have been here when your wife—'

'No, no. Not then.' He shook his head. 'I am speaking about earlier, when I was in prison the first time. She is a good girl, Vikki. She came home then to be with Ana.' And he added, 'Though they are very different, of course. Not a bit alike. But they respect each other, and Vikki is always conscious of the debt she owe us.' He nodded. 'Yes, she is a good young woman. She help Ana a lot in that difficult time. She has a very strong personality, a strong nature.' Then he said softly, 'She is also very clever.'

I asked him then where she had been. 'You say she came back to be with her mother. Came back from where?'

'Russia. She was in Moscow, at a special study place for computer technology. She is very clever with figures – what do you call it? Numerate? Yes, she is very numerate.' He seemed to like the word. 'But I have already told you.'

'She's a computer buff, then?' It puzzled me that he had mentioned that rather than her dancing, but when I asked him about it he said, 'Oh, yes, she is

dancing too. Nothing ever stop that young lady
dancing, not ever since she was little. But it was with
computers that she earned the roubles to pay her way
as a student. She work at night, you see. For an agency.
Temporary employment.'

'And she gave it all up to come back here and be
with your wife while you were in prison?'

He gave me an odd, almost surprised look. Then
nodded, covering it up by saying very quickly, 'No, she
don't give it up altogether. She has her own personal
computer. She bring it home here with her and every
night she is playing with it as though it is some new
toy. According to Ana, that is. And she pay for the
telephone, all the long and distant calls, and all out of
money she bring with her from her evening work in
Moscow.' He reached for the black raincoat then, help-
ing me into it. It was too big for me; the hat also.
'Leave those things in the car when you go into the
Intim.'

'Of course.' I nodded, hesitating a moment. But
there was nothing more to say, my throat constricted
by a sudden overwhelming affection for the man. 'God
keep you,' I muttered. Then I opened the door, closing
it gently behind me, not looking back. I was sure I
would never see him alive again and I was sorry as
I started down the stairs, listening intently for any
sound in the silence of the house.

There was no light on and it was very dark. I had
to feel my way, step by step, down six flights. Nobody
stopped me, and when I went out through the front
door the street seemed quite bright by comparison, lit

by the reflected glow of the port at the seaward end
and the glitter of stars above the housetops. It was
empty, absolutely deserted, everything still and very
silent.

I slipped across the road. The Dacia was unlocked
and I dived inside, closing the door gently. I sat quite
still for a moment, my eyes searching the street and
the windows and balconies of the houses, conscious
of a breathlessness and the beating of my heart. But
nobody took any notice. I began to relax then, concentrating on familiarizing myself with the car's controls.
Finally I switched on the ignition. It was a straightforward petrol engine and started almost at once. I
switched on the lights and watched as the fuel indicator climbed up the dial until it registered just over
one-third full.

The Intim Hotel was quite close, in one of the
transverse streets. There were several cars parked outside the Casa en Lei, a restaurant to which my Uncle
Jamie had taken me on several occasions. He liked it
because the atmosphere was old and solid, the food
quite good for Romania and, most important of all, it
was within walking distance of the main gate to the
docks. I parked the car between two of the vehicles
already there, locking it with the coat and hat, also
the bundle of papers Mihai had handed me, inside,
and walked the hundred metres or so to the hotel. The
door was firmly closed and I had to ring for the night
porter.

There were people in the bar, among them fortunately the cashier, so that I was able to settle my bill.

I asked for my key and with it she handed me a telephone message. It was from London, signed Alex, ordering me to return 'most immediate'. She had taken the call herself so that my decision to leave in a hurry came as no surprise to her. She made out my *nota* for one night only and I paid in dollars. That was the only time, I think, I showed nervousness, my fingers trembling as I counted out the notes.

She was a good-looking woman, black haired with a scarlet slash of a mouth, and I stood there chatting to her for a moment, determined to make my sudden departure seem as normal as possible. Because there were only three storeys to the hotel it had no lift, that being one of Ceauşescu's laws, and as I started up the heavily carpeted stairs she called to me to know if she should order me a taxi. It was a question I hadn't expected, and when, a little reluctantly, I said I already had a car, she looked again at her records and pointed out that I had not included the number of it on the form I had filled in. 'What is the number, please?' Her manner had suddenly become quite different.

I told her I didn't remember the number. I could feel the beginning of panic then. To be tripped up by such a little thing.

'If it is a hire car . . .'

'No, it is not a hire car.' And I told her it belonged to a friend. She began to argue that that was all the more reason why I should remember the number and without thinking I said he was picking me up at the Casa en Lei. I almost ran up the last two flights, and then on the top floor, which was in darkness, I couldn't

54

find the light switch. Finally, when I did locate it, all it gave me was the dim light of two coloured emergency bulbs so that it took time, fiddling with the key, before I could get my door open.

Once inside my room I had the comfort of proper lighting and I forced myself to calm down. But the Intim was a Government hotel and I couldn't help thinking about the men in the bar, wondering whether any of them were members of the *Securitate*. It was a double room, twin white-painted beds, white-painted furniture, lampshades to match and heavy drapes over the big windows from which I could look down into the street. I could see the Dacia where I had left it, tucked in amongst the other cars. There was nobody about.

Some member of staff had been in, turned the beds down and tidied up after me. All very well for Mihai to say no nervousness. I stuffed everything I could find into my suitcase, not caring how I packed in my haste, and was just leaving when I saw the telephone message from Alex Goodbody lying on the floor by the window. I picked it up, and before stuffing it in my pocket read it quickly through again. It was in Romanian, of course, the writing untidy and hard to read, but the gist of it was clear and I stood there for a moment, wondering about Zelinski. *Z gone walkabout*, it said. He must have spelled it out for her. Gone walkabout was obviously a cryptic way of saying he had disappeared. And it had to be Zelinski. There was nobody else on the staff whose name began with Z.

Alex Goodbody was Director, Resource Potentials,

an offshoot of OVL Aiden & Blair, a minerals finance company backed by Parsee and Arab money with headquarters in the City of London and an office in Islamabad. Presuming that Zelinski had really disappeared, it looked as though I was being recalled to take his place. The Resource Potentials staff was a small one, all of us language specialists as well as being either geologists or mining engineers.

But why me? I had only been with Resource Potentials just over two years. Less than any of the others, except Zelinski. Zelinski had been hired for a special operation. He was a professor at an American university with an intimate knowledge of Central Asia, apparently speaking most of the languages, even Chinese. Was that why I was being recalled, because of my knowledge of Asian languages?

Two months ago, when I had still been messing about with an old mining claim a dozen miles west of Kalgoorlie's Golden Mile, Z had been travelling the old Silk Road east of Kashgar in search of a Muslim fanatic who had been gunned down by a marauding band of Turkmen and left for dead. He had been found by some Tartar horsemen, who had taken him to their village where the women had nursed him back to health. It was there that Z had found him when he was trekking back from an expedition into the Taklamakan Desert that had proved both uncomfortable and totally unrewarding.

Alex had told me that much himself when briefing me on Operation Rust over a meal at his club. He just dropped it into the conversation, I suppose on the basis of *pour encourager les autres*, and I didn't question him about it, my mind on Romania at the time and how I was going to organize the type and quantity of scrap metal required by the Japanese steel company that had instructed us.

All this flashed through my mind as I walked to the bathroom, tearing the message into shreds. It had been scribbled on cheap, absorbent paper and it disappeared as soon as I flushed the toilet.

The Taklamakan, Samarkand, Kashgar – the old Silk Road. Was that where I was being sent? The road to Samarkand, all those ancient manuscripts unearthed by men like Hedin and Stein from the sand-buried temples of that terrible desert half ringed by towering mountain ranges. The old Silk Road! That was something I had always dreamed of.

But now I was carrying my suitcase down the stairs of the Intim Hotel bound for Bucharest in a black Dacia, the property of the *Securitate*, and the official who had signed for it was lying dead in the back of a truck. The Silk Road faded. I had other things to think about.

The hum of voices increased as I descended. The bar was still busy, but no sign of the receptionist, or of the night porter. I let myself out, my mind for some reason going back to the body in that truck, the way we had flung it out over the balcony parapet, wondering what the poor devil of a driver had done with it. And all the time I had to force myself to walk without haste, and when I came to the Dacia, to unlock it as though it really was my own car.

In less than a quarter of an hour I was at Basahabi, handing over Mihai's precious bundle of papers to a little sharp-nosed ferret of a man who answered to the name of Dumitru. He lived over the shop, just as Mihai had said. He asked me in for some coffee and a drink of something, but I declined. I had no desire to linger.

CHAPTER TWO

It was one thing for Alex Goodbody, in the security of his London office, to ring the Intim Hotel and instruct me to return *most immediate*, quite another to get myself out of the country. Later I discovered the telephone lines were still open at that time, but phoning him would not have helped. I would have to find my own way out. Otopeni was out of the question. Even if I could get a flight I didn't dare risk the airport's security, immigration and customs checks.

The Danube was a possible escape route, but there would almost certainly be patrols, and anyway the contact Mihai had given me lived in the outskirts of Bucharest. Moreover, I was in a car, and, after delivering his manuscript to Dumitru at Basahabi, I was already several kilometres out of Constantza on the main highway to Bucharest. I was tired, I think, emotionally drained. I took the easiest way out, stayed behind the wheel of the Dacia and drove straight on.

It was about two hundred and sixty kilometres

from Constantza to Bucharest, almost four hours' driving across the long, flat, dusty Danube plain, the road flanked by lines of maize stubble. Three hours later I still had no idea how to get out of the country, though I had thought of little else during the long drive. I was then approaching Fundulea, the last town before the outskirts of the capital. A silo loomed up, gaunt and black against the stars.

I pulled in to the dirt track leading to the silo and cut the engine. A donkey brayed, a shaggy little beast standing beside an ancient tractor, its head moving up and down as it rubbed its neck against one of the ploughshares. Apart from the moke, there was absolute silence, the plain stretching away either side of me, flat and unending, the maize stalks gleaming white with a touch of air frost.

I reached into the back for the map I had seen lying on the floor amongst a litter of cigarette stubs, crumbs and paper bags. It called itself, rather archaically, *The Tourist & Motor Car Map*, but it only told me what I already knew. To get out of the country by road was almost impossible. To the south the way into Bulgaria was blocked by the Danube, and the few crossings would be well guarded. Northward and westward the mountains of the Carpatii Meridionali and Orientali stood between me and the Soviet republics of the Ukraine and Moldavia. Hungary, or Yugoslavia, to the west was the best chance, but the direct Route 6 led through Timisoara, and Timisoara I knew was in a state of near civil war.

I was approaching the dangerous part of the

drive I had embarked on. The back of the map had information and plans of all the main towns, but even in the case of Bucharest only the main boulevards and squares were included, and most of these would surely have security checks on them, possibly roadblocks. I should have ignored Mihai's contact and stayed on the coast. I realized that now. It was crazy driving a *Securitate* Dacia into the heart of the capital.

I tossed the map on to the back seat and drove on through Fundulea and into the outskirts of Bucharest, the tension in me mounting. I drove slowly, peering ahead at every crossing, alert for the first sign of police or army.

Just before I left him Mihai had mentioned a man in the state fishing company. But that was in connection with scrap metal and the old ships laid up in the delta, particularly at Sulina which was the port of entry for vessels coming into the Danube from the Black Sea. In addition to their main office, which was in the docks at Constantza, they had a working base at Tulcea, and Tulcea was at the landward end of the long straight stretch of the Sulina Channel, little more than a hundred kilometres from Constantza. At Tulcea I might have been able to jump a ship heading south along the coast to the Bosporus and Istanbul, where I could of course get a plane direct to London.

But he had warned me the man might be unreliable, being in state employment, whereas the Bucharest contact he had given me was the brother of the man the *Securitate* had ambushed in the foothills of the Carpathians. Mihai had described him as an old friend and absolutely safe. I was very tired by then, and thinking of the Danube and the delta the water route seemed so much more attractive than sitting in the driving seat of this rattling vehicle, peering through the dusty windscreen along the pale beam of the headlights. I was low on fuel, dreaming of the delta as the scattered wayside booths gave place to houses, the narrow band of tarmac between the dirt verges stretching ahead to the first grey glimmer of concrete residential blocks.

I had taken to dinghy racing at an early age and on my second visit to Romania my uncle had taken me with him on a weekend sail up the coast as far as Sinoie, the nearest of the inland lakes. He wanted to have a look at the old Trajan settlement of Histria with its Iron Age remains. There, in the bright and very modern museum by the entrance, we had met a man who had just spent a month in a double-ended canoe-shaped boat exploring the reed-choked waterways of that huge area of silt brought down by Europe's greatest river. His description of it – the birds, the fish, the water lilies, the shallow lakes islanded with reeds and willow, and the fishermen, a lost race of Russian origin . . . So great was the impression it had made on me that every time I had looked upon the waters of the Danube, in Austria and once at Budapest, it was his picture of the delta that was in my mind. As a result I had gradually acquired an almost irresistible urge to see it for myself some day.

Perhaps I never would now. I was already into the outskirts of Bucharest, amongst the grey blocks of

Ceauşescu's concrete jungle, my exhausted mind wondering whether Luca Brasov really was safe. How
would he react to being told his brother Adrian had
been killed by the *Securitate* on the road from Timisoara? Anyway, I had no idea how to find the Strada
Plop, which was where he lived, and I was reluctant
to ask at this early hour, even though there were quite
a few people about, all walking towards the city centre.

The only hotel I knew was the Bucureşti, a solid
great pile of a place with dark marble staircases and
black leather chairs and couches. It was very close to
the main square, one side of which was taken up
by the Central Committee's white slab of a building.
Being such a large hotel nobody on duty at Reception
would be surprised at my asking for a room at this
hour of the morning. The fact that it was virtually the
Securitate's unofficial HQ gave a certain piquancy to
the situation, and if the Constantza authorities did
discover my connection with Miron Dinca's death, the
Bucureşti was the last place they would think of looking for me.

There was a certain amount of traffic, and people
walking under the trees or standing around talking in
little groups, as I drove into the wide boulevards leading to the centre. In fact, the Calea Victoriei proved
quite crowded, everybody moving towards the Piata
Revolutiei as it is now called. I left the Dacia in one
of the smaller streets at the back of the hotel and
walked the rest of the way, carrying my bag and everything else that belonged to me.

The Bucureşti was just as I remembered it when

staying there with my uncle; the huge, sombre foyer, the impressive marble staircase at the back and the long reception counter to the left, with one of the guests, a Frenchman, arguing with a taxi driver over the cost of hiring his vehicle for the day. Several other guests were slumped in the black leather armchairs, one of them fast asleep as though exhausted by a long wait.

The political situation had clearly caused a number of cancellations, for I had no difficulty in booking a room even though there would almost certainly have been additional reservations for *Securitate* personnel. I picked up my key and was just turning to retrieve my bag when the Frenchman gripped my elbow. '*Pardon, monsieur.* You are English, yes?'

I nodded briefly. He was looking at me very intently, his eyes large behind the gold-rimmed glasses, and I was suddenly tense, wondering what was coming. But all he wanted was help with the language. He had heard me talking Romanian to the clerk behind the counter. 'This man' – he indicated the taxi driver – 'he do not speak French, nor German, nor English neither, only Romanian. I do not speak Romanian.'

It turned out that he wanted the man to take him to Timisoara. He had offered him what he had been told was a reasonable fare, but the man had indicated that it was not enough. 'The clerk here agrees.' He thought perhaps the man got a percentage. 'So what is enough, plees?'

I suggested he tried one of the other drivers. There were at least half a dozen taxis waiting outside, their drivers in a huddle by the entrance. But he said they were all booked. 'Then why is this one free?' I asked.

He shrugged. 'I think per'aps his car is a very old one. Something is not right.'

'And you have to get to Timisoara?'

'That is where the action is. I am a photographer, you see.'

He was a freelance, based in London. He had flown in from Prague and at Otopeni Airport had taken the bus with a whole gang of journalists, all of them scenting political upheaval and in need of transport, most of their papers having no office in Romania. I told him to forget Timisoara. He might find all the action he wanted here in Bucharest.

'*Non, non.* Last night there is shooting in Timisoara. There are soldiers, and tanks with white flags. Here it is politics. You do not take pictures of politics. Not good pictures. Not my sort of pictures. I need bodies, hospitals with wounded, tanks with workers clambering over them, attacking with their bare hands. Now plees, fix me this man his damn car. The best price you can.'

So I fixed the car for him at almost twice the figure he had been given as reasonable for a day's hire, in dollars, of course, the petrol and any repairs to be his responsibility. A pity he wasn't going the other way, to Constantza, I might have taken a chance on it and driven him there myself. I wished him luck with his pictures and went up to my room. It was on the fourth floor looking out over the front of the hotel to a street where I could just see the façade of a rather nice-looking church. I dumped my case on a chair, took off my shoes and jacket and fell onto the bed, pulling the heavy coverlet over me.

I was exhausted, absolutely drained. So much had happened, and that damned car parked just a block away. The truck ... I kept thinking about the truck and the way the wretched man's head had stuck up out of the snow, just like Kasim's above the white surf of a breaking wave. Where was that truck now? Parked in some street above Constantza Port? Or up in the foothills, in some village, trees all round, a Christmas scene? I was thinking of Christmas then, my eyelids drooping – other Christmases. I had never had a Christmas like this would be.

But, tired though I was, I couldn't sleep. Christmas only four days away, and where would I spend it? In a battered tramp thumping my way down the Black Sea coast, or in some stinking jail?

My mind drifting, not fully awake nor yet unconscious, seeing two bodies as one and debating with myself as to whether it was better to die quickly, snuffed out in a matter of minutes, or to linger over a much longer period as my father had done. I could still remember his state of incontinence, the smell of urine, the periodic nauseous stink of vomit. I would not want to go like that, lingering. So had I done Kas a favour? Nice to think so. I had certainly done my mother one, though she wouldn't have thanked me for it had she known. She loved the man. She actually loved the man.

Why? In God's name, why? After all he had done to her.

There was a bloodstain on the ceiling, a faint pale red smear. Some previous occupant of the bed I was in had stood up on it and swatted some insect, a mosquito probably full of blood-suck. Somebody moved on the landing outside, a door slammed, the sound of a key turning, and then footsteps receding. Five thirty-seven. Time dragging and I lay there wondering if the owner of the footsteps was up early to catch a plane. Perhaps the planes were still running. Perhaps I could be in London six hours from now.

But I didn't stir. More likely a determined newspaper man out to beat the others to some exclusive. I turned over and closed my eyes again, wondering what death was like. Kas could tell me. So now could Miron Dinca. But that was done in self-preservation. Or rather, to preserve the life of Vikki's father as he was being throttled to death.

No, not her father. Of course not. He couldn't be. But then – did it matter? Where was she, anyway? And what did she look like? I couldn't remember. I couldn't imagine her now at twenty-five. That square forehead, those high cheekbones, and the eyes, those wide, almost protuberant emerald eyes. The fantasies I had woven around her, distortions of her real self, which was a much harder, much more positive personality than any man would want a woman to be in his dreams. *Fair, fair – fair is the rose. And the fairest rose is the English rose.* Who had written that? And suddenly I remembered. I had written it myself, years and years ago, it seemed, when I was still at school.

But though Vikki was fair, unlike most Romanian girls, she certainly wasn't English. Not Romany either. Dacian?

That is all I remembered of her – that and the fantasies I had woven about her, fantasies that totally ignored the strength of her personality, the finality of her every decision.

I was just seventeen when I lost my virginity to her. No, not lost – when she took it from me. We had been dancing in the big room on the floor below where Mihai and I killed Miron Dinca. I had been singing a wild Cossack song I had picked up on a brief Ukrainian exchange and we were dancing Cossack style. I was belting the words out at the top of my voice, the two of us dancing yards apart, and when it was over I sank to the floor, wet with sweat for it was high summer. I was absolutely exhausted. But not Vikki.

She was suddenly on top of me. I could smell her. Her body odour was almost overpowering as she groped for the zip of my trousers. Her hands seemed to be all over me then. Her skirt was up and she had hold of my right hand, forcing it up between her legs as she straddled me. She was wet, her skin all damp, her fair hair plastered dank across her face, her eyes ablaze with excitement.

Energy! That was what I chiefly remembered of Vikki, her abundant, inexhaustible energy.

Tired out as I was after the sleepless nightmare of the last few hours, I found myself aroused just at the thought of her, the strength of that hard, dance-conditioned body, her inexhaustible determination. She had raped me. And I had loved it, revelling in every minute – and then Mihai's wife, Ana, coming in, and the look on her face, not of censure, a look of pleasure almost.

I must have drifted off, for it was suddenly 8 a.m. I rolled off the bed, shaved and dressed, and then hurried to the mezzanine floor where there was already a small huddle of men round the coffee urn and help-yourself breakfast table – eggs, salami, meat, dark, almost black bread in thick slices, and the dull white cheese you find all over Romania. Cake, too, and chicken bones.

'You mind if I sit here with you?' It was the Frenchman. He had been getting himself some fruit juice and I was just settling down to my breakfast at an empty table.

I smiled and nodded. Better this photographer than some member of the *Securitate*. He pulled up a chair opposite me and sat down.

'So you didn't go to Timisoara after all?' I said.

'No. Ceauşescu return from Tehran yesterday afternoon and in the evening he is on the radio. Do you hear him?'

I shook my head.

'He is telling about events in Timisoara – terrorists and hooligans is how he describe the dissident element. And today, they tell me, he is to address the people direct, from the Central Committee Building. He is planning to bring in workers from the factories, so there will be a big demonstration this morning in the Place de la République with the army and the *Securitate* there in force to see that there is nothing like a repetition of what happen in Timisoara and some other provincial centres. And there will be tanks, water-cannon, all the paraphernalia of crowd control.'

The Frenchman's eyes gleamed with excitement. His name was Antoine Caminade and he was from Domme on the Dordogne River. He had lived with a situation very similar to that in which he now found himself all through his childhood, vicariously, through the eyes of his father and the stories he had told him.

The Dordogne rises in that part of France where the resistance to the Germans in the Second World War had been at its fiercest. His father, he told me, had been a member of the Maquis, had been caught up in an operation that had gone tragically wrong and had escaped capture by canoeing up the Dordogne almost to its source. He had joined a unit in the Massif Central and had then fought all through that last winter before the liberation of France, struggling for survival in the volcanic mountainous area beyond Le Puy. Antoine Caminade knew all about resistance, summary executions, torture and the sudden disappearance of friends and neighbours.

'You know Domme, monsieur?'

As it happened I did. I had stayed there one night, and in the early morning, with the mist lying like a bed of grey fungus along the whole stretch of the river, I had walked the deserted streets of that honey-coloured *bastide* town perched high above the

Dordogne. 'Yes, I know Domme,' I said, remembering the *Barre*, a treed terrace looking out over the mist to the hills that formed the opposite bank, the solidity of the church, the way it crouched on the topmost point of the medieval citadel, but particularly I remembered the graveyard behind, with names like Victor Hugo, and the Famille Emile Bach.

'You were born in Domme?' I asked him.

'No, but we are buried there, that is all. And today is the day of my father's death. Behind the church at Domme there are great grey stone *sarcophigues*, some in black or white marble.' His eyes were looking past me, seeing nothing but the picture in his mind. '*Ici repose*, and then the names, all our family, and the last one my father's, Rogér Caminade. He died last year. He was sixty-two. And, after his name, we have carved *Un homme de la Résistance – Le Jour de Gloire . . .*'

He sat silent for a moment, then suddenly smiled, apologizing to me for talking about his father. 'It is because' – he hesitated – 'because he is such a special person, to me most of all.'

He had a need to talk and I sat listening to him, but with only half my mind, my main concern being how to get out of the country. Mihai's words came back to me – *It is very near the end now.* What would be the situation if the Ceauşescu regime collapsed? Chaos? A struggle for power? And in those circumstances perhaps it would be possible to slip across the frontier.

I was thinking back to Hungary and Czechoslovakia, how Austria had opened its frontiers to the streams of people pouring out of those two countries, trainload after trainload. If anti-government demonstrations got out of hand, as they evidently had in Timisoara, then for a time at any rate Bucharest should be relatively easy to slip away from, and even if the frontier guards were still in position the Danube was an international waterway. The captains of vessels coming down the river would surely be more relaxed about a stranger asking for passage.

Constantza. Constantza would be the best bet. I cursed myself for having left the Intim Hotel. At breakfast – good God! was it only yesterday morning? – there had been a massive Greek god of a man waiting for his ship to complete her repairs. He had been wearing a brightly coloured seaman's jersey with the sleeves rolled up, his huge arms bristling with fair hair, his great head capped with a thickly curled blond mat, and he had a beard. He looked like Zeus. His ship, the *Patmos*, was a three-thousand tonner and he was sailing, he said, in two days. *Inshallah!* To Istanbul first, to unload a thousand cases of Murfatlar wine, thence to Piraeus with the main part of his cargo, which would be aluminium bars. I had thought he was the captain, but as we talked it became apparent that he was the owner, buying and selling cargoes wherever he could.

He would have taken me. I was sure of that. I even had his name – Yannis Michaelides. And he was from the islands, not the mainland of Greece.

'. . . after Moscow I go to Tashkent and on into the Taklamakan.'

'What did you say?' My mind suddenly refocused on my table companion. 'The Taklamakan?' That was the great desert north of the Pamirs where the Russians had tested many of their nuclear warheads. 'You've been there?'

'*Mais oui*. I tell you. After my father send me to Moscow and I learn Russian, I start to travel.'

'Kazakhstan?' I asked.

But he shook his head. 'No, not Kazakhstan.'

'Do you speak Chinese?' The Taklamakan was across the frontier into China.

'Not too much, but a little. Like I tell you, languages come easily to me.' He had been talking very fast, but somehow he had managed to finish all the food on his plate, and after gulping down the last of his coffee he jumped to his feet. 'More coffee?' He seized my half empty cup. 'I bring you also another egg. God knows when we eat again.' He came back with two plates piled with food as well as the coffee. 'You are right, you see.' He resumed his seat, leaning towards me across the table. 'The action has moved now to Bucharest, to the Central Committee Building. So that is where I go after I finish my *petit déjeuner* – not so *petit*, eh?'

Again that big-toothed grin. I was sure they were false. It was a description I should have applied to the man himself, but he was so friendly, so full of a bustling, eager excitement. 'Do you come? It will be interesting, I think. There is a rumour about some teleconference at the Party Headquarters in the Central Committee Building, Ceauşescu hooked up to all of

Romania's Party secretaries. They say – ' he nodded at the little group of foreign media people seated at two tables they had pushed together, a confusion of languages, all of them talking with great animation – 'that the whole monstrous regime is on the point of collapse. They also say that Vasile Milea, who is head of the armed forces, is unwilling to order the army to open fire on the people. There will be a great crowd in that square and if they did open fire . . .' He patted the camera on the chair beside him. 'And if they don't open fire, then there are still good pictures. We will see, eh?'

He brushed the last of his egg from his lips and got to his feet. 'Drink your coffee, *mon ami*, then we go together.'

'I'm sorry,' I said, 'but I have things I must do this morning.'

He hesitated, his eyes staring at me hard, and I got the impression that he was about to ask me what I was planning to do that was more urgent than accompanying him to the square to be part of the action. Instead, he got himself some more coffee and sat down again, switching abruptly to questions about my job. 'You are not a journalist, nor are you a photographer like myself. You are not here because this is the last of the Eastern Bloc countries to have a Communist dictatorship. So what is it you do here? Who do you work for?'

I didn't answer for a moment. It wasn't any of his business. 'Why do you want to know?' I asked him.

He shrugged. 'Curiosity.' He gave me a slightly

ingratiating smile, his eyes sliding away from me as he added, 'People, you know. I'm interested in people. That is what makes me a good photographer. The world is about people, eh?' He paused there, and then, his words gathering pace: 'I don't like to waste film like some photographers. When I take a picture that is that. And to achieve it I must know what is in their minds and then wait until they are in the right mood with the right expressions. You, for example. If I take a picture of you, then I wish to reveal the person you are. Do you understand?'

He did not wait for me to reply, but went straight on, 'I am like a painter, you see. My camera must do more than just reproduce the structure of the face. It must reach into the character behind the bone structure, and the eyes – the eyes are the most difficult, the key in fact. It is through them that my lens can reach into the mind of my subject.' Again that Gallic shrug, the little smile. 'C'est difficile, eh? It is an art.'

He finished his coffee and got to his feet again. 'Alors. You must excuse me, plees. Now I go to the Place de la République – to see what pictures there will be for me. Okay?'

'Yes, of course.' And I, too, got to my feet. We shook hands, I remember, very formally. 'Take care,' I said.

He grinned, a flash of those very white teeth. 'I do that.' He raised his hand. 'A bientôt. Per'aps we have dinner together tonight.'

He left then, and with nobody to talk to I found myself becoming nervous again, my mind going over my immediate plans and wondering whether the Dacia would be under surveillance, whether it would be safe to drive it out beyond the Gara de Nord with the city in such a dangerously volatile state. Luca Brasov lived in a little side street off the Bulevardul Bucureştii Noi.

The more I thought about it the more nervous I became. This was one of the main routes to the Ploesti oilfields. I could picture convoys of coaches bringing workers in to the city centre in support of Ceauşescu. They would almost certainly be accompanied by army patrols, and the police and the *Securitate* would be out in force.

I sat there for a long time, trying to make up my mind whether to go or not. In the end I went up to my room, got my briefcase and anorak and hurried out of the hotel before I could change my mind. There were a lot of people about, all of them headed for the square. There was a bakery open, the shelves already almost bare. All other shops seemed to be shut and there were military and police patrols at most of the street junctions, a group of water-cannon trucks parked in a side street.

The Dacia was where I had left. it. A little group of *politie* were smoking and talking close beside it, one of them actually leaning against it. The minutes ticked slowly by as I walked up and down, waiting for them to move off. A clock struck ten, and then shortly afterwards there was the sound of a shot. The demonstration was scheduled for noon. A man approached holding a bundle of placards. He handed me one. LONG LIVE THE PARTY. LONG LIVE CEAUŞESCU. Another shot, then the rattle of a sub-machine gun, shouts and people screaming. The little group of *politie* broke up, a cigarette end smouldering in the gutter as they hurried in the direction from which the outburst of firing had come. Suddenly the street was almost empty.

I walked quickly to the Dacia, taking the key from my pocket and stooping as though to do up my shoe-lace. Nobody was looking in my direction. I unlocked the car and slid into the driving seat, praying to God it would start first go. It did, and I drove quickly off, cutting through the side streets until I felt I could safely turn east into the Calea Victoriei, and so to the Piata Victoriei and the Bulevardul 1st Mai. From there it was a straight run to the Bulevardul Bucureştii.

Luca Brasov lived on the third floor of one of the Government's standard concrete apartment blocks. It was a four-storey building, so it had a lift, and it worked. It was his wife who opened the door to me, a small woman of indeterminate age, grey haired and with the most enormous brown eyes that fastened on me suspiciously when she realized from my accent that I was not Romanian. 'What do you want with my husband?'

'Is he in?' I asked.

But she would not answer that. 'Who are you? Where are you from?'

'England,' I said. 'I am English.'

Her gaze softened momentarily. 'But you speak Romanian.' She was still suspicious.

I started to explain, but then I stopped. It was too complicated. I reached into my pocket for the note Mihai had scribbled for me just before I had left him and handed it to her. 'Would you give that to him, please?'

She hesitated, staring down at it uncertainly, and I knew what was going on in her mind. If she agreed to give it to him, then she would be admitting he was there with her in the apartment. 'It is from Mihai Kikinda. You can read it if you still doubt me.'

The big brown eyes fastened on mine again, still hesitant. 'No, I don't want to read it.' She was still suspicious. 'I will give it to him when he returns.'

But I was quite certain he was there behind one of the shut doors leading off the narrow hallway with its drab paint. 'Please,' I said. 'He is the only man in Bucharest who can help me to get out of the country. I have to be back in England by . . .' But that was no good. I could see that. 'Mihai is an old friend of my uncle's. Before he died he was a ship surveyor. He brought me with him to Romania several times. That's why I speak the language. I became friendly with the daughter, with Vikki. We would dance together.'

She shook her head. 'Vikki don't dance with boys, only with herself. She dance alone – always.'

I nodded. 'But when I was in Constantza she let me dance with her.'

'Where?' The question was flung at me.

'At the restaurant Mihai and Ana frequented.'

'And the name? The name of the restaurant?'

'The Dunărea.'

'Where is that?' I told her, and then she asked me to describe it, and to describe Vikki, what she had been wearing that first time I had danced with her.

And when I had told her, she stared at me, wide-eyed again. And then in a whisper, she said, 'Then you are per'aps the boy Ana tell us . . .' A moment's hesitation and then she said, 'Wait here!' She said it abruptly and closed the door in my face.

She was gone a good five minutes so that I began to wonder whether I really had convinced her. In the state Bucharest was in I had no time to lose. At any moment the whole fragile edifice that was Ceauşescu's Romania, the republic he had built up with the dedicated determination of the ruthless peasant politician he was, might crumble into chaos. I didn't know what would happen then. Anybody's guess, all transport at a standstill, foreigners arrested as hostages, the army split and open civil war between all the various factions jostling for power. And I had virtually killed a man, a member of the *Securitate*, and there to prove it was that damned Dacia parked across the street. Quite apart from Goodbody's telephone message, I had to get out.

The door suddenly opened again and a grey-haired mountain of a man, who seemed to fill the whole aperture, stood there staring at me. He was unshaven and had a double chin to match his belly. He had slanted, almost Mongolian eyes and they stared at me hard. 'Is that your car out there?' He indicated the Dacia. 'Only the *Securitate* have that type, I think. What is your business with Mihai Kikinda?'

I started to explain, wondering how much I dared tell him. But I had only said a few words before he held up his hand. 'I think it is better I do not know. These are dangerous times. You see what they have done to Mihai.' And then in broken English, 'You come in now and then you tell me what it is you want from me.' He stood back to let me enter, but then he stopped me. 'No. First you get rid of that car. I do not like it there outside where I live. You must put it several streets away. Then you come back and you tell me what it is you want.'

That was how Vikki became my passport to freedom. Brasov's wife Tania was a friend of Ana's. And the account I gave them of my relationship with the Kikindas, particularly with Vikki, apparently matched what they had heard, so that with much laughter they brought out a bottle of *loza*, which is the same sort of plum brandy as the Yugoslav *slivovitz*. 'So. Why do you not marry the girl? That is what Ana want.' He turned to his wife. 'That is so, Tania?'

She agreed with a little nod of her head, her eyes fixed on mine. 'And Mihai too. Several times he say . . .' She gave a little sigh and let it go at that.

I stayed with them longer than I had intended. They were such a warm-hearted, friendly couple, and all the time working to help people in trouble with the authorities and living, I suppose, on the edge of fear. But, unlike Mihai, they never wrote anything down. I suppose that is something that is ingrained in most Jews – *my word is my bond*. The word only, never committing anything to paper.

I left shortly afterwards, Luca having promised to let me know what, if anything, he had been able to arrange for me. 'Per'aps I telephone you. At the Bucureşti. Some times after twenty-two hundred hours. Okay? I find you something.' And he patted the side of his big beak of a nose. 'Per'aps a nice fat woman, one of the immigration officers. They have females in Immigration. It helps.' He winked at me. 'You have dollars?' And when I told him yes, he said, 'Then not too much trouble. You give me twenty. Okay?'

I had given him two tens, and again he promised to phone me some time after 10 p.m. 'If not tonight, then tomorrow, or maybe the day after. It will take a little time, this.' He asked my room number, then gripped my shoulder. 'Make certain you write nothing down. Remember exactly what I say, which will be about a restaurant where we are going to have lunch, or perhaps dinner, together. It will include the name of the ship, the time and the place. We are two friends arranging to meet for a meal. That is all, and nothing written, you understand.'

I nodded and he gave me a great bear-hug. 'You find that girl – for Mihai's sake, for Ana's . . .'

'He thinks his wife is dead,' I said, and he gave a quick shrug.

'Maybe – maybe not. I don't know and he don't know, not for sure. Okay? You find out where Vikki is now and tell her, as soon as we have got rid of this creature who has been grinding the Romanian people to powder she is to come back and see her father. That is all I ask in return for what I do for you now.'

'Of course. I'll do my best.' And then I asked him what he had meant by referring to Mihai as Vikki's father. 'Is he or isn't he?'

'Of course not. Nor is Ana her mother. They adopt her. But never mention that to either of them. For them Vikki is their daughter.'

'And for her?' I asked.

He shrugged his massive shoulders, gave me another great hug, kissing me on both cheeks. 'You go now.'

'But who is she?' I asked. 'What were her real parents, what nationality?'

His heavy features broke into a smile. 'I don't know. They don't know. Maybe you find out – some day.' And with a quick, decisive nod he stepped back and shut the door.

CHAPTER THREE

Half an hour later I had manoeuvred the Dacia into a gap among a number of vehicles lining a side street between the Piata Victoriei and the Gara de Nord. The Bulevardul 1st Mai had been full of buses packed with oil workers from the Ploesti field, some of them armed with heavy wrenches and other roughneck tools, all of them periodically singing revolutionary songs. Shouts of *Ceauşescu – Romania* went on and on, busload after busload; *Ceauşescu our saviour, our leader*; *Romania libera – Romania libera*. I think those were the words, roared out in blind unison. And there were tanks, police cars, army vehicles full of soldiers, all the Communist paraphernalia of organized mob delivery. Increasingly, as I neared the railway station, I found there were army patrols guarding major intersections.

What finally decided me to join the growing crowd of pedestrians heading for the Central Committee Building was the sudden appearance of a Dacia like mine close alongside. It was black and the two men in it almost certainly *Securitate*. The driver reduced speed, so that we were travelling side by side, the man in the passenger seat staring at me. My suit, my tie, my shirt were all English and I cursed myself for not having left the car earlier. But the comfort of driving as a part of what was virtually a convoy . . . I lifted a hand in salute, staring at the man, my lips tight shut and unsmiling, hoping to God I could get away with it, and all the time my heart pounding, my nerves tightening the muscles in my face.

Then suddenly the moment of crisis was over, the officer returning my salutation with a quick lift of his hand, then nodding to his driver. The car shot ahead, weaving its way past the tank I was following and disappearing into the long line of buses beyond.

The Piata Victoriei would obviously be guarded, and though I was still quite a way from the Bucureşti, I took the next turning to the right, a side street of old-fashioned houses interspersed with shops. It was just after eleven by then. I drove on until I was nearing the next main intersection. An army detachment was setting up a checkpoint, so I swung into a narrow street that was little more than an alleyway. It proved to be a cul-de-sac, and when I got out of the car there was a pungent smell and the sound of grunting. I had parked almost alongside the home of a brown-backed boar, who glared at me through the railings of what had once been a tiny front garden. A curtain moved and an elderly woman stared out at me. I smiled at her and turned to lock the car, the pig grunting furiously – meat on the hoof and guardian to boot. The incongruity of it, and the fact that the *Securitate* had not stopped to question me, seemed all of a part with the chaotic dream world in which I was living.

A passage connected the cul-de-sac to a dusty street where I mingled with a crowd, all headed south, their numbers increasing all the time, their volubility too, and the atmosphere tense. At a guarded intersection the name of the street was posted on the side of an office block – Calea Grivitei. I knew where I was then. The crowd became thicker, spilling out into the road and moving even more slowly.

Somebody handed me a *Long live the Party* poster as I was carried along down the side streets behind the Bucureşti until, suddenly, we were pushing our way into the square with the white concrete mass of the Central Committee Building facing us, the whole open area in front of it a dense mass of humanity, with here and there the turret of a tank standing out like a half tide rock above the sea of heads. The crews were in many cases standing or sitting on the sides of their vehicles. One was even smoking a cigarette as I edged my way towards the Central Committee Building. There were flags, and the balcony on the first floor bristled with cameras and microphones, media men moving about as they put the final touches to their equipment. A man I spoke to confirmed what I had seen on a paper left on the bonnet of a car – Ceauşescu's speech would go out nationwide on both television and radio. The crowd seethed with the suspense of waiting, the tension growing as the time or the Party Leader's address passed.

After ten minutes hard pushing, when I had reached a position somewhere near the centre of the square, there was a sudden hush. Ceauşescu himself had appeared on the balcony. No crash of drums and cymbals, no fanfare of trumpets. He was suddenly there, a thin-faced man hunched in a black overcoat. And so insignificant. That was what struck me. For twenty years he and his wife had ruled Romania, over fifteen million people kept in absolute subjugation, a peasant ruling a mainly peasant nation. Remembering pictures of Balkan tyrants, I had expected a man of some physical stature, not a small ranter of a politician fumbling over his words, waving his arms about and delivering a speech that was full of slogans and platitudes, delivering it in a dull, monotonous voice. He even managed to look apprehensive, while his wife and the members of the Committee behind him faced the enormous gathering, tight-lipped, their features set hard.

His speech gradually gathered momentum, his fists pounding the air, and for a moment I felt a certain magnetism. But whatever it was that had been there for a moment gradually faded, his speech subsiding into old Party calls for unity, comradeship and dedication to the Cause. Romania. He constantly called on them to think of Romania and I could sense an uneasiness growing in the people around me. He was not getting through to them. They had heard it all before.

Then somebody, close by the steps leading to the main entrance, raised a cry of Timisoara. *Timisoara – Timisoara*. And *Toekes – Laszlo Toekes*. Then – *Killer. DRACULA*. The name of the dreaded count was caught up in a ripple of sound – *DRACULA, DRACULA, DRACULA*. And the bussed-in workers remained silent. All that effort to get them here from all over the country and they were not responding.

It silenced Ceauşescu, his face gone ashen, unable to believe what he was hearing. His wife, Elena, too. By then I was near enough to see their expressions, and to the crowd, as well as to myself, it was clear they were not only struck dumb with confusion, but were momentarily scared.

The scene in the great square was changing now, crews tumbling back into their tanks, a burst of noise as the engines started up, and then the sound of shots being fired. I did not see anybody fall, nor hear any cries of pain, but the shouts of abuse had ceased abruptly, and except for the roar of the tank engines revving up a sudden stillness settled over the crowd, everybody staring up at the balcony, which was now almost empty. The President and his wife had slipped back into the room behind.

When order was finally restored and they came out again, the speech was not the same. Ceauşescu's words were far more placatory. Now he was promising wage increases, improvements in pensions, a new scale of allowances. He was pandering to the mob, and they knew it. They were not appeased.

Murmurings grew to a groundswell of discontent

that the militia could not deal with, the President's speech increasingly interrupted by the shouts of agitators. Gradually his words were drowned, and at that point canned music blared forth from the speakers, and suddenly the crowd was in motion as water-cannon moved in, drenching the troublemakers.

That was when I caught a glimpse of Antoine. A gap had opened up to my left, and there he was, a tall figure, head turning as he searched the crowd. He saw me, waved, then turned abruptly, raising his camera above his head to take pictures of the water jets breaking up the crowd. The lane closed, people frantically trying to escape, a mass of humanity eddying in a great swirl as they were knocked off their feet by the force of the water.

I began to fight my way out of the square. And just in time, for the army and the *Securitate* were moving in. I caught a glimpse of one of the agitators, who had been trying to work the crowd into a frenzy. A marksman from somewhere high up in the Central Committee Building had shot him and he was screaming, his mouth wide and blood all over his face. But by then the crowd was pouring out of the square.

Clear of the shooting, the authorities lost control again. I passed a little crowd pouring petrol onto a pile of books, and the books all had Ceauşescu's face on the cover. A thousand faces of the Romanian President curling and blackening at the edges as a match was tossed into the centre of the pile and the flames took hold.

Though surrounded by a moving mass of people,

loneliness began to take hold again. Uncertainty lowers morale more effectively than anything else, and what I had just witnessed in the Piata Republica was a state on the point of collapse. It scared me. If the security forces lost control anything could happen and I found myself involuntarily looking around for my breakfast companion. I just did not want to be on my own.

In less than ten minutes I was back at the Bucureşti. No sign of Antoine Caminade. I asked at the desk for his room number, then went up to my own room and switched on the television. Nothing of interest, no indication of what had happened not half a mile away from where I lay on the bed, staring up at the ceiling, thinking of Luca Brasov and wondering how long it would take him to arrange some form of transport for me. I couldn't stay at the Bucureşti indefinitely. Three days? I would give it three days. After that I would have to see what I could arrange for myself. Tarom if possible. It was the only airline that flew direct to the UK – Bucharest to Stansted. So quick, so convenient. No stops, no changes, all over in four hours and the mess that was Romania behind me.

I must have drifted off to sleep for the next thing I knew the telephone was ringing. Luca! I snatched up the receiver. But it wasn't Luca. It was Antoine.

'*Ah, bon.* You are okay, then?' He seemed concerned.

Why he was ringing me was to say he had booked a table for us in the restaurant for eight fifteen. 'I have ordered sturgeon. No caviare. Too expensive, even here where the great big lovely fish is caught in the delta. I have it last night. But they bake it till it is dry, like an old shoe. I have arranged for it to be cooked the way I like. The way they cook it in Odessa – if you know where to go. So, eight fifteen. That okay for you?'

'So long as I am back in my room by ten.'

'Why?' He laughed. 'You have a gairl coming to see you, eh?'

'No,' I said. 'I am expecting a telephone call.'

I actually told him that. As I said it I realized it was stupid of me. I should have kept my mouth shut. But I had no reason to think it mattered to him, particularly as his next words were, 'If you have nothing to do now, watch the television. I think it may be interesting, what they do to cover up that poor little President and his dreadful speech.' Again that laugh, and he rang off.

When eventually the television station switched to a rebroadcast of Ceaușescu's speech they had managed quite a good cosmetic job, blotting out most of the original interruptions and dubbing in odds and ends of soundtrack lifted from the recording of an earlier and well-orchestrated rally in support of the Party and its leader. *Ceaușescu, Ceaușescu – Long live our esteemed, our much loved Leader* – or words to that effect. And music, a lot of stirring martial music. It was all very blatant and hardly likely to fool any of those who had been in the square. In the present climate I thought the truth would spread like wildfire.

I watched the programme right through, and then I had a bath, thinking, as I gradually relaxed in the warmth of the water, how he must have felt, standing there on that balcony, looking down on the dense-packed crowd and hearing his voice come blaring back at him out of the PA loudspeakers, amplified so that the sound of it filled the square. All those years, first as General Secretary of the Communist Youth, then, after four years in prison, through careful adherence to the Party line, he had been put in charge of the Party's organization. Some fifteen years later, nursing his power base and playing the part of a good administrator, he became Party Leader and one of the triumvirate that ruled Romania after the death of Ghorghiu-Dej in 1965. Within four years, by insidiously promoting his own people into positions of power, he had effectively become the country's ruler.

Looking back over my visits to Romania, it was obvious that Ceauşescu's hold over the people had been gradually slipping ever since the end of the sixties when he had been presenting himself as the modern equivalent of the Dacian hero Burebista, who had led the struggle against the Roman occupation, or as one of the later Romanian warlords who had endeavoured to fight off the Turks. That was when he had felt strong enough to break with Russia and train half a million factory workers for guerrilla warfare. He had called them the Patriotic Guard.

The man had been on a high then, lauded by the West. And now, twenty years later, I had stood in the central square of the capital and watched that same man trying to buy the support of his people, pathetically mouthing worn-out slogans, and all those around me knowing damn well that, apart from Albania and Cuba, his was the only state that still believed in Communism. No wonder he had looked scared, the whole of his life on the verge of ruin, all that he had believed in destroyed in a matter of a few months, and now his own position threatened. *Murderer – Timisoara* . . . However successfully the canned version of his speech was edited, however well the dubbing of loyal chants from the recordings of earlier rallies had been done, nothing could erase the fact that hostility, not abject subservience, was now the mood dominating the minds of his people. Nor could they erase the look on his face as he stared down at the great mob below that had turned suddenly hostile.

By the time I got out of the bath, it was past eight. I dressed and went down, still thinking about Ceauşescu and feeling almost light-hearted because I was no longer worrying about Luca failing to arrange a safe passage for me out of the country. I had dollars in my pocket, and if it was civil war, then I would have no difficulty.

The roar of voices coming from the dining room was audible the instant the lift doors opened, and when I went in the sound of everybody talking at once was overwhelming. The room was already full and the talk was all about the same thing as I threaded my way through the tables. Antoine Caminade was sitting alone at a table for two right at the far end.

'I think they are concerned that maybe they don't get another meal after tomorrow.' He already had a bottle on the table. 'I thought white, to go with the sturgeon.' We drank it slowly, talking like everybody else about what we had seen. We had each of us a different perspective and we had plenty of time to discuss our very disparate views. His was more of a media reaction, and he was better informed about what was going on behind the scenes, politically. The service was slow. The waiters were moving fast enough, but there were too few of them. Twice Antoine summoned one of them, getting me to protest in Romanian on his behalf, and each time the man gave me a sulky look and blamed the kitchen. And when finally he banged two plates down in front of us with the steaks of sturgeon criss-crossed in black lines, the fish overcooked and leathery, my companion launched into a very Gallic stream of protest.

The waiter merely shrugged. He didn't understand French, but he got the message all right and poured forth a stream of Romanian, speaking it so fast that I could barely follow what he was saying. It was a very proletarian type of speech, pointing the finger of contempt at us for being something capitalists – the adjective he used was one I had never heard before. Antoine got to his feet. I hadn't realized till then how tall he was. He towered over the angry little waiter. 'Come!' He picked up both our plates, thrust them into the man's hands and took hold of his arm. '*Pardon*,' he said to me over his shoulder. 'This afternoon I telephone the chef and speak with him personally. This is not our fish. I give him exact instructions, which of course he knew. Come,' he said again to the waiter and he led the way across the room to the swing doors that opened into the kitchens, the waiter trotting behind him with the two plates still held in his hands.

It was a good ten minutes before the two of them returned with Antoine carrying the plates himself and the waiter trotting behind with a bottle in his hand. '*Voilà*. I think you will find this very much better. The chef speaks French, of course.'

They were different steaks, not burnt at all, the flesh succulent and a sauce to complement it. 'The wine is the chef's own choice. He give it to me.' The grin on his face expressed a profound degree of satisfaction. 'Even here, in this ridiculous country, good can come out of tossing the weight about, eh?' He sat down, diving into his first experimental mouthful, then nodding enthusiastically and expressing his entire satisfaction. Still nodding and smiling, he dismissed the waiter, then turned the conversation to politics. 'We will see what happen tomorrow. If the foreign press boys are right, it will be touch and go for the Ceauşescus. You notice how the army don't shoot. It is only the *Securitate*, and perhaps some police.' And he went on to talk about Milea, Vasile Milea, the Minister of Defence. He had come up through the ranks and was very popular with the men. 'They say he refuse to order the military to open fire.' And then suddenly he asked me, very casually, 'When do you leave?'

'As soon as possible,' I said.

'And that is the phone call you are expecting

tonight?' It was said in a voice that was half statement, half question.

'Yes.'

Looking back on it, I realize he must have been sitting, waiting for me to come down to breakfast that morning so that he could join me. As a result, on the evening of the same day the two of us were now having dinner together. All this song and dance about the sturgeon and the way it had been cooked, he might have organized it in advance, for the effect of it was of course to bring us closer together – two men alone in a strange country, different nationalities, different backgrounds – and different jobs. I never had to ask him what his job was, why he was here. He had volunteered it. And anyway, his camera made it self-evident.

'So you go back to London.' He asked me where I would be staying, but I said I did not know. 'My firm will book me in at some hotel, I imagine, as soon as I can give them an ETA.'

'So you are not married? You do not have a house or a flat in London?' And when I shook my head, he added, 'You will fly out from Otopeni, is that what you plan? When – tomorrow?' And he added, 'There will be chaos tomorrow, I think. Unless you have some special pass I doubt you will get out through Otopeni. But maybe this phone call...' He hesitated. 'Do you have some important contact?'

I didn't answer that of course and after a moment's silence he went off at a tangent, talking about the political situation again, how delicately poised the Ceauşescus were. 'He is not accustomed to being challenged. So one minute he is giving orders to shoot and the next he is trying to appease the dissidents. You hear what he say today? He offer a wage increase.' He gave a quick, exaggerated shrug of the slightly padded shoulders. '*Alors!* If his wife Elena were the Party Leader, then there is per'aps no immediate problem. She would not hesitate. She is much harder, always pushing him to be firm. They say some of the worst excesses of the *Securitate* were initiated by her.' He leaned towards me. 'But do not misinterpret what I say. I don't think she is vicious like those women in the German horror camps. Just hard. She knows the Romanian people. They are peasants, bowing to any power stronger than themselves.'

He went on like that for some time, and just as he had finished his meal he suddenly switched back to my affairs, asking me a direct question – 'You puzzle me, Paul. You are here in this difficult time, but you are not a newspaper man or a part of the media. What are you? Are you here on business?'

It was put to me so direct that without being offensive there was no way I could avoid answering him. I simply nodded, and he said, 'So, you have a company – of your own?'

I shook my head. 'No, I act for others.' And because there seemed no reason not to tell him, I explained that I was out here to find out whether the people I was acting for could rely on a steady supply of scrap.

'If they were to run a steelworks in Russia – is that what you mean?' He looked puzzled. And when I did not reply, he said, 'And now you are trying to get home to England, so presumably you have the answer?'

'No,' I said. 'I think they want me for another job altogether.'

'Another job?' I think he was on the point of asking me for details, his eyes wide and very bright behind his gold-rimmed glasses. Even then it didn't occur to me that his questions could stem from anything other than a casual interest. Having been thrown together because we were neither of us part of any group, it seemed quite natural. I had never thought of my job as something important, something that others might be interested in. Scrap for a possible new steelworks, and before that, west of Kalgoorlie, an assessment of two old-time prospectors who had spent their lives in the Australian bush and now had a gold mine they wanted to sell in order to go chasing another pot of the stuff at the end of some rainbow of their imagination out beyond Alice Springs. It was routine as far as I was concerned, though I suppose the careful wording of the message should have alerted me. It just didn't occur to me that I might be entering a world where my movements would become of interest to others.

In any case, Antoine Caminade was no longer probing for information about my work. Instead, he had switched to an earlier conversation, talking about a visit he had made to Uzbekistan. He had travelled the old Silk Road from Merv through Bokhara and Samarkand as far east as Kashgar, then back via Yarkand and the southern route. Did I know the area? No, I said, but I had always been interested in the archaeological remains in the Taklamakan Desert. 'I speak Turkoman.' And I told him how as a student I had travelled from Iran into Azerbaijan as far as Baku on the Caspian Sea. 'I never got as far as the Taklamakan. I wish I had – those fabulous Buddhist manuscripts, the wall paintings, the sand-buried temples.'

'So per'aps you go there now?'

I laughed. 'Not a hope.'

'Why not? You say languages come easily to you, the same they do to me. What about Chinese? Do you speak any Chinese?'

I shook my head. 'Linguistically I don't go as far east as that. Anyway, why should my people send me to the Taklamakan area?'

'Why not? The Russians have bases there, for testing nuclear warheads.' He stared at me a moment, and then he began telling me about the forts, mosques and minarets he had photographed on his Silk Road journey.

Time passed quickly as we exchanged impressions of that lost area of south-central Asia. Then the coffee arrived and with it the apricot brandy he had ordered, a whole bottle of the stuff.

Just as we had started on the third glass, he leaned across to me with that toothy grin and said, 'You know we still have the evening ahead of us. You want a gairl?' And when I reminded him I was waiting for a phone call, he said, 'Yes, of course. But you must excuse, I do not intend to sleep alone in this morgue of a hotel.'

I wished him good hunting and he laughed. 'Oh, I don't go hunting for it.' He knocked back the brandy he had just poured and summoned the waiter, who looked quite scared when he told him to fetch the maître. Antoine got to his feet as a man with a head like a hard-boiled egg and dark little avaricious eyes came bustling towards us. 'There is something wrong, monsieur?'

'*Non, non.* A word with you, in private. That is all.' He took hold of the man's elbow, steering him towards the door. 'I will only be a moment,' he called to me over his shoulder.

I watched them disappear towards the foyer, then sat there alone, drinking my coffee and wondering about his motive for this elaborate charade. He was doing it to impress me. I realized that. But why?

After a few minutes he returned, alone, the grin back on his face. 'All is arranged. He has a cousin of course – very beautiful, very accommodating. In fact' – and he leaned down, almost whispering in my ear – 'in fact she has a sister.' He stared at me with a lift of the eyebrows. 'Don't look so doubtful. He says they are both clean, no clap, no HIV. They say this place is Government-run for the *Securitate*. Any gairl on their list is surely cleared for safe action.' He stared at me, waiting. 'So you don't want company for the night?' And when I shook my head, he called for his bill, signed it and, after pouring himself another glass of brandy and drinking it still standing, he left me with a quick wave of his hand.

I had another brandy myself then, drank the last of the coffee and went up to my room. It was just on ten o'clock. I had barely closed the door when the phone beside the bed rang. It was Reception with a message for me. It simply said: *Café-bar Dobrogea Strada Stirbei Voda twelve*. Nothing else. 'She do not give her name.' The brittle voice of the man at the desk sounded almost offended. 'You know who it is?'

'I think so,' I said. I thanked him and put the receiver down before he could ask any more questions.

I switched on the television, wondering why Luca had had a woman, his wife presumably, phone the message through instead of ringing himself and asking to be put through to me. I had given him my room number. Did that mean all direct communication with foreign visitors had been banned?

Romania TV was pumping out martial music larded with economic statistics, routine propaganda stuff. I switched the set off and sat in the big armchair watching the movement of people in the street leading to the little church. From far away came a burst of shooting. Suddenly people were running, a man in the middle of the road gesticulating, the crowd moving up towards the church and scattering. A moment later the street was empty and I was thinking about that phone call again. It was Luca, of course. It had to be. But why a meeting? Or was the café-bar just a safe contact point for me to be told what he had arranged? There was a simple map in the drawer of the telephone table.

The street was very close to the hotel. The twelve presumably referred to the time I was to meet him.

My dinner with Antoine Caminade seemed suddenly a far-off oasis of calm. Luca had said the name of the restaurant and its address, plus the time, would give me the name of the ship and where and when I should report. He had kept to the essentials of place and time, but what worried me was the change in his method of passing the information on to me. The phone to my room was working, and since he had phoned the message in to the switchboard the external lines were still open. So why the change?

Then, just as I was getting into bed, there came a knocking at the door and a harsh Romanian voice shouted, in English, 'Open up! Open up!'

'Who is it?' I swung my feet to the floor.

The knocking became the pounding of a fist. 'Open, open. *Securitate*.'

'Just a moment.' My voice was high and tense. 'What do you want?'

There was the sound of a key grating in the lock. 'There is a message for you.'

It was what I had feared. Or was this another message? I switched on the light and opened the door to find a short, sharp-featured man with an unruly mop of black hair standing in the corridor, one hand in the pocket of his jacket. His eyes watched me as though expecting me to make a break for it, or even attack him. '*D-nul* Paul Cartwright?' He didn't wait for a reply, pushing past me, his eyes searching the room. He slammed open the bathroom door, finally checking the heavy wardrobe. 'You are *Englez*?'

'*Da*.'

'And you are alone here in Romania?'

I nodded.

'Why are you here? You are not a journalist, I think. You have been in Constantza. At the Intim Hotel.'

I explained the nature of my business in Romania, gave him the names of two people I had contacted in Constantza before visiting Mihai, and then told him I would be going to the British Embassy in the morning to arrange further contacts. It was obvious he knew nothing about Mihai and what had happened in Constantza. He was a hotel security officer and he was here in my room, questioning me, simply because his orders were to check on any messages that could be classed as suspicious. I was a foreigner, the message I had received was anonymous. No name had been given. 'Who is this man you are to meet? Or is it the woman who telephone the message through to Reception?'

'I don't know,' I told him. And then, improvising quickly, I explained that one of the newspaper men here in the hotel had said he would arrange for me to meet someone he knew in insurance who would be able to put me in touch with an official of a state-owned shipping company. 'He did not say who the insurance man was. Just that he would contact me.' It was the best I could do on the spur of the moment.

But then, of course, he wanted to know the name of the newspaper man.

I told him the only name I knew: '*N-dul* Antoine Caminade.'

'And he is staying here in this hotel?'

'*Da.*'

He reached across the bed to the phone, had a brief word with Reception, then nodded. '*Foarte bino.* I leave you now. After you meet this insurance man you report to me. I have to know his name. Also what ships he offers to sell. You understand?'

When I had shut the door on him I found I was literally shaking. It hadn't shown while he was questioning me, I was certain of that. But now . . . I flung myself on the bed, all sorts of possibilities flitting through my mind. It was all so unreal, the whole bloody sequence of events like a bad dream. The windows of my room were tight shut against the cold outside, but I could still hear the sleepless people in the street below, a constant low murmur. It added to the tension that had been building up in me.

I had a bath, hoping it would relax me. But I had been living on my nerves ever since Mihai had let me into that room of his. Soaking up the warmth of the water, I could still feel the contraction of my muscles as I heaved the body onto the balcony rail, then thrust it hard into the night as the truck ground past. The Dacia, the hotel *Securitate* man, the night crowd in the streets, and Luca, the café-bar Dobrogea – where would I be this time tomorrow night? Steaming down the Danube and out into the Black Sea, pray God!

The bath must have done me some good, for once in bed I went off to sleep almost immediately, and I didn't wake until past nine. By the time I got down for breakfast the big room was almost empty. No sign of Antoine, or any of his media friends. With two and a half hours before my meeting with Luca I lingered over the meal, and then just as I was about to leave the Frenchman turned up, a plate piled high with food in one hand and his camera in the other, with a cup of slopped-over coffee balanced precariously.

'Did you have a good night?' I asked him. He looked thoroughly washed out.

'Oh, not so bad I suppose. I never sleep with a Romanian gairl before. She is well padded, like a feather bed.' He gave me that toothy grin, adding reflectively, 'Yes, a nice little woman – black hair, full lips. She would have been good, I think, but it is me that is no good. The brandy, per'aps.' He leaned across to me, holding up his forefinger and drooping it in front of my eyes. 'Like that, you know. I was no good.' He shrugged. 'No matter. She is comfortable and do not cost too much with the dollar–lei exchange rate the way it is. And then the bastards woke me.'

It was a tip-off, apparently. He had arranged with the *Paris Soir* stringer to alert him to anything exciting. 'I am there in the square when the helicopter land on the roof of the Central Committee Building. By then they are putting it out that Milea has committed suicide, but of course nobody is believing that. They all think he has been murdered. He is certainly dead because the army had no orders. Why are you not there? I try to phone your room, but they tell me to leave a message.' He stared at me, eating fast, and then without waiting for an answer, he went on, 'They came out on to the balcony, Nicolae and Elena, both. For a moment I think he was going to speak. The square was packed. We were shoulder to shoulder, some shouting, but mostly the crowd is quiet, waiting to see if it would be an exhibition like yesterday with more promises. The President is staring down at us, indecision written all over his face, and then his wife draws him to the back of the balcony and they disappear inside. Shortly afterwards the helicopter land on the roof and they take off.'

He went to get himself some more coffee, but came back saying the urn was empty. 'So, they are gone.'

'Where? Do you know?'

He shook his head. 'It is believed he is gone to the provinces, per'aps to Olt County where he come from.'

'Is that the end then? Is the Ceauşescu regime finished?'

He popped a whole peeled egg between his teeth, frowning. '*Ne sais pas*. Some say yes, some no – all I can tell you is that when I leave the square they have broken open the doors of the Central Committee Building and there are students on the balcony where the President and his wife have so recently been, and the army, the police, nobody do anything to stop them.' He pushed the rest of the egg into his mouth. 'You coming?'

I shook my head.

He leaned down, both hands on the table, peering

into my face. 'Why not? There will be chaos now.' His eyes gleamed and it was then I realized that the thought of chaos appealed to him. 'Are you afraid to be out on the streets with the mob?'

I didn't answer that.

'So you are waiting for somebody. Is that it?'

I glanced at my watch and got to my feet. 'I'm expecting a phone call.'

He stared at me, then smiled. 'You are a very busy man. And you have contacts.' He hesitated.

I didn't say anything, just raised my hand and left him there, hurrying up to my room. His persistence worried me to the extent that I thought perhaps he might be homosexual. It certainly was nothing to do with the fact that I was English. He wasn't an Anglophile, he hadn't even been to London.

I had with me a paperback copy of Hopkirk's *Foreign Devils on the Silk Road* and for an hour I tried to lose myself in the account of Sven Hedin's search for the lost cities of the Taklamakan and their Buddhist treasures, while all hell broke loose outside. And to think that my erstwhile little dancing partner had made her home somewhere over there.

But I couldn't concentrate; the endless tramp of feet, people pouring from the square, the sound of shots. There was gunfire in the distance, shouts, occasional screams. Finally the noise subsided, the sound of the mob drifting away. The phone rang.

It was Caminade. 'I think per'aps you like to know the helicopter I saw take off earlier was overloaded. They had two of their henchmen on board. They land by some small town and commandeer a car, but they are seen by military patrolling near Boteni Airport and arrested. They are now prisoners at the military garrison near Tirgoviste, which is some sixty or seventy kilometres north-west of here. You join me for lunch – one o'clock, okay?'

'Sorry,' I said.

'What is it now, another phone call? I have some more information by lunchtime.' A pause, and then he added, 'Is it your contact, then? You are meeting somebody?'

'I've got to go now,' I said, thanking him quickly for inviting me to join him for lunch, and put the receiver down. I went back to my book then, but though the noise of the crowd had subsided, I still could not concentrate, wondering all the time about Caminade. Why was he so interested in me, so persistent?

I had allowed myself half an hour to get to the Dobrogea. It was barely enough, for though the Strada Stirbei Voda ran straight into the Piata Republica, the Dobrogea was a long way down it, past the intersection with the Strada Schitu Magureandu, and there were crowds everywhere, the whole city, it seemed, in turmoil.

It was just after midday when I finally reached it, but no sign of Luca, the place deserted and boarded up. I stood there, waiting, and because of the ebb and flow of the crowd I did not feel conspicuous. The police and militia at the intersection took no notice of me.

A cyclist paused at the entrance to a side street, glanced in my direction, then pedalled towards me. I didn't recognize him at first, for he was huddled in a heavy greatcoat with a woollen scarf round his neck and a floppy brown woollen hat pulled round his ears and down over his eyes. He stopped just short of me and said, speaking English in quite a loud voice, 'You are being followed. Pale hair, long face.' His feet were on the ground and he was leaning forward. 'Walk on. Turn right, and right again, to back of Dobrogea. Somebody will be watching for you.' He was not looking at me, his head turned towards one of the crowd who had paused to light the stub of a cigarette. 'Walk slow and do not look behind. Okay?'

I gave a slight nod and he wheeled his bike across the road to a little group of youngsters standing in a close-knit huddle. They were very dark, with long black hair, like gypsies. I turned away, looking around me, pretending to search for my contact, then wandering slowly off as though disconsolate at his non-appearance.

I had walked barely a hundred metres, as far as the nearer turning to the right, when there was an outcry behind me. The gang of youths were gathered round a man with fair hair, shouting and gesticulating angrily. The man stood head and shoulders above them. It was Antoine Caminade.

I ducked down the side street, ran to the next right turn, and a moment later I was at the back of the

Dobrogea. He hadn't seen me. I was certain of that. There was a rear door, I beat on it, but nobody came. The place seemed deserted.

A window opened in the rear of the building next door and a woman's voice asked me my name. I told her and she said to wait, she would be right down. She was a small, dark, intense person with gimlet eyes and a quick, staccato way of talking. Was I *Englez*, where was I staying, could she see my passport? Then suddenly she asked me had I been to Constantza? Finally she nodded and let me in to what appeared to be some sort of office. 'You know Mihai, is that correct?'

I nodded.

'What is the name of his daughter?'

I hesitated. No reason I should not tell her. 'Vikki. And his wife's name is Ana.'

She smiled then, a quick readjustment of her features. 'Ana is dead.' She said it quite flatly, adding, 'And Mihai has been taken in for questioning.'

A knock at the door and Luca strode in, the bulk of him in his heavy coat and woollen cap seeming to fill the room. 'It is okay now,' he said to me. 'He don't see where you go.' And then to the woman, 'He will almost certainly try the back of the restaurant, may even come here. Watch for him. And don't let him see my bicycle.'

She left us and he shut the door. 'Sit down.' He waved me to a chair, pulling up another and squatting on it, his legs spread as though he were on a toilet. '*Acum*, listen carefully please, I have to go back to the Central Committee Building. I am a member of the NSF, the National Salvation Front. We have to form a government, so they are having a meeting. When I don't know. Nicolae Ceauşescu has been taken. You know that?'

I nodded.

'Okay. So we have to form a government.' He banged his fist down on the desk. 'And we don't have the people. Not people with the ability to govern. The *Communisti* will be regrouping. They have the experience. Our people don't. And there is Iliescu waiting his opportunity.' The massive shoulders heaved in a shrug. 'Not your problem, eh?' He shook his head, a sad, very massive gesture that said more than words. '*Acum*, listen carefully, please. You are not the only one I have promised to arrange for departure out of the country.'

'Mihai?' I asked. 'Are you arranging—'

'No, no. We will try to do something about Mihai, but later. We can do nothing about that until the *Securitate* release him.'

'What are they holding him for?' I asked. 'Is it because of Miron Dinca?'

'Yes, of course. They know he intended to visit Mihai, but they don't know what happen. Not yet. The forester found the body when he reached his home and start to unload his tools. He was scared, so he drive his truck up into the forest, but while he is still on the state highway he ran into an army patrol. That is how they arrest Mihai this morning.' He leaned forward quickly – all his movements were quick for such a heavy man. 'What happened?'

I told him, and he nodded. 'It had to happen, some day. God in heaven!' He slammed his fist down on the desk again. And then he was leaning forward again. 'Listen, please. But first, where is that motor of yours, that Dacia?'

I could only tell him roughly. 'I don't know the name of the street. It is a cul-de-sac.'

'A building, a shop, anything,' he demanded impatiently, 'anything that will identify the street you turned down.'

'I'm sorry,' I said, 'my mind was occupied by other things. But I can lead you to it.'

He shook his head. 'No good. I must check the car now, whether it is still there. I have to instruct the other person.' He stared at me. 'Think please.'

But I couldn't help him. The boar was all I could remember, the brown bristled back of it behind the railings, its angry grunting. At the mention of it his eyes lit up and he gave me a huge grin. 'Why do you not tell me that before? Everybody know Doamna Raceanu and her damn *porc*. His name is Boris. Not too original, eh? But he is near as big as a bear. Now, listen.' He gripped hold of my arm, garlic on his breath as he told me what he had arranged: 'Tomorrow night, or maybe the next night, there will be a small coastal ship coming down the Dunărea, down the Bratul Sulina. You go on board this vessel close by Crisan.'

'Where's it going?' I asked.

'To Cyprus. It is a Turkish ship. After you pass

through the Dardanelles you make your own arrangements to land. Okay?' He was getting to his feet. 'Now
I see about that Dacia car you borrow. If it is still
there, then no problem and I notify the person who is
to go with you.'

I asked him who it was, but all he said was, 'It is
somebody who has to leave Romania very quickly.
One of us,' he added, and then went on to give me
detailed instructions. These involved driving to Tulcea
where a fisherman from the little Russian community
in the Crisan area would meet us.

'But—'

He clapped me on the shoulder. 'Do not disturb
yourself. You will get through.' He gave a great guffaw.
'Your companion will see to that, and also look after
the matter of *benzina*.' And then as he was going out
he added, 'You will be good for each other.' Another
guffaw and then he said, 'Stay here until' – he glanced
at his watch – 'until it is one o'clock. Nicolina will
provide you with some food. Give her a dollar, something like that, and if I am not back by one you know
the car is okay. You meet your passenger at ten o'clock
tonight beside the Dacia, and watch out nobody follow
you. With your papers, all your baggage, you understand, and dollars, cash, you will require dollars.' He
stared at me hard for a second, then – '*Bun voiaj!*' A
quick nod and he was gone, closing the door behind
him and calling for Nicolina.

The little office seemed suddenly very empty. My
lunch consisted of black bread and the warmed-up
entrails of some animal, pig or goat, I wasn't sure

which, the dubious mess washed down with a glass of rough but quite drinkable red wine. Oddly enough, when I had finished it I realized the dish had been quite tasty. It also proved very satisfying, and the wine, being strong, gave me a rosier view of the journey ahead.

I was thinking then about the unknown passenger Luca had wished on me. The laconic way in which he had said *your companion will see to that*, when I had started to express my doubts about being allowed to drive through to Tulcea, had aroused my curiosity. And saying *You will be good for each other* – what had he meant by that?

The hesitant manner in which he had introduced the subject gave me an uneasy feeling that he wasn't quite sure about the arrangement. What sort of a man would my companion turn out to be? Somebody who could talk his way through any checkpoint, an ex-Communist high-up, an escaped political prisoner, a sharpshooter, a murderer, a man released from prison to do some of the dirty work for the anti-Communist dissidents?

Back at the hotel I phoned the Embassy. I asked for the ambassador. I didn't get him, of course. The very upmarket voice at the other end enquired my business, and when I told him, he said that was a commercial matter. He put me through to the relevant attaché so that I had to explain myself all over again. I also told him I had written from London before flying out to Romania. There was a long pause while somebody found the letter for him. 'Paul Cartwright, did you say?'

'Yes.'

Another pause and the sound of pages being turned, and then he said he was sorry he couldn't see me this week, which was hardly surprising since it was already Friday. 'At the moment everything is at sixes and sevens. I am sure you understand.'

We agreed a meeting at his office early Tuesday morning, and then he was good enough to say, 'If you get into any difficulties ring this number.' The number he gave me was quite different from the Embassy number. 'Keep your head down over the weekend. Don't play around with the girls or change money with anybody who comes up to you in the street offering above the official rate. In fact, I would advise you not to walk out of your hotel on your own, certainly not with anything of value on you. God knows who will be in power tomorrow or the day after. See you Tuesday.' And he rang off.

At least I had a number to ring if I did land myself in real trouble. And if I got out of the country safely I could always let him know.

It was already dusk now and the lights were coming on. I gave it until six and then I went down and settled my bill. They asked me, of course, where I was going and I gave the British Embassy as my address. 'I shall be staying there until Tuesday,' I said. 'Perhaps longer.'

It was sufficient to enable me to get my baggage out of the hotel and into a taxi without a fuss being made. They had doubtless checked with the switchboard and been told I had been talking to the Embassy.

The Dacia was still there, the boar still on guard and grunting. After paying off the taxi, the man drove right to the end of the cul-de-sac before turning. Then he stopped and began reading a paper. It was obvious he had been instructed to watch that I really did go to the Embassy. I had no alternative then but to drive off.

I had already got directions from him as to how to get to the Embassy and these I followed until I saw him turn off, presumably heading back to the hotel to report. I wondered how long it would be before somebody was bright enough to check the Dacia's number with *Securitate*. Or perhaps they wouldn't bother?

Once clear of the cul-de-sac the streets had been full of people, so that I had had to slow almost to a crawl. The petrol gauge showed the tank barely a quarter full. I parked in another side street near a shop half boarded up, where I was able to purchase a slice of almost black bread spread with what I took to be dripping interlarded with minute pieces of tripe, or perhaps it was brain.

Romania at any time was hardly a gourmet's paradise, but with fear stalking the streets and the distant sound of gunfire you grabbed what you could and considered yourself lucky to have anything with which to fill your belly. Dinner at the Bucureşti seemed suddenly the height of luxury! I spun that awful meal out as long as I could and then just sat there, wondering about the man who would join me when I returned to my original parking point and the grunting pig. I was wholly dependent on him to get me through any patrols, to find the *benzina* to top up the Dacia's tank, even to telling me where in Tulcea we would be picked up, the name of the ship. *You will be good for each other!*

I hoped so, for I was utterly in his hands.

I had planned to be back with the pig just before ten, but I was held up by a mass of people all shouting slogans. This was near one of the entrances to the Gradina Cismigiu, the big park just south-west of the Bucureşti, and the chanting was being led by a wild-looking character with shoulder-length black hair and the face and eyes of a fanatic. *NSF – NSF – Democratie, Democratie.*

It was well past ten before I reached my old parking place. It was now occupied by a small bus. As I passed it I saw with relief there was a figure in shapeless clothes and a broad-brimmed hat sitting on what looked like a bedroll with his back against the pig's railings.

I had to go almost to the end of the cul-de-sac before I found a place to park. Perhaps that was as well as it enabled me to check for anybody lurking in the shadows as I walked back. Apart from a couple sleeping on the opposite pavement the street seemed deserted. The figure seated against the railings stirred as I approached, then rose to its feet. I thought for a moment my companion-to-be was a cleric, but then I realized that the cassock was a long, ankle-length skirt.

It was a woman, the broad-brimmed hat fastened to her dark hair by two long hatpins.

If I hadn't been so appalled, I think I would have burst out laughing, for the hat reminded me of jackaroos I had met in the Australian bush. But she was much smaller, of course, a little shapeless bundle of a woman, and there were no corks dangling from the brim. I didn't know what to say and we stood for a moment facing each other in silence. Finally she asked me my name.

'Paul,' I said.

She nodded. 'I am needing a lift to Tulcea.' She had a soft, rather musical voice and she spoke English with almost no trace of an accent.

'Who sent you?' I asked.

A momentary hesitation and then she said, 'Luca.'

A woman! That's all I could think of as I turned and walked back to the Dacia. Why the hell had he landed me with a woman? The journey ahead was likely to present enough problems without the added complication of a female passenger. I cursed myself for not having got all the information I needed out of Luca when I had the opportunity, then I could have cleared out and left her and her bedroll with the pig. Damn it to hell! What was I supposed to do with her?

By the time I had turned the Dacia and driven back she was standing in the roadway, the bedroll at her feet. She flung it onto the rear seat and got in beside it. 'You know the way, do you?' I asked, wondering at the effort it had cost her to heave the bedroll in.

'Of course.' The voice was terse and I realized she

was about as angry as I was for some reason. 'You're late. I thought you would have had the sense to be early.'

'Who are you?' I asked her.

She didn't answer. I glanced round quickly and saw she was wrestling with the straps of her bedroll.

'Who are you?' I asked again.

'Why do you want to know?' The voice was sharp, almost agitated. 'It is no concern of yours who I am. You turn left here.'

'But when I drove into Bucharest from Constantza two days ago—'

'Do as I say. Turn left.' And she added, 'Just follow my instructions. So we avoid the crowds and maybe the military patrols.'

'If you're going to guide me out of the city by the side streets hadn't you better sit in front?'

'No. Here I can move more freely.' We were into one of the boulevards now and heading south. I knew that because at the last intersection I had caught a glimpse of the Plough. The North Star was behind us now.

'Who are you?' I asked again. 'I must know who you are. Or what your papers say you are. You do have papers – passport – whatever is necessary to satisfy the ship's captain, don't you? You'll need the equivalent of a passport to get into Cyprus.'

'I am not going to Cyprus.'

'Where, then?'

She didn't answer for a moment. Finally she said, 'I don't know. Not yet.'

I slowed the car. 'You haven't answered my original question. If you don't tell me who you are and why you're trying to smuggle yourself out of the country—'

'You will throw me out of the car. Is that it?' And she added, 'You just try, my friend. This car belongs to the *Securitate*, right? You do not have a hope of making Tulcea without me. You don't know where in Tulcea you are to rendezvous with Stefan or what ship it is will stop for you.' She leaned forward, her hand on my shoulder, the fingers digging in. 'Now drive on. Remember, please, I am much more desperate than you are to leave Romania behind.' Then in a more relaxed voice, almost with a tinkle of laughter in it, 'For the time being all you need know about me is that I am the other one. Now get on and drive.'

'We need some petrol,' I said.

'*Benzina!* You mean to tell me—' The words seemed to stick in her throat. 'What sort of a person are you? A journey like this, by car, and you don't have a full tank.'

'It's almost empty. Luca said you would see to it.'

'Did he!' There was a moment's silence, then she said, 'Turn left at the next intersection, then first right, and drive carefully.' She directed me through several side streets, stopping me at a motor-accessory shop. 'Bianca!' she called. Then to me, 'Dollars. You do have dollars, don't you?'

I nodded.

A large, grey-haired woman had appeared in the shop doorway. A flood of Romanian and a can was produced and a funnel. Filling the Dacia's tank was a furtive business with many glances up and down the street, but it remained empty, nobody about. Ten minutes and we were away. 'Bianca's husband runs a taxi service, she looks after the shop.' Then she was directing me on to Highway 3. 'You branch off to Tulcea immediately after the second bridge across the Danube, just before Cernavoda. That is where we could have trouble.'

But Cernavoda was well over a hundred kilometres away, and with very little traffic and enough fuel in the tank to get us to Tulcea my spirits rose. The click of metal on metal from behind caused me to turn my head. She had her bedroll half undone and was pulling an automatic rifle out of an untidy bundle of clothing. 'What is it?' I asked. 'A Kalashnikov?'

'Of course. What else? I got this one for six dollars.'

'And you know how to use it?' My heart sank, my hands tightening on the wheel.

'Of course I know how to use it. You think I'd lug the thing around if I didn't?' And she added, 'Why the hell do you think I have to leave the country this way and in such a hurry?' The tension was back in her voice.

I stared at the road ahead, thinking it out. It was the road by which I had come into Bucharest and the dust verge on either side of the narrow strip of tarmac still had the occasional cart piled high with maize stalks, presumably for fuel to give the hut dwellings some warmth.

'What did you mean when you said "the other one"?' I asked her.

There was a long silence, then she said, 'I don't think I tell you that until later. Maybe when we know each other better. I am going to get some sleep now. Wake me please if you see a patrol. Okay?'

'So you have killed somebody, is that it?'

There was no answer, and when I looked round again she was lying back, her eyes half closed and the Kalashnikov cradled on her lap, her finger on the trigger. 'That makes two of us,' I muttered.

'What did you say?' Her voice sounded very sleepy.

'Never mind. At least we have something in common. What do I call you?'

There was no reply. She was already fast asleep.

Some time later we began to wind our way through a forested area of sandhills, obviously the piled-up silt of the great river when its course had been a little further north, the pale sandy soil making splashes of silver that gleamed like water between the boles of the trees. Then back to the endless plain and shortly after midnight we reached the small town of Petesti. It was just after Petesti that we had our first brush with the militia. They were guarding the bridge across the western arm of the Danube where it flows north towards the delta. A figure draped in a grey greatcoat, his rifle slung over his back, stepped out into the middle of the bridge, his hand held up.

'Don't stop.'

But I was already slowing. 'I can't just run him down.'

'*Prost!* Do as I say.' Her voice was sharp with an edge to it. 'Drive on!'

'But I can't just—'

Her hand slapped hard against my right ear. She had a ring on her finger and it hurt. 'Go on, you fool!'

I turned on her, my foot on the brake. By then I had seen the man's face. 'He's just a kid.' I stopped, the front bumper almost touching him. He came round to the side of the car and I heard the rear door open. He was demanding our papers, his hand reaching out to open the passenger door. '*Autodocumenti.*' He never saw what hit him. She jabbed the butt hard into the side of his neck. Not once, but twice, seeking out and finding the carotid artery.

He was still buckling at the knees as she slid back into her seat. 'Go, go, go!' The door slammed shut as I revved the engine and let in the clutch. The Dacia leapt forward. A glimpse of the river below and we were across the bridge, fragments of the road surface leaping up, sparks flashing as the bullets flew. A rush of air, the blast of the Kalashnikov, then we were clear, off the bridge and back in open country.

The rear door slammed shut again. 'Faster!' she said. '*Rapid! Rapid!* The next bridge is where we will have real trouble. They will phone ahead.' She was breathing heavily as though she had been running. 'And don't worry. That boy is all right. His neck will be painful, that is all. But at the main bridge . . .' She left it at that, leaning forward, her head almost touching my shoulder, her eyes on the road, which the headlights showed running straight as a die beside the railway line. 'Turn left immediately you have crossed the bridge, and don't stop. Do you understand? Don't stop.' Silence, except for the roar of the car, the wind of our speed whistling in the cracks of the ill-fitting doors. 'Do you understand?'

I nodded. I could see the bridge now. There was a figure running to grab a couple of small steel barriers. STOP. It was large enough to read even at that distance. 'Don't stop,' she repeated, her voice suddenly pleading. 'Please, don't stop. Promise . . .'

But by then I did not need any encouragement. We were onto the bridge approach and the rest of the guard was running to take up their positions.

I jabbed my foot hard down, my hand on the horn button. We hit the flimsy barrier at something near maximum speed, a good hundred and ten, the militia-man on duty jumping for his life, the horn blaring, the wind of our passage blasting into the back of the car as she wound her window right down – and then she was firing, single shots.

'Left!' she screamed.

The buildings of Cernavoda were already closing in around us as I swung the wheel, braking at the same time, so that we took the corner at speed, the wheels locking in a tyre-shrieking skid. The back offside wheel hit something on the edge of the road and we straightened out with a jerk. Then the rear window closed, the rush of air cut off, and all was relatively peaceful as I reduced the speed to 100 k.p.h. We were heading north now.

'Well,' she said with what I took to be a sigh of

relief, 'we are across the Danube now. From here I think we stay on 22A rather than cutting across to the main coastal highway. It will take longer, but if we do that, we avoid Babadag.' Babadag, I remembered from the map, was quite a big place, but what she was really worried about was Tulcea. 'There is a big aluminium works there so they may still be supporting Ceauşescu, the *Communisti* for certain.'

I tried to insist that she would not use the Kalashnikov again, but all she said was, 'I promise Luca to get you through to the meeting with Stefan and if that is the only way . . .' When I protested again, she told me with some good fortune it might not be necessary, she knew Tulcea well and would guide me through backstreets until we were looking down on the Danube and the landing place. 'Anyway,' she added, 'I do not kill anyone. I fire only at their legs.' And she repeated that she had promised to get me through to Stefan. 'I also want to get through to him myself, safe.' She gave a little laugh. 'You forget perhaps that I am coming with you. Where are you going, after we board the ship?'

'London,' I told her.

'I know that. But where do you land yourself? Cyprus?'

'Istanbul, I was told.'

'*Bun!* That suit me fine.' She asked me whether I was all right to drive to Tulcea. 'Not tired? You don't fall asleep?'

'No, I'm okay,' I said.

'I think it is about one-twenty kilometres from

here. Less than two hours. You wake me please after one and a half hours. Okay? And you wake me very quick if those boys at Cernavoda send a car after us.' But she did not think they would, the military having to conserve *benzina* like everyone else. Anyway, it was easier and quicker for them to phone through to Tulcea. 'Then we become somebody else's problem.'

We were driving with the Danube close on our left side, a cold moon showing through drifts of cloud. I tried to find out something about her, but she said she was tired. 'It has been a very busy, very explosive week.'

'All right,' I said. 'You go to sleep. But first tell me what I call you, if I have to wake you suddenly.'

Silence then and I thought perhaps she had already gone back to sleep, but when I repeated the question, she said, 'All right. Then you had better call me Ana.'

'Ana? Did you say Ana?'

'Yes, that is my first name – Ana.' Her voice was barely audible above the noise of the engine and the rattle of the worn bodywork.

'Ana? How do you spell Ana?'

'A-n-a. Why?'

'I just wondered.'

'Oh, I see.' She suddenly sounded wide awake. 'You are still wondering what I mean by saying I am the other one.'

'Yes, what did you mean?'

'Later,' she said. 'We'll talk about that later perhaps. Perhaps I should not have said it . . .' Her voice trailed off into a yawn, and when I looked quickly round at her she was asleep – or perhaps she was feigning sleep. At any rate, I couldn't get anything more out of her and for the rest of the drive to Tulcea I was alone with my thoughts, all of which were somewhat chaotic. Once I caught sight of the outline of a ship, blurred in the moonlight, and shortly after that the road swung away from the river. Was it just a coincidence that her name, like Mihai's wife, was spelled with only one *n*? And what had she done that she had to get out of the country in such a hurry?

Thinking about that, and all the things that had happened, trying to visualize what the future held in store, kept my mind active and sleep at bay. By the little town of Saraiu we joined the 22A, an offshoot of the main Constantza highway. Here the road was bordered by walnut trees and in less than an hour we were approaching the main coastal highway and could see Tulcea Airport away to the right. 'Strada Babadag.' Her voice was blurred with sleep.

'Why are you so tired?' I asked her. 'What were you doing before I picked you up?'

But all she said was, 'Shortly you will see an autoservice station on the right. A little after turn left on to Strada Aurelian, then right, on to Mircea Voda and immediately left again. You are on Strada Lupeni then.' She gave a little laugh. 'I tell you I know my Tulcea. But that is enough for the moment. I give you more instructions when you turn off the Lupeni onto the Libertatii. We shall be very close to the river then.'

I glanced down at my watch. 'What time is he meeting us?' I asked.

'Any time after midnight. But he will be late. Stefan is always late.'

'Why?'

'His wife. They argue.'

'And the ship?' It was already past one, the clouds thinning, the moonlight stronger. 'When is the ship due to meet us?'

That she didn't know. 'Stefan will tell us. Not today I think.'

'Ana.'

'Yes?'

'Does the name Mihai mean anything to you? Mihai Kikinda?'

She ignored that, but when I asked her again, she said, 'Of course. Everybody who is dissident knows of Kikinda, admires him, reads his writing. You ask me questions, now I ask you. Why are you in Romania? I have been told nothing about you, only that suddenly you have to leave the country.' She wanted to know what I was doing there, what had happened to me that I had to escape from the country in such a hurry and so clandestinely. And why was I staying at the Bucureşti.

Answering her questions, fending off the more dangerous ones, took us on to the Strada Libertatii, and it was on the Libertatii that we passed a tank parked outside a tired-looking concrete residential block. Beside it was a blackened brew can on a make-shift fireplace constructed of rubble. The crew had either found billets in one of the neighbouring build-ings or were asleep inside their tank, on the side of which was a clever caricature of Ceauşescu draped in black with a dead white face and the fangs of a bloodsucker. The wings of a bat stretched over the whole side of the turret, the word *Dracula* in red paint and the red streaks pouring down from the fanged mouth of that dreadful white mask of a face seemed wholly superfluous. Nobody challenged us, nothing stirred as we drove past.

Neither of us spoke after that. It was such a vivid reminder of the superstitious nature of this country and the state of chaos that threatened. Five minutes later we dropped down to the riverside, which was screened by the massive blocks of hotels and apartments. 'It is where the cliff comes down to the water, downriver from the main building. There are some stone steps.' She directed me to a dilapidated track that dropped very steeply. There were old shacks, cheap prefab offices and workshops, the debris end of a river port.

We sat there staring down at the ruin of an old stone staircase that terminated at a timber-planked jetty half awash. There was nobody there, no boat – all that rush to get here, all the risk, and Stefan not there to meet us. 'What do you expect?' she said when I voiced my exasperation. 'This is Romania. Romania after almost half a century of Communist mismanagement.'

But it wasn't only exasperation I felt. I had been party to the killing of a senior security official, and now suddenly I was faced with the possibility that I might not get out of the country, the blank emptiness of that dilapidated jetty lapped by the black waters of the Danube staring me in the face. Suppose the ship didn't come, or worse, it steamed past us and no boat to take us out to it? 'You say this fellow Stefan is always late.' She was out of the car now, had already dumped her bedroll on the dusty surface of a roadway that was made up of rocks and age-old silt. 'Suppose he doesn't come?'

'He will.' She yanked open my door. 'Come on! I have to park the car. Anybody seeing it here, and the luggage – these black Dacias, it is very conspicuous.'

'It's almost two in the morning. Everybody will be asleep. What are you going to do with the car?'

'The Gara Fluviala, I think. Now get out, please. With everything that belongs to you. We have to be hidden away down the river before it is daylight.'

'And then?'

She reached over and grabbed my arm, half pulling me out. 'Get your things, then lug everything down to the quay. Okay?'

'God! You're a bossy woman.' I meant it as a joke, but she took it seriously. 'Somebody got to look after you.'

I cleared all my things out of the car and she climbed in behind the wheel, flicking the headlights on and off – short short short, long long long, short short short. I wondered where, and why, she had learned Morse. And she could drive. She backed the car up the precipitous gravel track, weaving it through the jungle of prefabs, faster than I could have done it myself.

PART TWO

THE OTHER ONE

CHAPTER ONE

She was gone almost half an hour, and after I had taken the baggage down to the jetty I had nothing to do but sit on my suitcase and consider the situation. Ahead of me now lay the delta. I knew quite a lot about it, from books I had read, from talking to men who had been there on fishing or shooting expeditions, some who had camped in clearings among the willow trees, steering the long, narrow local boats through the endless labyrinth of giant reeds that blocked off so many of the waterways. There was boar and otter, even a strange-looking beast called the enot dog that was peculiar to this wild wetland constructed of the silt brought down by Europe's greatest river. And there was the sturgeon, of course, also a fish called the sheat, and all sorts of birds; pelicans, ibis, ducks and grebes, sea eagles, too.

To pass the time I began to hum the tune of 'The Virgin Sturgeon needs no urgin''. Soon I was singing it softly to myself: 'I fed caviare to my sister, She was a virgin pure and shy, Now she stands on Piccadilly, Selling what men want to buy.' And the only other verse I knew, about feeding caviare 'to my Grandpa: He is nigh on ninety-three. Screams are coming from the garden, He's got Grandma up a tree.'

Alas, I had no caviare to send me wild about the woman who had been thrust on me.

Nothing moved on the river, except the current carrying debris, and the moon now shone out of a clear sky, the stars with a frosty look. Would I be able to catch sight of a real live sturgeon, or that enot dog I had never seen? To pass the time I began making up sturgeon verses – 'I fed caviare to my koala bear, And all it did was stare at me. Then when I thought it would never move, It tried to roger the tree.' I had just got that one worked out when I saw her walking towards me down the track.

She walked with a limp, her right leg stiff as if in an iron brace. 'Any sign of Stefan?'

'No.' I was staring at her face, clear in the moonlight as she came close to me. She was younger than I had thought, and she was possessed of a certain beauty, her features very regular, like the sculptured head of a Greek goddess. 'What are you staring at?'

She knew damn well, of course. So many people must have stared at her, in pity or revulsion. 'I'm sorry,' I said. 'It came as a bit of a shock.'

'It usually does.' She said it flatly, a tone of weariness. 'I do have other features . . .' This on a lighter note, but her voice tailed away. She lifted her head. 'Listen!'

Faintly I could hear the creak and paddle of oars. A moment later the long, planklike line of one of those double-ended delta fishing craft came into view round the stern of a motor tourist boat moored to the end of a wooden jetty a little further downstream. The moon was now so bright I could see every detail of it, and of the figure rowing with his back to us. 'It looks more like a boy than a man,' I said. 'Where's he come from?'

'Crisan.'

Crisan I had seen on the map. 'That's more than halfway down the Sulina Channel.' No wonder he was late if he had had to row all the way. The Bratul Sulina, from Crisan up to where we were now standing on the Tulcea arm, would be almost forty kilometres. 'Who is he?'

'Stefan's son, Rudi.'

His craft, built of broad steam-bent planks of cedar smothered in pitch, was like a cross between an early Viking boat, a skiff and an Indian canoe. One long sweep of the oars and he let go of them, moving quickly to the bows in time to leap on to the jetty and slip the painter through a metal ring. He was a slim, fair-haired boy with a nut-brown face already setting into the lines of maturity. He greeted Ana with a broad smile full of very white teeth. They obviously knew each other. 'You the *Englez*, eh?' The smile was gone, a scowl on his face, very blue eyes catching the moonlight as he stared at me.

I held out my hand, conscious that I was being summed up by a kid who had already acquired a fair knowledge of human nature. Suddenly he took my hand in both of his, bent down and kissed it. 'You are . . .' He hesitated, searching for the right word, then shrugged. '*Bun venit, domnule.*'

I took my hand away, feeling slightly embarrassed by this serflike greeting from another world, the salaam of a Russian peasant to somebody in authority. I replied in Romanian and he flashed me a large grin, jumping back into the boat, effortlessly balancing himself as we handed him our baggage. He piled most of it in the narrow V of the bows, put a dirty piece of black plastic over it, then helped me in. Since I was the heaviest he asked me to sit up for'ard to balance the outboard engine cocked up on the stern. Ana he placed on the centre thwart. There was a motor boat moving somewhere out in the centre of the river, the wash of it spilling over the jetty and rocking us. I thought for a moment it might be a patrol boat out looking for us, but gradually the sound of it faded away upriver, then died out completely towards the Delta Hotel and the curve of the esplanade.

Rudi paddled us out into the current, slipped the rope loops over the thole-pins again and began to row, still standing. In this way we slid very quietly down the Bratul Tulcea, river and oars giving us about three knots over the ground, and only the sound of the blades in the water and the occasional slap of a fish fighting for its life in the bottom of the boat to break the quiet of the river.

Occasionally we spoke, in whispers, and in Romanian. Mostly I was asking him questions, about

Crisan and the Russian fishing community. 'They are the Lipoveni,' Ana intervened. 'Very Orthodox. They get their name from the lime trees of the Ukraine.' Apparently new religious practices introduced by Peter the Great were the cause of their exodus from Russia. 'They are still quite strict, with many icons in the houses. You will see, if we have to wait for the ship at Crisan and sleep ashore.'

But Rudi said his father had ordered him not to stop at Crisan, but to take us to a secret place, an island hideout in the middle of a lake. 'You will be safe there and nobody know you are here waiting for a ship. Okay?' I caught Ana's eye and I swear she winked at me. Suddenly she was smiling. She protested of course, but he said he had food, some blankets and two goatskin rugs. He was sitting on them. The ship would come tomorrow, about noon. That would be December 24 – Christmas Eve. I got the impression that it was no use arguing with him. His father's word was law to him, a being supreme under God. 'There are matches with the food and some dry paper. You will have a fire and when there is no more fire you hold each other close, then you keep warm.' He was grinning.

'Bundling,' I said, looking at my minder and seeing only the harelip.

'What is bundling, please?'

'Doing what he has just suggested,' I told her.

A light showed straight ahead, the gleam of a mast. Gradually a jumbled mass of metal, half blocking the channel, resolved itself into two or three quite large vessels, all apparently grounded. The current was sluicing past them, a swirl of water glinting in the moonlight, and as soon as we were clear of them Rudi leaned across the stern and swung the big Seagull into the vertical position. One pull of the starter cord and the buzz-saw sound of the outboard effectively drowned any attempt at conversation, virtually isolating me in the bows.

The built-up banks slid by faster now. Milă 28. I remember catching sight of that particular board – twenty-eight nautical miles to the Black Sea. So small a distance to safety, and by the way the reeds, the trees, the telegraph posts were slipping by we must be doing all of seven knots over the ground, the channel ahead dead straight, a white gleaming sword of water reflecting the moon.

I don't think it was freezing, but the wind of our passage made it seem very cold. Roofs along the left bank, some of them reed-thatched, marked first the village of Vulturu, then Gorgova, and after that there was nothing but reed and willow and the channel running straight ahead. Now and then I glimpsed a small side channel clogged with reeds and water lilies, willows weeping their branches down to the pan-leaved surface of the water. We passed a hotel with wooden shutters closed against the winter, and shortly after five, or was it six? – it was too dark for me to be certain – Rudi cut the engine and we slid silently into the rough rock bank.

We had arrived at Crisan. 'Stay in the boat please and do not talk.' He scrambled ashore, jumping from rock to rock, which at this point were piled up into the form of a primitive stone jetty half demolished by long usage. Ashore, the vague outline of houses showed against the first dim pallor of the dawn. Most of them were of part board construction topped with either reed or what looked like cedar-wood tiling.

He disappeared through a gate in a wall a hundred yards or so downstream. He was gone about ten minutes, throughout which Ana and I remained absolutely silent. But I think we were both of us very conscious of each other, thinking of the day ahead and the loneliness of this wild waste of reeds with only the dredged channel to the free port of Sulina and the Black Sea to provide a point of contact with civilization.

Rudi came back, balancing like a goat on the jetty of precariously piled stones. He waved a big torch at us, flashing his wide-mouthed grin. 'Where we go now you will need this. I forgot to bring it. And some more paper.' He had a roll of it tucked under his arm. All this in a whisper as he jumped into the boat, barely rocking it. A quick shove of an oar and we were out into the current, drifting rapidly past the line of houses that was Crisan. He started the engine again and by the time it was light enough to see the face of my watch clearly we were turning across the current into a channel running north-east, the boy weaving us through the shallows marked by the leaf-pans of the water lilies, the tall reeds an impenetrable wall on either side and willow branches drooping over us.

'Where are we going?' Ana asked.

'You see.'

We turned into a side channel, the beam of the torch flashing on and off as he navigated his way through the vegetation. A sharp turn and the darkness of the gut we were in became palely luminous, the reed wall falling back on either side and dawn light ahead. Everywhere fish were jumping, rippling the flat surface of the water into concentric rings that caught the light. Suddenly the reeds were gone and we were puttering out into open water, fishnet-poles on either side. It was a lake and there were the floats of nets. We drifted over them and then, at full power, we motored out into the open water, towards a dim-seen wall of vegetation. Trees ahead and a great flapping of wings, followed by a slow rhythmic beat. 'Pelican. You see many birds here – cormorant, grebe, egret, heron, stork per'aps.' He slowed the engine and it ticked over as he probed for a landing place.

Even with his help, getting out of the boat and unloading it was not easy, the narrow craft rocking precariously. A fish jumped, the plop of it leaving a small wave circle on the lake's limpid surface. He had poled us in with an oar until the reeds that formed the island were matted into an almost solid floor, and there were trees whose roots were probably fastened to the lake bottom.

'I get you some fish,' he said when everything was stowed well clear of the water, and we watched as he paddled to a fish-pole, reaching down into the water and grabbing the first of the metal rings that spread the captive net trunklike over the surface of the lake.

A dozen or so silver-shining fish were flapping about below the last ring.

'Bream,' Ana said, still in a whisper. 'That is good. If we can get a fire we can spit-roast them.'

Rudi got the fire going for her, and then he left. 'I come back this evening or per'aps tomorrow, soon as I know when the ship come to take you away. Okay?' Again he kissed my hand, and then he was gone, the buzz of the Seagull fading away across the lake.

We were on our own then. 'Tomorrow is Christmas Eve,' I said.

'I know. What do you want for a present?' She gave a quick, giggling laugh. 'I think all you get is a poor little bream blackened by fire.' She had half a dozen of them skewered on slivers of dead reed, and as she laughed she looked round at me. For a moment we were looking full at each other, the light from the suddenly sun-burnished lake showing the split break of her upper lip, dark hairs fringing it and growing up into the vertical gap.

I heard myself echo her laughter and at that moment the disfigurement did not matter. It was the whole face I was looking at, and it was a nice face, full of the sunrise glow and the knowledge that we were alone on a reed island, lost in the middle of a lake in the no man's land of the Danube delta. It was like being at the end of the world, or on a desert island, and across a gap in the reeds that was like a window onto the lake a roseate pelican glided slowly into view, the pink of its body accentuated by the orange tip of the sun just showing. 'A pity it's so cold,'

I murmured. 'If it wasn't for that this would be idyllic. It reminds me of Canada, the same cold sense of being the last human left alive.'

'You have been there?'

'Yes. It was in a float plane with a bunch of gold prospectors, and we came down on a lost lake like this. It was a lot colder, there was ice forming.'

'You have travelled, then.'

'Yes, I suppose so.'

'To many places?'

'No, not so many. From the Yukon I flew down to WA. The change in temperature nearly killed me. We were out in the desert, you see, and I was checking a seismological survey.' The fire was without flame now, only the embers glowing, and I got to my feet. 'I'll get some more wood.'

It was difficult walking on the island, my feet were constantly breaking through the floor of reed debris, and the only branches I could break off were rotten with the dampness of the air. When I got back, having walked round most of the island, she had found a large round loaf of home-made bread in the food sack. We tore off chunks and ate it with the ember-hot flesh of the bream, peeling it off the backbone with our fingers. Again I was reminded of the Canadian north, campfires and fish, always fish out of the lakes. *Ouananish*. That was in the Labrador, the land-locked salmon, sucking fingers burnt by the pink of fire-hot flesh.

The day passed in a chill dream, neither of us talking much, the silence of the wet world around

us broken only by the occasional splash of a fish jumping or the beat of heavy wings as a pelican flew over,
the wash of its splayed feet landing making a noise
like a surfboard riding a wave. Once, after she had
disappeared behind a tree to relieve herself, Ana called
to me. Lying in a tangle of undergrowth, half buried
in a mat of sodden reed debris, the rusty teeth of a
huge iron trap grinned up at me.

'Boar,' she said.

'Or man?' I had once seen a trap like that set for
rustlers at a sheep station in the Kimberleys.

'No, boar,' she insisted. 'But I don't know why it
is here, on a small island in the middle of a lake.'

Our conversation, what little there was of it, was
confined almost entirely to observations about the
world in which we found ourselves temporarily
marooned. She showed no curiosity about my life and
background, and my own attempts to find out about
her were either sidetracked by a conversational non
sequitur or by a blank stare, or the stone wall of
silence. She seemed unwilling to admit me to any
degree of personal intimacy, as if the revelation of
any knowledge of herself would breach the wall she
had built around her. It was a mental wall, and in the
end I stopped trying to get inside it, contenting myself
with the comfort of her presence and the occasional
word or two. The fact that she had bothered to show
me the trap she had stumbled on was the closest I got
to her.

It didn't matter. I had so much to think about. It
was not just the uncertainty about getting out of the

country, Sulina and the Black Sea becoming a beacon in my mind. It was what was to happen to me afterwards. Why the urgency of my recall? And Zelinski, what had happened to 'Z' – an illness? But he had been travelling the high mountains and the deserts of Central Asia most of his life. Or had he been murdered? I knew one member of the staff of Resource Potentials had been killed, a man named Galliano, an Italian. He had been drowned in a lake somewhere in Peru, and there was a woman, I couldn't remember her name – or perhaps I never knew it. She had been killed in a car crash on the M4 in England. That was just after she had returned from Iran, something to do with oil rights in the land of the marsh Arabs.

My female minder had wrapped herself in a blanket and was fast asleep. Time passed slowly. A wind got up, rattling the hard stalks of the reeds, and looking through our 'window' on to the lake I could see the water whitening into little breaking waves. It was suddenly much colder, so I got to my feet and set off on an exploration of the island. It did not take me long, though the going was wetly treacherous, and whenever I peered out through the vegetation I saw water, and beyond the water, reeds, nothing but reeds, and a jungle of stunted willows. When I got back to our camp, I replenished the fire, gathered a pile of wood and sat in front of the wet-sizzling logs with a blanket that reeked of fish wrapped round me. It was still only just after midday.

I must have dozed off. When I opened my eyes again she was bent over the fire, a blackened pot in her hand. 'I found this, so I'm making fish cakes with the crumbled crust of the bread. Rudi's mother must have packed the food sack. There is even some salt, and a small bottle of oil. I think olive oil.' She held it out to me. 'Too thick for sunflower, don't you think?'

'You've taken your hat off,' I said.

She smiled at me, the black hair falling over her eyes. It was not an unattractive smile. 'Are you hungry?'

I hadn't thought about it till then, but – 'Yes,' I said, sitting up and realizing that I was, very hungry. 'The cold air,' I murmured. And then I asked about the hat. 'It doesn't exactly . . .' I hesitated. 'It's not exactly you,' I said.

She laughed. She seemed more relaxed. Perhaps it was the fact that she was totally absorbed in the cooking of a meal, but for the moment she was no longer shut in on herself, the wall of silence broken. 'My work takes me into dangerous places. Places where there are no women, only men, and prostitutes. It is best I don't try to make myself attractive. The hat is concealment, and the pins . . .' She told me then how she had managed to go to England for six months as an *au pair*.

'Do you know Seven Dials? There is a pub there and on the wall behind the bar are group photographs of the flower girls of Covent Garden.' Again that little, relaxed laugh. 'They are not really girls, of course, and the photographs were made when Edward VII is on the throne of England. The neighbourhood is very rough then. When it is dark, anyone who is decently dressed is pulled into a doorway and lucky if he is thrown back into the street with anything on to cover his nakedness. Girls the same, even the older flower women. So the hat and the long hatpins.' She reached down, picked up the hat and pulled out one of the pins. It had a stud at one end and a point as sharp as the knife Mihai had rammed into Miron Dinca's guts at the other. 'You see, it will go through the thickest cloth, no problem.' She smiled, a flash of something that was almost arch in the dark, luminous eyes.

Strange, but that was the closest we came the whole day. I took it partly as a warning. No liberties. No advances. She replaced the needle-sharp pin, then tossed the black hair away from her eyes and put the hat back on her head. 'There. Is that better?' She laughed then. 'Now I look like a – *zeita*, don't you think?'

'Goddess?'

'Yes, goddess. Don't you think?'

'Not exactly.'

She threw back her head and laughed, and I saw that the stretch of her lips above the very white teeth almost obliterated her disfigurement. 'Not exactly,' she mimicked, and then, as our eyes met, her mouth shut tight and she turned abruptly away to the fire.

The moon was waning now, but still close to the full. The fish cakes were good and a dark powder wrapped in a twist of paper turned out to be ersatz coffee, acorns, or some other nut ground up fine. Stewed in the old pot she had found, it was dark and hot, not coffee, but a bearable imitation. Unfortunately we had no sugar to take off the bitterness, but it warmed us and we sat holding the tin mugs, our fingers wrapped tight round the scalding enamel.

We talked for a time as the lopsided moon rose and the vegetation that hemmed us in took on an intricate pattern of reflections. 'Glad I am not alone here.' Her voice sounded drowsy. 'I think if I were alone I would try to write a children's story, about witches and fairies, or hobgoblins perhaps – something on the lines of Grimm.'

'Grimm was a German writer,' I said. 'In Romania you would surely write about vampires.'

'Bram Stoker's Count Dracula – Vlad the Impaler?' The tinkle of her laughter was lost in the old goatskin she was wrapping close round her. 'As so often the truth is far more horrible than Bram Stoker's fiction. Vlad Dracula was murdered by the ruler of Transylvania. It was his son, Vlad Tepes, released by the Turks from incarceration as a hostage, who did the impaling – any criminal, anyone who opposed his rule, had a wooden stake rammed up the rectum and then he was hoisted up for all the world to watch the agony of his death. The size of the stake depended on rank. You can imagine the size of the wooden fence post that was rammed into the arse of a really important noble-man! But that is Transylvania, Walachia, in fact. Here we are in the delta where there are no castles perched on crags. So you can accept Vlad Tepes as Ceauşescu saw him, a Romanian folk hero who practised ethnic cleansing and defeated the Turks. Do you know how he defeated them?'

'No,' I said. 'All I know about Dracula is the horror films I had a passion for as a kid.'

'So you enjoy horror? Well, you will enjoy what I tell you now. When he had staked out all opposition to his rule, he started in on the Turkish garrisons on both sides of the river. The Turks then invaded Walachia with a large army, but they found the whole country destroyed by Vlad's ruthless scorched earth policy, no food and the water poisoned. At Tirgoviste, before the Turkish army had even reached the frontiers of Transylvania, they were faced with a great barrier of stakes. I have read somewhere that the barrier was a kilometre deep and three broad, and on every stake was impaled the body of either a Turk or a Bulgar. It was too much even for Turkish troops. Though cruel themselves, and accustomed to cruelty, they retreated without a fight, scared out of their wits by the mass horror that had faced them in that valley.'

She leaned forward, threw a big log onto the fire, and then snuggled down under the fur cape. 'Do not dream too much about the dreadful Vlad.' And she added in a whisper, 'I just wish sometimes I could have . . .' She shook her head. 'Never mind. I should not have thought like that, but it is not just Ceauşescu who followed in the pattern of Vlad Tepes.'

After that she didn't speak and I was left to my own thoughts, the moon pattern changing all the time as it climbed the sky, ragged clouds slipping across it, the wind in the reeds sounding like surf, the thrash of the willow branches like waves breaking. The force of it had been rising steadily for the last few hours and the rough water it kicked up on the lake made a constant hissing sound, surging in sudden rushes into the little slot where we had landed from the boat. The boy Rudi couldn't possibly come for us until the wind subsided, so that for the time being we might just as well have been marooned on a desert island. And we were so tantalizingly close to freedom, Sulina and the Black Sea not fifteen miles away.

Twice I tried to question her as to why she needed to get out of the country so urgently. I thought at first she was refusing to answer, but then I realized she had fallen into a deep sleep. Hobgoblins! She had talked about witches and fairies and then she had mentioned hobgoblins. Strange that she should use that word – was it of Celtic origin, the little demons whose haunts were the dark corners of the great courts, coming into their own on Walpurgis Night and getting up to all sorts of devilry? That was German folklore. Welsh too – the *Mabinogion*, but Walpurgis, the witches' sabbath, and hobgoblins sounded Anglo-Saxon. I dreamed of a boat poking its bows into the little gut so close to our fire, riding a white-water wave surge, and that dreadful Viking leaping ashore, the same man who had sacrificed his wife to Thor at the launching of his long ship, binding the wretched girl to the logs that rolled the keel into the water, laughing at the crunch of her bones and the piercing agony of her screams.

Then the weight of his armour and his weapons broke through the reed crust and he disappeared. I woke at that point to a tearing, splitting sound and the scream of a bird as a branch was ripped off a nearby tree, the noise of the wind louder, a solid, seething roar. The wings went flapping over my head, panic in the wild cry of a pelican, or a heron perhaps, desperately trying to get airborne through the moon-wracked tangle of the undergrowth.

'You cold?' She was sitting up, hugging the fur skin close about her.

It was only then I realized how bitter the night had become. 'Yes,' I said, suddenly conscious that I was shivering.

'It's the wind.' She leaned forward, trying to stir the fire into a blaze. But the embers were quite burnt out, the fire dead.

'Did the bird wake you?' I asked her.

'No. It was the cold. And then you.'

'Me?'

'Yes, you – you shout something. What I don't know, but is not Romanian, or English.' She rolled over, gathering up the plastic sheet she had been lying on. 'I think we now take Rudi's advice and – what is the word you use – bundle?' She was kneeling up, her fingers, white with the cold, holding two corners of the plastic. 'You don't mind, do you?'

A few hours back she had been firing a Kalashnikov at an army patrol, now her eyes were pleading with me not to reject her offer of body warmth. I didn't say anything, simply pulling my blanket covering back, a silent invitation, and she crept into my arms, arranging both coverings over us and pressing herself against me like an animal seeking warmth and protection.

Holding her like that I could feel the shivering of her body. 'What were you dreaming – when you cry out?'

I didn't answer. I certainly was not going to tell her about that, and as I held her closer, the warmth of her body gradually seeping through to me, I began to sing that ballad Britten had set to music for Pears, 'The Foggy Foggy Dew'. 'Are you married?' I asked as I put a hand over one of her breasts. She took it away instantly, but gently, so that I knew she was not offended.

'No, of course not.'

'Children?' I asked her.

I felt her body tense and there was an awful silence. 'One,' she said. 'Why? Do you know anything about him?'

'No, of course not.'

'Then why do you ask?'

So she had had a child, a boy. 'And you're not married?'

'Many women now satisfy their need of children without feeling any compulsion to marry the father.'

I asked about her family. 'Brothers? Sisters?'

I felt her shake her head.

'Father?'

A long silence. It was like getting blood out of a stone to discover something of her background. Then, in a small voice, 'I thought you had guessed.'

The other one! 'So Vikki *is* your sister.'

'No, she is not my sister.' And she added, 'Now stop it, please. How would you like it if I ask you so many personal questions?'

I tightened my hold on her waist. 'I must know about you. We are thrown together for – how long I don't know. Or what will happen to us. It's important we understand each other.'

'You tell me nothing about yourself.'

'You don't ask, so I presume you are well briefed already. Luca, or more probably his wife, will have told you why I have to slip out of the country, unofficially.'

I waited. I could hear her breathing, but that was all.

Suddenly she turned to me. 'Yes. He tell me you have helped to kill somebody, an official of the *Securitate*. Right? The man whose car we use to get to Tulcea.' Her hand reached up to my mouth. 'No. Don't tell me. Is better I don't know who he is. Is better I don't know anything. Then if we are stopped from leaving Romania . . .' She took her hand from my mouth and turned away again.

'That doesn't make sense,' I said. 'You hit that militiaman, and later, at the bridge, you opened fire on a patrol. If we're caught we're in it together. So why are you so desperate to leave the country?'

There was a long silence. Finally she said, 'It is nothing that concern you. It is all personal – very personal.' Her voice trembled. 'Very personal, very shocking.'

'You killed somebody?'

I felt her body tense. 'Of course I kill him.' In that moment her tone was quite violent.

'Why?' I asked.

'Why? You ask me why!' She was trembling and I

could feel her fingers digging into the flesh of my arm. 'It is a long story,' she murmured.

'It's not three o'clock yet. We have all the rest of the night.' It was cruel, but I felt I had to know. 'Why?' I repeated. 'Why did you kill him?'

There was a long pause. Then – 'My baby. Because he take my baby.' That was all she would tell me and after a while I must have fallen asleep. For how long I don't know. It was too dark to see my watch. Slowly I became conscious of the trembling warmth of a body pressed close against me and a queer snuffling sound. The noise of the storm was so loud that it took me a little while to realize that she was crying, a muffled sobbing that shook her whole body. 'What is it?' I asked.

The trembling stopped abruptly and she gave a gulp. 'What do you think? I can't sleep!'

I tightened my hold on her. 'You're cold. Is that it?'

'Cold? Do you think I care about the cold? I have been cold half my life. Every winter . . .' She suddenly pushed me away and got up. 'I need a pee.' She found the torch and in its light I watched the shapeless bundle of clothing blown by the wind to the nearest tree.

When she returned she seemed to have got a grip on herself. 'It's the cold,' I said, and followed her example. The time was just after four.

'It is not the cold,' she said on my return, her voice tense with anger.

I suppose I was still half asleep for I said, 'What is it, then?'

'Oh, for Chri'sake, don't you hear what I told you?' She was blazing with fury now. 'I tell you my baby is taken from me. You force me to tell you, and then you are so stupid you don't think what it mean to have your child wrenched from your arms. And I was still breastfeeding him.'

The wind-chill was so intense now that we were both of us shivering quite violently. 'Better try and keep warm,' I said, and she nodded. However angry she was, the fear of hypothermia overrode it. Once again we snuggled up to each other, glad of what warmth our half frozen bodies could provide. 'One more question,' I said.

'No.'

'Who took your baby from you?'

'I tell you, the man I kill. Now go to sleep.'

'What about your own parents? Couldn't they do anything for you? Your father, for instance?'

A long silence, and then, her voice a whisper that was muffled by the fur of her goatskin covering, 'He was in prison.'

'The *Securitate*?'

She didn't answer.

'Who is he?'

'Stop it!' Her body had stiffened. 'You know damn well who he is. Now go to sleep.'

'Mihai Kikinda?' It had to be. 'And your name is Ana, the same as your mother's.'

'Anamaria. I prefer to be called by both my names.' Her voice was very tense, her body trembling.

'Remember what you said to me when I picked

you up in the Dacia and introduced myself? You wouldn't give your name. You simply said all I needed to know was that you were the *other one*. When you said that you were referring to Vikki. Is that right?'

Silence then and I thought she wasn't going to answer, but then she said, 'Of course.' And the tone of her voice had changed. It was cold and hard. 'That is enough questions.' She rolled over onto her other side. 'Go to sleep now. It will be dawn soon.'

But I couldn't sleep, not now that I knew she was Mihai's daughter. It began to rain, a hard, wind-driven rain. We lay, bundled close, with the black plastic spread over us and one of the goatskins between us and the sodden reed debris that was our bed. She didn't like Vikki. That much was obvious from the tone of her voice. Why? Just because Vikki's features were unblemished and she didn't limp, but danced the hours away? But the hardness, the coldness of her voice. I tried to visualize what it had been like coming back to a home that was already occupied by a wild, unnatural daughter adopted out of one of Ceauşescu's orphanages – that set of the face, those hard, imperious eyes and the mouth that had kissed me so fiercely – hard, hard, hard. She was such a hard little thing.

Time passed on wet-leaden wings as I thought back to that first time I had seen the Kikindas with Vikki dancing out to the compulsive beat of the music, that rapt look on her face, her eyes glazed as though in a state of ecstasy. Back and forth, back and forth, her own steps created on impulse, her little hands beating time, the ribbon in her hair bowing to the rhythm of her body. But I couldn't remember what Ana Kikinda had looked like.

Later, the second or third visit, when Uncle Jamie and Mihai were deep in conversation and I was dancing with that hard little-girl body pressed against me, I could remember her then, the sadness of her expression. I think that was when the thought first entered my head that she wasn't Vikki's mother. She was so withdrawn, and no warmth between them.

Ana Kikinda. The face was one of considerable beauty. I realized that now. But there was no life in it. Mihai, on the other hand, talking about the *Communisti*, and about Ceauşescu and his regime, how it had promised so much and then fallen under the dead hand of a tyrannical bureaucracy, Mihai's face, though the lines of life were deep-etched, would light up as though with some inner fire. But his wife's face showed no emotion, a strangely dead face that somehow frightened me as a little boy.

Now I began to understand. A gust of wind and a surflike roar as it swept through the island's reeds, shaking the moisture-laden trees, large drops of water spattering my face. My companion in misery stirred. 'What is the time, please?'

I could just see my watch now. It was past eight, so I must have slept in the end. The cloud base was very low, tattered wisps like smoke writhing across the whitened water of the lake, but it was no longer raining. 'The wind has changed,' I said.

'*Da*. And it is not so cold.'

I slipped out from under the plastic sheet and squelched across to our window onto the lake. A queer sun glow was turning the whirling cloud vapour to a dull red so that the reed edge to the lake seemed to smoulder. I called to her, it was such an extraordinary sight, and we watched it together, the vapour like steam from a volcano, twisting and turning, forming strange shapes that were constantly changing. The sun glow began to fade and suddenly it was snuffed out, the shapes all gone and only a grey murk lying over the water.

'I will try and relight the fire.'

Her words were almost lost in the roar of the wind as she fought her way through the reeds to a tree that must at some time have been struck by lightning. What was left of the trunk had fallen in on itself, and digging into the hollow of it she came out with a handful of fibre that was still dry. 'You get some reeds, where they are dead and brittle.' It took time, but we finally got a fire going, the flames fanned by the wind and the two of us huddling close, our arms held out like two cormorants drying their wings.

All that morning it blew hard from the south. We made toast of the last of the bread, sucking at the fish bones we had discarded the night before. That was all we had, and afterwards we sat there, dozing fitfully, periodically gathering dead reeds or twigs, piling them beside the fire and feeding them into it as they dried out.

There is something very primitive about a fire, the life-giving warmth and the terrible power of it, the speed at which it can travel. I had nearly been overrun once by a bushfire in WA, not far from Perth. The next day I flew over it in a company plane and watched as the strong westerly sent it chasing after a bunch of big roos. First one tree, then another, burst into flame like a petrol bomb, and then suddenly the wall of fire overran the poor wretched animals and in a moment all that was left of that beautiful, bounding action was the black lumps of their charred flesh writhing and kicking in the agony of death.

And then the pilot pointed, shouting, 'Dingo! Watch!', and he had banked his aircraft so that we had a clear view of this lone animal as it turned to face the wall of flame, no longer running. It lay there, flat on the ground, its head tucked into its paws, waiting. 'You watch,' the pilot said. 'He'll make it. The only animal in all Australia who knows by some strange instinct what it must do to survive when all the others are being burnt alive.'

That dingo had waited until the heat of the flames caused the brown hairs of its coat to smoke, then, at the moment of being engulfed, it rose to its feet and raced forward, straight into the furnace heat. For a moment we lost sight of it in that tide of fire, and then a small charred rag of a thing burst out from the holocaust of flames, still travelling at speed across the blackened smoking embers of a world that had once been green and full of life.

I tried to tell my companion about it, but it is difficult for somebody who has never seen a bushfire to understand what it is like. She had got the Kalashnikov out of the clothing she had wrapped it in and was squatting cross-legged beside our own little fire, cleaning it with paper from the roll Rudi had brought us when he had stopped off at Crisan for the torch. 'What is dingo?' was her only comment. And when I told her it was the wild dog originally bred by the Abos, she said, 'And the Abos, what are they?'

I was soon into the Dreamtime, and that was when I realized she was a political animal and very much her father's daughter. Try explaining the Dreamtime to somebody so battered by life that her only dream was the destruction of Ceauşescu and the whole ghastly regime. 'You talk of a dog facing a wall of fire. You should talk of humans – in Romania, in Hungary, in Poland, in all the places where men, and women, deliberately, and of their own free will, fight – not just for survival like your dingo, but for the things they believe in. Men like my father. That is bravery, real bravery. And now they have hold of that monster Ceauşescu and his wife I hope they kill them. That is the only way. And I hope they burn in hell.' It was said with such venom that I instantly had a picture in my mind of Ana Kikinda slapping the man's face and calling him a monster, and the members of his personal guard flinging themselves on the poor wretched woman and carting her away, legs and arms stretched tight and her face screwed up in agony.

After that we seemed to withdraw into ourselves, only occasionally speaking, and then only about mundane matters. Somehow we managed to keep a small glow of heat in the fire and we stayed huddled close, half awake, half asleep as the clouds lifted and the light strengthened. A fierce, grey, blustery day. I think we were really too tired to talk, too tired to think even, exhausted by the December cold. At last, some time after ten, the sun began to glimmer through the rampaging wrack of cloud, streaks of blue and a bright glare appearing to the south-east. But no warmth. No warmth until around midday the wind began to ease.

Several times I tried to get her to talk – about herself, about her father, particularly about her mother; but to all my questions she remained obstinately silent. Finally I got up and started to do some arm-swinging exercises. I dared not jump about for fear of breaking through the fragile crust of the island's reed floor. Gradually my body warmed up as the blood began to flow, the sun and the lessening wind-chill raising the air temperature.

My companion stirred. 'What is the time, please?'

I looked at my watch. 'Twelve thirty-seven.'

She nodded, still half asleep. 'Rudi will be here soon.'

'I hope so.' I thought perhaps that this was the moment I could surprise her into answering some of the questions that had been wandering through my mind during the hours of cold and darkness. 'Why don't you like Vikki?' I asked her.

She threw off her goatskin cape and was on her feet in a flash, facing me with an angry flush on her cheeks. 'I never say I don't like her.'

'Jealous of her, then?'

'No.'

'Aren't you envious of the fact that she can dance, and you can't?'

She turned away from me, saying nothing.

'But you're afraid of her, aren't you? Is that why you hate her?' I don't know why I put it so bluntly. Perhaps I wanted to be brutal. Anything to get her talking.

But of course it had the reverse effect. She gathered up the goatskin, flung it round her shoulders and stumbled away into the undergrowth, her every movement a declaration of the emotional disturbance my questions had caused her. I watched as she fought her way towards the far side of the island and my mind switched to Vikki, wondering where she was now, what she was doing. All that I knew of her was what Mihai had told me, that she had found herself a protector and had disappeared into the post-Communist chaos of southern Asia.

All these years and the fascination of my mysterious little dancing partner had remained. I found myself humming Ravel's *Bolero*, my feet automatically picking up the beat. For her, *Bolero* had been a sort of signature tune. *DUM, DUM – dum, dum, dum, DUM*. God! She could dance! My arms reached out as though to clasp hold of her again, my body swaying to the beat of the music I was humming. And I could hear my voice. The wind had gone completely now. Everything so still. *DUM, DUM – dum, dum, dum, DUM*.

'What are you doing?' She was back, those big eyes of hers staring at me. 'Why are you humming that tune?'

'I don't know. The storm, I suppose.'

'It is not storm music, Ravel's *Bolero*. It is the pounding of blood in the veins, the excitement of—' She stopped there, standing very still, the harelip somehow more noticeable. 'You were thinking of Vikki, weren't you?'

I hesitated. 'Yes. Yes, I suppose I was. I was thinking of Vikki. Why not?'

This might have developed into an intimate discussion revealing more of the relationship between her and the adopted sister she had found waiting for her at that house in Constantza when she finally returned to her family, but at that moment there was a sudden burst of wing-flapping from the lake, a whole flock of pelicans on the move, thrashing the water as they got themselves airborne. And when the noise of their departure had subsided and all was quiet again, I heard the distant buzz of an outboard. 'Rudi?'

She nodded. 'That is what I came to tell you. I saw a fishing boat moving out from the shore.'

It was Rudi, thank God, not some Lipovenian stranger, and he had news of our ship. It had left Rousse shortly after dawn the previous day and was expected off Crisan some time around midnight.

'You have good night?' He was grinning. 'Mama send you bread she bake this morning, also some *nuca*.' He dumped a fishnet bag at Anamaria's feet. 'You fix fire good and I get fish. Okay?'

Tonight. By midnight tonight, with luck, we might be steaming past Sulina out into the Black Sea. Rousse was a big town, the fourth largest in Bulgaria, and the country's most important port. I knew about it because I had planned to visit it in my scrap-metal enquiries. It was all swampland, and, with the chemical works across the river at Guirgiu in Romania, this agro-industrial beehive turned the waters of the Danube to the sick colour of macro-pollution and the chlorine-poisoned air to something that people could barely breathe.

That's what I had read and I wondered what the ship would be carrying. It was a Bulgarian ship, its name *Baba Tonka*. I asked Rudi whether it had been loading at Rousse, and he said yes, but he didn't know what the cargo would be.

By the time he returned from raiding one of the family fishnets Anamaria had got the fire blazing brightly. Bream again, and some carp, the fresh white flesh wonderful eating, a replenishment of the energy-warmth we had lost during the bitter hours of dark-ness. And when we had finished, we sat in a somnolent daze cracking *nuca*, the walnuts Rudi's mother had included in the food bag.

The mist had gone now and the world was a golden haze. The boy went off again, hunting with a catapult. Incredibly, the sun was warm, warm enough to burn the moisture out of the sky, so that by the time he returned with some more fish and a mallard he had killed with a stone from his catapult, the sky was a clear pale blue and I was lying on the black plastic sheet in my shirtsleeves.

We both of us wolfed the food whilst Rudi sat laughing at us and making jokes in pidgin English.

'Some day I speak good. Then I have big boat, many fish. Per'aps fish factory also. Then we get good monai for our fish, not the miserable seven lei for one kilo we get now.'

He left shortly afterwards to go the rounds of his father's fishnets, and then take the catch to the cooperative. Dusk was closing in on the lake by the time he got back, the bottom of the boat gleaming silver with fish scales. There were still a dozen or so bream flapping about on the wooden ribs, the planks slippery with oil and everything stinking of fish. 'All into *barca* now, please.' He wanted to have everything stowed so that we could cross the lake while it was still light enough to see the tall withies that marked the channel by which we had entered this secret world.

Again I had the bow position. The surface of the water was flat calm and leaden now, marked only by the innumerable rippled circles of fish jumping, the gale and the white wind-whipped water already a distant memory. But the cold was returning. I could feel the breeze icy on my cheeks as the Seagull started into life, the bows cutting smoothly through the water, heading for the distant reed line.

A torch was thrust into my hand, Rudi wanting me to guide him through the shallows at the entrance to the channel. Withies supporting fish-traps closed round us, the floats of nets, and then the wall of reeds. I switched on the torch, which was waterproof so that I was able to thrust it below the surface of the black, oily-looking water. I could just make out the bottom then, lying flat on my stomach and guiding Rudi by hand signals.

That's how I saw it, a massive, grey-green armadillo of a thing barely visible against the mud. The slow movement of the rear end of the beast was the only indication that it was moving. It seemed to be feeding on the bottom vegetation. I called to Rudi and he scrambled for'ard, peering over my shoulder. '*Nisetru!*'

It was the first time I had ever seen a sturgeon, and this was a big one. It was about the size of a thickset man, with a skin like an alligator's, rough and knobbly. Anamaria had also come for'ard. The bows dipped and the creature suddenly came to life. A flick of its tail and it had slid away across the mud floor and disappeared.

'No caviare for the ship captain.' Rudi's teeth showed white in the gloom of the overhanging branches and he scrambled back to the outboard.

It was slow work feeling our way between rafts of tangled water lily roots, grounding periodically and having to pole our way out with the oars. Finally we made it to the main channel and by seven thirty we were into the broad, straight waterway of the Bratul Sulina. We went ashore then, and in a clearing under some trees squatted down beside a smoke-blackened stone fireplace. '*Turisti!*' There was contempt and a certain hostility in the way Rudi said it.

We got a fire going and ate our last *al* very *fresco* delta meal – home-baked bread, fresh-caught bream, olive oil and some dreadful, stinking, spidery minilangoustes that were all shell and legs with just a small bit at the base of the tail that was edible. Rudi produced from the depths of his fish bag a bottle of wine that tasted like retsina. We sat drinking it until, shortly after ten, it was time to move out into the Sulina waterway, drifting down on the current and keeping close in to the shore. Just short of the first of the line of houses that was Crisan we nosed in among the stones that protected the canal bank. 'You pay Rudi now, I think,' Anamaria whispered to me.

I asked him what I owed him, but he shook his head. 'Luca is friend of my family and you are friend of Luca. I don't want any monai. Very happy to know you.' The teeth flashed in the glimmer of moonlight just beginning to climb above the eastern horizon. A long argument ensued, and in the end he said, 'You give me five dollars. That is for the *benzina*.' He said it sullenly as though I was forcing him to do something discreditable.

In the end I managed to get him to take ten and a further five. 'That is for your mother. Understand? For Mama, and thank her please for the food and for thinking what we should need for spending a night in the open.' I think it was the fact that I had thought of his mother that made the whole transaction acceptable to him, for after that he chattered away, happily practising his English on us.

Waiting for a ship you do not know will come, sitting cold and uneasy in a little boat with its bows on to a stone bank at the mouth of a river that stretches back across half the countries of Europe produced in me a strangely disembodied feeling, a sense almost of unreality. I think it was more out of a desire to force an emotional contact with the only person who could talk to me in my own language that I again put the question to Anamaria that I had asked before – 'Why do you hate Vikki?' And as before it raised in her an immediate reaction:

'I don't hate her. I never said I hated her.'

'But you don't like her. You made that plain enough.' I could see the whites of her eyes in the moonlight as she stared at me, and when she didn't answer, I said, 'It isn't just because she can dance and you can't, is it? Or because of your lip?'

Silence, but the sullen, almost puzzled look on her face told me I had got through to her. 'Your lip can be dealt with, you know that? A good plastic surgeon . . .'

'And who pays – you?' There was contempt and anger in her voice. I had touched her on the raw.

'So why don't you like her?' I asked, reverting to my original question. 'Is it because of her different temperament? You have both had to face up to personal disaster. As children you have both had to cope with appalling difficulties. Is it because you feel she has coped more successfully?'

She stared at me sullenly.

'For God's sake!' I said angrily. 'There has to be a reason . . . Is it because of your mother? When she saw your lip, and then found she couldn't have another child herself . . . That was when they adopted Vikki, wasn't it? That was why. You must have felt rejected then. Was that the cause—'

'Stop it! Stop it, do you hear!'

'So it was that, was it? She lavished the love that should have been yours on Vikki and you felt rejected.'

She was staring at me, her eyes so wide the whites shone quite bright in the moonlight. 'You don't know Vikki, do you? Not really.' There was an awful note of dejection in her voice. 'Our little sultana. That's what she claimed she was. Did she never tell you that? A little Muslim princess. That's why the orphanage was so glad to be rid of her. She acted out her fantasies to such a vivid degree that it affected her behaviour. The people who ran the place made her life hell, but it only hardened her. She lived in a dream world. That, and her dancing, were her refuge. Her fantasies became reality. And because she was so strong-willed, believing so absolutely in the background she had created for herself, there was nothing the authorities could do. It is only later she discover the computer. Do you understand?'

'I suppose so.' Both her parents – I still thought of them as that – had been quite open about her conviction that she was descended from the khans of some obscure offshoot of the rampaging Mongolian hordes that had swept through southern Asia in the thirteenth century. Several times my uncle and I had listened to them discussing whether her imperious manner was inherent in her genes or whether it was an act she had developed from her need to cope with the institutional world into which she had been plunged at such an early age. Did she remember the world she had been born into? I had never asked her. And whether it was inherited or assumed, it only accounted for a part of what I remembered as a very complex and volatile character.

I was vaguely conscious of Rudi saying something, but I did not hear what, my mind going back as it so often did over my memories of her. I could recall almost everything she had said, the way she had looked, and what we had done together. And yes, she had a way with her that was imperious. But it didn't matter. I had accepted it as a natural part of her make-up, never bothering to question why she was like she was. She was just Vikki, and when we were together that was all that mattered.

A hand reached out and touched me, Anamaria leaning forward and whispering urgently, 'The ship! It is coming now. Turn your head.'

I didn't see it at first, the ghostly line of the waterway blurred with mist. But then my eyes became focused on a vague pinpoint of white, which gradually hardened, and a moment later I could make out the red and green of the navigation lights, confirming that what we had seen first was the steaming light at the masthead. I turned to Rudi. 'The *Baba Tonka*?'

He shrugged. 'I think, yes. It is the time Papa say he come.' Anamaria started to say something, but he silenced her. 'Listen, please.' Faint through the mist came the sound of a ship's engines strangely eerie in the still dampness of the night air.

'Do you know the captain's name?' I asked.

'No, Papa don't say. Only that you pay fifty dollars for passage.'

'For both of us?'

'No, I don't think.' He looked at Anamaria. 'It is between you and the captain. That is what Luca say to me.'

'And where will he be taking us?' But I had asked him that earlier and his answer was still the same – he didn't know, neither his father nor Luca had told him. 'Is all very difficult now. Not too many ships on the Dunărea.'

He pushed the boat away from the bank and out into the stream, then scrambled quickly up into the bows, lying close beside me and shining the torch, not directly at the ship, but down into the water as though we were fishing. 'We know soon,' he whispered.

The beat of the engines was getting louder now, the ship's lights brighter, little coloured haloes gleaming in the mist. Suddenly we could see the dark shape of her looming towards us. The engine sound dropped to a gentle hum. Rudi clutched my arm. 'Baba Tonka. You are okay now.'

He twisted round and like an eel slid into a kneeling position amidships, pushing Anamaria aside and seizing hold of both the oars. We were bows-on to the current, the ship seeming to move faster. A thresh of water from its stern, froth from the reversed prop glinting in the moonlight. With a deft stroke of the oars Rudi swung our little craft round, letting the current drift us alongside. A ladder hurtled down from above, uncoiling its wooden slats as it fell. Rudi grabbed it, motioning Anamaria to start climbing. She glanced up, not moving. But I knew it wasn't the vertical climb that made her hesitate. It was her sudden fear of the unknown, the realization that up there, on the deck of this Bulgarian vessel, she would be among strangers, facing an uncertain future, no longer with any control over her destiny. She glanced quickly round at me.

'It's all right,' I said. 'You'll still have me and I'll be right behind you.'

She hesitated. Then I saw the line of her mouth tighten so that the cleft in the upper lip was barely visible. She looked suddenly like the person she really was, a fighter, and throwing her head back, she gripped hold of the rope ladder and began to climb, swinging herself out from the ship's black-painted side and using her feet.

'Goodbye, sir.' Rudi said it in English, then seized hold of my hand, kissed it, and with that white-toothed grin of his held the end of the ladder out to give me a ready foothold. I thanked him and swung myself up, keeping an eye on the feminine bundle above me, hoping to God she wouldn't fall.

Stupidly they had fixed the top of the ladder to a lookout point just below the wheelhouse so that the climb was longer than it need have been. But it had one advantage: the ship being a small bulk carrier, we were handy for the accommodation unit when we finally completed the precarious ascent. A seaman and an officer were there to help us over the rail, the officer rigged out in uniform jacket and grey polo neck. '*Salaam*.'

'*Salaam alaikum*.' We shook hands.

As soon as the cargo net with our baggage was

swinging clear, the beat of the engines increased and I leaned over the rail to wave goodbye to Rudi. The boat and the boy looked very small as he pulled clear of the churned-up water astern and drifted away into the mist.

A sudden altercation broke out between Anamaria and the seaman who had hold of her case. 'No!' She grabbed hold of it, shouting at him to let go.

'What's the trouble?' I asked. And then it dawned on me. The Kalashnikov! 'My God! You haven't brought it with you, have you?'

'Of course. It is my safety.' With her black hair falling over her eyes she looked quite wild.

The officer had already given the seaman his orders, and though I did not speak Bulgarian, I had got the gist of it. 'The man is taking you to a vacant cabin,' I told her. 'You and your baggage. We will discuss what you do about the contents later.'

She nodded, seemingly satisfied. 'I don't mind so much after we leave Sulina. Then Romania is behind me.'

'And if we are stopped at Sulina . . .' I had a sudden mental picture of this wild-eyed creature with her Kalashnikov pointed at the captain, holding up the whole bridge and demanding that they make full speed out of the Bratul Sulina and into the Black Sea. I asked the officer what the *Baba Tonka*'s first port of call would be and he replied, 'Istanbul.'

So the captain had been given our hoped-for destination. From Istanbul I could probably get a flight direct to London. I glanced back at Anamaria, who was now being led through a door into the accommodation section of the bridge housing. I was wondering what she would do with herself when we reached Istanbul. She had said she had papers, but did she have friends there, money, a credit card perhaps? I knew so little about her despite the time we had spent alone together on that island.

The officer tapped my arm. 'You come now. Talk with *capitan.*'

He was in the wheelhouse, a small man with a lot of black hair, seated in a battered armchair. 'So. You are . . . ?'

'Paul Cartwright,' I said. He heaved himself up and shook my hand.

'And you seek voyage to, where – Istanbul, Ródhos, Izmir? After Izmir . . .' He shrugged his shoulders at me, dark eyebrows raised and what looked like false teeth flashing white under a very dark moustache. 'After Izmir, Famagusta possible. Where you want to go?'

I told him Istanbul would suit me fine, and he took me through into a little cubbyhole of a cabin just aft of the wheelhouse on the starboard side. 'You have papers?' I handed him my passport into which I had slipped five ten-dollar notes. 'Good.' He nodded, pocketing the money. 'And your little friend?' I explained that we were travelling separately.

He didn't like that. 'You are together. Nobody tell me different.'

My guess is he had been watching our behaviour after climbing the ladder. He wanted me to pay. And when I started to argue with him he said, 'You escape from a country like Romania. Fifty dollars is not too much. It is cheap to take your woman to Istanbul.'

'She is not my woman,' I insisted.

He only smiled. 'Perhaps I keep this.' He indicated my passport, firmly clamped in his delicate, hairy-backed fingers. Then, lifting his head, he nodded towards a scattering of lights glimmering in the dark rectangle of the only window. 'There is Sulina, coming near. I stop my ship and send you ashore, eh?'

We haggled for a while, finally settling the girl's passage for half what I had already paid him. Once I had given him the dollars, two tens and a five, he was all smiles, handing me back my passport and shaking my hand, even patting me on the shoulder as he led me back into the wheelhouse.

There must have been an onshore breeze drifting in, for Sulina was almost clear of mist, a straggling little waterside port with several ships lying alongside a dusty, potholed road. A few shops and houses, several warehouses, everything looking worn and dilapidated, and nobody about, nothing moving except a few stray cats, one or two dogs. No pilot or port launch came out to meet us. The whole place seemed dead.

That was my overriding impression as Sulina slid by on our starboard side, that and the rust. There was rust everywhere, the ships, the dredgers, the few cars parked in dusty side streets, only a naval ship looking as though it was cared for. And at the end of the built-up section of the port a line of laid-up vessels lay in rust-brown dereliction strung out along a gut dredged out of the Danube silt. I could see the old lighthouse standing solitary in the moonlight, the land stretching flat into infinity, and further out to the east the flash of the new lighthouse marking the way in to the dredged channel. I picked up a pair of binoculars lying on a ledge beside the radar and focused them on the vessels in the wet gut, wondering who owned them, how much they would want for them. If Alex hadn't sent me that urgent recall message the scene of dereliction I was now looking at was enough to make the whole trip worthwhile.

With the current behind us, the flash of the new lighthouse was soon dropping astern, and shortly after that the bows swung through almost ninety degrees, heading south on a direct course for the entrance to the Bosporus. The captain straightened up from the chart table. 'Come. I show you cabin.' It was one deck below the wheelhouse along a short alleyway on the port side, a double cabin which I was to share with the first officer, the one who had met us at the head of the ladder. He had vacated his own cabin for the benefit of Anamaria and was already in his bunk and asleep.

'When do you expect to reach Istanbul?' I asked the captain as I said goodnight to him.

'The Bosporus I think a little after 2400 hours tomorrow. But Istanbul . . .' He shrugged. 'I don't know when we are to dock. Sometimes soon, sometimes it is necessary to anchor off and there is long wait.' He patted my shoulder. 'Do not be in too much hurry.'

That was when I asked him whether I might use the radio-telephone in the morning. 'I have to report to my office in London.'

'To tell them you have escape from Romania, eh?' He smiled, and I knew he was wondering what I had done and what my office in London was, thinking probably that he could have charged me more – though fifty dollars at the lei rate of exchange was a lot of money, and hard currency at that.

The cabin was hot and airless, but after about thirty-six hours of bitter cold on that reed island I did not complain. I just put my head down and slept, lulled by the throb of the engines. Even the persistent rattle of a glass in its holder, or the pounding of feet in answer to some order shouted in a language I did not understand, barely touched my consciousness, and I never heard the first officer turn out in the middle of the night to take his watch.

He left the light on, but it wasn't the light that woke me, it was Anamaria. 'Problem,' she said. 'They wish to search our baggage.' She was dressed with a dark scarf over her head that accentuated the pallor of her face, and she looked worried.

'You should have buried it on the island,' I told her.

'Yes, but I don't. So what do I do now?'

'Ditch it.' She stared at me uncomprehendingly. 'Throw the damn thing overboard.' I was still half asleep and not in the mood to be disturbed.

'I cannot walk about the ship with a Russian automatic weapon in my hands. If they see me . . .'

'What do you expect me to do, then?' Damn the woman! I rubbed my eyes, staring at the porthole. 'Turn the light out.' I swung myself off the bunk, glancing quickly at my watch. Six twenty-seven and dawn not yet broken. I rubbed the porthole glass clear of steam, peering out at a cloud-black morning, the white of the bow wave turned faintly red by the glimmer of the port navigation light. 'When are they going to carry out this baggage check?'

But she didn't know. After leaving me the captain had gone to her cabin, ostensibly to check that she had everything she needed. It was just as he was leaving that he had told her about the baggage check. 'He tell me they are very strict at Istanbul and some time in the morning he must see for himself that we have nothing in our baggage that we should not have. I have been thinking about it half the night, wondering what I must do.'

'Ditch it,' I said again. 'Throw it overboard. And any ammunition, any other weapon. You have a porthole?'

'No, a small window.'

'Does it open?' Apparently it was slid back several centimetres to let the air in, but she didn't know how much further it would go. I told her to see if she could put her head out. 'If it is a straight drop to the sea then you have the solution to your problem. If not come and tell me and we will think again.'

'And if I cannot put my head out to look down . . .'

'Oh, for God's sake, you've got a mirror, haven't you? Use that.' I got back into my bunk. She stood there for a moment, staring at me angrily, and then she left. She did not return and I slept through until the sun woke me, a bright blaze slanting in through the porthole and shining intermittently on my face as the ship rolled.

The captain and the first officer were still finishing their breakfast in the little cubbyhole of a saloon when I entered after having had a quick shave and a shower. They were discussing cargo arrangements, but before they left I was able to confirm his permission to use the radio-telephone. This was on the bridge and I made the call to Alex's home shortly after 1500 hours London time. There was a delay, of course, but finally I got through.

'Alex Goodbody.' His voice was so clear I might almost have been speaking to him direct. 'Where are you phoning from?'

I told him the name of the ship and that I was clear of Romania and out in the Black Sea. I even wished him a happy Christmas and was just going on to give him a rough idea of my ETA at Istanbul when he cut in sharply, 'I asked where you were phoning from – your cabin?' And when I told him I was on the RT from the ship's bridge, he asked whether there was anyone within earshot. 'The watch on duty,' I said. 'But I don't imagine they understand—'

He cut me short. 'Don't talk. Just listen. On arrival Istanbul go to the Bolu Agency in the big covered bazaar. There will be a packet waiting for you. It will contain your airline tickets, destination and your next contact—'

'But I'll see you in London. I can probably get a direct flight—'

'Don't interrupt, and don't say anything more. Go to the Agency, collect your mail and follow the instructions. Is that understood?'

'Yes, but—'

'Did you hear me? Have you got the message? Just say yes if you have.'

'Yes. Only I don't understand—'

But he had rung off, and I was left standing there holding the receiver. I could of course have claimed I had been cut off, but I knew by the tone of his voice that it would serve no purpose. I left the wheelhouse and went down the ladder to the main deck, standing in the shelter of the bridge housing and looking out across the waste of glittering water, wondering what the hell they had dreamed up for me. It was blowing quite hard now, the waves breaking and the ship beginning to pound. That reference to Z in the curt message dictated over the phone to the receptionist at the Intim in Constantza . . . So far, in WA, BC and the Yukon my assignments had all been straightforward research into the financial prospects and involvements of certain companies in particular projects. That would have been true of the Romanian assignment, a simple assessment of the prospects of a company shipping out scrap for a new, jointly owned Russian steel mill.

I think I had known all along that there was another, darker side to Resource Potentials. Nobody had told me so, not specifically. I just felt it was there whenever I was in touch with any of the old hands, men, and one or two women, who had been recruited, mostly from the Services, after Korea, Borneo and the Gulf, any of the lesser wars we had been involved in after the Second World War. On the occasions when I had been briefed by Alex himself, I had always been conscious of a certain reserve, and those eyes of his that seemed always probing beyond whatever it was he was saying. Talking to him, I always had the feeling I was under observation.

A crash up for'ard as the bows slammed into a wave and a sluice of water pouring along the deck made me realize the wind was rising fast. One of the officers and a member of the crew came out of the forepeak and began cautiously moving along the deck checking the hatch-cover fastenings. A heavy belt of cloud was climbing above the horizon, ink black against the lingering sun glare. Then the brightness and the glare, the sparkle of the breaking wavetops, was abruptly snuffed out. The Black Sea glowered black, and in that moment I was suddenly conscious of a presence. Somebody had come up behind me. And because of the nature of my thoughts, and perhaps the threatening look of the sea, I whirled round, prepared for – I don't know what – anything.

But it was only Anamaria, standing quite still and muffled against the cold wind in that now ridiculous-looking goatskin cape. She was a bare two metres from me, a shocked look on her face, and I realized I had ducked quite instinctively into a crouch. A little shame-facedly I straightened up.

'What were you expecting?' The whisper of her

question was barely audible against the noise of the wind and sea.

'Nothing.' I smiled, trying to make light of what had been a nervous reaction prompted by the thoughts racing through my head following that brief exchange of words on the RT.

'I did as you advise,' she said.

It took me a moment to realize what she was talking about.

'I drop it into the sea. Nobody saw.'

I nodded. Thank God for that. She was nothing to do with me, but coming aboard the *Baba Tonka* together the way we had we would inevitably be linked. And on the island, the closeness, that feeling of being responsible . . . I had been thinking of what Alex had said, the way he had decided abruptly, and on the spur of the moment, to send me instructions via an agency instead of telling me direct while I was on the line to him. Nobody would then know my destination or who I was to contact.

'You are not going to London, are you?'

'What?' I turned again to face her, those big eyes fixed on me, that disfiguring lip. She had a sudden lost look, and I wondered what her plans were, whether she had any friends outside Romania. And lei. Lei would be no good to her in Istanbul. And how did she know I wasn't going to London? But when I asked her, she shrugged.

'It is all over the ship.'

'How?'

'The radio operator, of course.' And she added,

'What you do is of great interest to these people, so much of Bulgaria facing Romania across the Dunărea.'

'And I suppose they know where I am being posted?'

She laughed. 'No. Not exactly. But the *capitan* say to me that you will pick up your instructions at a well-known agency in the Kapali Carsi. The Bolu, I think he say. Is that so?'

I nodded.

'And something else,' she went on. 'Ceauşescu is dead. He is executed by firing squad this afternoon. Both Nicolae and his wife Elena. They are both of them gunned down in the courtyard of the garrison headquarters.'

I stared at her, wondering whether it was true or just wishful thinking on her part. 'Who told you?'

'The *capitan*.'

'Christmas Day!' I murmured. It seemed somehow very fitting. He hadn't believed in Christ. Probably he hadn't believed in anything other than himself.

'Now there is only Albania,' she said.

And Cuba, I thought. China and North Korea, Cambodia and the Khmer Rouge. That was just about all that was left of the great Communist bloc. Russia, the Soviet republics, Poland, East Germany, Hungary, Czechoslovakia, the Baltic states – all gone in less than half a year. It was unbelievable. And now Romania. 'Then you've nothing to worry about,' I said.

But I knew she had. I could see it in her eyes, in the haggard, haunted look in her face. And myself? Well, I could still walk away from this new assignment, whatever it was. But I knew I wouldn't. Curiosity, if nothing else, would keep me following whatever the instructions were that would be waiting for me at the Bolu Agency in the Kapali Carsi, Istanbul's great covered bazaar.

CHAPTER TWO

You will take over from Z. His body was brought down to Gilgit by Laun Said, who will brief you and will thereafter be your guide. He has all the details and will meet you at Dean's Hotel on your arrival in Peshawar. If you have to overnight at Karachi stay at the Metropole and contact Shaikh Arshad, or at Rawalpindi Syed Ali Lari, Flashman's Hotel. Priority air tickets enclosed. Proceed with utmost dispatch.

It was signed AG, that was all.

I can still remember the shock the fax gave me as I read it, standing there in the agent's stuffy little office with the noise of the bazaar coming to me like the sound of a roaring torrent from the covered street outside. So Zelinski was dead. That was the thought uppermost in my mind.

'Sit down, please.' The agent, a small, dark-featured man, watched me intently through gold-rimmed glasses as he waved me to the chair set facing him across the desk. 'I send my clerk out to get the reservations as soon as you telephone your arrival. He will not be long.' His hand reached into the breast pocket of his sky-blue jacket and produced what I took to be a silver cigarette case, but it was difficult to tell, it was so covered in intricate hieroglyphic patterns. He offered me one, but I shook my head, still thinking about that fax. 'Is okay if I smoke?' he asked, his English very precisely spoken.

'Of course.' I was staring down at the fax again . . . Had he died a natural death, cholera, typhus, an aggravated form of hepatitis, or had he been killed in some border scuffle? But the trouble spots were Armenia, Georgia and Azerbaijan, the smaller republics of the Caucasus between the Black Sea and the Caspian. And Afghanistan of course. Only Afghanistan was anywhere near Gilgit and the fax referred to his body being brought *down*, which presumably meant from the high mountains of the Himalayas – the Karakoram, the Hindu Kush, the Pamirs.

I thought perhaps the owner of the agency would be able to fill in for me since it was perfectly obvious from the way I was being treated that Resource Potentials had used his agency before. But Mustapha Bolu had never heard of Zelinski. He did, however, have some financial gossip via a business contact in Tajikistan: the Russians were rumoured to be spending vast sums on exploration and on the development of the necessary infrastructure preparatory to large-scale production. This was in the Zeravshan Valley. I had no idea where that was, but the Tajik Republic, I knew, was north of the Hindu Kush and the Pamirs with China its eastern neighbour.

Was this what Z had been checking over? It would certainly be the sort of project for which a big mining company might employ us to carry out a covert investigation. Z was not only an expert on early religious scripts, and both a desert and a mountain wanderer, he had also, like me, been trained as a mining engineer.

Our conversation was interrupted by the arrival of a little bazaar boy, immaculately clad in white with two small cups and a metal jug resting on a glittering brass tray. Bolu introduced the child as his son. The boy placed the tray down carefully on the desk, bowed to me and left. But as he went out, he turned and gave me a long, hard look, as though to implant my features in his memory, or perhaps trying to assess what I was worth to the agency.

'A bright boy, your son,' I said.

Bolu smiled and inclined his head. 'Thank you. He is very bright, I think.'

The coffee was, of course, Turkish, thick and sweet with the grounds lying like a mud pack in the bottom of the cup. Politely we talked of things in general, the financial outlook for the Turkish pound, the situation in Russia, and then Bolu wanted to hear my views on Romania's future. Would Britain resume her one-time close association now that Ceauşescu was dead? It was while we were discussing this that his clerk, a big man with a muscular face who looked more like a bodyguard, came in with the tickets and my reservation for a flight leaving for Karachi next day.

'I am sorry,' Bolu said after an animated discussion
with his clerk, 'but apparently PIA – that is the Pakistan International Airline – cannot make for you a
reservation onward to Peshawar. That is internal, of
course, but Emin has arranged for them to notify Karachi of your arrival flight and also of your standing as
a friend of Turkey and of the Turkish people.'

I thanked both him and the clerk and got to my
feet. To be classed as *a friend of the Turkish people*
was, he explained, to be given the highest commen-
dation. He personally accompanied me out into the
vibrant mêlée of the great bazaar, assuring me that
anything I wanted of him he would do instantly. For
instance, did I wish him to book hotel accommodation
here in Istanbul? I thanked him, but said I had already
booked in at the Hilton. After that reed island, I felt
the company owed me an expensive night in Istanbul.
However, I did ask him to be kind enough to notify
Alex Goodbody of my travel plans and he assured me
he would do so. 'I already make a note to do that
when Emin bring me the airline reservation, and I will
fax the Metropole in Karachi to give you a good room
for tomorrow night. Okay? Is there something else?
Money?'

I told him I had Amex and Visa cards.

He nodded. 'I will instruct Shaikh Arshad to see
that you have the currency monies you will need in
Pakistan.' We had stopped and again he asked if there
was anything else.

'No,' I said. 'You have been very kind and helpful.'
We shook hands and I left him, launching myself into

the torrent of humanity, my mind completely absorbed in the extraordinary shift of activity that now faced me. As a result I would have walked right past her if she had not caught hold of my sleeve.

'Plees.'

Presuming it was a beggar I automatically shrugged off the clutching hand, but the fingers closed more urgently.

'Paul – plees. I must talk to you.'

I stopped then. She looked quite haggard, dark rings under her eyes and the split lip even more noticeable. 'What is it?'

'You said you would help me . . .' Her voice trailed off. She was staring up at me and I saw her lip trembling. Then her eyes went blank and she turned away. 'It does not matter.' It was said in a whisper, so that I barely heard, but I caught the note of despair, saw the sudden remembered squaring of her shoulders.

'What is it?' I reached out, grabbing hold of her arm. 'What trouble have you got yourself into now?'

'Nothing. It does not matter.' And almost angrily she shrugged off my hand and began to walk away. A moment more and she would have been lost in the crowd, but I couldn't let her go like that. A few quick strides and I had caught up with her, seizing hold of her arm and jerking her round.

'What is it?' I insisted.

She shook her head, biting her lower lip and trying to break free of my grip.

If she wanted money, why the hell didn't she say so? But instead of saying what the trouble was she was almost cringing away from me and I found myself looking down at her, down at that ridiculous hat and the pins. 'What have you done?' Had she killed somebody else? The possibility was suddenly in my mind and I thought: My God! I can't get involved with this. Not now. Tomorrow I would be in Karachi. Then Peshawar. And after that . . . 'You surely didn't come here without money.' I didn't mean lei. By money I meant hard currency.

'No, of course not.' She said it with an angry toss of her head. 'I am not a fool.'

'Then what is it? I suppose you have killed somebody else.' I tried to make it sound humorous, but of course she didn't take it that way.

'You are so stupid. Have you no imagination? Can you not understand what it is like for a woman to be . . .' She stopped abruptly and turned, for she had backed into a Japanese couple. She apologized, first in Romanian, then in English but they stared at her uncomprehendingly, then retreated quickly into the crowd. They had seen the split lip. Probably they regarded her as an ill omen. I had met several Japanese in WA – always polite, always smiling. But I didn't understand them and these two were not smiling as they disappeared into the human tide that flowed past us.

There was that unhappy look that I'd seen in her eyes before as she faced me again, holding out her hand. 'Goodbye, Paul. I am sorry. You have been kind and I have been rude. You have problems of your own, I think.'

That little speech of hers touched something deep inside me. She hadn't been thinking of herself, but about me. She looked tired. Those rings under her eyes. And waiting for me outside the Bolu Agency. I couldn't just leave her. Not after what we had been through together. 'Would you like a coffee?'

I saw the sudden eagerness in those dark brown eyes of hers. They were so damned expressive. And then they went suddenly blank and she said, 'No. It is very kind of you, but thank you, no – it does not matter.' And she smiled as she held out her hand again. She actually managed a smile. 'Goodbye,' she said again.

As luck would have it I could see a coffee bar sign quite near, the neon light flashing over the heads of the crowd. 'Come and have a coffee,' I said, ignoring her outstretched hand. 'I want one and I don't want to sit alone.'

I saw the sudden eagerness leap back into her eyes, but she shook her head. 'You have already had coffee. I watch the little boy bring it in to the agency. You cannot want another so soon.'

But by then I had hold of her arm. 'You said you had not been to Istanbul before, so we are both of us alone in a strange city. Come on. I think you could do with a coffee. Or an arrack, perhaps?'

We didn't talk after that, not until we were seated at a little table and I had ordered the coffee. She had left her baggage with a refuge run by nuns. She was a Catholic, so at least she had somewhere to go. But when I asked her why she was wearing that ridiculous hat again she smiled and shook her head. I got it out of her in the end. That was after the coffee came, when I said jokingly, 'If you think that hat suits you, I have to tell you I disagree, most strongly.'

She didn't smile, though I knew she had a good sense of humour. She just shook her head. And when I pressed her she suddenly flared up: 'You think I don't know what it does for me? But it is necessary.'

'Why?'

She stared at me angrily. 'Why do you think? It is an excuse to have the pins.'

I suppose I was being very obtuse, but I still didn't understand. Finally she said furiously, 'Do I have to spell it out to you? I am a woman and I am alone in a Turkish city.'

'But at the Catholic Mission—'

'You fool! Don't you understand? I am not at the refuge. I am sleeping rough.'

Her words left me speechless and appalled. 'Where?' I finally murmured. 'Do you mean you slept out last night?'

She nodded.

'Why?'

'There is no room for me at the refuge and they said it was better for me to sleep out than in any of the Turkish "hostelries". They lend me an old sleeping bag and I had my sheep coat.'

A waiter passed with a tray of coffee, the cups surrounding a plate piled with what looked like baklavas. I saw her eyes fasten on it and when the waiter came past again I ordered a plate of them. Her eyes thanked me, but she didn't say anything, bending her head to stare down at her coffee. I asked her when she had last fed, but all she said was, 'It does not matter.'

In fact she hadn't had a proper meal since we had breakfasted together on board the previous day. She had lei, of course, but only a few thousand because the export of Romanian currency was strictly limited and she had feared the ship might be stopped at Sulina, in which case she would probably be interrogated by exchange control officers. Anyway, the lei was worth so little outside Romania, and the dollars she had she was hoarding for her air fares to Kazakhstan. The only way she could get there was to fly and she had not enough hard currency to pay for the tickets.

'They tell me if I go out to the airport each day sooner or later there will be a vacant seat on take-off, that will cost many less dollars. But then there is the travelling. That costs money. Also I will have to feed myself. And if there is no vacant seat for several days . . .' She left it at that, her eyes fixed on me sombrely. 'This is something I do not expect.'

'What did you expect?'

'I thought the ship would go to Russia, to Odessa probably. I have people I know in Odessa. People who will help me.'

'But nobody in Istanbul?'

She shrugged. 'Yes, I have one contact. A woman. But she is a Kurd. They are both Kurds and now her husband is arrested since a week back, and the police take all the money she have in the house. They even freeze her bank account.' She gave a quick shrug. 'It is what you call one of those things.' She smiled, but her lips trembled as she added quickly, 'I believe I had thought of everything, but now this.' Those brown eyes of hers had a liquid quality as she stared across the table at me. 'I don't like to ask you, but have you some dollars you can spare? A loan. I pay you back. I promise. Very soon. It is just for now I need the money.'

Kazakhstan was where Vikki had gone, but when I asked her if she had been in touch with her sister she shook her head. 'She is no longer there, but she has rich friends in the capital, Alma-Ata.' That was all she would say. She didn't know where Vikki was, but she was quite confident that if she could just get to Alma-Ata everything would be all right.

In the end I didn't lend her money. I took her to the travel agents whose address in a street just off the bazaar was stamped on my own reservation and booked her to Alma-Ata via Tehran. Goodbody wouldn't like it. A night at the Hilton and the cost of a flight from Istanbul to Tehran and on to Alma-Ata that he hadn't sanctioned . . . But at least it would be the end of January before he knew anything about it, for I used my Amex card to pay for the reservation, and by the end of next month anything could have happened. Like Z, I could be dead by then.

'What is it? You look so serious. And I am so happy. Thank you.' She had hold of my arm and was looking up into my face, smiling, her pale features alight with relief, the eyes gleaming. 'I pay you back, as soon as I contact Vikki. And if I don't contact her

I find some work. But I pay you back. That is the first thing I do.'

I handed her the tickets, and as we went out into the street she rattled on, her voice full of excitement. 'Do you know Alma-Ata? Vikki dance there once. In the Hall of the People I think, in front of all the local Communist leaders. That was three or four years ago. She dance in Moscow, too. Did you know?'

'And now?' I asked. 'Is she dancing in Alma-Ata now?'

But she didn't know. 'I have no knowledge where she is now. But it does not matter. She has contacts there and they will replace the money the secret police take when they raid her Kurdish friends' house here in Istanbul. Then I pay you back. I promise.'

Her repeated insistence on repayment confirmed something in her character that seemed at odds with her desperate situation. She was determinedly independent. So much so that she resented my paying for anything. Seeing the voracity with which she dealt with the baklavas, I had already decided to ask her to dine with me, but now I explained the invitation as a kindness to me. 'Only one thing I ask.'

'What, plees?'

'That you take those pins out and roll them up in that dreadful hat. I am not taking you out to dinner with that thing on your head.'

'Of course not, but I am not dressed—'

'Never mind. Just get rid of the hat.'

'It is I who should take you to dinner.' And she

added quickly, 'Now that you have paid for my tickets—'

'Don't be silly,' I told her. 'I'm not paying for the dinner, the company is.'

'For your dinner, yes. But not for mine. We are both alone here so I will have dinner with you. I will like that. But I pay for mine. I can afford it now, you see.'

It took a deal of arguing before she would consent to be my guest, and then, when we were in the taxi and I told the driver the Hilton Hotel she said, 'No. I can't come with you to the Hilton. I have no clothes for that sort of place. It is for tourists and business people, and the women will all be in evening gowns, their hair just done, and jewellery – no. I cannot possibly. I am not even washed properly.'

'Then we go up to my room and you have a bath.' And I added quickly, 'There is a lock on the door. You will be perfectly safe.'

She stared at me a moment, very seriously, then she burst out laughing. 'I lie in the bath and you sit reading or writing or something in the room.' She shook her head. 'You are like no man I ever meet before. And I believe you. It is like when we were by that fire and holding each other to fight off the cold . . . But I could not go into the dining saloon, or anywhere in the Hilton, not with my clothes. And when they see my face . . .'

'All right,' I said. 'While you're having your bath I'll ring Room Service and order our dinner. That takes care of your little problem. Now all we have to decide is what we have to eat.'

'But—'

I leaned towards her and put my hand over her mouth. 'No buts,' I said. 'You're on your own. So am I. And I doubt it will be the first time the Hilton has served a meal for two in a room reserved for one.'

I didn't tell her mine was a double room. When the man with my baggage threw open the door I saw her check as she caught sight of the second bed. But then I pointed to the window with its view out over the great city that was old Constantinople. The sun was low in the sky now, the Sea of Marmara beginning to flush red and the minarets of the Blue Mosque standing like gigantic spears, black in silhouette around the piled-up domes of Constantinople's architectural wonder. And there were other minarets, and other domes, some blue, some gold, and the great bulk of Santa Sophia.

I caught the sudden intake of her breath, and after that silence, until she whispered, 'It is so beautiful.' The door clicked shut as the man left and she gripped hold of my arm. 'Oh, thank you. Thank you. I never expected . . .' Her voice trailed away. 'I don't have the words, but to be here, in this hotel with this view – if only for a moment. It is like a dream.'

The Marmara was changing colour all the time, very subtle changes, almost pastel, and the sky above changed with it. And where the sea narrowed and the Bosporus began, the inlet called the Golden Horn was alive with the bustle of ships and small craft, ferries plying back and forth, and the bridge above them full of traffic streaming like little toys between Europe and Asia.

I used the bathroom briefly, then handed it over to her. Also the dressing gown out of my case and a clean pair of pyjamas. 'What are these for?'

I knew what she was thinking so I told her she needn't wear them if she didn't want to. She laughed.

'You are curious to know whether I have any other blemishes, is that it?'

I pushed her into the bathroom and shut the door, telling her I would order drinks. 'What would you like? Champagne, I think.' The only answer I got was the sound of water as she ran her bath.

The champagne, when it arrived, was in an ice bucket and beautifully cold. I called to her that I was putting her glass outside the door, but she said, 'No. Give it to me, plees. I like to drink it in my bath. The door is not locked.'

I found her sitting in a cloud of steam with a towel draped round her shoulders. 'This is such dissipation.' She grinned at me as I put the glass into her out-stretched hand and went back to my seat by the bed-room window, strangely disturbed and no longer thinking about the future. Her behaviour had reminded me that at some time in her life, after she had left the orphanage, she had earned her living on the streets. *How does any girl live if she has no home, no job and a lip like mine?* That was what she had said on the drive down to Tulcea. I could remember her exact words, the way she had said it, the anger in her voice and the look on her face. Something else she had said. *You learn very fast, about all kinds of thing, but about men in particular.*

The minarets and domes were illuminated now, the city full of lights, and beyond the city with its many headlights the blackness of the water was scored by the slower movement of ships. Just to sit there looking down on all that lit activity was to be tutored in the long history of mankind now culminating in a population explosion that was beyond the world's ability to cope. Laun Said. A strange name. Said was a courtesy title like sir or esquire, but the man himself, what would he be like? He had all the details, would brief me and be my guide – guide to where?

I sat there at the window imagining all sorts of things as I tried to probe the future. And suddenly I was thinking of the Rus, those Swedish Vikings who had sailed their long ships down the Dnieper and, when there was no more water to float them, had used log rollers to get them across the height of land, then sailed them down the Volga into the Caspian. In the course of a hundred years or so they had fathered the Russians and could gather a fleet of over a thousand ships to attack Byzantium. Looking down on this ancient city I thought I ought to be able to muster some of their courage, not worrying about the future, but filling my mind with the excitement of the unknown.

A hand touched my shoulder and I started from my reverie to find her standing beside me wearing my pyjamas, the bottoms rolled up, and my dressing gown hugged round her. 'You were far away.' She smiled the awkward grimacing of the lips that was becoming so familiar I barely noticed. 'What are you thinking?'

I got up and poured us both another glass. It wasn't fair. I knew that. She had had so little to eat it was bound to go to her head. But I had to get her talking somehow. And to go with the meal we had chosen from the menu the waiter had left with the champagne I ordered one of the heavier reds, a Rioja. Also a cognac each, a Delamain, to go with the coffee.

The first thing I needed to know was why she had been forced to leave Romania. She had killed somebody. I knew that. But who?

Perhaps my first attempt was too direct. She clammed up on me. 'It is nothing that concern you.' There was a long silence, and when I persisted, she said angrily, 'I tell you it don't concern you. This is all personal, very personal.' Her voice shook. 'Very personal, and very shocking.'

'But you killed somebody and I must know who.'

'Why? Why do you need to know who he is? It is not your business.' And when I said it was because I wanted to understand her, to feel that she wasn't hiding things from me, she burst out: 'Of course I kill him. What do you expect?'

'But why?'

'Why? You ask me why?' Her whole body was suddenly shaking with the violence of her emotion. 'I already tell you why. He is a monster.' She gulped down the rest of her drink. 'You are not built to have a baby, so you never know, never understand – my baby. It was because of my baby. He take him from me. I was feeding him with my breast – to keep him quiet. But I don't have enough milk and when little Ion start to cry again he seize hold of his legs and pull him away from me. I think he is going to dash his head against the wall, but I scream so loud he runs out of the room, slamming the door and locking me in. That is the last I see of my baby. I don't know where he is or even if he is alive. But when Gregor come to take me again, I have one of those pins ready and I thrust it down between the brute's bottoms. Now do you understand?'

I didn't have to answer that, for the waiter came with our meal, and with the food she gradually relaxed. It wasn't until the end of the meal, over the coffee and cognac, when we were sitting in armchairs by the big window looking out over the city, that I returned to the subject of her baby. 'Was it his?'

'No. The baby was mine.' Her voice was suddenly trembling with emotion. 'Ion was my baby. Mine.'

'Yes, but was Gregor the father?'

'Maybe. I cannot be sure.' And she added, her voice rising, 'I know how to look after myself, but I tell you, he is a monster. He rape me and I was not prepared. You understand what I mean?' And then, without any further prompting from me, the whole ghastly story came out, a rush of words that was almost overwhelming, all about her life after leaving the orphanage and this man Gregor, who was apparently the younger brother of Miron Dinca. She described him as a pale, vicious copy of Miron. 'Whatever Miron did he try to do better.'

It was Miron who had had her put in an orphanage. Her father was in prison and her mother was living with the man in one of those concrete apartment blocks in the north of Bucharest. But he couldn't stand Anamaria's presence. She was always crying or screaming at him, her hatred of him, caught doubtless from her mother, made very plain for him to see. Finally, he had got rid of the child by persuading an orphanage in the Carpathian foothills to take her – 'a dreadful place, no heating and bitterly cold in winter. I do not complain and stay there for over two years, for the sake of my mother. After that it is three more years before I can arrange to get out with somewhere to go.' And she added, 'That is not so easy when you are a young girl and have a mouth like mine.'

All this poured out of her in an emotional outburst, and in order to steady her I asked her how old she was then.

'About thirteen, I think, maybe fourteen.'

'And now?'

'Now?' There was a long pause. 'Now I am very, very old, I think. That is how I feel sometimes. And then, at other times' – she gave a sad little laugh – 'at other times I can pretend I am just a little girl that life has passed by and left unblemished.' She sighed, staring out of the window at the lights of the city sprawled out below. She was near to tears then, I think.

'But life has not passed me by,' she went on, speaking slowly now. 'I was born scarred. Sometimes I think it is because of what happen to my mother before I was born, or more like when I was growing in her womb. And then, after I leave the orphanage—' She stopped there, her eyes gone blank. 'It was a grim little town,' she murmured. 'And the men . . .' Again that blank look. 'It was up in the Carpatii, the Meridionali.'

'You had a job there, did you?'

'Sometimes I work in a café-bar.'

'You lived there?'

'No, of course I don't live there. I live the way I am living now.'

'On the streets?'

She nodded.

And then I made the mistake of asking her how she had earned her living if the café-bar was only occasional employment.

She flared up at me then. 'How do you think I earn a living? How does any young girl buy her food when she has no money and is living on the streets? It was a bad, dirty place, and that café-bar . . .' The harelip suddenly opened in a smile. Or perhaps it was just a grimace. I couldn't be sure. 'Then the trouble started and they send the army in. Things were a little better then. I take up with a young officer . . .' But then one day, when she had gone out to wait in the bread queue, she and the others in the queue were caught in crossfire. There was a burst of rifle fire and a bullet had smashed into her leg.

She had been patched up, the leg put in plaster by a young Red Cross worker. To recuperate she had been sent to a government camp where she had been given crutches and told to make her own way as best she could. 'I didn't tell them I had no relatives.'

'Didn't you know where your mother was? And your father—'

'He was in prison, and my mother—' She gave a harsh little laugh. 'My mother took me in. She felt she had to, I suppose, but she did not like it. My lip, I think. It reminded her—' She gave a little shrug. 'I don't blame her, and anyway she had changed a great deal. She was alone in the apartment, but after a few weeks' duty on the Hungarian border, Gregor came back. It was his apartment now, rented from his brother. He didn't throw me out. He used me.' Her voice was trembling and had dropped almost to a whisper. 'In all sorts of ways. He had no regard for my leg. That is why it never healed properly. And then his brother came and there was a fight. Over my mother, and Miron took her away.'

I felt the clutch of her fingers. I hadn't realized it till then, but she had my hand clasped in hers. 'That left me alone with Gregor, and the bastard took it out on me. So – do you wonder that I kill him when I can, and I don't regret what I did. He was a filthy, dirty, beast of a man.'

'And your mother?' I asked. 'What happened to her?'

I thought she wasn't going to tell me, but then she suddenly said, 'It is Miron who had her operated on, by an abortionist. I think it must be after I am born. I don't know. But I do know this. She can never have children afterwards. I don't think she could ever enjoy sex again.' And she added quickly, 'But that I only learn later, of course. Miron and Gregor – I don't know which was the worst of those brothers. Miron, I suppose. They were both of them in the *Securitate*, but Miron move up the promotion ladder more quickly than Gregor.' She reached for the big balloon glass and downed the rest of her cognac, her eyes fixed on nothing, deadened, I thought, with the wretchedness of her memories.

So her father and I had killed Miron, and she had killed Miron's brother, Gregor. I stared at her, at the disfigurement that she thought could have happened in the womb. God! What a tangled mess! But that was Romania under Ceauşescu, Miron and Gregor the sort of men who would be attracted to an outfit like the *Securitate*. The same sort of men who had doubtless been attracted to Hitler's SS or the KGB or East Germany's *Stasi*.

I wondered how old she really was. She looked in her thirties, but life had been hard on her. Or perhaps it was that I had no way of understanding what that sort of life had done to her. And I was getting involved. I turned my head, looking past her to the traffic on the bridge, the constant flow of headlights. Not so many now it was getting late, but enough to have a mesmeric effect.

I was still thinking about my involvement with this strange creature, wondering what I was going to do about it, when there was a soft thud. Her brandy glass had fallen to the floor and she was leaning back, her face very white and her eyes closed, the hand that had held the glass hanging limp and the dressing gown pulled to one side to reveal the round swell of a breast. She had passed out, but whether through drink or exhaustion I wasn't sure – a bit of both, probably. But that settled it.

I picked her up and put her to bed. There seemed no weight in her at all, and as I lowered her down she made little sounds in the back of her throat, but she didn't wake.

I was more than ready for bed myself, but I had a bath first, lying there in the soothing warmth of the water, thinking about the future. My involvement was a very temporary one. Tomorrow would be another day. She had the ticket she needed. We would go our separate ways, and that would be that. I drifted off to sleep, still thinking of her and of where I should be in two days' time.

I woke to find myself in bed with a damp towel round me and a figure standing between me and the subdued glimmer of light from the window. For a moment I wasn't sure where I was, then the figure bent down, fingers closing round the hand I had automatically lifted to protect my face and her lips brushing against the back of it, a peasant gesture of submission and thanks. She was fully clothed, the Paddington Bear hat gripped in her other hand. '*Adio*,' she whispered. 'I am going now.'

I sat up, starting to protest, but she pushed me back. 'Thank you,' she said, her voice strangely hoarse. 'You have been very kind. I shall always remember, and what I owe you I will repay through your firm's agency. I have the address.'

It flashed through my mind what it might cost her to earn those dollars, but then she said, 'Something I have not told you. I do not want to spoil last night. You are still being followed. The same man. I catch a glimpse of him in the bazaar when I am waiting for you outside the Bolu Agency.' She opened my fingers and pressed something small and hard into the palm of my hand, and as she closed my fingers again I felt a tiny thread attached to it. '*Adio, prieten.*' She let go of my hand and went to the door.

I didn't attempt to stop her. What would be the use? We were going different ways. The door opened, a shaft of subdued light from the landing outside outlining her figure for an instant as she turned for a last look at the room and the faint flush of dawn showing a pale streak beyond the city. I could guess what she was thinking – this brief, cosy respite, and the harsh world waiting for her outside. Her face showed briefly as a pale oval.

'Good luck!' I breathed.

'I will pray for you,' was her answer. A strange choice of words. The pale oval vanished, the door closed, and she was gone.

I got out of bed and went to the window, opening my hand, already guessing what she had given me. It was a little gold crucifix on a golden thread of a chain. Her most treasured possession, probably. A gift from who? From a nun at the orphanage? A gift from God that she would rather starve than pawn.

Looking back, I now know why she gave it to me. Genetically part Romany, she had that intuitive perception of what the future might hold in store for me. At any rate, there would be times in the weeks to come that I would clutch at it as sailors and flyers clutch at the good-luck charms presented to them by their loved ones.

I was near to tears as I hung it round my neck. And once it was there the loneliness I had felt as the door closed behind her seemed to fade. It was as though something of her strength of will, her determination to survive, had been passed on to me.

A little over four hours later I was at the airport. A glance at the departure indicator showed that her plane had already left, and since there was no sign of that dreadful hat anywhere amongst the crowd of Europeans and Asiatics sprawled over the seats, I presumed she had got away all right.

I still had almost two hours before take-off and after a quick look at some of the shops, I went through the departure formalities and settled myself at a table with some coffee. I was actually looking straight at the entrance to the loos when he came out. He stood there for a moment, the lighting reflected on his gold-rimmed glasses as he surveyed the mass of humanity sprawled over the seats and overflowing on to the floor. Then he saw me and waved, pushing his way towards me through the crowd. '*Alors*. You are leaving this beautiful city, eh? Or is it that you just arrive?'

'Leaving,' I said. 'What about you? Where are you off to?'

'An assignment. I have to photograph some politicals. They have a meeting in Karachi. You know Karachi?'

He said it so easily, in such an offhand manner, that if it hadn't been for Anamaria I would have accepted his explanation. 'No. I don't know it. I have staged through once, that's all. An engine failure.' I was playing for time, giving my brain a chance to decide what line I should take. But we were obviously booked out on the same flight so there was really no point in trying to conceal my destination. Anyway, if he was following me he knew it already, having presumably got it out of the travel agency staff.

He was banging on about Karachi and the dangers of disease, something to do with the main water supply running close alongside the underground sewage system. And then he asked me where I was staying.

By then I had made up my mind and, without any hesitation, I told him.

He nodded as though that was what he had expected. 'I will be staying at the Sind Club, which is just across the road from the Metropole. It has a beautiful old-world flavour, a touch of your Raj, I think. Also it is much more comfortable. But the Metropole is perhaps better for you, all those offices on the first and second floors.' And then he took me by surprise, saying, quite abruptly, 'Have your people told you about me – you know, how old I am, what my position is, why I am engaged in this rather bizarre activity, eh? Have they told you I have four children, all girls, all at convent school, and a very beautiful, very expensive wife? They don't tell you that?' He was smiling, a slightly impish smile. 'No, of course not. These are personal matters, and they are bureaucrats. They run desks. They don't live in the real world, eh? They have no emotions. Or, if they have, they don't show them.'

He gripped my arm. 'So stupid. It is the personal that is of importance, the involvements, the relationships – if a man keeps some mistresses, then there are extra mouths to feed, bodies to clothe. You understand what I am telling you? Our activities are governed by our involvements – sexual, emotional, but chiefly sexual, for it is involvement with the other sex, or in some cases, of course, the same sex, that govern the actions of the male. And power, of course. For the woman it is different. There is a biological urge to fulfil, the eggs must be fertilized, eh?' The impish smile broadened to a grin. 'That, my friend, is the end of my little lecture, now you know something about me you did not know before. I think I talk too much.'

The grip on my arm tightened. 'Now you tell me something about yourself. Why do you get yourself into this dangerous game? Or don't you know it is dangerous?' His blue-grey eyes were fixed on mine. 'You are a mining engineer, also a project assessor – Resource Potentials. Your life is govern by a man named Alex Goodbody, right? He holds the strings of your purse so you do what he say, go where he tell you. Okay? But you are not the killing type. Or are you? Is there another man inside you I don't see?' He stared at me, laughing. But his eyes remained fixed on mine. He was deadly serious, and the levity with which he had flung those questions at me gave me a chill feeling deep down. And he was right. That was what scared me, the fact that I was going into something I didn't understand, going into it blind.

'Well? You don't answer. Don't you ever stand back and take a hard look at yourself? In life there are stages – seven ages, your great Elizabethan play man wrote, but there are more, I think. Every so often a man must stand back and think where he is going. You must take control of your destiny, isn't it?' And then, quite suddenly, and gripping my arm again, he asked me where I thought I was going. 'Or don't you know?'

'Of course I know. And you know.' I was deliberately seeking refuge in a literal reply. 'You know where I'm going. The travel agency—'

'Peshawar,' he said. 'Of course. But after Peshawar, eh?'

I turned my head away, looking out of the terminal windows to the aircraft parked on the tarmac, gleaming wet after a sudden flurry of rain. A Turkish Airlines jumbo was being disconnected from its tow bar, the engines crinkling the air with their vapour as it began to taxi, and there was a smaller aircraft away to the right with two busloads of passengers boarding. It was just the view from an airport terminal, any airport, planes standing with their snouts tucked into the boarding ramps, vehicles shifting people, baggage, fuel

– everything so ordinary, so very twentieth century.
And after Peshawar – what? I didn't know. After
Peshawar it was a blank, except for a man with the
improbable name of Laun Said. I should have refused
the assignment, thrown up my job and walked away
from this unknown. But there was Mihai and the body
I had thrown down into the snow-covered back of
that truck.

'*Sans fait rien.*' I turned to catch the end of his
shrug. 'I think you per'aps do not know. Is that right?'

I didn't say anything, and after a moment he
nodded. 'You do not know, do you? Which means that
at Peshawar you meet somebody.' He sighed. 'That is
a pity. I was thinking that per'aps we can make a deal.'
He leaned forward. 'Listen, my friend. I have some
information, but not reliable. It is all rumour, bazaar
gossip. After your meeting in Peshawar I think you
have more certain information. We meet then, eh?'
And without waiting for a reply he rattled straight on,
'Peshawar is the gateway to the high mountains and
the great deserts beyond. From Peshawar you go up
to Chitral and Gilgit, to all those impossible passes,
which are now being closed by snow and ice, or
through the Khyber to Afghanistan. I remember at the
Bucureşti you say something about languages coming
easy for you and that you go on a student exchange,
first to a family in Georgia, then another in Uzbekistan.
Do you visit Tajikistan?'

I nodded. 'But very briefly, just a week or two in
Dushanbe.'

'The capital. It will be very rich, I think. Tajikistan

is the doorstep to the Pamirs.' He shook his head. 'That is somewhere I would like to have been. I was very young at the time, backpacking with a friend, travelling by local buses across into China by way of Kashgar. I was following the old Silk Road, the great caravan route from Kubla Khan's capital to Byzantium and the Mediterranean. My excuse was the study of the way of life in the caravanserai along the old trading route. But it is my grandfather, Pierre Caminade, who was the real reason. He was a journalist, and with the financial support of *The Times* of London, maybe also the Quai d'Orsay, he followed the Silk Road's northern route from Yarkand round the Taklamakan Desert, then north of the Lop and into the great Gobi Desert.'

He was leaning forward, very intent on what he was saying, and I had a glimpse then of quite a different man, his mind now on the track of some deep-felt enthusiasm. 'Do you ever hear of those two intrepid missionary women, Cable and French? No? A very strange pair, extraordinary stamina. They write several books about their travels, which was mostly between the wars, and Pierre Caminade believed they were something more than missionaries. The people of the Gobi he thought far too wild and primitive to be susceptible to Christianity. He believed the two women were treasure seekers rather than teachers of the Christian faith, that they were hoping to find a still-undiscovered city buried deep in the Gobi sands with a temple stuffed with Buddhist manuscripts.'

He shook his head. 'A pity my grandfather don't

follow the young Swedish explorer Sven Hedin into the Taklamakan, but it was the story of the two missionary women in the Gobi that gave him the newspaper backing he needed, so he goes into the Gobi. Then, for some reason I very much wish to discover, his notes become very scrappy after he leave the Gobi, then cease abruptly in the middle of a sentence, and at the end of a page, so that I believe some pages have been removed. It is a loose-leaf notebook and the pages are not numbered, so there is no way I can be certain.'

He paused there and shook his head. 'A very tough, very remarkable man. I wish I had known him. Did he discover something of importance? The notes do not start again until he is stormbound in the snow hole where he died. He is in the Pamirs then, the northeast part on the China border. His description of those storm-wracked days is the most dramatic of all his writings. He was at the highest point of the Khunjerab Pass, buried deep in a snow hole he had made with his bare hands, a candle fabricated from yak fat his only light and source of warmth. He froze to death of course, his notes brought out by the Russian party that found him and sent by the French Embassy in Moscow to his relatives. Attached was a covering letter from the ambassador himself dated 5th March 1939, the year war broke out. I found that notebook in a much-worn portmanteau at the top of our house in Domme when I was clearing up after my father's death. My mother had died four years before . . .'

He went on about the notes, something to do with an archaeologist and the remains of a Buddhist stupa that marked the site of an ancient city. But I wasn't really listening. I was trying to decide whether I should ask him about the man who would meet me at Peshawar. Antoine's own journeys had taken him across the Gobi round the Taklamakan, keeping to the Silk Road, and up into the foothills of the great mountains to the west, his camera his excuse and his introduction to the local Turkoman and Tajik people. And then he was talking of the geologists, oil men, and officials, both Chinese and local, he had met on the way, the story of his journey pouring out of him as he dug back into his memory.

I was still trying to make up my mind about asking him if he had ever met or heard of Laun Said when a movement among the bodies reclining on the seats around us stopped him. Our flight was boarding and we gathered up our things, back again in the present world of air travel. That was when I finally made up my mind. I might not have another opportunity.

We were held up in the queue waiting at the boarding ramp. 'Laun Said,' I said. 'Does the name mean anything to you?'

'Laun Said! Did you say Laun Said?' The quickness of his response, the sudden keenness in his voice, the flash in his eyes, made me realize I had made a mistake. 'Sir Launcelot Peregrine Cellan-Manners. The old spelling, I think, and Cellan pronounced *Kethlan*. Welsh, you see.' He laughed, an excited little laugh. 'So that is who you are meeting. The Great Game. You know about the Great Game? Russia and your imperial gem of India.' And he added, 'Your empire is no more, but the Game still go on, and Laun Said is part of it. He is Wellington and Sandhurst, your Queen's Guards one time, I think, but Intelligence always. That I know for sure.'

He glanced quickly to the head of the queue where the passengers were being checked on to the plane by two stewardesses. 'I will see if we can change our seats, so we can sit together. I have a suggestion I like to make to you. Give me your boarding pass.' I had it in my hand and he grabbed it, pushing his way past a group of Pakistanis and buttonholing the senior stewardess. He was still talking to her when I reached the entrance to the aircraft. 'She will try,' he said, handing me back my boarding card.

The change of seats was effected after we had levelled out at some thirty-seven thousand feet. We were then over the Mediterranean with the Cyprus panhandle just visible away to our right. 'So! I 'ope you have an expensive wife, like me, then per'aps you consider what I have to offer with more enthusiasm, eh?'

'I'm not married,' I said.

'Some girl friends per'aps, some children, a mistress?'

I shook my head.

'Gambling debts, then. No?' He laughed. 'Oh, well, I tell you a little of what I know. But only a little. The situation in the Soviet republics, as I am sure you know, is very uncertain at the moment. The Armenians and the Azerbaijani are at the other's throat, the Baltics are urgent for independence. But it is in Central Asia, the southern part, that area between Mongolia and the high mountains that are the boundary with India, where the trouble will come. I am in Tashkent recently, the bazaar and all the business community throbbing with rumour. So much is a problem of religion, the population predominantly Muslim, but the Russians Orthodox. Nobody like the Russians, and they are everywhere. The Communism they plan was to supplant this religious split, but they forget the racial differences, the people of Asia having their roots in the Mongolian empire of those two great khans, Genghis and his son Kubla. Think, my friend, what Stalin did, great swaths of ethnic cleansing. And just now the Afghan War, a whole decade, and at the end of it the Russians forced to pull out and the guerrilla fighters, the mujahedin harassing them, even the tanks, all the way to the point where they disappear into that two-and-a-half-kilometre tunnel they drive under the Hindu Kush.'

He had hold of my arm now, the grip of his fingers tight in the excitement of what he was trying to tell me. 'It is that withdrawal which begin the crumbling of Russian Communism, eh? The realization that the Muslim people, led by fundamentalists, as in Iran, need not for ever be slaves to Russia.' And then, just as the stewardess was trundling the curried airline meal down the aisle, he said, 'You see. The old Soviet republics now plan a Commonwealth-type federation, and it is largely a federation of the Muslim states. There are wild men, too, like in the Caucasus, where the Chechens are pushing for independence. I hear that when I pass through Baku. Do you know Baku?'

I shook my head.

'All they talk about there is oil. The place stink of it. But before that I am in the Caucasus, in a world of hate and ethnic-cleanse – very Balkan. I go there to see a man who can tell me something I wish to know. But he is dead before I arrive. His wife, who is a big woman with a moustache and many layers of clothing, plead with me to tell the media people that before he die he has seen a great light and a voice has called to him, saying the dead will rise with weapons undreamed-of and there will be a great slaughter of their enemies. The Azerbaijani, she say, will be destroyed absolutely, and there will be no more war. I hear this story several times in the Caucasus.'

He paused, his brows lifted, smiling. 'Why am I telling you this? Because, however bad things are, the eternal optimism of the human race will always, out of its brain, produce a spark to keep the flame of hope alive.' He leaned forward, gripping my arm again in that urgent manner of his. 'I was not old enough to fight in the last great war. Nor were you, I think.' He grinned. 'But you and I, we both know about the holocaust the deliberate destruction of thousands upon thousands of innocent people. And that little girl writing in her secret hideout at the top of that house in Amsterdam . . . Did Christ die for nothing? Can the vile side of man's nature be burned out of him by war?' He shook his head. 'Ethnic cleansing – it goes on and on through the ages. Violence leading to violence, the world infected by territorial greed.'

His outburst was so unexpected I could think of nothing to say for the moment. And then the reek of curry announced the arrival of the meal trolley at my side. 'After we eat,' he said as I lowered my flap table, 'I tell you something about the Mafia. I meet one of the capi in Moscow.'

He was silent after that, concentrating on his food. There was wine for those that were not barred from drinking by their religion. No whisky, but there was arrack and vodka. The curry was very hot, the lamb (I think it was lamb) very tough, my piled-up plate shining with fat. The best part was the rice, basmati by the texture of it, but the halva, when I came to it, was like chewing the plastic container in which it was served.

'In Tashkent, in Dushanbe, among the merchants, the journalists, the professional people, they are all quite sure that war is coming to Transcaspia – a jihad – Muslim against Rus . . .' He leaned back with a sigh and a very subdued belch, snatching the paper serviette from his collar and mopping his brow with it as he went on, speaking even more rapidly, as though the curry had fuelled his brain: 'And there is this dancer they talk of, who claim to be a relative of some sultan – sultana. She is in Alma-Ata. You know it?'

'No.'

'Kazakhstan. It is the capital of that big sprawl of a Soviet republic.' And he added, 'I think you don't miss much, the environment, the lifestyle – ugh!' He had taken off his jacket now and in his shirtsleeves the Gallic shrug was less noticeable.

'What was she like?' Alma-Ata was the destination on the ticket I had bought for Anamaria. 'This dancer,' I said. 'Did you see her?'

'No.' He was on to the halva now, chewing doggedly. 'No, I don't see her. She is gone before I arrive.'

The sweat was breaking out at the roots of my hair. It could have been Vikki, I thought. 'Was she dancing solo?'

He shrugged. 'I don't think so, but I tell you, I never see her dance.'

'What sort of age?'

'How do I know? I tell you, she is not there when I am in Alma-Ata.' He turned his head, a quick glance. 'Why do you ask? Do you think you know her?' His eyes were fixed on me, curious now.

'No,' I said hastily. 'I thought perhaps . . . I thought maybe she was a gypsy dancer I saw in Romania. No, not gypsy. The gypsies you see in Constantza and Bucharest are said to be Egyptians. They are certainly not Romanies, the women all dressed up in gaudy colours.'

He nodded. 'Gypsies!' The mention of gypsies seemed to spark him off again. 'One time, I am surrounded by several, all importuning, very noisily. And then their men appear, wild looking, black haired, dark skinned and aquiline, demanding money.' He smiled, then began to chuckle to himself. 'It takes them very much by surprise when I use a few tricks on them, a karate chop for one, a kung-fu kick in the testicles for another. And then, when I produce one of those long flick knives that jump out with a flash of sharp steel – *pouff!*' He spread his hands. 'They vanish, the men like shadows, their women cackling and screaming in a cloud of red drapery and tinkling golden gewgaws.' He crammed some more of the cloying sweetmeat into his mouth, his cheek bulging as he champed, and said something about her having a Russian general for a lover. 'When the time come he will lead a whole division into battle on the side of freedom.'

And when I said I thought it most unlikely that Russian would fight Russian, he shrugged. 'That is the story anyway. And who can say? So many of them are conscripts. I tell you this, the real soldiers are all the time looking over their shoulder wondering where their pay come from next week. And they like their vodka, eh!'

As I finished my meal he returned to the subject of rumour and dreams, telling me that way back, when he was travelling in the footsteps of those two missionaries, Mildred Cable and Francesca French, scratching around in the remains of ancient cities overwhelmed by time and the wind-blown sand, looking for the dry, scratched vellum of ancient manuscripts, he had heard men wishing that the stranger who had come to them out of the beyond to give them water for their ponies and the livestock on which their lives depended had stayed. 'That man was an engineer named Broz. He had been offered the daughter of their khan in marriage if he stayed, had even been promised the succession when the old man died.'

He stared at me, his lips stretched in that impish smile. 'That was the man who became known as Tito. They want him back. He, and no one else, they said, had the strength of character, the ruthless determination, to hold the people together.' He gave a sad little shrug. 'He is dead now, his Yugoslavia breaking apart, but when I am staying with these people their wish for his return is so great they believe he will really come again and save them from the Russians. Read Pasternak or Solzhenitsyn, think what Stalin did, whole tribes, races even, uprooted and dispatched into oblivion, mostly to Siberia. When the yoke is too heavy to bear, then the Mongol, the Tartar, the Turkoman and the Tajik, they invent another world, a promised land, and a leader, even one who is returned from the dead. You have only to think of the story of the Israelites escaping out of Egypt. The more desperate they became the wilder the dreams, like that dancer they claim can control the movement of a whole division. And they really believe she can do that just by opening her legs to some four-star general.' He laughed. 'That is how wild the stories have become, which is, of course, a warning of the breakdown of Russian dominance.'

I had finished my meal now and I leaned back, his voice going on and on, talking now about Europe and the future of the Single Market, asking me why Britain did not ally herself with France. 'The EU is dominated by Germany, and Chancellor Kohl, now he has East Germany, he is looking, not in our direction, but to the east. Russia is a land-based power. What have we in common? What have we ever had? France is a maritime nation. The British islands are by their geographical nature maritime. And when the tunnel is fully operating and we are tied together as by an umbilical cord . . .'

The sound of his voice merged with the steady drone of the engines. My eyes, heavy-lidded, were beginning to close. I was thinking of Vikki, wondering whether the dancer he had been talking about could possibly be her.

Sitting at over thirty thousand feet, half asleep in a rarefied atmosphere where no human had any right to be, and all these people, strangers slumped shoulder-to-shoulder watching a film shot in Lahore, saris and pale military uniforms, flowing robes and white-laundered shirt-tails . . . Anything seemed possible, particularly when the camera panned across the front of the Lahore Museum to fasten on a child playing with a Space Age toy under the ornate barrel of Zamzama, the great gun that Kim played on. Viewed like that, even the idea that Vikki, by the simple act of sleeping with a Russian general, could influence the destiny of a whole community of people did not seem too far-fetched. But where was the general to send his division? Which of the old Soviet republics was he to support?

The sun was slanting down on a brilliant white plain of cotton-wool cloud far below us. That, and the vodka, and Antoine Caminade going on again about France and Britain dropping out of the EU, gave me a sense of detachment. 'It's better for both our countries that we trade in the Middle and Far East, and round the Pacific Reem. It is a so much bigger market . . .'

And I sat there, half asleep and wondering why he felt so strongly about the EU. Two great wars, the occupation of France, jackboots in Paris – it was a very tenuous alliance we had had. Before that there had been Napoleon, Nelson, Henry V and Agincourt, the Black Prince and Crécy, our goddams rampaging through Aquitaine – France and Britain, William of Normandy – how could we ever combine?

'Concorde,' he said suddenly, reading my thoughts. 'And soon we have the Airbus, also that thing you people call the Chunnel . . .' He leaned suddenly forward, his hand gripping my arm again. 'Who is Z?' he asked abruptly.

The question took me by surprise, my eyes opening wide. 'It doesn't matter,' I said. 'He's dead.'

'Okay, so he is dead. But what is he doing, getting himself killed up there on the Roof of the World?'

I shook my head.

'He is a mining engineer, and a metallurgist like you. He is killed, eh? By the Mafia?'

A long silence while I considered how he knew about Z. The Intim in Constantza. He must have got it from the receptionist. But how much else did he know?

The trolley came down the aisle again, collecting the last trays and selling cigarettes, scent and watches from Hong Kong or Singapore. 'You like a drink with me?' His hand was on my arm, shaking me. 'Then I tell you about the Mafia, eh?' The false teeth grinned at me. 'I make you creep.' He laughed. 'Whatever your game I think you will find yourself dealing with the Mafia.'

I asked for a tomato juice. The stewardess ripped the top of the can open for me and slapped a miniature bottle of vodka down beside it. The trolley had moved on so I didn't argue. 'Everywhere in Asia you find the politicians and the businessmen with dreams of wealth. And where there is the probability of wealth, there is the Mafia also. Those cities of the Gobi and the Taklamakan now lost in the sand, they were rich in their high days, their oasis water brought to them by the melt of glacier ice six thousand, seven thousand metres up in the high ranges of the Tien Shan, the Pamirs and the Karakoram . . .' He was leaning slightly forward, head twisted towards me, watching as I drank the Bloody Mary he had landed me with. 'They dream of new cities built with the oil and mineral wealth they are sure is waiting for them in the high ranges, waiting to be discovered and developed by modern technology . . .'

The lights dimmed and the next thing I knew the film had ended and passengers were queuing for the toilets. Antoine was silent now, slumped in his seat and fast asleep. The lights were switched out, only the reading spots remaining. I waited until the queue had thinned, and then, having relieved myself, I fell into my seat and slept. I was still very tired, a nervous reaction rather than physical exhaustion.

Dawn was beginning to break as we started the long descent into Karachi. We had been held up by a strong headwind. My companion, it seemed, had the capacity of a camel. He hadn't stirred all night and he was still fast asleep.

We hardly spoke as we completed our immigration cards and the aircraft came to a halt. He was ahead of me as we left the plane, but he waited for me as we entered the terminal building. 'I have to meet somebody now,' he said. 'If you want me, you know where I am – the Sind. If not, then I see you in Peshawar. *A bientôt.*' And with a casual wave of the hand he turned and left me, elbowing his way up the queue to the immigration desk. His baggage must have had some sort of priority, for there was no sign of him by the time I reached the baggage-claim carousel for our flight.

At the Metropole there was a message requesting me to contact the Arshad Agency immediately on arrival. This I did by phone as soon as I was installed in my room. There was no answer, nor did I have any luck when I tried to contact Caminade at the Sind to arrange for us to meet for dinner. There was no answer from his room and after paging him they finally reported that he was not in either the bar or the dining room, nor was he on the terrace. They thought the sahib had probably gone out to dine with the friend who was with him when he arrived.

The Metropole proved a strange, rather impersonal place, my room large and cooled by a slowly revolving fan positioned like a chandelier in the centre of the ceiling. The windows looked out on to a parade-ground-sized square courtyard peopled by the large black kites that were forever planing and circling overhead as they rode the thermals. It was dusk now and there were fairy lights among the shrubs in the far corner, the wail of Indian music throbbing on the still-warm air and waiters with glasses and dishes of sweet-meats hurrying to and fro among the crowd of guests, all dressed up, the women in their best saris, some in what might be described as old-fashioned cocktail frocks, the men in variously coloured suits, some with bow ties and sharp jackets with padded shoulders. And there was a bride and bridegroom by the door into the hotel looking both excited and embarrassed.

I stripped off and had a bath. The plumbing made strange noises and the compo-stone floor sloped from the walls inwards to a central drain. The couple in the room next door were also having a bath, the chatter of their voices quite audible through the thin partition, talking very fast in a language I did not know.

When I was dressed I went downstairs and checked Reception for any message. There was none. It was a fine night, the air still warm, and since I had an excuse, I strolled across the big open square and through the gardens to the Sind Club. The windows were open to the terrace and I sat at a table there and ordered a whisky sour, my mind running back over the events of the past few days. I was being required to step into a dead man's shoes and nobody had told me why, or what it was all about.

I paid for my drink and walked back to the Metro-pole. The thought of dining alone in an unknown restaurant did not appeal. Instead, I went up to my room, rang room service and ordered a meal. Looking through the drawers of the table on which the telephone stood, I found the usual Gideon Bible, also, below a telephone directory, several tourist brochures left presumably by a previous occupier. There was one of Baltistan which contained a map showing the course of the Indus River and the peaks and glaciers barring the way into China, peaks with names like Trango Towers, Baltoro Cathidrals and Muztagh Tower. There was also a brochure of Swat and the Chitral Valley, another of Gilgit and the Kashmir borders.

Inevitably, with a job like mine, maps have a great fascination. To have these brochures to study over my meal was a stroke of luck and a perfect introduction to the country into which I was heading. Gilgit itself was at 5,700 feet with the pyramidal peak of Rakahposhi towering over it, and less than forty miles to the south loomed the slightly higher 26,660 foot mass of Nanga Parbat. They were old brochures and I could only just trace the route of the Karakoram highway leading into China, but they gave me a mental picture of the colossal mountain sprawl that lay beyond Peshawar barring any thought of winter travel to the north.

That, and what little I had been told of my guide, produced in me a tingle of nervous excitement so that I found it difficult to sleep.

I was woken by the telephone, and a deep, rumbling voice announcing itself as Shaikh Arshad. He had been informed of my arrival, but had not attempted to contact me as he thought I might be tired after my journeys. He would be at his office shortly after nine if that was not too early. He gave me the number of his room on the first floor and he looked forward to meeting me. 'I think, Sir Cartwright, you have a busy day ahead.' And he rang off.

The Metropole, as might be expected with its mixture of offices on the lower floors, was a very commercial hotel, the stone corridors and broad stone stairways echoing to the footsteps of all sorts of people. *The Shaikh Arshad Import–Export Agency* was painted in large gold letters on the door to his room, the proportions of which were exactly the same as my own. He was a large, bearded man, the backs of his hands covered with black hair. Two big armchairs were set on either side of a low table. The double bed had not been slept in so presumably he had a house in Karachi. A young man with very thick smarmed-back hair and a neat little moustache got up from a desk by the window and hurried out.

'He is gone for the coffee,' Arshad said, and as soon as the door was shut he produced from the breast pocket of his voluminous jacket a folded slip of paper. 'A message from Laun Said,' he said in his heavily accented voice. 'I read it to you. He is telling you he will be in Peshawar when you arrive and will meet you at the airport. Also he warns you to be careful and not to talk about your plans with anybody. He says you are to hurry, so I have found a seat for you on the afternoon flight today. And you are to take with you climbing boots and cold-weather clothing. Do you know the Brigadier?'

'No.' I shook my head.

He smiled. 'Then I think maybe you find it an interesting experience.' He had apparently acted for Laun Said on two or three occasions. 'And always he is going high, so I think you must be prepared.' He had arranged for his assistant to escort me to the 'shoppings'. 'You do not have to concern yourself with tent, sleeping bag, rope, ice axe or any of the actual climbing impediment. The Sahib will have everything if it is necessary.'

The assistant came back with the coffee and for a moment I was happy to linger over it while Arshad gave the young man more detailed instructions, speaking to my surprise in Pashtu. Then he turned to me. 'I think you go now, or you miss the plane.'

I very nearly did miss it, the 'shoppings' involving more than one bazaar and taking longer than expected. And then, when we landed at Peshawar, nobody came up to me and introduced himself as Laun Said, nor was there any message either at the desk or at Dean's Hotel where Arshad had booked me a room.

I was now in a vacuum, my mood of tense expectancy on landing reduced to one of angry frustration. In the taxi from the airport I had glimpsed the old cantonments of the regiments that had held India's North-West Frontier in the days of the Raj. They were still there, so that in my imagination I could hear the bugle calls, the stamp of men on parade, the sound of gunfire. The Guides, the Scouts, the Gurkhas, the Khyber Rifles, Probyn's Horse – I had grown up in a household littered with books about the world my father had lived in as a youngster, a mixture of fact and fiction that had coloured my thinking ever since the receptionist at the Intim had given me that message and I had realized my destination was Peshawar and the snow-covered heights beyond that were generally regarded as the Himalayas.

The room I had been allocated was in the old part of the hotel and matched the sombre mood that now gripped me. It had been built to cope with a hot climate in the days when fans or punkahs were the only means of keeping cool, walls up to a yard thick composed of what looked like a dark brown-grey clay and a window aperture that was more like an embrasure. And the hell of it was there was nobody I could contact. All I could do was have a meal and go to bed. Tomorrow I could phone Arshad, or better still, because he was nearer, Syed Ali Lari at Flashman's Hotel in Rawalpindi.

I had dinner at the Inter-Continental, which is on the Khyber Road and looks across to the huge battlemented red pile of the Balahisar Fort. On my own, with nobody to talk to, my mood was such that I drank rather too much. I vaguely remember being helped from the taxi to my room and falling into bed with my clothes on. The call of nature got me up around four and I changed into pyjamas. It was very cold. The next thing I knew there was a pounding on the door and a high-pitched voice shouting, 'Wake up, sahib! Wake up! Are you all right, plees?'

I must have muttered some sort of reply, for the door opened and the voice, much closer now, yelled,

'Me, I am Abdullah, sahib, and I have here my car waiting to take you to Jamrud.'

I opened my eyes. A shaft of sunlight was slanting in through the window embrasure, illuminating a pockmarked face leaning over me. It had a front tooth missing. 'Hurry plees, sahib. I have brought you tea.' He was thrusting a large cup and saucer at me.

'What's the time?' I asked him.

'Is just after eight.'

'So why the hurry?'

'The Sahib Laun Said, he say to meet him at Jamrud. He is expecting to be there about one hour from now.' I asked him how far it was to Jamrud and he said, 'Nine miles, sahib. But is on the Khyber Road and there are very many refugits.' He sucked at the tooth gap and spread his hands with a shrug. 'We could be on that road an hour to Fort Jamrud. He says to meet him at the Arch and to clear yourself for entering the Tribal Lands.'

The sunlight, the gap-toothed Abdullah and his car, the knowledge that the meeting with my guide was very close now and I had not been abandoned . . . Abdullah had disappeared into the bathroom and there was the sound of running water. I jumped out of bed, no hangover and suddenly full of energy and a feeling of optimism. Little did I know!

PART THREE

THE GREAT GAME

CHAPTER ONE

It was a beautiful morning, a cloudless sky and the Sulaiman range an arid backdrop in the distance, the brown of bare rock tinged with the blue of morning mist rising from the plain.

I was sitting in front with Abdullah, who wore his round Pathan hat at a jaunty angle as though he too was affected by the freshness of the morning. He was a very silent man, and even when I spoke to him in his native Pashtu, his answers were monosyllabic so that I felt I was having to drag each scrap of information out of him. And when his reply was not monosyllabic it was because he was being evasive. To the simple question how long had he worked for Laun Said he replied, 'I am not working for Brigadier. I am taxi-man. This my car.'

'And where were you and the Brigadier when he told you to pick me up at the hotel here and take me to Jamrud?'

A long silence, and when I repeated the question, he said, 'I don't know where is Brigadier.'

'You mean he telephoned you. Where from?'

No answer, and when I persisted, he shrugged and said he didn't know. A boy had arrived. 'No telephone. Only message.'

'What time was that?' I asked him.

Another shrug. In the end he admitted it had been some time in the early hours of the morning. 'So it was the boy who said I was to hurry.' I was wondering where the hell the man had got to.

Abdullah smiled. 'No need for boy to say that. Brigadier Sahib always in hurry when he require my services.'

I asked him about the boy then, where he lived. The answer was another shrug. 'He is just a boy.' Finally, after a lot of probing, I learned that he was an Afghan refugee, a teenager who travelled the Malakand Pass road picking up a job here, a job there. In other words, living on his wits. He was called Nuri after the district he came from, which was Nuristan on the borders of Chitral and Afghanistan, close under the great mountain range of the Hindu Kush.

I think my questions worried Abdullah, for he suddenly became quite talkative, complaining how the cruel bombing of the Afghan villages had caused a stream of 'refugits' to pour across the frontier into Pakistan – old men, women and children, even babies carried on their mothers' backs – 'They come through Landi Kotal and down the Khyber to camp here in the plain, and we have to pay for them. They live on us.

They eat our taxes. It is a great disaster, and it is the Russians who have done this.' Like most Muslims he loathed the Russians – the Nicolais, he called them.

Every now and then we were stopped by the volume of traffic, anything from gaily painted closed-in smuggler's trucks, each with its individual name and mascot of bright wool dancing in front of the driver's eyes, to slow-wandering flocks of flop-eared sheep or shaggy, horned goats. The approach to Jamrud was packed with people, the road a ribbon development of bazaar stalls serving those refugees who had not been transferred to permanent camps much deeper in Pakistan.

The crowd became thicker as we came within sight of the turreted stone arch built across the road to mark the end of Pakistan proper. To our right gaily caparisoned buses, brown with dust, stood like patient beasts of burden amongst the milling mob as more bundles and battered fibre suitcases were piled on the roofs. Most of the men had guns slung across their shoulders, old Lee-Enfields mainly, but quite a few Kalashnikovs, and many of them had their hair, even their beards, dyed red. Extending along the road edge from the right-hand tower was a line of mainly single-storey buildings. These housed the administration and transport offices.

'You get bus here to many places – if you have monai.' Abdullah gave a gap-toothed grin. 'Not so many have monai. See you guard your pockets, eh? Refugits.' He said it with contempt. 'Why don't they fight? They should join the mujahedin. But no, these are the rabble who come across the border from Afghanistan because they are afraid for their lives. They are not true Afghani, not Afridi, not Pathan or Waziristani, they are the no-goods who take our money, and when that is not enough they take more by threat of gun. You understand, sahib?'

I nodded, searching the crowd for somebody who would fit the picture of Laun Said I had formed in my mind. Abdullah was inching the car forward, forcing a way through the press of people towards the last of the makeshift offices. 'I don't see your Brigadier,' I said.

'He will come. Is not yet nine and he say to wait for him here.'

I asked him what sort of a vehicle the Brigadier would be driving.

'Land Rover. Long wheelbase and four spare tyres, also jerrycan. And he flies the flag of your country – if he is dressed correct.'

'How do you mean, dressed correctly?'

'Sometime he wear uniform. But often he play at being a tribesman. I pick him up once and he is dressed as a mullah. Very strange man Laun Said, sahib. Been in what he calls the Great Game country many years. But you watch his hands.'

'Why?'

He hesitated, then said very quickly, 'Grab you by the balls is why. He is that sort of man – sometimes.' He was grinning at me and I felt myself beginning to flush, conscious of my ruddy colouring. I had always looked younger than my age. I turned away to hide my embarrassment and found myself looking straight into the eyes of a man with a great head of bright red hair and a beard that covered most of his face. He had a jezail, one of those long-barrelled muzzle-loaders, in one hand, and in the other he held the hand of a young man, almost a boy, with a long, bronzed face and curved nose that gave his features the sort of aristocratic beauty I had seen in museums of Asiatic art.

The man's eyes held mine for a moment and I thought he was on the point of speaking to me, but his young companion was tugging at his sleeve, whispering urgently in his ear. He turned his head, a deliberate, casual movement, then a muscle of his jaw tightened. He said something and the boy nodded, drifting off towards one of the stalls.

I thought for a moment I must have imagined that sense of sudden tension in the man, my eyes searching through gaps in the crowd, trying to understand what it was they had been looking at. But all I could see was the long curve of the stone wall that half circled a paved terrace to the left of the archway. Set into the stonework was a series of marble panels, about half a dozen of them, each one inscribed with an important facet of the Khyber's history, starting with the Gandhara period, which rang a faint bell. I asked Abdullah what it was and he said, 'Many tourists ask me what is Gandhara. Is name for this area, in Bronze Age.' A Russian-style jeep with two men in it had parked below the last panel. The top was down and the vehicle was covered with a dark brown, almost red layer of dust.

'Your passport, plees, sahib.' Abdullah had his door open and in a rush he explained he had to visit the guardpost and fill in the necessary papers to clear me for entry into the tribal area. He also asked me for 'monai' to pay the dues – not for himself since I would be going on alone with the Brigadier, and for the same reason he would not have to register the number of his car. I asked him how he was going to explain my visit. 'Does tourist cover it? Journalist, perhaps?'

'No, no. Is sufficient I tell them you are with Brigadier.'

I watched as he pushed his way through the crowd and entered the guardpost. Tourist, journalist, a VSO administrator perhaps, but for that he would have to produce an identity card, preferably plastic and with a photograph. A host of possibilities tumbled through my mind, all equally improbable, and when I finally turned back to look at the man with the bright red hair he had vanished, and so had the boy.

A flash of light caused me to turn my head to the left. The two men were out of the jeep now and one of them was scanning the crowd through a pair of binoculars. It was the binoculars that were reflecting the low-slanting sunlight. They looked like Iranians, or Libyans perhaps, both of them dressed in loose-fitting suits and both of them with very black hair and moustaches. The binoculars steadied, trained on the bus parked almost underneath the archway. I thought I saw a glint of red hair, but I couldn't be sure. No sign of the boy. The bus doors closed and it began to move. I got out, thinking to follow it.

Standing just in front of me was a man I took to be one of the mujahedin. He had an old .303 slung over his shoulder and a bandolier of ammunition, the brass cases catching the sun and flashing every time he moved. His hair and beard were hennaed a particularly bright red.

The bus passed quite close to me and the man who had seemed to want to speak with me was sitting on my side. Once again our eyes met. Then he turned away. But for a second his head was directly behind and above the man just in front of me with the brightly hennaed hair and beard. I had a shock then, for the hair and beard of the man on the bus was quite different, so that I realized it wasn't dyed. It was natural. He had ginger hair of a brightness that I had only seen before in Australia.

'Sahib. Your passport.' Abdullah was back, holding it out to me. 'Also the necessary paper. You are now clear to enter the tribal area. You can go to Landi Kotal, stock yourself with all the drugs you desire, and down to Torkham, which is the border post, the point of entry for Afghanistan. But I must tell you it is not permitted for you to enter Afghanistan, or any part of Baluchistan territory. Barra, which is the great bazaar for contraband, is also no-go.' And then, with a little clucking of his tongue, he said, 'You should not have left the car. The refugits. Is not like the old days, like the golden days of our slavery under your administrators. Then we could leave car unattended and everything safe. Now, thieves everywhere, especially in place like this.' He caught hold of my sleeve. 'Now we go back to car, plees.'

We sat there, waiting, and the minutes ticked by with nothing to do but watch the shifting pattern of the crowd. A motley, mixed lot, very wild looking some of them, particularly the Afridi, and I would have been happy just watching them if I had not been so concerned about the non-appearance of my guide. By nine thirty I was getting edgy.

'Do not concern yourself, sahib. He will come.' And with a smile Abdullah added, 'When he does, you will see – he will be in hell of a hurry.'

I pushed my door open. 'Well, when he does come, you can tell him he'll find me over there looking at those marble tablets.'

By then I was almost trembling with suppressed anger. No good cursing Abdullah. It wasn't his fault. But wasting time like this . . . What infuriated me was that this army type with the fancy rank was clearly being paid by Resource Potentials to do a job, and that job was to brief me and act as my guide. That made me in a sense his employer, and after all I'd been through to get myself here . . . curiosity and the sense of uncertainty had my nerves on edge.

But then, standing in front of those marble tablets, my eyes taking in what was inscribed on them in English, invasion after invasion, the simple words stirring my imagination, a calm descended on me. The Persians, the Greeks under Alexander, the Parthians, the Moguls, the Sikhs and finally the British, and turning my gaze to the archway and the mountains beyond,

I began to realize what a deadly trap of a gash the Khyber River had carved out of them, the blood of thousands upon thousands of fighting men mingled with the dry dust of eroded rock.

The whole story of those two millennia of constant conflict was so concisely told that I could think of nothing else for the moment, hurrying back to get my camera.

'Be careful,' Abdullah admonished me on a note of near panic. 'No women, nothing military. And hurry! You must hurry, plees.'

'It's your Brigadier who should hurry,' I told him.

'Per'aps he go down to the station. It is the day for the train and the bus has already left.'

'Well, if he comes before I return he can bloody well wait.' Abdullah looked so shocked I added, 'I won't be long.'

The light was just right, and back at the tablets I took careful photographs of each of them. Then I wandered round the stalls. They sold all sorts of things – fruit, vegetables, frames for photographs, rolls of cloth and silks for saris, clothes for men, those funny round pancake hats the Pathans wore, also conical fur hats for the high mountains, some with earflaps. It was while I was at a stall full of beads and bangles for women that a hooter blared away to my left, then a sudden outburst of steam and the sound of wheels straining at the steel of the track. The train was leaving, clouds of black smoke rising in the still air.

Somebody tried to sell me a Lee-Enfield and a little boy pointed to my camera and wanted me to make him a picture of himself. He knew about Polaroids and it was hard to get him to understand that my camera was not a Polaroid and could not take pictures that spouted out a print in about five minutes that he could take back to his mates and flourish with pride.

It was when I was taking a close-up of a wooden booth full of cheap cooking utensils, the tin gleaming bright in the sunlight, and brass, some of the trays intricately worked, that a horn blared. I turned to see a battered Land Rover covered in dust pulled up close alongside Abdullah's old Merc, and then Abdullah himself waving to me frantically.

I made my way back then, but I didn't hurry. Why should I? When I finally got back to the car I found myself faced with what looked like a Pathan tribes-man, sand-coloured shirt-tails hanging loose over baggy trousers, dark glasses bridging a formidable nose and a grizzled moustache above a little goatee beard. He was standing by the lowered tailboard of his Land Rover, while Abdullah slung my gear in. 'Where the devil have you been, man?'

He wasn't a Pathan at all. He was Welsh by the sound of it, and appeared to be in a foul temper.

'Laun Said?' I asked.

He nodded curtly, yelling at Abdullah to hurry with my valise.

'You're late,' I said.

He had taken his glasses off, to get a better look at me, I suppose. The tension in him, and the furious temper he was in, took me by surprise. 'What do you mean, boy – late? It's you . . .' But then he took a deep breath. 'I've been driving all night. So what were you doing over there? Looking for him?'

'Who?'

'Gingin, for God's sake.' He turned to Abdullah. 'Didn't you tell him?' And then he shrugged. 'Oh, well, doesn't matter. Ginger McCrae.' He turned before I had a chance to ask him what he was talking about, pulled a loose fur cape round his shoulders and got into the driving seat. The engine roared. 'Move it, for God's sake!' Abdullah was round at the passenger door, holding it open for me. 'Good journey, sahibs,' he said as I climbed in.

'Good journey! You know damn well it won't be a good journey, you old fool.' The 'old fool' was spoken as an endearment. The gear lever shifted against my knee, the horn blaring as we swung towards the archway.

Once our papers were checked and we were through, I asked him about McCrae.

He didn't say anything, concentrating on the road ahead. A bend, and then suddenly he put his foot on the brake, flashing headlights and sounding his horn as a big truck decorated with great splashes of crimson thundered down on us, holding to the middle of the road. 'Been like that all night,' he growled as we scraped past. 'An ammunition run, I wouldn't wonder. That's an empty one going back to Karachi.'

'McCrae,' I said again. 'Who is he, and what's he to do with us?'

'He's our guide.'

I stared at him, the whole venture suddenly seeming crazy. 'What do you mean? You're the guide.'

He shook his head. His foot hard down on the accelerator again, stones clattering against the mudguards, a perpetual din.

'But the instructions given me when I reached Karachi—'

'From London?'

'Yes. You would brief me and act as guide.'

'Hah! Fine if I knew where we were going.'

'You don't?' With the ground suddenly cut from under my feet all I found to say was, 'Does this man McCrae know?'

He shrugged. 'I don't know. Maybe.' Silence then, and when I tried to discover why he had taken the job if he didn't know where we were going, all he said was, 'Because I needed it.' A smudge of black smoke appeared between us and the Sulaiman range. He was leaning forward now as though the Land Rover were some sort of steed that could be urged into a faster gallop.

'He's on that train, is he?'

'Yes.'

There were so many questions I needed to ask him, but he shouted to me above the noise of the engine and the rattle of the stones, 'Shut up, can't you. You see that picket—' He was pointing. 'About ten o'clock and just showing against the skyline.' A small tower, like that of a medieval church, showed pale above the brown shoulders of the foothills just to the left of the direction in which we were travelling. 'Shortly after

that the rail-track gets really steep. My guess is he'll
jump the train then. Now keep quiet and let me concentrate. There'll be some nasty bends soon, not the
place to meet a heavy truck . . .'

'At least tell me—'

But he didn't let me finish. 'Later, damn you!' He
turned his head briefly, glaring at me, the cobalt blue
of his eyes glinting in the sun. 'Do as you're told, boy!'
The bark of his voice and his use of the word 'boy'
again hit me like a blow and for an instant my mind
blanked and I was in the bows of the *Waltzing Matilda*,
reaching down to fling Kasim over the yacht's pulpit.
I saw once again the surprised look on his face, the
mouth agape in the break of a wave as he called for
me to help him in words I could not hear, the roar of
the waves merging into the clatter of fallen stones as
we entered the first long bend and began to climb. The
train had disappeared, hidden by the shoulders of the
crumbling mountainside up which we were climbing,
the crags above dappled white by the previous evening's rain, which the altitude had turned to snow,
now melting in the sun's warmth.

Something had happened – but what? And the
patronizing way he had addressed me, as though I was
some junior subaltern of his. Was that why Abdullah
referred to him as the Brigadier? Or was he really a
brigadier?

Looking at him, crouched over the wheel, his
round flat Pathan hat tipped to one side as the sun
caught us on a bend, his weather-beaten face scorched
dark by years of near-tropical heat, the hooked nose

above the bristling moustache, the beetling brows, the clipped, military tone of his voice as he told me to shut up . . . I could just see him on some dusty parade ground, like the ones we had passed in the old imperial cantonments on the outskirts of Peshawar, barking out orders at a bunch of Gurkhas or a company of the Khyber Rifles. I was just opening my mouth to remind him that I was in effect his employer on this expedition and demand an explanation when he swung into a tight hairpin and seconds later another of those gaily painted trucks was taking up most of the road.

By the time it had passed us I had thought better of it and said nothing, remembering what Antoine Caminade had told me about him. He knew this country. I didn't. And there was plenty of time.

I sat back then, forcing myself to relax, my mind running over the other things the Frenchman had told me – about his grandfather, his wanderings in the Gobi following the trail of those two strange Englishwomen, and about his snow-hole death in the high Pamirs, the missing pages from his diary. Pierre Caminade.

Another bend and then a straight stretch with the picket close now, its square stone tower standing almost white against the cloudless blue of the sky. 'Ever heard of Pierre Caminade?' I thought if I sprang the name on him suddenly like that he might give me a straight answer.

He glanced at me quickly, but said nothing. If he really was Intelligence, and the Pamirs his territory, then surely he must have heard about the man's death.

'Well?' I said. 'Does the name mean anything to you, or not?'

'Yes.' His eyes were on the road again, the next hairpin coming up. 'We'll stop at the picket. How do you know about Pierre Caminade? You've come from Australia, isn't that right, with a brief stop in Romania? That's what your CV says. Caminade died in the Pamirs, trying to cross the Khunjerab Pass. A long time ago now. So how do you know about him? Your people in London, did they tell you?'

'No,' I said. 'His grandson, Antoine Caminade. I met him in Bucharest and again in Karachi.'

'I see.'

We were climbing the stony aridity of the shoulder on which the picket was built, neither of us speaking now. We were getting high and, looking past his shoulder, the mountain ridges were a brown moonscape of steep slopes cascading with scree and slashed by the carved-out bed of the rail-track. Black holes like stone-embellished entrances to cave dwellings marked a tunnel, and below that was the road snaking upwards and marked by more cascades of stone. A bus bore down on us trailing a streamer of dust. It was packed tight with men, most of them wounded, bloodstained bandages and fierce, battle-weary faces staring zombielike out of the windows, seeing nothing but their own pain. And there were others lying sprawled on the top of the bus where the luggage would normally be strapped. The whole vehicle, crammed full of wounded, was a stark reminder of the war the mujahedin were fighting across the border in Afghanistan now barely thirty miles away.

'Know how to use a handgun?' The question, barked at me as we topped a rise, took me by surprise.

'How do you mean? What sort of handgun?'

'Any sort. Have you ever fired a gun?' He was slowing now, pulling off the road onto the sand and gravel of the verge.

'In Australia,' I said. 'Shooting roo and wallaby.' And I added, 'For food only. On seismological and geological expeditions. A lot of the boys just did it for fun. I didn't see the point of killing for killing's sake.'

'Doesn't matter. You fired the thing. You know the mechanism. Good shot, are you?'

'Not bad,' I said, remembering how we had lost our way once, just the two of us, and Mike, a young mining engineer straight from England and an office job. Taught me a lesson. It was almost a week before they found us and if I hadn't bagged that female roo . . . 'Why?' I asked.

He reached under the instrument panel, let down a flap and produced a nasty looking little revolver, handing it to me. 'I like to know I've got my back covered.' The locker also contained a rifle and two shotguns. He took the rifle as he pushed open his side door. It had telescopic sights. 'We'll wait for the train over there by the picket.' He nodded and I turned my head to find we were now slightly above the tower and only about a hundred metres from it. 'It's a good lookout point and I want to see how the train has been made up today.'

'Two or three coaches,' I said, 'and five or six long-wheelbase wagons, one at least crammed full of armed men. You were negotiating the first bend at the time. And there are guards riding the engines, both front and rear. Why? What do you plan to do?'

He fumbled under his brown woollen robe and produced a scrap of paper. 'This was slipped into my hand by a young Afridi boy at Jamrud Station just after the train had pulled out.' He handed me a creased and grubby scrap of paper on which was scrawled L K and beside it a little sketch or perhaps a hieroglyphic. 'Only just missed the bloody thing,' he muttered angrily.

'L K presumably stands for Landi Kotal?'

He nodded.

'And the little drawing?'

'At the top here the gradient is at its steepest and there is a guardpost and a signal to warn the driver if the bridge ahead has been washed away or blown up. Or perhaps they put it in for military purposes when they bridged the roadway.' The drawing suddenly fell into place, recognizable as a guardpost and a signal in the down position.

The picket was on the downward slope of the shoulder. 'We'll give it five – no, ten minutes. I'm sure I am ahead of it now . . .' He went round to the far side of the tower and folded himself at the knees. He didn't sit, he squatted, his back to the stonework, his eyes slitted against the sun. With that big nose, baggy trousers and the silly little hat that looked like a rather burnt pizza case worn as though it was a Para beret, nobody would have guessed he was from the UK. Or was he?

'Were you born out here?' I asked him.

'Of course.'

Out of the wind and in the sun the stone at my back was quite warm and I was relaxed. 'What about McCrae?' I asked. 'Is he a friend of yours?'

He nodded. 'I told you – we recruited him out of the Guides. A long time ago. Since then we've been in and out of trouble together God knows how many times.' He turned his head and looked at me with those startling cobalt eyes. 'Wondering why I called him in for this little bit of fun, eh? We've got to get through the mountains to the north of Afghanistan. It's his patch, he knows the terrain and the people. Got a lot of contacts. With him to guide us we might even talk our way through the Salang Tunnel. We both speak Russian and between us we can talk most of the local patois.'

'I thought you said you didn't know where we were going.'

'I don't. Not for sure. But I can guess.'

He was silent for a moment, then he said, 'Since you've been in Australia you probably don't even realize there's a war on just over the Khyber there. From Landi Kotal it's only a few short miles to the border at Torkham. The Russians, bless their little Nicoline hearts, drown themselves in vodka and hope the Hueys and the MiGs can win the war for them. But as we found to our cost, and all the others who have invaded this country, the people here, once they're fighting a jihad, never give in – no invader can ever win against the Pathans, the Afridis, the Nuristanis. Allah says if they die fighting the infidel, then they go to that lovely, heavenly place where it's always springtime with houris on tap . . .' He stopped there, listening. Then turned to me again. 'Did you hear it?'

'Hear what?' I asked, staring into the dust-hazed distance. The view from the picket embraced the whole of the Kabul River's descent to the Jamrud plain, a desiccated wilderness of burnt scrub, scree and stony embankments. It looked like the worst of the mining scenes I had witnessed in Australia.

'Listen!' He cocked his head on one side, listening intently. But the only sound was the sound of the wind whistling in the open embrasure halfway up the tower. It was the only means of ingress or egress, the tower impregnable except to a tossed grenade, and any attacker who got that far would be a dead man. Finally he shook his head. 'The train can't have got here before us, unless . . .' He paused, then added, 'It depends, I suppose, what weight of munitions they're railing up to the mujahedin in those goods wagons you mentioned.' He shook his head again, and still talking virtually to himself, he said, 'Dammit, we were right below it just as we entered the start of the pass. We surely must be ahead of it here. If not we'll have to pick him up at Landi Kotal. And that could be too late.'

'How do you mean?' I asked him.

'Ginger wouldn't send a cryptic little note like that unless he was in trouble. That's why—'

His legs straightened suddenly under him, bringing him to his feet in one fluid movement, one hand holding the rifle, the other raised to shade his eyes. 'There it is again. You must have heard it that time.'

'It sounded like a clap of thunder to me,' I said.

'There's a cutting a little further up,' he went on, still talking more to himself than to me. 'He knows it, I know it, and if he's in trouble . . .' He was leaning slightly forward now, staring back down at the road snaking up the dry river-bed below us. 'There, did you see it – a puff of smoke?' He relaxed then, straightening up and smiling, whistling a tune between his teeth, then putting it into words – 'She'll be comin' up the Khyber when she comes, when she comes. She'll be comin' up the Khyber— We've made it. We're ahead of 'em, praise be to Allah.'

B-O-O-M . . .

A sound like distant gunfire echoed round the bare, brown, desiccated hills.

'Hear it now?'

I nodded.

'That's the engines.' There was an almost boyish excitement in his voice.

The sound went on repeating itself— *BOOM – Boom – boom*. Then *Ps-ss-sht*. The hiss of steam was a long-drawn sigh, faint on the still air.

'There are two of them, one at each end, arse-about-face to each other.'

Suddenly I saw it, thick black smoke spouting out of what I had taken to be the shadow of a distant rock, but was in fact the exit from a tunnel. 'She'll be comin' up the Khyber—' He turned his strangely shaped head towards me, grinning hugely, one big hand gripping my arm as he pointed away to the left. 'See where the track runs up the shoulder there? No room to turn, so they run it up to some buffers, switch points, then the other locomotive takes the lead and they'll be on their way here. Unfortunately there was no way I could get the Land Rover up there. All gravel and scree, you see.'

I could see the whole train now, one engine in front, another at the rear, both belching their way along a barely discernible track that seemed to have been bulldozed out of a hillside that was all scree, right down to the dry river gully below us. And then it was gone, into another tunnel, and we waited, following its progress by the booming pant of the engines. Minutes passed, and then it reappeared higher up the brown scree slope and moving in the opposite direction. The whole scene was like a clip from the publicity film they had made of the huge opencast copper mine I had once had to assess for pollution in Papua New Guinea.

'Won't be long now. As soon as it changes direction at the switch we'll move.'

The lead engine had disappeared into another tunnel. A short one this time, two columns of black smoke hanging in the air as it reappeared, only to vanish again into the stone-arched entrance to another black hole of a tunnel, this one driven through the whole side of the mountain, which was humped above the track so that it swallowed the train completely, leaving only the dying murk of its smoke hanging in the air and the muffled drumbeat of the engines struggling up the gradient.

'How old are you?'

I was still concentrating on the train's progress, my mind wondering about the man we were waiting to meet. He repeated the question and it annoyed me. 'Does that matter?' I asked him.

He hesitated. 'No, perhaps not. More a question of experience. It's experience that counts on a job like this.' And when I didn't say anything, he tried another tack. 'Who are you working for? Who employs you?'

'Same people that engaged you, I presume.'

He laughed, and shook his head. 'I don't think so. My agents are a bit specialized.'

The black cloud in the valley below was suddenly more concentrated, and the first of the two engines appeared with a great belch that came up to us with shattering loudness. The engines were really pushing it now, the tom-tom beat of their struggle up the gradient more laboured as they pull-pushed the five packed carriages across the gully in a wide curve, climbing slowly up to the switchback. He handed me the glasses that had been hanging round his neck. 'The guard will drop off in a moment. You'll see.'

The lead engine was now approaching a metal lever that I hadn't been able to see with the naked eye. Slowly it ground its way up to the buffers on the ridge of the shoulder. *Ps-ss-sht.* The train was suddenly stationary, the lead engine close up to the buffers, the two of them panting as though with exhaustion. A

Pathan had dropped off by the long-handled lever and was switching the rails. The panting increased, black smoke pouring out as gunfire explosions shook the air again and the wheels slithered for a grip on the rails. The train began to move, slowly climbing the top of the shoulder, the guard mounting as the last carriage before the rear engine reached him.

'Okay, let's go. We've got a few minutes yet, but I'd like to be in position with time to choose my spot.'

We went back to the Land Rover. 'What's he do now? For a living, I mean?' I asked as we drove off up the road.

'Gingin? Same as the rest of us.'

'Us? Who's us?'

'A few old Frontier hands who've gone a bit native. That about sums us up.' And he added with a laugh, 'It's the fun of it, you know, rather than the money. That's why we do it.'

'Do what?'

'What I'm doing now. Things like this. As long as I can get to Goodwood once a year, and perhaps Ascot . . .' He patted my arm. 'If you're not careful, man, you'll start growing a trunk.'

I pushed his hand away and asked him what the hell he meant by that.

'You're like that little heffalump, too many bloody questions.' He grinned at me.

Back at the Land Rover we drove on up the road. It was full of bends, the pale brown hills above us precariously poised on slopes of wind-scoured scree, patched almost black in places where stones cast a myriad individual shadows. A bridge gave a glimpse of the railway line, above us now. A concrete guard-post and a signal, then the rails disappeared into the first of a series of cuttings that had been blasted out of rock. We stopped a little further on. 'We'll wait for him up there.'

He pocketed the ignition key and nodded to the steep bank above us. It was all loose stone, our feet trampling down the rubble as though we were scree walking. For the last few yards we were clawing our way up on hands and knees. I found a stunted little bush that was like wire and I grabbed hold of it and hauled myself up. Suddenly my head was above the top of the bank, my eyes on a level with the rails. To my left was the exit from one of the cuttings. I could see down the length of it to the signal, which was down, to the guardpost with its peculiar rounded hat of concrete, and beyond that to the bridge. The panting boom of the engines came up to us from down the gully, and away to our right the twin lines of steel made a big sweep round the end of the gully, climbing all the time.

'The gradient's just about maximum at this point and the train will be moving at little more than a walking pace.'

'He's going to jump then?'

'If he can.' And he added, 'We need him. He knows the passes between Afghanistan and Tajikistan, I don't.'

'But I thought—'

'My stamping ground is the Pamirs and the

Karakoram, the borders of China. To get where I think we have to get, that's hard going, and it's late in the season for fooling around on the Roof of the World. Through Afghanistan it's relatively simple, but you need friends among the mujahedin so you can be passed from one khan's territory to the next. Gingin is from the Paghman Valley. He knows the country and he has friends everywhere. Now that the Soviets have withdrawn I don't think he really knows what to do with himself. He's a fighter, and that's how I managed to engage him for this little venture. Before the Soviets invaded he worked the contraband route up from the coast to Landi Kotal, using mules mainly, sometimes camels, on mountain tracks that bypass the customs posts.'

He paused there, listening, and then said quietly, 'Somebody has been talking. That's the only—' He slid his body forward, reaching up for the stones of the trackbed. 'Wait here.' In one lithe movement he had reached the edge of the track, one hand stretched out to grip the nearest rail.

He stayed like that for perhaps a minute, while the sound of the train came to us as a distant drumbeat, moving slowly closer. He turned his head. 'Get back a bit. Stay here, out of sight.' He stood up then and moved to where the cutting to our left ended, leaning his body close against the buttress formation of blasted rock.

BOOM-churr-pssht . . . Suddenly it was there, in the cutting, filling the whole space; a black monster, its round breastplate gleaming almost silver in the sun, star and crescent glittering bright in the fierce light, and men in loose drab clothes crowding the carriage roofs, some with guns, and from the engine's short funnel volumes of black smoke appearing in great belly-thundering gasps.

Half hidden by a piece of rock that was blasted smooth by years of wind-driven dust, I watched as first the pistons then the coach wheels ground their way up the track above me. More pistons, the rear engine struggling past, and then a shout. More shouts, and I lifted my head to see a man jump from the last coach, rolling down the embankment side. His rag of a turban flew off. Red hair, red beard, the details of his appearance glimpsed in a flash. He found a grip where a patch of brittle vegetation struggled to survive and pushed himself to his feet, his body leaning forward to thrust himself down the rest of the embankment to the waiting Land Rover.

And at that moment there was a burst of automatic fire.

He was running, giant strides, his feet driving to catch up with each other, and for a moment he went on running as though nothing had happened. Then suddenly he folded at the waist where the bullets had caught him and pitched forward, face down, the stones tearing the skin of his face to shreds until that bright ginger head hit the road.

There was another shot and I ducked. The crack of it was closer, but no zing of a ricochet off the rubble around me and I lifted my head again just in time to see the man who had blasted those bullets at McCrae lose his balance in an open doorway of the last coach and pitch head first on to the track, his body jerking like a rabbit caught in a trap. His contortions thrust him backwards and suddenly he was still, just the lower half of his body showing as the rear engine, facing backwards with the driver leaning out of the cab, ran over him, blood and guts spurting out onto his trousers. The mountains round us echoed to the agitated sounding-off of the engine's steam hooter, the train's brake shoes emitting sparks as they clamped down on the steel rims of the wheels.

'Catch!'

A bunch of keys almost hit me in the face, Laun Said running past me and shouting— 'The Land Rover – quick, man. Get him into it. Engine running, and my door open.' And just audible above the hubbub from the train, now grinding to a halt, I heard a cry that sounded like '*Guides ki-jai!*' and then he fell, sprawled face down behind a piece of rock that had fallen from the slope above. Shots rang out from the train, a burst of firing, and the bloody fool lying there, motionless. I thought for a moment he must be dead, but then his rifle moved, slowly, almost imperceptibly.

The train had stopped now, heads peering out from half-open carriage windows, men spilling onto the track, and the man who had fired that burst had stepped back, crouched in the doorway. I didn't wait then, I grabbed the keys and ran for it.

I think everybody on the train, except for the man who had just fired at Laun Said, was too surprised to do anything, momentarily caught off balance. I didn't see what happened after that. I heard a shot, just a single shot, but by then I was running full tilt for the Land Rover and no time to turn my head.

I hit the road still running, grabbed the handle of the rear door and, holding McCrae by the shoulders, I somehow managed to thrust the dead weight of him into the back. I expected some protest from him, a cry, a scream of agony. But he made no sound, and as I slammed the door shut his face was turned towards me, blood mixing a different red with the beard, and his eyes, a bright, piercing blue, staring straight at me.

The keys? They had been in my hand when I was struggling to get McCrae into the Land Rover. They weren't on the ground, or in my pockets. A shot rang out as I yanked open the rear door again. Another shot and no sign of the keys. A feeling almost of panic then. In desperation I turned McCrae's body over, there was a clank of metal on metal, the keys lying bright on the aluminium floor. Another shot, followed by a whole scattering of shots. But by then I had shut the back and was scrambling into the driving seat.

It was as I pushed open the passenger door that I saw Laun Said sliding down the embankment, shifting himself from side to side, using the barrel of his gun to steady himself. I had the wheels turning as he flung himself into the seat beside me. 'Go!' he hissed at me, as he pulled the door shut, cutting off the sound of the sporadic firing from the stationary train. 'Move it, man! Move it!' This said as an order, but quietly, as he sat back in his seat, relaxing.

I put my foot hard down, the engine roaring. There

was a ping as a spent bullet hit the metal side of the
vehicle. 'Got them both, the bastards!' And he added,
'Doesn't help poor old Gingin, though. Dead, I
suppose?'

I nodded.

'Sure?'

''Fraid so.'

He didn't say anything, merely nodded. 'What gear
are you in?'

'No idea,' I said.

He was peering down at the lever. 'You're in third.
Change up.'

He put his hand over mine, guiding me as I worked
the clutch. 'Thought you said you could drive the
thing.'

'They were old Land Rovers. This is a lot newer.'

He went through the gears with me, showing me
the lever that operated the subsidiary gear range, then
going over the controls. After that he sat there, his
face set, not saying anything and his eyes on the road
as it twisted and turned, climbing steadily upwards.
Twice I asked him about McCrae, what we were going
to do about the body. But he didn't answer; just sat
there, staring ahead, quite content apparently to let
me go on driving, though we had left the train far
behind.

Driving up the pass was hard work, the road constantly bending and the gay-painted trucks kept on
coming, most of them driven fast and with great
abandon.

Suddenly the crags on either side of us opened out

and straight ahead was a massive structure of what looked like red clay. 'Shagai,' he said. 'Khyber Rifles. This was their stronghold.' And as we drove past it, 'The cemetery is not far now.'

'You mean you're going to bury him out here?'

No answer, and we drove in silence through another defile. Then suddenly he told me to slow down and pull over onto the verge. 'It's up there.' He nodded to the left. 'Give me a hand.'

We opened up the back to find the body had been thrown against the side, the knees bent double and blood all over the floor. 'Where's that handgun I gave you?'

'I put it back in the dashboard locker.'

'Keep it on you.' He took the keys from the ignition, opened the locker and handed me the gun, replacing the rifle he had used and locking the flap.

Even with two of us it was hot, hard work carrying McCrae up to that little sun-baked cluster of head-stones. There were about a dozen of them, but only one of the men buried there had been killed in action. One had been drowned, the rest died of cholera. Laun Said pulled a knife from under his shirt-tails, jabbing it at the ground until he found a soft spot. 'There are tools in the rack on the back of the rear door. Get a couple of spades and anything else you think we may need.' He was kneeling on the ground, pulling McCrae's body round until the red mop of hair was resting in his lap. The blood was clotting dark and the flies had arrived. 'Go on, man. Hurry! We've got to be through the Narrows ahead of the train.' He spoke softly, his head bent over the battered face of the dead man. 'Ginnie and I, we've known each other a long time. Been in some tight spots together. And to end like this. So fucking unnecessary.' He raised his head, looking up at me. 'Such a waste.' There were tears in his eyes.

I turned and ran the short distance back to the road. A truck roared past just as I reached the Land Rover. The driver waved to me, a dark face under an oily rag of a turban. I grabbed two spades and a mattock, hurrying back. He was still sitting there as I had left him, one hand stroking the red-matted hair. He seemed in a trance, but at the sound of the tools hitting the ground he put the head of the corpse gently to one side and got to his feet in that graceful, fluid movement I would learn to recognize as one of the characteristics of the man.

The spot he had chosen was close beside the grave of the man who had drowned. Why the ground was softer there I have no idea, for they had all died in the same year, 1919. It didn't take long to bury him, for we dug only a shallow grave and the mattock, with its blade and its pick, made short work of scratching out the hollow into which we laid him. Laun Said had taken the shoulders and before we started to pile the earth back he knelt down. 'Dust to dust,' he murmured, and his voice shook. Then he bent over the corpse, kissed the face on both cheeks, then on the lips, finally closing those blue eyes now gone dull with no life in them.

Abruptly he got to his feet, that same fluid

movement, and seizing one of the two spades began to throw the earth back, covering the face first and working with desperate energy. He left me to stamp it down and cover the worked earth with tufts of grass, walking slowly back down to the road.

Down the pass I heard the thick, heavy panting of the train, very faint at first, but by the time I reached the road and had replaced the tools and shut the door, the sound of it was filling the defile. He had the engine running, the Land Rover moving before I was properly in my seat. 'Where are we going?' I asked him.

'Landi Kotal.' He didn't tell me why and he didn't say anything after that, driving as though the devil were after us, his face set. In a moment, it seemed, we were into the Narrows, road, river and rail-track compressed into a gully that looked to be barely fifty metres wide, the rock cliffs on either side appearing at times to be leaning over us. 'The killing ground.' He said it abruptly, in a voice devoid of any feeling, as the defile opened out into a flat area that was blocked at the far end by the closing in of the heights to form another defile. Here the road split into an upper and a lower route, one-way traffic and the river flowing fast. There were cave dwellings, some of them perched precariously among the rocks, and higher up there were patches of snow shining white in the sunlight.

He pulled in to the verge, parking the Land Rover close against an outcrop. He glanced at me quickly. 'First time you've been in the Khyber?'

'Yes.'

'Well, there you are then. Got a nasty history, the sand here soaked in blood, and not just soldiers' blood, women and children, too. You speak Pashtu, don't you? I'm surprised then you haven't been here before.' He got out, and I followed him. 'We'll wait here for the train.' He wanted a close look at it in case there was anyone in the carriages that he recognized.

We walked back a little way and climbed an outcrop. Lying flat on the sun-baked sandstone we should be only a few feet away from the train when it passed us. 'Not quite so spectacular as the Bolan, but this is the pass the Russians would have used in any breakthrough to the fertile plains of the Punjab, this is where the blood was spilled, here in the Khyber.' Then he began talking about a forebear of his, a doctor, travelling from Jalalabad down into India disguised as a Persian merchant. The description of the doctor's journey, taken from his diaries, came pouring out of him as though to drown the memory of the friend he had just buried.

Disguised as a Baluchi trader, Dr Manners had attached himself to a party of women and children with an escort of a dozen sepoys under a lieutenant provided by the garrison. 'This is about the spot where they were ambushed. Suddenly the oven-baked heights above them, that had seemed so empty a moment ago, came alive with Pathan tribesmen. They rose up out of the ground on which they had been lying, their deadly jezails pointing down and picking off the redcoats one by one. The long-barrelled jezails, you see, had a much longer range than the British Army muskets. And when all the escort were dead or wounded, they came running and yelling down a dry watercourse, falling on the women and children, slashing at them with their long knives.'

The doctor had apparently been wounded and lay on the ground, feigning death. When it was dark he had washed his wound in the river, searched the bodies for food, and then begun the long trek down the pass to Jodrum Fort.

He went on, talking about the Afghan wars, and about his own experiences, until, faint on the wind, came the soft panting of the train. 'It wasn't only the British who were ambushed here. There were the Sikhs, and before them the Moguls.' His hand shifted, gripping my arm. 'This and the Bolan are the plugholes through this particular mountain mass. The Great Game, which is what Gingin and I were playing, is not only about politics, and the military strength to keep Russia out of India and away from the Gulf. There is trade, you see. Drugs. Opium and hashish. The hub of all this huge mass of mountains is the Pamir, a high-altitude plateau with passes running out in all directions. That is my special province. Gingin's was Afghanistan. He knew all the local warlords. He would have got us through, either up the Pahgman or by way of the Salang Tunnel. It's two and a half miles long, guardposts at either end. No way I could get you through.'

'The Russians have gone now,' I said.

'For God's sake, man! I thought you had at least some knowledge of this part of the world. Afghanistan is not a country in our sense of the word. It's a loose confederation of armed and warlike tribes, each with its own leader, and only drawn together during the last ten years to save themselves from being dominated by people they hate. Without they know and trust you, there's no hope of getting through to the north side of the Hindu Kush.'

'Is that where we're going? I thought you said—'

'That's right. I said I didn't know, and I still don't. But there's a woman I want to meet. A whole new ball game has opened up following the Russian departure, and the word is she is the key.' He glanced at me quickly. 'Precious stones. Is that your field?' But he didn't wait for an answer, raising his hand. 'Listen.'

The sound of the approaching train was growing more distinct every moment, and it was no longer the deep-throated pant of locomotives struggling with a steep gradient. It had found the more level section of the pass and was steaming with a swish-swish of escaping pressure and fast-moving pistons.

His grip on my arm tightened, and then I saw it, thrusting its black barrel of a boiler out from between the brown, toppling cliffs, black smoke pouring from its funnel, the star and crescent gleaming in a shaft of sunlight and steam hissing from the jerking pistons. And all around, in the limestone cave mouths, there were people come out to stare, men, most of them, some armed, and one I saw with a rocket launcher.

'One day,' Laun Said whispered in my ear, 'they'll stop the train and loot it.'

The noise was suddenly deafening. The whole

train, including the rear engine, was emerging from
the defile, the noise of it reaching up to the crags
above, reverberating along the pass in a monstrous
cacophony of sound, so that I expected any moment
the steam-hammer roar of it would start an avalanche
from the snow-encrusted tops of those brown, sun-
blasted crags.

In a moment the lead locomotive was upon us, so
close I could almost reach out my hand and touch it
as the iron boiler thundered past. Then the cab, and
the driver peering out, seeming to look straight at me.
Whether he saw us or not I don't know. But a man in
the first of the carriages did, and I saw his eyes widen
in the shock of recognition. And then, almost unbelievably, he smiled at me.

I felt my mouth respond in an answering smile,
and then he was gone and the open trucks were clattering past, followed by two more carriages and the rear
engine, the cacophony of sound gradually fading as
the train entered the jaws of the next defile.

Laun Said was scrambling to his feet, peace
descending in the deadly open space between the
defiles, a peace broken only by the grinding clatter of
a truck on the east-going section of road immediately
above us.

'No hurry,' he said. 'We'll let the train get ahead
of us and out of the Narrows.'

'Did you recognize somebody then?' I asked him.

'No. Waste of time hanging around.'

'Not for me,' I said. 'Caminade was on the train.
In the first coach.'

'Caminade?'

'The Frenchman I told you about. Antoine Caminade.'

'I see. Did he recognize you?'

'Yes.'

He nodded and walked quickly on to the Land Rover, not saying anything until he had pulled out on to the road again, driving fast. 'Will he talk, do you think? If we can catch up with him.'

'He'll talk,' I said. 'He's a great talker. But whether he'll tell us what we want to know . . .'

'Cock and bull, eh?' He glanced at me quickly. 'And what do we want to know? Have you thought about that?' And he added, 'Beginning to look like a bit of a human jigsaw puzzle, you see. There's you, and there's me, and this man Caminade whose grandfather dies of hypothermia in a snow cave up near the Khunjerab Pass. Dies with pages ripped out of his travel diary. Why? What was in those pages? His grandson doesn't know – or does he? And then there's those two thugs. Not Russian. No, I don't think so. Difficult to tell, dressed as they were in standard off-the-peg Moscow suits. Ex-KGB?'

'Could be,' I nodded, thinking of all the Cold War Russian units breaking up and spilling unemployable agents round the country, redundancy rife.

'Caucasian,' he muttered. 'That's what they looked like to me. Chechens most like. They tell me Moscow is crawling with them. They run most of the rackets, drugs, currency, arms, anything that will turn in a quick dollar.'

'So why were they gunning for McCrae?'

'I wish I knew.' He was silent then. A beat-up old bus crowded with bodies roared past us in a cloud of dust, another following it. And then, as we left the Ali Majud pumping station behind and the dust settled, we were out on a flat plain full of what looked like mud-walled villages with towers, some round, some square, and massive wooden gates in the wall that faced away from Kabul, and in the distance, away to the right, was a huge, wind-eroded Buddhist stupa.

'These villages,' he said, nodding away to the left, 'they're not really villages at all. They are family fortresses, great treasure houses stacked with Sèvres and Dresden, icons by the dozen, silver, gold and precious stones, silks, marble – to visit one of those sheikhs is to meet Aladdin in person.' He swerved to avoid a bunch of women walking with great pots balanced on cloth rings on top of their heads. All of them were veiled. 'I think we'll go and see Ahmed bin Kazakh. He has a godown in Landi Kotal and contacts or agents everywhere. But his HQ is right here, almost the first of the fortified enclaves. If anybody knows what that woman's up to he will.'

He was silent then, peering across the waste of grit and stone to our left. 'Ah! There it is.' And a moment later he pulled off the road onto a rough track. There were tyre marks everywhere, and shimmering through the haze ahead was another of those fortified enclaves, the largest that we had seen so far. 'Precious stones,' he said suddenly, reminding me that a little time back he had asked me whether I was any sort of an authority.

'No,' I said, 'not an authority. But I do know something about the subject.'

'Good! Tell me this, then, what would you expect to find up here? No,' he added quickly as I started to ask him about the geology of the area, 'further north, and east. In the Hindu Kush and north-east up into the Pamirs.'

Sitting there, with the walled enclave coming rapidly nearer, I searched my mind, but not very successfully, for though I had travelled the north-west fringe of the area I realized I knew very little about it. 'I thought the Pamirs were your province,' I said.

He nodded. 'But I'm not a geologist. There's marble there and the higher ridges are so grimly bare that they shriek aloud their volcanic origin. Larval folds and some quite startling fissures. It's clear that the rock formations are fairly recent vintage. That's all I can tell you.'

'Limestone?' I was dredging back in my memory to the books I had studied.

'Limestone?' He thought about it for a moment, then nodded. 'Yes, I suppose so. Sedimentary rock, certainly. The water from the melting snows has carved great valleys out of the plateau. Very fertile valleys. Lapis lazuli.' He was frowning. 'That's what I was trying to remember. That's what they trade in more than anything. Special marbles, too.'

'Corundum,' I said. And when he asked me what that was, I explained to him that it could be anything from abrasives, emery paper for instance, to sapphire and ruby gemstones. It was coming back to me then. 'Kashmir and the north-east of Afghanistan. Tajikistan. You know the land of the Tajiks?'

'Of course. They make all sorts of things of the lapis lazuli – little trinket boxes, necklaces, pendants. The bazaars are full of lapis jewellery, even bowls and vases, and in one place I have seen panels of the stuff for sale. With one of those panels you can do a DIY job. If you've got the skill you can make the most beautiful ornaments.'

It was really coming back to me now, things I had learned way back. 'Garnets and agate. Amethyst, too. And, of course, rubies and sapphires.'

'It's sapphires I've been hearing about.' He eased up on the accelerator. 'Ahmed bin Kazakh.' The clay walls were close now – thirty or more feet high – the track leading straight up to the great gateway with its twin guard towers. The doors were of massive sections of cedar wood. 'You'll find him very polished, very charismatic. Educated partly at my old school, then Sandhurst and a term or two at Oxford. He's very persuasive and you'll think him an Anglophile, but just remember, he's an Afghan. Anything he says, take it with a pinch of salt.'

He cut the engine and got out as a loudspeaker, set in one of the firing slits of the right-hand tower, asked for our names and who we wanted to see, first in Pashtu, then in what I took to be Dari, finally in English. Laun Said went to the intercom set into the support of the right-hand door.

'That's a new gadget,' he said as he climbed back into the driving seat. 'Some time since I was last here. Then you had to yell your business up to a guard in the tower there.' The doors were swinging open, operated mechanically, and we drove through the archway into a large compound, flat like a parade ground and surrounded by single-storey buildings separated by narrow, winding alleyways. Peering over the rooftop of the stuccoed building was a dome in sand-worn tiles and a stubby little minaret. A man in what looked like an immaculately laundered nightdress, a turban on his head, had appeared on the veranda of a nearby house.

'Ahmed's secretary.' Laun Said swung the Land Rover round and stopped it facing towards the gateway, a move that I guessed was habitual, on the basis of being prepared for any eventuality. 'You wait here. I'll see what the trouble is. I don't think Ahmed Khan is in residence. And remember, he likes to be referred to as Ahmed Khan.'

The secretary didn't come forward to meet him. He let him come to him, standing silent on the veranda. He wore a long, curved knife in his belt. It was rather like a scimitar, the scabbard encrusted with silver, one slim, long-fingered hand resting on the hilt of it. Several men, armed with AK47s, had appeared on a neighbouring rooftop. There was tension in the air and I didn't like it.

Leaning across, I got hold of the ignition key and unlocked the armoury locker below the dashboard. They were both of them talking. An argument? I wasn't sure. The secretary's face was very dark, the skin drawn tight across the high cheekbones and the thin, hooked nose, the full, loose lips and black eyebrows giving him a very Semitic look. He might have just come down from the Golan Heights.

Watching them, my mind involuntarily went back to the scene in that balcony room looking out over Constantza Port and the wretched Miron, his limbs convulsed in the agony of death. And then that island of reed, the night spent with a harelipped cripple girl who had not hesitated to fire on Romanian militiamen guarding a roadblock, had admitted to having killed Miron's brother, stabbing him to death with a long steel hatpin. And now, here on the edge of Afghanistan . . .

It was getting hard to recognize myself. There was Kasim, too, the sudden impulse to seize his legs and throw him over the pulpit into the sea. And I was just a very ordinary young man, a mineralogist with a degree in economics . . . It didn't make sense. Nothing made sense. For God's sake, I wasn't a killer.

Or was I? Was that what my life was all about, what I was born for? Kasim, Miron – if only I hadn't taken that rust job in Romania. And now, here on the North-West Frontier of India, two Russians dead, blood and guts spewed from a man's stomach onto his boots as that iron-bellied locomotive cut him in half. And the ginger-haired doll's head of the dead McCrae cradled in the lap of his ex-lover. I didn't kill them, of course. Not even Kasim. It was the sea did that. But I was the catalyst.

So where now? Where would it all end?

I reached across for the map sticking up out of the pocket in the driver's door. He had marked in the Salang Tunnel north-north-west of Jalalabad and east of Termez, south-south-east of Samarkand. The map showed the road from Kabul running through the Hindu Kush and on across the Oxus River to Tajikistan, all Uzbek and Tajik country. And to the east the high Pamirs. The Roof of the World. So where the hell would we land up?

I wished I knew more about the area, but all I knew was the country between Tashkent and the Caspian. I knew nothing about the Pamirs, and since that was the stamping ground of the man Alex had hired to act as my guide, our destination had to be somewhere in that region.

Lapis lazuli – but the value of that had dropped since the deep blue of the natural lazurite was synthesized some time in the early 1800s. There was turquoise, of course, but Alex wouldn't have sent me hot-footing up here to assess the possibility of digging not very profitable stones out of crevices in degraded Tertiary rock formations.

Laun Said had come out on to the veranda, Ahmed Khan's secretary close behind him, palms together and a bow as they made their farewell salaams. No, if it was gemstones I was looking for, it had to be corundum, either rubies or sapphires. I remembered the gemstone textbooks I had read gave north-eastern Afghanistan and the Pamirs as one of the prime sources of the best corundums, some of the rubies as big as carbuncles. Was that what Caminade's grandfather had written in the missing pages of his diary? And McCrae – if his Russian killers were really Mafia, then greed would explain his capture and final end.

'Ahmed is at his godown in Landi Kotal.' Laun Said had his door open and was climbing in behind the wheel. 'Secretary Mansur will inform him of our arrival.'

The great gate had swung open and with a movement of the hand that was half a salute and half a farewell wave he drove out of the compound, bumping and bouncing down the gravel-rutted track till we got back to the highway. The stupa was behind us now, the narrow, stony plain opening up, and there were people about, distant figures walking or riding. I could see several camels, but only here and there was the brown aridity of the land relieved by the green of vegetation. 'What do they all live on?' I asked as we passed a long line of mules heavily loaded.

'Trade. Most of it trucked in. This road is the main lifeline. They pay for food, equipment, arms, ammunition, everything they need, by whatever gives them the best return in the way of smuggled goods. Since the start of the Soviet–Afghan War ten years ago the main traffic has been drugs, arms and all the fiddles that economic and social chaos spawn. But now that the Russians have withdrawn—' He shrugged. 'Who knows? Precious stones and minerals are a possibility, but more likely concentrated agricultural products, anything that is transportable along the mountain tracks pioneered by the smugglers. Ever hear of Bara?' he asked me. 'No? Well, now, when I first saw Bara it was no more than a village. Since then it has grown into a huge entrepôt dépôt stacked full of contraband, what you'd call a free port, and it wasn't long before there was a mini-Bara operating clandestinely in the Pathan capital of Peshawar.'

He had been so silent on the way up the Khyber, but now it seemed he had the need to talk, doubtless to block the memory of what had happened that morning out of his mind. He began talking about the Torkham–Landi Kotal–Bara smuggling route, how it had needed a modern road with competent civil engineers to drive it through the mountain passes. 'And roads in a warlike area such as this need defending. That leads to pacification. So there you are, man. There's a political element to almost any development in what used to be called the North-West Frontier before we pulled out in '47. As it is, the whole elaborate smuggling set-up is a throwback to historic times when every patch had its warlord, his followers collecting dues from each caravan passing through. You see – another year and there will be a new government in Kabul and little wars starting up like bushfires all over Afghanistan. And we will not be driving along this road, not in the carefree manner we are driving along it now. There will be checkpoints in each of the Khyber Narrows, baksheesh the only way of getting through.' He laughed. 'Maybe I'll have retired myself by then. Gingin isn't going to be the last of us to lose his life. It's getting dangerous. Always has been, but more so now. Gingin did well to survive as long as he did.' And he added thoughtfully, 'He and I, we're the same age.'

I wished Alex Goodbody were here with me now, then perhaps he would understand what he had pitched me into.

'What did that secretary tell you?'

He glanced at me, but didn't answer my question, his eyes switching quickly back to the road.

'He must have told you something. You were gone five or ten minutes . . . Come on, for God's sake. You talked about something – what?'

A crowd of men, all of them armed, were sprawled across the road ahead and he slowed. 'Mujahedin.' They gazed at us curiously as we drove slowly through them, their dark eyes wary in their deep brown faces – not hostile, just wary. One of them had an old blood-stained bandage round his head, another was shaking uncontrollably. Strangely, not a word was uttered by any one of them.

'Shell-shock,' Laun Said said as he drove on. 'Even the Pathans crack in the end.' He was fishing around in the pocket of his jacket. 'What do you make of this?' He pulled out a crumpled piece of paper and handed it to me.

How is it that one recognizes blood so readily when one sees it? Not by smell, as would be the case with most other animals, but by the colour and consistency of it. Or is it by some sixth sense? As soon as I opened the scrap of paper and smoothed the creases out I knew what it was that had been used to draw the two smudged and shaky lines.

'McCrae?' I asked.

He nodded. 'Up in that cholera cemetery, while

you were down at the Land Rover getting the tools. I knew where to look, you see.'

So he had been wounded before he jumped from the train. 'And he knew if he died, when he jumped out onto that embankment, there was a good chance you'd find it.'

'Yes. I think that's a reasonable assumption. What do you make of it?'

By then I was holding the paper up to the sun and well away from me, my eyes slitted for focus concentration. 'Initials?' I said. 'It has to be initials.' I turned to him then. 'This is where you earn your pay.' It was stupid of me, but the uncertainty was eating at my nerves. I didn't know what lay ahead, how far I could trust him. For all I knew he might be in the pay of some organization other than Resource Potentials. In which case . . .

'All right, the two figures are initials. We agree on that. Now, what are they?'

'You're better able to read them than I am,' I said. 'You knew where to look for this message, so you must have had some idea what to expect.'

'On the contrary, I had no idea at all. I knew where to look because we had played hide-and-seek in the mountains of the North-West Frontier for twenty years and more.' He looked at me, a cold, searching stare that gave me the feeling he was trying to make up his mind how to handle me. I suppose the difference in our ages made it inevitable that his first approach should have been on a CO/junior officer basis. 'We were very close, you see,' was all he said. And then, seeking the neutral ground of a straight question, with the Welsh intonation even more marked, 'The initials, man. What do you make of them?'

I hesitated, one half of me wanting to needle him further in the hope that he would be forced to explain what he had meant by 'playing hide-and-seek in the mountains of the North-West Frontier'. The Pamirs presumably, or the Hindu Kush. I looked down at the paper again. The two figures McCrae had traced in were appallingly shaky. 'He must have done it in the train.'

'Yes, in the train, I think,' he agreed. 'Hadn't a pen, or else he didn't dare reach into his pocket, so he scrawled them with a fingernail, having first scratched at his wound. Just the sort of thing Gingin would do,' he added with a sigh. 'Never explicit. A tortuous mind. There you are, then, whatever that scrawl represents, it will still be a puzzle to decipher its meaning.' He reached for the piece of paper. 'L-C,' he suggested. 'Or it could, of course, be 1-1. A bit of a numbers man, you see.'

'The second figure,' I said, 'could certainly be a 1. But the first . . . if that's a 1 the train must have jolted him badly, which means it was going at speed and the carriage was passing over some points.' And I added, doubtfully, 'Alternatively, it could be an S, or even a G. More likely than an I. A C, perhaps?'

'Just those two squiggles,' he muttered, 'and so many possibilities.' He put the piece of paper back in his pocket, pulling onto the verge to let several coaches pass, all of them very battered, full of people and thick with dust. 'There you are, then, we won't get any further till I've talked with Ahmed.'

The gravel plain had widened out still further now, old army tents dotted everywhere like a khaki sea lapping at the walls of old villages and contraband enclaves, the road winding up to the sprawling outskirts of Landi Kotal. 'One question before I talk with Ahmed,' he said. 'This man Zelinski. What do you know about him?'

'Nothing really. I met him once, very briefly. That's all.'

'What did you talk about?'

I shook my head. 'I can't remember. It was in Alex Goodbody's office. He introduced us. That was all. I was on my way out to Australia, Zelinski going back to Dushanbe, the capital of Tajikistan.'

'I don't need to be told that,' he said irritably. 'It's the man I want to know about now.'

I told him I couldn't help him, and he nodded as though that was what he had expected.

'I don't even know where he died,' I said. 'Or how.'

'In the northern approaches to the Khunjerab Pass.'

'That was where Pierre Caminade froze to death. Was that what happened to Z?'

'Not quite. He died of hypothermia, yes. But he had also been shot. It was a Gurkha patrol found him, and according to the officer's report he had a bullet lodged in the left buttock and a second bullet had passed between two of his ribs and gone through one of his kidneys, coming out at the back in a big hole that resulted in some damage to the vertebrae. The poor fellow must have been in agony, but he managed to struggle to a snowbank and scrape a hole big enough to protect himself from the wind. That was where the Gurkhas found him. They had been following his tracks, which were still apparently just visible despite several falls of fresh snow. And there were other tracks, in places superimposed upon his. The body had been turned over, his clothes disarranged as though the killers had been searching him for something.'

'Did the Gurkhas find any clue as to his killers?' I asked.

'No. But the officer had the sense to dig about in the wounds and extract the bullet lodged in his buttock. It had been fired from an AK47, which does not help a great deal. Kalashnikovs are now common currency. Anybody can pick one up if he's got a few dollars.'

He didn't say anything after that. We were into the beginnings of Landi Kotal, the road half blocked with parked coaches, taxi cars too, and a noisy mass of humanity. The train had already arrived, its position marked by dark wisps of smoke rising from behind some low buildings. Spare rolling stock stood sidetracked just above us. We pushed our way through the crowd and drove into a town that was full of concrete utilitarian buildings with heavily barred windows. Some had steel shutters. It was outside one of these that Laun Said stopped. He got out, went to the door and spoke into the intercom. Almost immediately the door opened and a local boy came out. He had a Kalashnikov slung casually over his shoulder.

'We walk from here,' Laun Said said as he parked the Land Rover close against the building, handing the keys to the boy who grinned and nodded as he listened to his instructions. He looked about twelve.

We started back then, the way we had just come, the sun quite hot in the shelter of the buildings. After a hundred metres or so we turned right, into a street that was little more than an alleyway dropping steeply between tall buildings two or three storeys high. Here again there were iron bars and metal shutters. 'Godowns, all of them,' Laun Said said.

There were shops on the ground floors, one of them a Pathan version of a takeaway with great pans and iron cauldrons steaming, some sort of animal skewered on a spit and turning slowly as it roasted. There were three men there, all of them tough looking and wearing nondescript clothing, one with an old sports jacket over a long shirt that looked more like a skirt and a length of calico-like cloth slung round his shoulders as though he were playing the part of a Roman senator. All of them wore the flat pancake cap of the Pathan; the Roman senator had his pushed to the back of his head so that it appeared as a brown halo.

I felt Laun Said's fingers grip my arm. 'This is it,' he said, guiding me over what was almost a kerb and pushing me past the man crouched over the bubbling cauldron. '*Salaam*, Khalid.'

'*Salaam*, Laun Said.' A flash of white teeth and the

janitor's dark visage was suddenly all smiles. 'A long time we don't see. You wanting Ahmed Khan, yes?' And when my companion nodded, he said, 'Okay. Is expecting you, sahib.'

CHAPTER TWO

The warehouse ran a long way back, three floors,
all stacked with wooden crates and boxes. Ahmed
Khan's office was at the top of the building, a screened-
off corner, the interior hung with beautiful rugs, some
of them silk, the floor carpeted with what looked like
hard-worn Bokharas. Silk lounging cushions were
spread about the two walls of the actual building.
There was also a desk with a full bank of electronic
equipment, and it was from behind this desk that
Ahmed bin Kazakh rose to greet us.

He was a small man. That was my first impression.
I couldn't see his features very clearly for he had his
back to an open door leading on to a flat rooftop, the
glare from which hit me in the eyes. Two things struck
me immediately as he came round the desk and clasped
my companion's hand in both of his and then
embraced him; first, that the desk was heavy-duty steel
and would act as a very efficient barrier if he needed
something protective to duck behind; second, that

seated at his desk with the light behind him he commanded the cargo lift and the stairway up which we had climbed, and with a quick turn of the head could see anyone approaching across the flat roof.

'My dear fellow. It's good to see you again.' His English was perfect, so was his accent. But even as he embraced Laun Said I could see the quick flicker of his eyes in my direction, the momentary assessment of a man accustomed to making instant decisions about people. His reaction to me was not exactly hostile, but it certainly was not friendly, so that my gut reaction to him was one of relief that he was not a man with whom I had to do business. There were no salaams, not even a handshake as Laun Said introduced us.

'Do you speak Pashtu?' Ahmed Khan asked me.

I nodded, my mind still absorbing his personality and the bizarre surroundings.

He turned back to Laun Said, speaking fast in a language I did not understand, but knew to be Dari, the old Persian language. He waved us to the deep-piled cushions arranged against the far wall, using an intercom to order Khalid to bring the refreshments, then seating himself cross-legged in front of us. His dress was a peculiar mixture of Eastern and European. He wore the sort of buttoned-up tunic that Jinnah had worn in so many of the pictures I had seen of him, bright cream silk with the shirt-tails hanging out, and instead of trousers he wore jodhpurs and beautifully shone handmade boots.

But it was the jacket that held my gaze.

When Resource Potentials first gave me a job, which was virtually that of an office boy, the best I could afford by way of accommodation was a bedsit in an area full of Asians just off the Portobello Road. To get home in the evenings I very often took the Central Line to Notting Hill Gate, walking from the office to either Bond Street Station or Oxford Circus by routes that were lined with some of the most expensive shops in the West End. Particularly I liked strolling up Savile Row, and it was this that educated me to the finest cloths, the best-cut suits, cashmere sweaters and handmade shoes. Only when a lesser shop was running a sale did I get an idea of the prices these places charged and I swore that one day I would earn enough to feel I could walk boldly in to any of them and order what I wanted.

Ahmed Khan, without of course the jodhpurs and the shirt-tails, would have been accepted, his impeccable accent and the perfect fit of that jacket, the obviously expensive cloth, would have seen to that. And since I couldn't understand what they were saying my mind was free to roam, dreaming that perhaps this would be the project that would make me rich enough for my dreams to come true. No point in my listening to them, but every now and then the name of a place slipped into my consciousness: Salang was mentioned several times and the Malakand Pass. And another word too, an English word, a title, which is probably why it particularly caught my attention. The word was sultana.

'Sultana!' I exclaimed. 'Who are you talking about?'

The two heads snapped round, four eyes fastened on mine in surprise. I really believe they had been so engrossed in their conversation that they had quite forgotten about me.

'What sultana?' My voice was suddenly urgent. Something Anamaria had said, way back, in another existence it seemed.

Though I had put the question to Ahmed Khan, since he was the one who had referred to a sultana, it was Laun Said who answered me, in a voice that was unpleasantly tense. 'We'll talk about that later. Meantime, I would ask you to keep quiet and let me do the talking. Is that understood?'

'Ahmed Khan speaks extremely good English,' I reminded him, 'so why don't you carry on your discussion in English? Then I could—'

'For God's sake, man! Use your intelligence.' He turned back to Ahmed Khan, switching back into Dari, and from the tone of his voice I knew he was apologizing for my interruption. Then he turned back to me: 'Most ill mannered of you. Now, of course, he wants to know why you are so interested in his reference to this unknown sultana. He has never met her. Have you?'

'How can I answer that when I don't know who you are talking about?'

'There you are, then. So perhaps you will now let me continue to find out all the things we need to know. In particular, I am trying to arrange for a guide to one of the secret smuggling routes that cuts across the Hindu Kush by a pass that from what I am told is little more than a deep crevice.' His voice was suddenly modulated as he added, 'Please understand, I am not trying to arrange anything that you or Goodbody would find offensive. The cost of the guide I take it is immaterial?' His eyebrows lifted, and when I made no answer, he nodded and turned back to Ahmed Khan, who was looking at me. His eyes were not brown like most Pathans and Afridi tribesmen. They were blue, a surprisingly opaque duck's egg blue, almost the colour of turquoise. In his very elegant, very clipped English he said, 'Since you are so interested, I take it you have a particular lady in mind. Perhaps you could tell me where this sultana of yours is now residing?'

'I don't know. Somewhere in South-central Asia, I think. Kazakhstan perhaps, Tashkent probably. She is a dancer.' And I added defensively, 'I think she only claimed the title sultana to give her some standing in a foreign country. We danced together when we were small.' I explained then about her adoption and the sort of life she had led with the Kikindas.

'How old?'

I said I didn't know for sure. 'A little younger than myself, I think.'

'And her name?'

'Vikki.'

'No, her surname.'

'Kikinda. I have already told you that.'

'After they adopted her, yes. But her own family name?'

But I couldn't help him there. 'She was always very reticent about her origins. Except for the title. She was very insistent about that, very determined that everyone should know that she belonged to a royal tribal family, and was the daughter of a sultan.'

'But you don't know what sultan.'

'No. I wasn't really interested. We were dancing partners, that's all.' And I explained how infrequent my visits to Romania had been.

Khalid came in with the tea then, I think in answer to a bell push hidden away among the cushions against which Ahmed Khan was lounging. The tea was China and unbelievably, in addition to the usual sweet cakes, there were cucumber sandwiches, and when I commented on it, he gave me a little smile of pleasure. Over tea they talked in English, which was a relief, mostly about the changes that had occurred at Landi Kotal and the western end of the Khyber since Laun Said's last visit, and then Laun Said was telling him about McCrae's death and the killing of the two men he thought were Mafia agents.

All this was in English, with many tributes from Ahmed Khan to the man they both referred to as Gingin. 'So sad. I shall miss him. This was one of his best listening points and he called me regularly.' Ahmed Khan nodded. 'A good fighter, too. And in earlier days, up at Gilgit, he could beat the locals at their own game. Nobody better on a pony. It must have been the last chukka he played, up there under Rakaposhi with the snow coming down – beat those

Gilgit devils at their own game, and at his age. I think perhaps he was almost fifty then.'

'More,' Laun Said said tersely. 'Nearer sixty.'

Ahmed Khan nodded in agreement. 'A great man – at mountaineering and at polo.' And suddenly he was quoting from Kipling – ' "Something lost behind the ranges. Lost and waiting for you. Go!" Or perhaps you prefer "One man in a thousand, Solomon say, will stick more close than a brother, but the Thousandth Man will stand by your side to the gallows-fall – and after." ' – He leaned forward, a quick dart of the head like a cobra striking. 'Tell me, you went to find out where he had gone, but you never caught up with him, did you? You never found out where he'd gone to and why? He was supposed to meet you in Pindi. I sent a message. Didn't he get it?'

Laun Said shrugged. 'He couldn't tell me, poor fellow.'

'Khalid picks up all the gossip, and rumour has it that he went north up the Malakand to meet someone.'

'Who?' The question was almost a CO's bark.

Ahmed didn't know.

'Somebody from Gilgit, perhaps, or Chitral?'

Ahmed Khan shook his head. 'Not Chitral. Khalid says there has been some avalanches up near Chitral. The place is cut off. Up here it has been a warm winter – so far.'

'And Gilgit?'

'Gilgit is just possible – for the moment. So we hear on the radio. There is no telephone. You know what the VHF is like up here. Even ultra-high frequency waves cannot penetrate beyond the high mountains.' He poured more tea, a third cup, and as in the deserts of Arabia, the third cup was the sign for us to leave. 'You look after yourself, Laun. And look after this young man.' He had turned to me and clasped my hand in a surprisingly hard grip. 'It is winter up there.' Another flood of Dari, a quick embrace and then he was seeing us to the head of the stairs. '*Salaam*.'

'*Salaam alaikum*, Ahmed Khan. Now we go to see if we can find your sultana lady, eh?' And Laun Said laughed.

A moment later we were out in the steep alleyway again, no indication from the outside that we had been anywhere unusual.

'One point, when you were talking about dancing, I think he thought you were some sort of juvenile gigolo.' Laun Said gave me a sly, sidelong glance, his teeth showing in a smile between the neat military moustache and the beard.

'I'm neither a gigolo, nor am I homosexual,' I said tersely.

He laughed. 'Defensive barricades in place, eh? Well, there we are, then. No fun and games on the way up the south face of the Hindu Kush. I wonder what Ahmed's Nuristani will be like.' His left eye winked at me. I hadn't noticed it before, but that was when I first realized it was glass. I was going up into the Pamirs with a one-eyed Welshman. *Taffy was a Welshman, Taffy was a thief* – I wondered how much I could trust him. 'Not to worry, man. Up where we're going there's lots of other ways of keeping ourselves amused.' And he added, 'I doubt we'll either of us have much energy to spare until we're out of the other end of the tunnel.'

'What tunnel?' I asked him. 'I thought you hadn't the nerve to go into Afghanistan, through Jalalabad and on to the Salang Tunnel.'

He jostled past a couple of heavily armed locals, stretched out a hand and grabbed my arm. 'Watch it, young man. You're trying to needle me again. Don't push your luck. You get my dander up and see what happens. I can get quite rough.' He smiled at me and then said, 'Mebbe it would help if we move on to Christian names. Certainly it will be necessary when we get into the belly of the Hindu Kush. One word is better than two when alerting the other feller to danger. Okay, Paul?'

'Right,' I said.

'Laun. Got it?'

'Okay, Laun.'

He nodded. 'That's better. And don't try roughing me up again. I've seen a lot more of life than you and I'm told by people who don't like me too much that I have a very short fuse.'

'I'll remember that.' I said it laughingly and he relaxed so that I was able to ask what he had meant by the other end of the Salang Tunnel. 'You said you wouldn't attempt it without McCrae to talk us past the local warlords.'

'That's Salang II. What Ahmed and I were talking about was Salang I, the tunnel they started and had to abandon.' He stopped there, for we had reached the Land Rover. The sun had gone again and it was snowing; it was also blowing quite hard, straight down the main street. Suddenly it was very cold. 'I think that's what Gingin scribbled with a bloody fingernail – S I.'

The kid we had left guarding the Land Rover was sitting on the bonnet. He jumped down when he heard our voices. 'Everything okay, sahib. Nobody steal. Ali Raja take care of everything, right?' The broad grin again and the flash of teeth in a narrow, sharp-beaked brown face as Laun unlocked the Land Rover. I saw him slip a ten-rupee note to the boy, patting him on the shoulder, then shaking him formally by the dark, wiry-boned little hand. 'See you again soon, Ali. You keep your nose clean, no mischief, eh?'

Grins all round as he climbed in and started the engine, and then, as we moved off, continuing in the direction we had come, he said to me, 'Up here in the North-West Frontier, if a guard does his job well, always pay him handsomely. You may think Ali the Raja hardly did anything to earn what I paid him. Okay, so nothing happened. But if a couple of thugs had tried something, the little Ali would have earned that note and more. He would have gone into action as an automatic reflex, and he'd have done it without thinking whether it would cost him his life. He has a gun, and up here that makes him a man, even if he isn't yet screwing the ladies.'

We then drove out of Landi Kotal straight on towards the Afghan frontier, a sudden burst of sun in our eyes so that all I could see through light flurries of snow was the whitened ribbon of the road winding down what appeared to be an escarpment. No sign of the frontier post, the road just vanishing into a mist of driven snow. 'I brought you out here to give you some idea of what we'll be going into very soon now.'

'And afterwards. Where are we headed, what's our destination – the tunnel under the Hindu Kush?'

He shook his head. 'Not a chance. Ahmed made that perfectly clear. Salang I yes, but not Salang II.' And in answer to my query as to why he had chosen to discuss our programme in a language he knew I would not understand, he turned on me and said, 'Don't you understand? No, probably not. I suppose I take it for granted that anybody fit to accompany me on an expedition will understand the nature of a man like Ahmed, even if he is of a different race.' And then abruptly he asked me what sort of a man I thought Ahmed was.

'Tricky,' I said. 'A bit of a barrow boy with an English public school background.'

He laughed. 'Not bad. For the last ten years, all through the Afghan–Russian War, that man has lived on a knife edge.' He leaned forward, peering into the snow. 'Ah, here we are.' He pulled into the side, stopping with his left-side wheels up against the edge of what could have been a bottomless pit, for I was looking straight down into a white, flake-swirling nothingness. 'We'll give it half an hour. There's a superb view from here.'

'No doubt,' I said, 'if the sun were shining.' He had switched off the engine and I could feel the cold creeping in. Snow was already settling on the windscreen wipers, blurring our vision for'ard.

'Not to worry, man. That little Nuristani, Ali Raja, has a direct line to Allah. He said there would be "plenty blue", but snowstorms coming and going all day. We'll see.'

So we sat there, the cab getting colder and colder. Taxi cars went by, packed with bodies, men standing outside clinging to the luggage racks, sprawled on the roofs, even standing three or four deep in the lidless boots. And every now and then a heavily loaded truck came grinding up out of the snow, a white ghost of a vehicle with two black eyes where the windscreen wipers had swept the clinging mantle of snow clear. There were armed guards crouched on high-piled sacks, and on the roofs of the occasional overcrowded coach. All this endless stream of traffic jostling for road space in the face of overloaded trucks grinding their way down the steep gradient, stacked high with crates that could only be weapons in transit, the snow thickening, covering everything with a heavy blanket of white powder that blew in long blizzard streamers.

'We were talking in Dari,' Laun said suddenly.

'Yes, I know that.'

He looked at me, nodding almost approvingly. 'You're good at languages, eh?'

'Yes,' I said. 'I pick them up very quickly. But I don't know Dari.'

'No reason why you should. It's like the Welsh, you see. It's been overtaken by the modern Persian, just as the name of the country has been overtaken by the present usage. Iran. Damn silly, really. You understand Welsh?'

'No. Gaelic. I can understand what they're saying in the Hebrides. Or I could once,' I added. 'That was when I was at Bristol and studying the long-ship explosion of the Scandinavian peoples.'

'The Rus?'

'Yes, of course. The Rus, what the Baltic Vikings were called when they sailed south, raiding deep into the mouths of the rivers until they found the Volga.'

'I know all that, man.' Laun gripped my arm, his good eye alight with a sudden enthusiasm. 'Rolling their long ships across the height of land until they found the Volga.' He nodded. 'There you have it, man. Then down through the lakes to the Volga delta and so into the Caspian. Ten or eleven centuries ago, that was, and there were others of them who found the Don, taking their ships westward to the Dnieper and so into the Black Sea – Odessa, Sevastopol.' He let go my arm, leaning back and smiling to himself. '*Dammo Dai*, man!' he exclaimed, that boyish enthusiasm back again in his voice as he murmured, 'What an age to have been born into – raping the women, slaughtering the men, building a new race, the Russian people. And they're still made in the same mould. Look at the history of the Russian Revolution, the Stalinist–Brezhnev periods. Nothing has changed. Except, of course, the weapons. Races don't change – not easily.'

'No, but they do evolve,' I said.

'*Da*.' He nodded. 'But not in my lifetime. Not fast enough, not in years. Unless we're given a second bite of the cherry we'll never see the evolution of the people we're meeting now. It's too slow a process.' And then he suddenly asked me, did I believe in reincarnation. His face was turned towards me, that one eye gleaming very bright.

I hesitated. It was gone now, but the gleam had been almost too bright. 'I don't know,' I said, wondering what it was like to be a secret agent in a foreign land. My mind switched to Kipling's Kim and the man who had taught him how to survive as an agent, how to gather the information that could be worth a whole division or more if it were got to the right person at the right time. And that was going back almost a hundred years to the India of the Raj.

There was a sudden thinning of the snow, a glow away to my left. A wind had got up, a burst of hail rattling on the metalwork of the Land Rover, the driven ice particles reflecting the sun's rays in a blinding refraction of light. The sun gleam lasted barely a minute, then the hail turned to snow again, the wind falling light and the flakes so large that it was almost as though dusk had fallen, a grey-white world that was in itself a warning of the unpredictable meteorology of the great mountain ranges ahead of us.

'How are you on skis?' The question was almost barked at me, so that I wondered whether perhaps he too was feeling a twinge of nervous tension.

'Canada,' I told him. 'I had part of a winter in Canada, up in the Yukon. Four-by-four travel, most of it, but there were two old-timers up above a frozen lake called the Squaw. I was up there just over a month, assessing a gold prospect. Alluvial. The weather closed in on us, so it was skis and then snowshoes mostly. Why?'

'After the Karakoram – if we get that far – we'll be on skis more than snowshoes. We'll take both. Also a skidoo if they have one up at Chitral or Gilgit.'

'So we're not going down into Afghanistan?'

'Don't be daft, man. Didn't you hear what Ahmed Khan said?' He looked at me then, that glass eye of his dull as a pebble that has dried in the wind. 'No, of course not. I keep forgetting. Used to travelling either on my own or with men that talk the language.'

'How many do you know who speak Dari?' The tension building in me made me rap the question out. 'McCrae, I suppose. Who else?'

He didn't answer me.

'Well, go on,' I said. 'How many?'

He gave a quick, irritable shrug, and I switched back to the gear. 'Snowshoes, skis, a skidoo if they have one, an Everest-type tent, I presume, winter mountain clothing, cold-weather bedroll or sleeping bag – where are we going to pick all this gear up?'

'Peshawar. Military stores.' And he added, 'Got most of it already. But we'll need nylon ropes, ice axes, spare torch batteries . . .'

'So where *are* we going?'

He sat back, staring straight ahead into the flake-filled gloom. 'Don't know that I should tell you that. Not yet. Not till we're up in the high mountains away from all other humans.'

'Why not?' I was quite unable to keep the impatience and anger I felt out of my voice.

'Why not?' he repeated, turning his head, the glass eye staring at me, his voice a speculative murmur. 'I don't know enough about you, do I? That's why Ahmed refused to talk English in front of you, or even Pashtu. He doesn't trust people he doesn't know. And nor do I,' he added, almost to himself. 'I'll tell you everything in due course.' And then he suddenly laughed. 'You see, I don't want to frighten you.'

'I'm just a passenger, is that it?' And when he didn't say anything, I went on, 'I take it the tunnel you call Salang II is the one the Russians used as their supply line when they invaded Afghanistan. That's a road tunnel. All their armour, the last of the rearguard troops, that's the route the whole army took when they abandoned the country and ten years of bloody fighting. They all went out by the military highway that ran under the Hindu Kush through that tunnel. So what is Salang I? A tote-road, or just a probe? Why did they abandon it and go and start all over again – a new tunnel, the one they finally used?'

He shook his head, sitting silent and very still.

'They came up against some obstacle, is that it?' I was thinking aloud. 'What was it?' And when he still didn't say anything I lost my temper. 'Okay. Forget all about the Hindu Kush and those bloody tunnels!' I shouted at him. 'Drive me back to Peshawar, anywhere where I can telephone Alex Goodbody. If you won't be open with me I'll advise him that I'm not prepared to go on with you as my guide. You understand?'

I thought for a moment he was going to lash out at me. Remembering his phrase about a short fuse, I kept my eyes on his hands, which were off the wheel now and both of them balled up into fists, the knuckles white. A man used to having his own way. He could be dangerous, and if we were going to cross the Hindu Kush on skis, nights together in a tent small enough to backpack ... and ropes. How much would they weigh?

Suddenly I found myself hoping he would force me to the point where I really would phone Alex in London and call the whole thing off. But instead of lashing out at me, or worse still, retreating into his shell and leaving me to force the issue, he said, 'A couple of things I can tell you. You ask why they abandoned the first tunnel – we call it Salang I to put it into chronological perspective with the second tunnel, the one they finished and named the Salang Tunnel. The first attempt was made further east. It's not shown on any map – at least, I don't know of any—'

He was interrupted by a bearded face rapping with mittened knuckles on the glass of his side window. He was the driver of a truck that had pulled up just behind us and he wanted to know what it would be like in the Khyber Pass, had there been any snow there when we drove through it?

He told the driver what he could and the face disappeared, the white ghost of a man scuttling back to the shelter of his truck, which was piled with sacks, men on top beating with their arms to recover their circulation. 'Poor buggers!' Laun said. 'They'll be perished by the time they get through the Khyber.' And he went on to tell me that what had stopped the Russians in their first attempt to tunnel under the Hindu Kush, and so open a secure lifeline into the Afghan plain, was an underground river.

Of course, he hadn't needed Ahmed Khan to tell him about that. Scouting through the Pamirs in his Land Rover, he had heard about the abandonment of the tunnel enterprise a long time back, but his informants had never been inside it, so they hadn't been able to tell him whether the completed section was a full-width road or not. What they had been able to tell him was that the entrance, which he had seen for himself, was big enough for trucks to enter, and that it was now absolutely sealed, huge steel shutters.

'How long is it?'

He shook his head. 'I don't know. In fact, I don't think anybody but the engineers know that, and they have been warned that it's Siberia if they talk about it.' It was the usual Russian clampdown. They had made a costly mistake and it was as much as a man's life was worth to let it be known.

'The snow is thinning. Any minute now and with luck you'll be able to see why I've brought you to this lookout point.' And then he was telling me the reason he thought Alex Goodbody had arranged for us to meet. 'Lapis lazuli,' he said, reminding me that there had been an unexpected increase in the amount of the stone coming on to the market, source unknown. 'But Ahmed was talking about sapphires. Couldn't say where they were coming from, but not out of Tajikistan. Big stones. Uncut, of course. But of superb quality. The source is something we have got to discover.' He pointed ahead, beyond the bright gleam of a truck going down to Torkham. 'Look! It's clearing now.'

The wind had fallen away, the snowflakes thinning and falling lazily, shimmering with the blaze of the sun that was bursting forth like a great burnished shield. Suddenly I could see the whole length of the road as it snaked down the side of the Sulaiman's northern escarpment. The Torkham border post emerged, and a white band up the sheer crags that hung over it. I asked him what it was, and he said, 'The Durand Line. It's the boundary Sir Mortimer Durand negotiated way back in 1873 so that Afghanistan would act as a buffer state between Tsarist Russia and the Indian subcontinent. And it still holds, thank God, Afghanistan's still a buffer state – of a sort! Ten years and the Russians couldn't destroy them, finally going back the way they came.' He suddenly gripped my hand. 'My God, just look at it – the whole range visible now! The great barrier of the Hindu Kush.'

The snow had suddenly ceased, the sky a pale blue, and there, where the plain ended, a massive barrier was flung across the flat land leading up to it, pinnacles and ridges all brilliant white against the sky's blue. 'Like a breaking wave, man.'

'And we're going up over that lot?'

He nodded. 'But further east, where I am afraid it's quite a bit higher.' He passed me his binoculars and through them I could see the rampart's summit, the whirling of wind-whipped snow. 'I thought you'd better see it for yourself,' he said. 'Just so you can duck out if you want to. I wouldn't blame you if you did. Not certain I wouldn't be glad if you did call it off. It's not going to be at all comfy when we get really high. Here we're only around two, three thousand feet. Up there the peaks run as high as twenty plus.' He let go my hand. 'Okay? Seen enough, have you?'

I nodded. 'Quite enough, thank you.'

'So what's your decision – scrub it, wait for the warmer weather or go ahead as planned? It's up to you. You're the boss.' His head was turned towards me, watching intently.

I don't know why, but almost without thinking I said, 'Now. We go now. No point in putting it off.'

'Good. This time of year the cold will cut down on the snowfall. Less chance of an avalanche, more chance of some good ski runs.'

'You know how to get to Salang I?'

'Not from this direction, but I know who to ask.'

He turned the Land Rover and we went back through Landi Kotal, across the plain with the great stupa, then into the Khyber. This way it was all down-hill and he drove fast, his whole being concentrated on the road, the sun low now and hazy, the defiles in shadow, black, gaping gashes. At Jamrud we checked out of the tribal territory, and after that the traffic was less and quite shortly it seemed we were into Peshawar. He didn't stop, but drove straight through. 'Pindi,' he said, his voice sharp and crisp, the natural Welsh lilt seemingly overlaid by memories of the old cantonments we had passed along the eastern approaches to the town.

'Drop you off at Flashman's. You should be able to pick up some gossip there, and then tomorrow, get out and about in the bazaars, pick up what you can.'

'And you? Where are you going?'

'Don't worry about me. I have my contacts.'

I had to be content with that, for he refused to answer any questions about his movements. My guess was he was planning to search back along the route McCrae had taken, but a glance at the map showed that the road north over the Malakand Pass and up the Swat Valley to the Pamirs turned off at Noswhera, several miles short of Rawalpindi. I told him this, but all he said was, 'Don't try and organize me, young man. I know what I'm doing.'

That was the end of that, and after we got to Rawalpindi I didn't see him for almost a week. And when he did show up, all he would say was, 'I think I know the answer now. We'll see.'

'I wonder,' I said, 'if your information is the same as mine.'

'How d'you mean?'

I strung him along for a little longer by telling him of my activities during the time he had been away. I had concentrated on the gold, silver and jewellery bazaars, seeking information about the seven preciosities used in the decoration of Buddhist temples long, long ago. The preciosities are gold, silver, lapis lazuli, crystal, ruby, emerald and coral. The information I picked up mostly concerned lapis lazuli and the corundums – rubies and sapphires. For the last year and more the flow of lapis lazuli and corundums into the bazaars had increased quite dramatically.

'Nothing new in that. Ahmed Khan had already told me—'

'I'm talking now about the Sultan of Borbikstan.'

He stared at me, his eyes wide, and I found it distracting to have to read the mind of the man through the single window of his good eye. 'What do you know about Borbikstan? Where did you get hold of the name?'

'Is that what you were going to tell me?' I asked him. 'The saga of the lost ships of Erik Villman? The saga. The lost Rus de Burgsvik?'

'I don't know anything about a saga, but yes, a chieftain of the Rus from Gotland, the big island off the south-east coast of Sweden. It's a very confused story handed down by word of mouth among some of the people of the Pamir valleys. How did you come to hear of it? Not through bazaar gossip, surely.'

'No.'

'The saga, then. There are several stories about lost ships and parties of Vikings who lost their way and vanished in the high mountains. All word of mouth. I don't know of any written evidence to back them up.' He wanted to know if I had acquired a copy of the saga. But of course I hadn't. Nor had I even seen a copy.

'So how do you know about it?'

'Caminade,' I said. And I told him of the sudden appearance of the Frenchman in the hotel dining room.

It was I think the fourth day of my stay at Flashman's and I was just ordering my meal when the door was flung open and Antoine stood there searching the room. He saw me and came hurrying over. '*Alors*. We meet again, my friend.' He pulled up an empty chair and sat himself down opposite me. 'I have news for you.' He asked me what I was having to eat and when I said curry he nodded. 'Ah yes, always they must disguise their meat.' And he ordered the same. 'You know Swat?'

I shook my head.

'But you know where it is. You are going there, per'aps?'

'Maybe.'

He smiled and nodded. He was very excited, bubbling over with the news he had picked up and was dying to tell me. 'The capital of Swat is Saidu Sharif and a little outside the town is this hotel. Very beautiful old Raj hotel, a pillared colonial building with – you do not believe this, per'aps – but there is a place for dancing among the columns on the *premier étage*, on a floor that is brown-yellow of a sort of soapstone. Above is a vast, flat roof. There was a moon the two nights I was there and the view of the mountains was marvellous. You must go some time. It is very, very beautiful.'

And then he was talking about a valley, up beyond Chitral, where there was a lost settlement of people descended from the men of Alexander's army, language, customs, features all reflecting the Greek influence. 'I tell you this,' he said as our food arrived, 'because then per'aps you find it is easier to believe what I tell you now. But first let us eat. I have been on the road all day. The Malakand is much over a thousand metres and conditions at the top of the pass are bad.'

After that he didn't say much and I didn't press him until we had finished our meal. I was tempted to order brandy in the hope that a good stiff drink might loosen his tongue. As visitors the ban on drink did not apply to us. But with a man like Antoine alcoholic stimulation to talk was quite unnecessary. Even so, as soon as the coffee arrived he ordered a double brandy for each of us, and in virtually the same breath launched into an account of his activities since I had last seen him in Karachi.

He had flown straight to Peshawar, then by car to Landi Kotal where he had spent the night, visiting various contacts, including Ahmed Khan. From there he had gone back to Peshawar. Laun told me he had picked up his trail at the Inter-Continental, which is on the Khyber Road at the edge of the golf course and the polo ground looking across to the great red mass of the Balahisar Fort.

'In the old city,' Antoine went on, 'close to the Balahisar, is the Oissa Khawani Bazaar. I have a friend there who dates from my journeys in search of the missing pages of my grandfather's travel notes. The Oissa Khawani is the street of the storytellers and, *mon ami*, he is still there. A little older, of course' – he gave that infuriating cackle of a laugh – 'but still telling stories. Now,' he leaned quickly forward, his eyes radiating his barely suppressed excitement, 'you will never guess . . .'

I couldn't spoil it for him. I didn't say anything, just sat there, waiting. At last he said with a flash of those very white teeth, now darkened by stringy bits of curried meat still sticking to them, '*Alors*. I think per'aps you do suspect what I am now going to tell you: this man, this friend of my backpack travels along the Silk Road and then down the old Great Trunk Road so immortalized by your Kipling, he remember the story I told him of my grandfather's journeyings. Well, of course, he would, eh? – being a storyteller. And because it is a good story he tell it to others. That is how he come to obtain the missing pages. Yes, those pages that I am looking for, they are given into his possession, quite freely. But he don't tell nobody. He could have made a small fortune, could have taken his family to Lahore and sat on a rooftop there doing nothing, just lying on his *charpai*, his feet up, thinking beautiful thoughts and dreaming of the houris that wait for him in the Abode of the Almighty.'

He stopped there, a pause to let the information sink in, his eyes sparkling now with a sort of Gallic devilry. I kept my mouth shut, knowing he had to round the story off. But whether it would be the truth or not, how could I possibly tell!

'So!' Those strange blue-grey eyes had hardened now. ''Ow much, my friend? 'Ow much you give to know the end of my story?'

I hadn't expected that. It was put so crudely, with such an abrupt switch of mood, from the excitement of the adventurer who has stumbled on the solution of a mystery to the glint of business avarice. ''Ow much you think your people pay for the location of this new gem wealth that is flooding the bazaars, spreading out into the great world beyond?' And he added, barely pausing for breath, 'You do know about that, eh? You know about the rubies and sapphires—'

'Yes,' I said. 'And the lapis lazuli. Though for the value of that to take off, the buyer would have to recreate a fashion for it.'

'*D'accord, d'accord.* But the rubies, the sapphires—' His eyes gleamed.

'You have the location?'

'But of course, of course. It is all there in Pierre Caminade's notes. In his own writing. All in his own hand.'

'Okay,' I said. 'Then you had better take me to see this storyteller friend of yours.'

But he wasn't going to fall for that. He laughed and shook his head. 'It is not necessary. He no longer has the writings. I have them. And I don't have to buy them. He give them to me because of all the business he has gained telling the story of my grandfather, Pierre Caminade.' And he added, 'I am Family, you see.' And then, leaning quickly forward with a speed that reminded me again of a cobra I had once seen striking at a pye-dog that came too close, he said, 'But you – you are not my family. You are an agent for buyers as yet unknown. Is that not so? But you know about stones and metals, you know the market values.'

And when I sat there, saying nothing, just staring

at him, he gave a nervous little laugh. 'I don't want much. Just enough to tell my people I am finish with them. I like to see their faces when I tell them to go to hell.'

'How much do you want, then?' We had to start somewhere, and I never doubted the truth of what he had told me.

Again that infuriating little laugh. 'You want an auction? Here? Now?' A pause, and then he said, 'All right. I give you a figure, a starting price. Say twenty millions. Dollars, you understand. Transferred to an account I will open in a Swiss bank, the deal complete only after I have notification from them in writing that your cheque has been accepted.' He laughed again, a big show of teeth. 'Also that the money is clean, not the laundering of some Capo de Mafia or one of the Russian drug barons. Okay?'

I shook my head. 'Sorry. Not okay.' The price was much too high, a try on. Anyway, I was not authorized to deal direct with him. But to keep him talking I explained there was a great deal to be settled before we reached the point when I could present him with a cheque. 'To start with,' I said, 'I doubt whether my people have the slightest idea what you are trying to sell them.'

'But they rely on you, yes? That is why you were sent out to Romania, to check the scrap-metal situation. They must have had confidence in your knowledge and judgement. And now, to make you their front runner in this . . .' He hesitated and I could sense the wheels turning as he tried to decide what line to take.

'You replace a man like Zelinski, an agent of such experience.' And he went on as though talking to himself, 'But then you are in position and available, also you have the necessary language and something of the right background.' He nodded. 'Yes, of course. It makes sense. And then to get the Brigadier to hold your hand . . . That makes sense too.' He signalled to the waiter and ordered two brandies, and some more mineral water. And then, without a pause, still looking at the waiter, he asked me who had killed Zelinski. 'You know he is murdered?'

I nodded. 'At least, I presume he was.'

'Ah, so you don't know for sure. And if he was murdered, you don't know who killed him.'

'No.'

'The Brigadier, per'aps. Have you thought of that?' It was a ridiculous suggestion and I told him so, but he just smiled and shrugged. 'Zelinski is on his territory and he, too, per'aps is playing the Game. Suppose he is playing it for Russia.' He was smiling again. It was a smile of satisfaction, almost of smugness. 'It fits, eh?'

Maybe it did, from the point of view of a Frenchman. 'Nonsense,' I murmured. But even as I said it I realized there was no way I could explain to him why I regarded his suggestion as out of the question. It was a matter of birth and upbringing. Only somebody of the same race could understand a man like Laun Said.

The Frenchman took my meditative silence for obtuseness, I think, because he went on, 'He is a killer. You know that?'

'When it is necessary, perhaps,' I said.

'No per'aps. You know damn well he kill for his country, for revenge – he is a self-appointed executioner.' I wanted to challenge him on that, but he said, 'The other day the Khyber Express is stopped at a defile near the top of the pass. I have it from the driver of the rear engine. There was a man with red hair who was shot as he ran from the train to a four-wheel-drive vehicle on the roadway. And then there are two more shots, not from the train, but at passengers on the train, each shot most deadly accurate.'

The waiter reappeared, putting a bottle that was half full on the table beside him and another bottle that was mineral water.

Antoine poured a couple of fingers of brandy into his empty glass, sniffed at it and wrinkled his nose. 'Not exactly a *fin*, eh? Not even a cognac. Ah well—' And he raised his glass to me and poured a large gulp of it down his throat. 'Where were we? Ah yes. Three men dead. I saw two of them. Russians, they said. They looked like Chechens to me. Mafia?' he asked with a lift of his eyebrows.

'I wouldn't know,' I said. 'Does it matter?'

'Why did they kill McCrae?' He pronounced it *Mak-Kry*.

'How the hell would I know?' I was beginning to tire of his questions.

'So. You don't know why Zelinski is killed. You don't know why McCrae is killed.' He leaned forward, his eyes fastening on mine. 'You think you know what drive this "Brigadier" of yours, Laun Said. But you don't, do you? When you are killed I wonder if you will know why he does it?' He left the question hanging in the air, just letting it sink in.

I could see what he was after. He wanted to drive a wedge between Laun and myself by instilling in me an element of uncertainty and fear. I wondered why. And then he said, 'We were talking about sapphires and rubies, lapis lazuli, even marble. But that is not what this thing is all about.' He held up his hand as I opened my mouth to argue with him. 'But yes, of course, there has been an increase in these items coming out of this area into the local bazaars and from there onto the world market. That you must already know from your Brigadier, from Ahmed Khan, from all the conversations you have had here among the jewellery merchants of Rawalpindi. But that is – what d'you call it? – small beer, eh? It brings in the cash that is necessary to fuel the thing they are building.'

'What thing?' I asked. 'What the hell you are talking about?'

'Ah! So you don't know. You really don't know what this is all about. That Goodbody chappie . . .' He was smiling at his use of this old-fashioned colloquialism and I wondered if he had picked it up from Laun.

'You tell me,' I said. 'If it isn't about precious stones, then what is it about?'

But he shook his head. 'You ask your Brigadier – if he knows, that is. Or Goodbody. But I don't think they know over in London. Pity!' he added. 'Zelinski knew. Must have known. Otherwise, why would they kill him? And if the Brigadier knows, then I do not make a bet on him to live very long.'

'But you know.'

He shook his head. 'No, not for sure. But I think I can make a guess and be somewhere near the reality of it.'

And with that I had to be content. He finished his coffee, downed the rest of his drink and got to his feet. 'I must go now. I have someone else to see. No, it is not a woman.' He gave me that media grin of his, and as he shook my hand, he said, smiling still, 'When you speak with Monsieur Goodbody again please convey to him my thanks for the hospitality of his organization.' And then, just as he was leaving the room, he turned and came back to me. 'Because I like you, *mon ami*, I will make you a present of some advice. To get the information you need you will have to go under the ground. Have you experience of . . .' He frowned, searching for the word. 'What is it you English call exploring rock canals under the surface?'

'Potholing?' I suggested.

'*Oui. C'est ça.*' He looked at me a moment, his head on one side. 'And do you pothole yourself?'

'No,' I said. 'I have never done any potholing.'

'Ah. But if you are to get to the bottom of this thing I fear you must pothole. There is a river under the earth there among the rocks at the bottom of a glacier, a river and a lake, and there are the *troglodytes*, the lost Rus de Burgsvik. Take my advice. Go home. Forget the whole thing. Then you are safe.' And he added, 'But if you go down the rock holes and' –

he paused and shrugged, his palms spread – 'then I think you do not return. To handle this thing a big organization is required, an oil company, or a financial conglomerate with cash to invest. Twenty million, tell your friend Goodbody. That is the price I am wanting for Pierre Caminade's missing notes.'

A quick nod and a smile, and then he was gone.

I glanced at my watch. In London it would be 0230. No point in phoning now. I went to bed and set my wristwatch alarm for 0500. But when I got through his secretary said he was out seeing a client and she did not know when he would be back. 'Well, get him on his mobile,' I said. 'It's very urgent.' She came back to me some time later, when I was shaving, to say she thought he must have switched his mobile off. She wouldn't give me the number, of course, so I told her to ring me as soon as he returned. But though I waited in my room until lunchtime she did not ring back. I phoned her several times myself, but all I got was a promise that she would make certain he rang me first thing in the morning.

I was fast asleep when the call came through. He was ringing from the office and the time by my watch was 0514. Because of the necessity of putting my information in code, I had kept it very short. All he said, when I had finished dictating the jumble of letters, was, 'Okay. Phone me again when you have all the answers, then I can tell you whether the price is right. I think you will have to bargain with the man, but that is a matter for our prospective client. Keep in touch.' This all in clear, and he rang off.

'Sod the bugger!' I said, slamming the phone down. Not a word of thanks, not even a grudging 'Good luck'. Didn't he know what it would be like up there on the Roof of the World in winter? Surely he would have looked it up in a geophysical map. He must have been informed where Z had been killed. And even if he were such a bloody, bone-headed Saxon as to have no imagination at all, there were photographs, endless pictures of the whole stretch of the Himalayan ranges, videos and documentaries made by climbers.

I found it impossible to get back to sleep, my mind going over and over a whole scenario of desperate situations, the nerves of my body literally shivering to the imagined cold. And the wind, it was there in my dreams, dark clouds racing and the snow – snow and rocks, great pinnacles thrusting up out of the blown snow-spray, so that I might have been back in the Cornwall of my youth, lying prone on my stomach and looking down at the great rollers surging amongst the rocks, piling up the face of Gurnard's Head and other iron-black cliffs, a full gale screaming over my head.

And then a hand gripped my shoulder and I started up to find myself looking up into the face of Laun Said. 'Get dressed,' he said. 'And hurry. We're leaving. Now.'

I stared at him. God! he looked tired. 'What's the hurry?' I mumbled.

'The hurry is that there are some Russians arrived in Peshawar and making enquiries.'

Apparently they were security officers from the

Russian steelworks a few miles outside Karachi. 'KGB?' I asked him. The huge complex had been pointed out to me by a fellow passenger as our flight from Istanbul had come in to land. It was close to a long line of gaily painted trucks queueing nose-to-tail for over a mile at the grain godowns, and on the opposite side of the Karachi–Babhore road was the company town known locally as KGB City.

'KGB or Mafia, what's it matter? They're making enquiries about my movements, so shift it.' And he ripped the bedclothes off me.

He had come in from Darra, driving through the tail end of the night. The Land Rover was waiting outside the front entrance and we left as soon as my bags were packed and loaded and I had settled the bill, heading back east on the road to Peshawar. A little Gurkha was at the wheel now and Laun was already fast asleep in the back. We took the Grand Trunk Road north-west as far as Attock, where the Kabul River joins the Indus, and at Noswhera turned right across the Kabul, heading north.

The time was 0756. 'Anybody following us, Kuki?'

'*Naheen, sahib.* Nobody follow us. Road all empty.'

'Achh-chha.'

I turned in my seat. 'Urdu?' I asked. His face was just visible, pale in a welter of blankets and foul weather gear.

'Yes, Urdu. But don't worry, Kuki speaks quite good English.' And when I asked him how he had suddenly been able to produce a driver, he said, 'He's a taxi wallah. In the Pak capital, Islamabad. My batman way back.' And he closed his eyes and was asleep again on the instant.

Silence then and the only sound the Land Rover grinding up the long incline that led to the Malakand Pass. It began to snow, the occasional headlights of a truck or a bus peering at us through the murk. The going became gradually worse, the cab colder, progress slower, wheels spinning on stretches of packed ice.

The voice from the back said, 'How high are we now?'

'Now a thousand metres plus, sahib.'

A glimmer of sun seen through a white gauze curtain of moving flakes. It was low down in the east, a hazy dish of burnished gold. And then, as though by magic, the curtain of snowflakes seemed to be pulled back and there was the pass, rugged and bitter-cold looking, but bathed in slanting sunlight.

The condition of the road got worse as we climbed, the ruts deeper and Kuki fighting the wheel as he drove back and forth across them, choosing his route with unerring precision. The clouds were thin white wisps tinged with pink that sailed over our heads, the sky gradually becoming visible, blue gaps that came and went. We were passing cars now that had been abandoned, an occasional truck or bus, and once or twice men tramping through the snow, pleading for a lift out of their misery.

By the time we reached the top of the pass, the whole sky was a washed-out pastel blue, and all along the horizon ahead was the great white wall of the big mountains, tier upon tier. Wedding-cake stuff, the whole scene a chocolate-box picture, and here we were in a vehicle at something less than five thousand feet and already I was shivering at the cold and remembering with longing the avenues of tamarisk-type trees and walnuts that lined the road beside the Kabul, the relative warmth of the cab as we had travelled into the dawn before heading north across the river.

Two bulldozers were fighting a losing battle to keep the top of the pass open. The snow, driven into drifts by the wind, obscured the depth of the ruts so that even some of the larger vehicles had become stranded; one, a big ten-wheeler, engine grinding, driving wheels spinning, was going nowhere, only cutting deeper and deeper into the blackened icy mush of the road's surface.

We finally made it, the road flattening out, then beginning to descend towards the Swat, which now wound through a flat land of cultivated fields squeezed between stony foothills on either side.

'Opium country,' said the voice from the back. 'Not all of it rice and wheat. There's a lot of money in this valley, a lot of rupees by peasant standards.' And then he was leaning forward, tapping me on the shoulder and pointing away to the right. 'The Churchill picket. Churchill was here, y'see. And so was Buddha,' he added. 'It's a most beautiful valley and it goes right back into the Himalayas.'

'So we follow the river to its source, right?'

But he had started giving instructions to the driver to pull off the road when we reached the level of the river. Away to the left was the entrance tunnel of an irrigation canal, stone-stepped to break the force of the water, but now ice-bound, so that it had a stippled look. And against the chill blue of the sky the Churchill picket glowered down at us. It was not just a single tower like the one from which we had watched for the train in the Khyber Pass, but was square and solid, more like a small Crusader castle. Near where we parked a man stood fishing through a hole in the ice, his Pathan hat worn at a rakish angle and a bright embroidered blanket thrown over his shoulder.

Out of the Land Rover it was bitter cold. Laun flexed his knees and swung his arms, turning his back to the biting wind. Unzipping, he pulled out a large, misshapen cock and began to urinate. I was shocked by the sight of it and he grinned at me, a glint of teeth below the little moustache. 'Tibetan army. A bunch of Mongol types on the Chinese border. Thought I was a Rus.' And he added as he shook the last drops from the mutilated foreskin, 'I'd have been dismembered if a company of Chinese regulars hadn't arrived on the scene.'

'Is that where we're going?' I asked him. 'Across the border into Tibet?'

He pushed the battered object back into the warmth of his trousers, shaking his head. 'No.'

'Then where?'

'Breakfast,' he said. 'Tell you later. There's a jumble of rocks down there by the water if you want a shit.' He dived back into the Land Rover where Kuki had already produced on old wicker picnic basket. Coffee, hot coffee! And three aluminium mess tins packed with eggs, pilau rice coated with a half-congealed curry gravy. And to finish, there were flabby slices of bread, butter and a pot of Chivers Old English Marmalade.

He wouldn't talk during the meal, wolfing down his food, then settling full length in the back. 'We'll spend the night at Saidu. Saidu Sharif. There's a man there you should meet. We'll talk then. Meantime, a suggestion – don't be offended, young man. You look flabby, and we're quite high up here. Take the opportunity, get acclimatized to the altitude. The one thing I don't want is you going down with mountain sickness. At the same time get some exercise. See if you can make it up to the picket. That'll be enough for an initial workout. Kuki will keep an eye on you.' And he lay back, closing his eyes. A deep sigh and he was gone.

The way that man could fall asleep on the instant was a constant cause of amazement to me. There were times in the days ahead when I wished to God I had that facility.

CHAPTER THREE

It took me almost two hours to climb up to the shoulder on which the picket stood through the snowdrifts and finally up the rock face to the picket itself. It was an extraordinary place. Perched on a knoll at the end of the shoulder reaching down from heights that glimmered white against the blue above me, it was a massive little stone fortress, loopholes everywhere. A company with mortars and small arms could hold it against an army. Coming down proved even more difficult than going up, but at least I had some photographs to prove that I had been inside the picket, and also pictures of the view from the embrasures.

I was barely halfway down when I heard Laun's voice, faint on the still breeze, calling me to hurry. By then my wristwatch said 1548 and the sun was beginning to drop behind the mountains above me. 'Took your time,' he said as I was finally able to flop back into my seat in the Land Rover, wet and steamy, my legs literally trembling. Dancing normally kept my leg muscles in trim, but I hadn't had time for that recently, or the opportunity.

He was at the wheel himself now and I had barely closed the door before he had the Land Rover moving. 'Snow,' he said, nodding his head to the clouds building up over the serried mass of mountains ahead of us to the north.

We just made it to Saidu Sharif before snow began to blot everything out, and by the time we had settled in to the rest house it was dark. I lay on the bed for a time, easing the lassitude in my legs and worrying over the fact that I wasn't fully fit for this sort of venture. I worried, too, about Laun. From things he had talked about, people he had known, I reckoned he was nearer sixty than fifty. It seemed daft of AG to have picked a man whose age might make it difficult for him to stand up to a winter struggle across the Pamir passes, and he was supposed to guide and support me, not the reverse.

It was the snow, of course, the white blackness of the night outside, that started me thinking again that if I had any sense I would get through on the local radio-telephone to my boss and tell him the whole thing was off.

What decided me to do nothing was something Laun said when we met over the evening meal. It was curry, of course, the meat tough and stringy. 'Goat,' Kuki said. 'Is all I could buy. Shops very empty.'

'You'll get used to it,' Laun said to me. 'Nothing much else up here in the mountains unless we shoot and barbecue a deer.' And then he said, 'There's some of the Pioneer Corps quartered up at Bahrain. An avalanche has blocked the road up towards Kalam. The officer in charge will be joining us for coffee. His name is Yakob Pirbux. A bit of luck finding him here in Saidu. He's the one who found the body of your man Zelinski and brought it out. He has in his possession something Zelinski jotted down in a notebook. It concerns the lost band of Rus I told you about and the young woman who has joined them in their troglodytic existence.'

He wouldn't say anything more than that. 'Later. Later.' That same parrot phrase. But the food and the cold, and the three hours I had spent struggling through snow and climbing up that last stretch to the high-perched picket, made me unwilling to argue with him. I closed my eyes, chewing the tough meat absently, like an animal chewing the cud, only opening them to scoop up more of the pilau rice and chilli-hot curry.

I woke to a nudge. A glass, half full of a golden liquid, had miraculously appeared beside a mug of steaming coffee. 'Drink up,' Laun said.

It was a malt. No sign of the bottle. 'Yakob Pirbux will be here in a moment.' With the malt inside me, not even a full mug of very black coffee could keep me awake. And then Laun's voice again, telling me to get to my feet.

Standing beside me was a tall, very slim Pakistani captain in immaculate camouflage kit, his cap under his arm. Dark features, nicotine-stained teeth under a very black little moustache, sharp, very brown eyes below a head of thick black hair sleeked down with water. Yakob Pirbux was a Gurkha captain on secondment to the Pioneer Corps and in charge of the detachment detailed to clear the road through to Chitral.

Laun pulled up a chair. 'Drink, Yakob?' A knowing wink. 'Only orange juice, I am afraid.'

'Of course.' The captain nodded and smiled as Laun reached down, pouring the drink surreptitiously under the table. Two fingers of the same golden liquid that I had just drunk. The Pakistani captain reached for it eagerly, then raising his glass, he said, 'Chin-chin!'

'Down the hatch!' Laun said, and we drank to the clearing of the road that connected with Kalam and the jeep track to Chitral. 'I guess we'll be through to Chitters before the week is out, Brigadier.' The man was washed so clean, his uniform so immaculately pressed and his voice so clipped that I guessed at once he was Sandhurst trained. No indication that he had been working since dawn with a large number of Sikhs shovelling snow and boulders with a toppling snowfield above them.

More coffee, a big jug of it. Another slug of malt from the surreptitious bar under the table, and Laun said, 'Now, Yakob, would you be good enough to repeat, for the benefit of friend Paul here, what you told me a few days back. Paul is here as Zelinski's replacement.' He turned to me. 'Y'see, your man was alive when Yakob and his patrol caught up with him.'

'Not very much alive, I am afraid,' the captain said. 'He had burrowed into the snow, but even so, he was suffering from hypothermia. And of course he was badly wounded. In the stomach, and one leg. He could talk, but only just. He had false teeth, I recall, and he had lost the upper plate, so it is not very easy to understand what he is trying to say. Also I am tired. We had been on a patrol along the Tibetan and Chinese borders and were heading south for either Nisa Gul or, if we could, direct to Chitral. It was winter, conditions about as they are now, and we were travelling on skis, with one sledge between the three of us. The only thing in our minds then was the need to reach either a settlement or Chitral where we could sleep secure and warm.'

A compass had been playing up and they were too far to the west. When at last they had a clear spell and could fix their position roughly by the stars, they decided to edge further westward, cross the Hindu Kush at either the Agram or Dorah passes into Afghanistan, and hope that in the turmoil following the Russian withdrawal, they would be able to hitch a ride south through the Salang Tunnel. That was how they came to cross Zelinski's tracks.

'We just do not believe at first. We think it is a yeti. Some form of prehistoric ape perhaps, isolated for centuries in the loneliness of the high mountains. But then we see the clear mark of a boot. More footmarks that waver from side to side, and there is blood here and there. That was when we realize it is the staggering steps of a man we have picked up, and that he is wounded.'

By then it was getting late, the light beginning to

fade, and they had been watching for a suitable place to bivouac. That was how they found Z. Those staggered footsteps led them to the bottom of a recent avalanche where a great rock the size of a small house gave shelter from the wind, and in the lee of it the snow had piled up. It was into this drift that Z had burrowed, using the last of his remaining strength to dig himself a cold bed that he must have been sure would be his last resting place.

Captain Pirbux reached for the knapsack he had brought with him. 'You asked for the loan of a GPS, Brigadier.' He was feeling around in the interior of it. 'Here.' He passed a dark little plastic container across to Laun. 'You take it, sir. I think maybe it is important. But I do not know how to work it, and I do not quite know why I think it is important.'

Laun looked at it, extending the little aerial, then turning to me holding the lightweight box of tricks out. 'Know how to work one of these?'

I nodded. 'Of course.' There had been one on Kas's boat. But an older model. This was the latest, very lightweight even with the battery. 'Global Positioning System. We used them regularly when working in the outback of WA, particularly in the southern part of the Simpson. Not a desert to get lost in!'

'Western Australia, eh?' Laun smiled, nodding his head as though pleased. 'You boys certainly get around.'

'Don't start playing with it – please, sir.' The captain's voice was quite urgent. 'There is a digital recorder attached to the back. It is set exactly as we found it. The coordinates, I think, give the position where he was shot.'

'But not why, eh? And you've no idea who?'

'No. We talked of this when you were here before.'

'Yes, I know. And you thought it might be those Rus lost in the Pamir ranges.' Laun had turned the GPS over and was reading aloud the figures on the back. 'This gives his position at the time he was shot. That what you think?'

The captain nodded. 'Yes. The position is very near to where we find him.'

Laun reached for one of the maps he had placed on the table at his side. 'You were where? Show me.'

But Pirbux could not be certain. 'Somewhere about here.' He took a pencil from the left breast pocket of his tunic and drew a circle covering two or three hundred square kilometres of mountain terrain to the south and west of Faizabad.

Laun nodded. 'So you reckoned you were east of the Salang Tunnel?'

Another shrug. 'Do you mind if I smoke? You see, even if drink is forbidden to us we can still smoke.' He smiled as he offered a crumpled packet to us, then lit one himself. 'If that little gadget is accurate, and I am told it is, almost to the metre—'

Laun reached for the man's pencil and marked in the coordinates. The lines crossed a long way east of the Salang Tunnel proper. 'You said yesterday, when we talked, you thought you were almost over the line of the tunnel the Russians abandoned. That correct?'

'Yes.'

'In other words, what you're suggesting is that Zelinski had been probing for a means of gaining access to the abandoned tunnel from above.'

'It's a supposition, no more.'

Laun turned to me. 'What do you think?'

But it was just guesswork. 'It's possible, I suppose.' And then, voicing a sudden thought that came into my head, I said, 'What about Caminade?' I turned to the captain. 'French,' I said, and described Antoine to him.

But he had not seen him. 'I don't see anybody answering to the description in the villages between here and the roadblock we are clearing just south of Kalam. I will ask when I drive up in the morning.' He looked at his watch. 'Now it is time for me to go. It is very tiring looking after about a hundred men up there at nearly two thousand metres – the cold and the damp. It is the valley of the Swat all the way, but very constricted where we are working, big peaks close above us. Also many big, very smooth boulders, like wallowing hippopotami. You'll see when you get up there.' He got to his feet and, with something near to a click of his heels and a little bow, he thanked Laun for the 'orange juice'. 'Very comforting.'

'And I can keep this?' Laun waved the GPS recorder. 'For the time being, anyway.'

'Yes, of course.'

There followed a short exchange in Urdu and then Captain Pirbux left us. We heard him down below calling for his driver, and then the sound of the truck's engine. It was a four-wheel-drive pick-up and I didn't envy him, for he was billeted at Shangla fifty kilometres up the road.

Nor did I envy myself when Laun said, 'You understand what he was telling me just before he left, about the avalanche his men are clearing. He reckons it will be at least five days before they've dug their way through so that vehicles can get up to Kalam. That'll give you a chance to acclimatize yourself to the altitude and tone up your muscles.'

He had it all planned, like a military exercise, and we started the regime next morning, taking the Land Rover as far as Shangla, then trekking along the road with pack, bedroll, ropes and skis on our backs as far as Bahrain, a distance of sixteen kilometres and then back to Shangla with nothing to eat.

That night I didn't mind that it was goat and I slept like a log despite the ache in muscles I had forgotten I had. It was the same routine the following day, but walking faster and with forays into the glens that rose steeply up to the right. The few villages were perched on the valley side, the houses seeming to grow out of the rock, some of the poorer-looking dwellings mere fronts to living quarters that were hewn out of the solid hillside, sometimes out of a cliff face.

Laun obviously knew the area well. He had friends he greeted along the road and several offers of refreshment. It was on the third day, after we had marched well beyond Bahrain into an area that was heavily timbered, with the mountains closing in on either side and flimsily balanced log bridges across the icy and much diminished Swat, that he accepted the hospitality of a little gnomelike man, who looked so wild he might have been a character out of *Peer Gynt*. The exterior of his abode reminded me of the Yukon, being built of logs cut from the surrounding forest.

But the log cabin effect was no more than a façade. Behind it, the main living quarters reached back into a natural cavern, and at the back was a log-burning stove with a blackened kettle steaming gently. The bare stone walls had bright-coloured cloths, intricately worked with stitched patterns, propped up on wooden supports so that they could be carried outside to air. The whole cave dwelling, which is really what the place was, not only felt warm from the stove, but looked warm. And water was laid on, a crevice in the rock delivering it to a stone basin with an outlet pipe to the hill slope and the river. This, and the cooking and eating utensils, seemed at a glance the only concession to the modern world.

The man was a forester. Both he and his wife, who suddenly appeared wrapped in a homespun shawl with a small child in her arms, had wrinkled, nut-brown skins. 'Nice people,' Laun said. 'I have been here before.' He told me their names, but I cannot remember them now. What I do remember is that they had kindly faces and smiled readily. Also they gave us soup with nuts in it and what I took to be some form of woodland fungi.

By the time we continued our route march my muscles had stiffened up. The Swat was on our right now, a solid shaft of ice, and rising up behind it was one of the high mountain peaks which Laun said were nineteen thousand feet and more. We crossed by a log bridge, climbed about a thousand feet, then put on our skis and slalomed down. We then tried sidestepping up with our skis on, then angling down the slope so that we finished up by the little huddle of dwellings called Laikot.

'That's enough for today.' And Laun added, 'At least I shan't have to carry you.' It was the nearest he got to a compliment, but it pleased me enormously.

By the time we got back to Saidu I was cold and tired, leg and thigh muscles screaming at the hammering they had been given. My one desire was to fall into a hot bath. But to get to our room we had to go through the communal area where dinner was already being served. 'So, there you are, *mon ami*!' He was sitting at a table in the corner. 'Where have you been?' He put down the French paperback he had been reading and rose to his feet. 'Getting ready for the big trek, eh? Or have you been hole-potting?' That cackle of a laugh and the teeth gleaming as he shook my hand.

I started to introduce him to Laun, but they had already met. Their paths had crossed a few days ago and I was conscious at once of an atmosphere of unease between them that bordered on hostility. I thought at first it was just a clash of personalities, their backgrounds and their racial origins so entirely opposite. But when we went to our rooms and I was able to ask him what the trouble between them was, all he said was, 'I've nothing against the man personally. I just don't trust him, that's all. He's French. It's nothing more than that. They play their own game, and it's different from ours, you understand – always has been.'

However, they managed to get on well enough during the meal. Antoine was, as always, a fast talker, his conversation larded with little anecdotes, colourful vignettes that illustrated the point he was making. And of course, his voice, so quick and lively, so full of odd little phrases, the result of speaking fast in a foreign language, seemed in some extraordinary way to complement the slower, more musical lilt of Laun's Welsh accent.

When we got to the coffee stage, a bottle appeared from under Antoine's chair. I can see it now, a presentation half-bottle, flat and chunky, and gleaming golden in the lamplight – Hine VSOP. He grabbed three glasses from a side table and poured the liquid gold with the sort of flourish an actor would use at the moment of embarking on his big scene. Still standing, he raised his glass: 'To us, and to the success of our venture.'

I looked at Laun. His moustache was suddenly bristling, one deep blue eye glaring at the Frenchman. 'What the hell are you talking about?'

Antoine took another sip of his drink, holding the cognac in his mouth for a moment, savouring it. Then he put his glass down gently, swallowed and leaning forward, both fists on the table, said, 'Either we are in this together or we abandon the whole idea, eh? You' – he was staring down at Laun, their eyes locked – 'you and Paul, you cannot go to where you want to go without me. I, Antoine Caminade, have the directions. I know where the entrance is. You don't.'

'You have the coordinates?' Laun barked.

'The coordinates? Oh, yes, the long. and the lat. No, I do not have the coordinates.'

'So what do you have?'

'The missing pages of my grandfather's diary. Without them you cannot find what you are seeking.'

'And what are we seeking?' I asked, keeping my voice low and gentle in the hopes that I could lessen the tension between them.

He unlocked his gaze from Laun's almost reluctantly, and after a moment's hesitation, he relaxed. He was smiling now, not looking at either of us. The smile, I think, was for something in his mind. 'A good question, I think. Per'aps it is that thing your poets called the Holy Grail. Per'aps it is just that you are full of greed, like two hungry merchants. For me—' He shrugged. 'I don't know. I follow the lead of my grandfather. I don't know where it will take me. All I know is that is where I must go. You understand?'

'I think so,' I said. 'But it was you who demanded twenty million dollars, just for the sight of whatever it was that your grandfather wrote. You are the greedy one.'

'No, no. Absolutely *non*. I tell you – I have four lovely daughters and an expensive, very beautiful wife.' He shrugged. 'Trouble is, I do not see her too much.' He paused, then went on, speaking slowly as though to a couple of backward children, 'Y'see, my grandfather, Pierre Caminade, is following the route of the two English women missionaries when he stumble upon an ancient city. This is in the south-west of the Gobi Desert. He is thinking all the time that Mesdemoiselles Cable and French are, like Sven Hedin and the French archaeologist Paul Pelliot, really looking for Buddhist manuscripts, and this is a city not recorded in the books he is carrying with him. There are many houses there, the tops just showing above the sand in some places, and a larger building where the sand is mounded up like a dune. This is where they start to dig. He has two camel drivers with him, both Chinese from Hami, and it is not long before they find the fresco head of a young monk or abbot painted on the wall they are just beginning to uncover. It is slow work. The sand is so dry and fine it just trickle back into the hole they dig, like water.'

He stopped there, not looking at us, but staring up at the ceiling. Neither Laun nor I made any comment. I think both of us were afraid that if we said anything it would interrupt his train of thought, and both of us knew he had reached the crucial point of what he wanted to tell us.

Finally he came back to earth as it were, his gaze fixing on us as he said, quietly and very matter-of-factly: 'That is where he find the man's body.' A pause for effect, and then he went on, slowly now, 'He is lying at the feet of the abbot, or whatever his Buddhist rank is, his body a little shrivelled, but otherwise preserved in the sand. The long woollen garment he is wearing remains intact, his sandals and his feet also, and the expression on his face is described by my grandfather as being "serene". No fear, y'see, as though he has died in his sleep. And in his left hand he is grasping a leather satchel, much sand-worn by long use in desert conditions.'

He paused again, his eyes switching from Laun to me. The theatricality of it was typical of the man, a dramatic moment of silence to emphasize the importance of what he was about to reveal.

'It was in the satchel that he found the record of the religious wanderings of that unknown body, the day, the month, the year, and anything that had struck him as unusual or important.'

Antoine reached into his briefcase, producing an envelope that contained pages of typescript pierced at the top right-hand corner and tied with a twist of crimson ribbon. This he undid and laid the pages out on the table in front of us. 'There! The original is in French, of course, but I have it translated into English and typed. For your benefit. So you can read it.'

Another dramatic pause, and then he added, 'It is the story of a follower of Buddha who finds himself entering the troglodyte world of a tribe whose appearance he has never seen before – not Mongoloid, not Slav. Closer perhaps to the Magyars of Hungary. The mummified wanderer of southern Asia my grandfather uncovered from the sand had spent almost his whole life walking with Buddha through lost worlds of heat and ice, desert and great mountain ranges. He must have been a man of incredible hardness. In the words of Pierre Caminade, *il est très simple, très fort, très religieus* – in brief, a man of most enormous strength of purpose, very persuasive, very charismatic, for he claims to have converted these pagan dwellers of the underground to Mahayana, which, as you know, is a late and somewhat debased form of Buddhism.'

Silence again and a slow smile. 'Whether he did, or did not convert them, we may never discover. It is the year 1220, the time of Genghis Khan and the great Mongol advance across Asia to the Black Sea.'

'The position?' Laun said briskly. 'Where was it he met these people? Other than in his imagination, that is.'

'It was not in his imagination,' Antoine declared, the tone of his voice moving up a notch.

'How do you know?' And Laun added, 'A man working in the dry, desiccating heat of the desert, alone except for his two camel drivers – God Almighty! How would you react? He could be utterly and completely round the bend for all you know.'

'No!' The exclamation was quite violent, an outburst of Gallic fury as he leapt to the defence of his forebear. 'My grandfather would never lose his senses. He was a hardened traveller. In fact, I imagine, not unlike that shrivelled wanderer of the thirteenth century whose body had yielded such an important and fascinating record. You need have no doubt in regard to the authenticity of what he recorded in his notes of which you have the most important part there.' And he added, his voice still full of anger, 'It is very offensive of you to doubt him.' He reached for the pages of typescript. 'You do not believe me, then—' But I was before him and had picked up the pages.

'Just one point—' And I added hastily, 'I believe you, Antoine. I am sure that . . .' I stopped there, my eyes glued to the second page. In the middle of it was a longish paragraph that was not Pierre Caminade. It was a direct quote from the ancient traveller's manuscript, and here it was – not the coordinates, of course, but a full and detailed description of where he had met this lost tribe of fair-haired pagans. That is how he described them – fair-haired pagans. That paragraph took me back to the thought that had been in my head when I had begun to raise the one question that had been bothering me. I pulled the sheet closer, gripping it tight as I looked across at the Frenchman. 'What language was this written in, do you know? I am referring to this paragraph which your grandfather wrote as a direct quote, presumably just as the ancient had written it. What was the original language?'

His reply confirmed what had been in my mind. 'Chinese, of course. Some ancient form.'

'And your grandfather quoted it in his notes, copying it down straight from the original.'

'But of course. He did not intend to take the whole manuscript with him. The vellum, or whatever it was written on, would have been too fragile, I imagine. In any case, if you read the next page you will see that his interest at that point in time was centred on the wall fresco, not on the sand mummy's notes – more colourful, eh? The picture is in colour, natural colours, condensed out of desert plants in the rare moments of their blooming.'

'And you have the original of his notes?'

'But naturally. Not here, but I have them at home in Domme.'

'And this paragraph,' I went on, 'this reference to fair-haired pagans – he copied it down exactly as the ancient wanderer had written it?'

'I have already told you—'

'Yes, but here' – I turned the sheet round for him to see – 'here it is in English. So you had somebody translate it. Unless of course you can translate from the Chinese yourself, and an ancient form of the language at that?'

'No, of course I cannot.'

'Then who?' I saw Laun leaning forward now, and Antoine's face had suddenly gone tense. 'Who translated it for you?'

He didn't want to tell me at first, but I finally got it out of him. He had had a photocopy of his grandfather's entry made and had taken it to an expert on Sino-Tibetan languages at the University of the Punjab in Lahore. He would have had it translated into French, but of course the professor, or whatever he was, would have been an elderly man who did not speak French, having studied under English tutors in the aftermath of the Raj. The English was slightly pedantic, but as I was reading it, the question at the back of my mind was, of course, why had he made us a present of such an important piece of information. It didn't make sense in view of his original demand for a very large sum of money.

Here are the exact words of the Sino-Tibetan

linguist's translation of the original, words that my
eyes devoured with great excitement:

> *It was with greatest hope and very considerable
> excitement that I looked down upon that enor-
> mous hidden valley. It was not of too much width,
> but it went on for ever, or so it seemed to me with
> the sun beating down and the snow all round on
> the high mountains. There was mulberry there,
> almonds in bloom, rice also and the gleam of water
> in a distant lake that was bright emerald. And then
> the cloud came down and I only see the sides of
> that valley, which were very steep, either loose rock
> or impossible cliff, a most sombre and forbidding
> place, yet the floor of it already showing green with
> the growing rice. There were ditches and dykes
> that carried water to all the things they grew. And
> around it, in the cliff faces, there were the dark
> holes of caves, but no movement, no peasants,
> nobody. There was no way I could see of descend-
> ing. It was just as the fair man had said, and
> following his instructions, I looked around in a
> brief gap in the clouds to see if I could see the
> most black of the surrounding mountains. It was
> the time of day. He had said that was important.
> And I think I see it, away towards the sunrise,
> towards my homeland, a massive great peak, all of
> one side in shadow so that from where I stood, my
> back to the sun, it is black – very black and very
> terrible to look upon.*
>
> *The journey to the bottom of that peak takes*

me three whole days. And two and a half more to struggle up to the point where, after waiting a long time, the sun glow is on my back as it sets behind the far mountains. That is when I see it, a black line, a crack, and there is movement. There are men there watching me.

I dare not write any more, and in case they seize me I will hide this that I have written in a pile of rocks that somebody has made and hope I shall recover it later, for I see they are coming for me. They are tall men with golden hair worn long, and their weapons, which are great two-handed axes and long swords, shine out in a sudden shaft of sun.

If they kill me it does not matter. In two years I have been wandering I think perhaps I achieve tranquillity and peace, and so I will name this great valley Nirvana, committing it to Buddha as my Gate to that state of Heavenly Grace. What I have heard of these men is that they live in the mountain and inside of that mountain there are steps hewn out of the rock that go down into the bowels, where is a strange god who has a great hammer in his hand and with this he crushes those who are sacrificed to him. Then they are like the pulp of trampled mulberries. So ...

It ended there. Or rather that section of the MS. The typescript continued for another five pages. I turned to the last page. The writer was a different man. Like his predecessor, he was a wanderer of the great spaces of desert and high mountain that cover so much of southern Asia, and he had come upon the old original manuscript by chance. The phraseology was different in these final pages, the information more sparse, almost cryptic. The writer had read what the earlier traveller had written, and since the manuscript had still been there, hidden under the cairn of stones, it was obvious he had never returned from the 'bowels' of what I, too, was beginning to regard as the Black Mountain.

'In the circumstances,' Antoine said, 'it is hardly surprising that the finder of that manuscript did not linger there, but turned abruptly round and headed east, away from the Black Mountain and the great valley that lies to the east of it.'

'The Pamirs,' Laun said. 'I have seen such a valley. But only once. The whole place is bedevilled by cloud that hangs over the surrounding peaks. Not a place to spend your leave!'

'So you don't see the Black Mountain?' Antoine was leaning forwards, his eyes strangely bright as though he had seen some sort of a vision. 'Only the valley the wanderer named Nirvana?'

'Yes. I have seen the valley. At least I think I have. A long, narrow valley, and at the northern end of it a lake, strangely shaped like a crescent, where the water is a vivid, emerald green.'

'And irrigation canals?'

'Yes, I think so. From where I stood, at something over fifteen thousand feet, they looked like pencil marks on the flat surface of a map.'

'The caves?' I asked. 'What about the caves, and the mulberry trees, the crops?'

Laun shook his head. 'I only saw it momentarily. A gap in the clouds that closed so suddenly I couldn't be certain the valley had been there at all. But the valley was there. Of that I am certain, because to get back to Bozai Gombas I had to struggle round the edge of it. I went clockwise, the deadly black shale sloping always away to my right, dropping steeply out of sight into the cloud. I cannot remember how long it took. It was several years ago and I was so tired, so goddamned tired. I was moving in a daze, you see. And I was scared. Twice I caught brief glimpses of the lake, its position changing so that I had some measure of my progress.'

He sat back, half closing his eyes. 'I tell you, it had a strange atmosphere, that valley. The best description of the area is *spooky*. I couldn't get away from it fast enough.'

He stopped there and I saw by his face that he was reliving the experience. 'Voices in the night. Strange voices. I had a one-man Everest-type tent and I was too tired to sleep properly. My breathing was bad. I was pretty near the end of my tether, you see. And those voices. All round me, they were.'

'In your head. Delusions.' Antoine's voice was very quiet now. 'My grandfather had the same sort of experience. But that was in the Taklamakan, not high up in the mountains. It is all in the head.'

'No. Not in the head. Not in mine, anyway.' The bark was back in Laun's voice. 'I do not suffer from delusions, man. Not even on occasions when I have been wounded. Not when I am exhausted, either. Never. Those voices were real. I could not understand anything they were saying. It was very strange, not a lingo I have ever heard before. And they weren't ghosts, those men. They were real people. I tell you, it was all very spooky.' And he added, 'Once, when they seemed all round my little tent, I tried to confront them. But by the time I had found my way out of the tent they were gone. Vanished into the black of the cloud-mist.'

'All in your mind,' Antoine insisted.

'No. Damn you, man! Not in my mind. I heard the clink of stones moving as they melted away, and I thought I glimpsed a movement. The next night it was the same, voices and movement all round the tent. That time I didn't attempt to struggle out of my sleeping bag. Instead, I tried talking to them from inside the tent. But the result was the same. As soon as they realized I was awake the voices ceased and I heard them moving away.' He shifted angrily in his chair, then leaned forward again. 'Look, man, I'm supporting you, or rather your grandfather. So why try and rubbish me? Is it because you are responsible already for two deaths? Four, if you count the two Russians I shot. And God knows how many more there will be!'

'I don't understand.' The sudden intake of Antoine's breath was quite audible. 'I am not the cause of any deaths.' But he understood very well. I could see it in his face, in the shocked look in his eyes. He knew what Laun was driving at. All three of us had realized the implication of his having had the ancient Chinese script translated. But he was unwilling to accept responsibility for the chain of events that had followed – the murder of Zelinski, the McCrae shooting and then the two men on the train.

'Your fault,' Laun said. 'Four men dead, and all four on account of your thoughtlessness, your stupidity. If I read you right, your background is something rather similar to mine. And yet you go to an Indian academic in Lahore to have that passage translated. Didn't it even cross your mind that the translator would take a copy of it and pass it across to his cronies? Not for money. I'm not suggesting he sold it to them. But academics are very concerned with their standing within the university of which they are a part. He would have known it would be of extreme interest to those of his colleagues in the Chinese language and religious disciplines, also in the department of archaeology. It would have gone the rounds in those departments like a bushfire. Somebody along the line would almost certainly smell money, and the Russians would be the obvious market. It might even have got to someone in Intelligence. That's where the money is for something as unusual as that, bearing in mind the mineral wealth of the Tajik and Pamir area.'

'I do not accept that.' Antoine was on his feet, his face white and tense. 'Why do you accuse me? There is Paul here. He is working for a company whose interests are in minerals. And before him there is Zelinski. No, you don't blame me.' He suddenly bent forward, staring at me, his clenched fists supporting him on the table top. 'It is your man Zelinski. He is passing it to the Russians. That is my thought.' He turned abruptly to Laun. 'And now I think about it, you are also employed by Resource Potentials. You kill two people, just like that!' He snapped his fingers in front of Laun's face. 'And up there in the Pamir ranges, that is your territory. My thought now is that it is you who kill Zelinski.'

'Don't be daft, man.' Laun's voice was very quiet, an attempt to reduce the tension. 'At the time of Zelinski's death I knew nothing about Resource Potentials. Or about Zelinski. I knew he had been killed, of course. This is my patch and I keep my ear to the ground. But I didn't kill him. Of course I didn't. Why should I? I didn't even know the man was in the area, not until I had the report of his death.'

And then he asked Antoine the question that had been on the tip of my own tongue – why was he making us a present of the vital passage in the ancient manuscript? 'Two days ago you tell Paul you want twenty million in US dollars for it. Now you give it to us free.'

There was a long pause, Antoine apparently considering all the various answers he could give, but in the end he simply said with a little shrug, 'You have the means to reach the Black Mountain. I don't. I do not even have a jeep because my funds are so limited. So—' Another shrug and the long, pale hands moving expressively. 'This is your patch, as you already tell me. You have the contacts, the equipment, all the things I lack because I am alone and am not *au fait* with the

Indian military. You let me come with you, and when we see the Black Mountain, I take you to the underground entrance – okay?'

Laun looked across at me, those strangely upturned eyebrows lifted. 'I think we need to talk this over, don't you?' I nodded and he turned back to Antoine: 'If things go according to plan, we should be leaving for the upper part of the Chitral Valley in three days' time. Meet us here with what equipment you have been able to scrounge, and then we will see.' And he added, 'It could be we have all the information we need. In which case . . .'

'Okay, okay, you want it all to yourself, is that it?' His voice had risen again, his face flushed.

'Want what?' I asked. 'What do you think we want to keep for ourselves?'

The Frenchman laughed, not very pleasantly. 'You don't know, do you? You are risking your lives and you don't know for sure what it is for. Mad dogs and Englishmen, isn't that so? You are both of you so very typical.'

'I am not English,' Laun said in an icy voice. 'I am Welsh. And Paul here is half Scots. Now, if you will kindly stop trying to trade insults, perhaps we can reach an agreement.'

It was a verbal agreement, of course. It had to be, I suppose. But I didn't like it. In the end, it was something he said that decided me to accept. He wasn't looking at Laun when he said it, he was looking at me. 'That little sultana of yours, do you know where she is?' And he laughed as he watched my face. 'Yes, your little dancing partner. You see, I have a very comprehensive dossier on you. I know about a man named Kasim, for instance. Your mother's paramour, what you call toyboy, I think. And after they marry he ill-treat her. I know also he is drowned sailing his boat, and you are on board. And then there is the death of that *Securitate* official. Again, you are there with the father of that little dancing girl who calls herself a sultana. You want to find her, don't you?' His eyes were on me, gleaming with a cruel enjoyment.

'I embarrass you, eh? Then you listen. There is a sultan in the cave dwellings under the Black Mountain. Did you know that? And he has a dancing girl with him who insists on being called his sultana. Ah, that intrigues you, does it?'

He paused there, his eyes still on me, still with that mischievous gleam. Then suddenly he threw back his head, his teeth a white gash in his skull as he gave that cackling laugh. 'I think we all go together, eh? To the Black Mountain.' He turned to Laun. '*Au revoir*, Brigadier. We meet here in three days' time, okay? And no funny business, otherwise I have you both locked up for murder.'

We made no promise and watched in silence as he turned and strode out.

PART FOUR

UNDERNEATH THE ROOF OF THE WORLD

CHAPTER ONE

We left the next day, just the two of us. It was Laun who had insisted on pushing on fast without waiting for Antoine. 'I don't know what his game is, and you're no help – you don't know either. Yet he's been following you ever since he caught up with you in Bucharest. And all that information about you. Where did he get it from? See what I mean? There's an organization behind him.'

His voice had risen as he developed his reasons for pushing on immediately, the Welsh intonation more pronounced. And then he added, 'And he's French, you see.' That seemed to clinch it as far as he was concerned, and I didn't argue.

It was to take us twenty-seven days to reach the Pamir region. That was allowing for recuperative stops at several mountain villages. And it took us another five days to cross to the far side of the mountainous plateau known as the Roof of the World. The Pamirs, the focal point of the great Himalayan ranges of the

Tien Shan, the Karakorams, the Hindu Kush, were in the depth of winter. It was then early February, the sun beginning to climb the sky, and in the moments when there was no cloud-mist our world was a white jumble of jagged peaks that faced us from all points of the compass, serried ranks of them, their slopes bare rock in places where avalanches had peeled the snow away.

It was a hell of a place, warm one moment, bitter cold the next, and there was wind, almost always there was wind. The wind-chill factor governed our lives, and the constant struggle to cross the ridges, always either climbing upwards or sliding and scree-walking precariously down, was utterly exhausting.

Looking at the violence of the terrain I was glad we had failed to locate a skidoo for hire. We were better off dragging the two small sledges Laun had scrounged out of Indian Army stores. With so few places where we could have made better progress using skidoos, we would have found them an encumbrance and would probably have had to dump them. Yak transport would have been the answer, but when I suggested it to Laun, he shook his head. 'The poor beasts have got to be fuelled, and fodder is only to be found in the valley bottoms. We have got to stay high where we're away from people and where the snow is firm.'

He was thinking, of course, of the Russians who had been making enquiries about him. And there was Antoine, too. Even so, there were moments when I wished we had waited for him. His ebullience, and his loquacity, would have done something to relieve the monotony of my companion's military adherence to planned marches. Each day had its objective and a timetable, discussed with me the night before, and whatever the terrain, he stuck to it rigidly. 'If we don't stick to the plan then we never get there. If you're lax about a set march, then sooner or later you give up. Believe me, I know.' And that was that. We went on, day after grinding day, dragging the sledges up impossible slopes, with only the relief of an occasional ski run over safe snow.

The night before we left Saidu Sharif we had spent a good hour discussing whether or not to wait for Caminade. We owed him something. We were both agreed on that. But Laun was adamant that in having the ancient manuscript translated he had forfeited any right to our consideration. He was thinking, of course, of McCrae's death. As for locating the Black Mountain, Pierre Caminade had found it without any GPS facility. Had McCrae found it? But Laun didn't know. He claimed he didn't know any more than I did what his friend had discovered. 'Something,' he said. 'But what, I don't know.'

I asked him then whether that was the reason he had gone off and left me at Rawalpindi. 'You were looking for McCrae?'

'Of course.'

'And that was when you first talked with Captain Pirbux.'

'He hadn't seen Gingin.' And he added, 'But he had heard about him. He knew he was in the area.'

'And those two Russians? The men you shot?'

'No. I don't think they got as far as that. Not the types to go looking for trouble in that sort of country.'

We had had another long talk with Captain Pirbux while waiting for the Pioneers to clear the final section of the road. Yes, he had noticed a rocky peak, very black, in the hour before sunset. This just before they had found Zelinski's body. He had even taken a bearing on it, just to confirm the GPS position. 'It is very prominent,' he said, 'like a colossal stone needle pointing skyward – but the blackness of it only stands out at that one particular time of day.'

The Black Mountain was on the north-west side of the Pamir. 'It's the right position,' Laun had said. I suppose it is force of habit with those who play at Kipling's Great Game, but he didn't tell me then what he told me later. All I got out of him was confirmation that the first Russian attempt at tunnelling had run into an old subterranean watercourse leading right back to the point where the Hindu Kush linked up with the Pamir mountain mass. 'It might even have been fed from the Emerald Lake.' But then he shook his head. 'Just possible, I suppose. But still a longish tramp from the point where the Russians abandoned that first tunnel.'

If we hadn't had Zelinski's GPS receiver, I don't think we would have found the mountain. Several miles short of the position where he had been wounded we walked into a bitter cold bank of cloud, which was very frustrating, for it was almost 1600 hours, just about the time when the last rays of the sun would pick out the crack that marked the way in to the mountain. The mist came down so thick that even with the GPS pinpointing the position of the cairn we could not locate it. Pirbux had said the cairn was still there. He thought it must have been added to, for the loose stones had been cleared from around it and it was larger than he had expected.

We checked and rechecked our position. It coincided exactly with the coordinates the captain had given us. There was nothing for it but to camp right there and wait for the cloud to clear, for it was now so thick that if we walked even a few metres away, the little tent was obliterated, totally. 'If you have to get out for a pee,' Laun said, 'catch hold of the end of this rope, and hang onto it for dear life.' He was knotting one end of it round a loose rock, then he walked away, paying it out as he went. Almost instantly his ghostly shape was swallowed in the mist. It was very peculiar, an instant vanishing act as though he had never been. I could hear the splash of his water, but it didn't come from the direction he had taken.

'Do you know where I am?' he called to me.

'No.' His voice, strangely disembodied, had seemed to come to me from almost all points of the compass, as though it were floating around me in the mist.

When I told him this even his laughter floated round me. 'I am experiencing the same sound disorientation,' he said. Then suddenly he was back, a shadowy shape that resolved itself abruptly into a human being only when I had moved so close to him I could reach out and touch him. 'That's how dangerous it is to walk out of sight up here in these conditions. And at night . . .' He left that to my imagination.

The evening dusk was with us for barely a moment it seemed. Suddenly it was dark. Not the normal darkness of the night, but a black, black, impenetrable nothingness, a sort of blackness I had never experienced before, not even when sailing the English Channel in thick fog.

He flashed his torch in the direction of the tent, but there was nothing there, only the beam's luminous circle, the moisture drops so large and thick it was as though we were under water.

Like two blind men we groped our way along the thin thread of the guide rope, one hand held out in front of us. At the moment mine touched the fine, silklike fabric I could see it, but only just the section of it that was illuminated by the torch beam. We unzipped it and crawled in to the relative warmth of the interior. We were dreadfully cold by then, for a wind had sprung up. But despite the wind there had been no movement of the mist. It was as though the wet blanket that pressed down on us was so heavy that only a hurricane force wind would shift it.

'Why?' I asked, as we burrowed in to the relative warmth of our sleeping bags. 'It was blowing quite hard, yet no movement in the mist.'

'I don't know why,' he answered, reaching out to zip up the inner lining of the tent. 'But I have a theory.' He was closing the side of his sleeping bag. 'The Russians stopped tunnelling because they ran into water, an underground river, in fact. That you already know.

What you don't know is that the water in that river was quite hot. Hot enough for it to steam.' His theory was that its course passed through an area of volcanic rock that was still in a state of instability. 'It's warm down there, I can tell you that.'

It was the first indication I had that at some stage he had managed to get inside the abandoned tunnel.

By then he had switched off the little solar night light he had unearthed from his kit, and, lying there so intimately close, I was reminded of the night Ana-maria and I had 'bundled' to get some warmth into our cold bodies. I tensed myself, prepared to fight him off, but apparently he was now resigned to the fact that I wasn't the sort to play 'fun and games' with him. He kept his hands to himself and the only effect of the closeness of our bodies was a grateful sense of warmth that loosened his tongue. He began telling me what it had been like, all those years ago, when the Russians had been trucked back to wherever they had come from and engineers and building workers had arrived to install the huge prefabricated steel doors that were to seal off the entrance to all but the mining managers who would periodically check the condition of the empty workings. 'There was some talk of it being used as a *gulag*,' he said. 'But I don't think anything came of that. Certainly when I was there I saw nothing being brought in that would suggest the incarceration of even long-stay prisoners.'

His visit had been accidental rather than planned. He had been doing his national service then, a wet-behind-the-ears subaltern on his first leave, and was hitch-hiking back from Kashgar dressed as a Tajik silk trader. He had planned to travel by camel with a caravan bound for Samarkand and Bokhara, but at the first serai they stopped at he found himself making up his bed next to the driver of a truck loaded with steel shuttering. They got talking over the evening meal, and when he discovered the shuttering was for sealing up the entrance to the tunnel the Russian engineers had just abandoned, he arranged for the driver to give him a lift to Termez. Next day he sold his camel and, riding the cab of this ex-army truck, headed south. By the time they reached Termez he had persuaded the driver to take him on as his mate. The shuttering was heavy and the driver, who was also the owner of the truck, would otherwise have had to pay somebody to help him.

At Termez they turned back east, following the course of the Oxus River. Two nights later they were at the entrance to the old tunnel. It took them two whole days to unload the truck by hand, and it was as they stood around, watching the engineers measuring up and positioning the shutters, that he had slipped away with his pack and bedroll. Somewhere along the tunnel the Tajik merchant's clothing was thrown off and he emerged, like an insect from its chrysalis, in the full splendour of a Red Army staff officer.

'Good God!' I said. 'If you'd been arrested . . . Why the hell didn't you wear your own uniform?'

'Don't be daft, man. How else could I have got the information I wanted? The only men left in the tunnel were engineers and labourers. There wasn't a soldier amongst them, and if there had been, he would have accepted me as a staff major. It was a KGB uniform, y'see, taken from a body I had stumbled on, frozen stiff as a board, in the Taklamakan.' He shook his head, laughing. 'The crazy things we do when we're young, eh?' I felt a finger jab at my ribs through the two layers of thermal quilting. 'Don't you worry your little head, boyo – I wouldn't do it now.'

That uniform had given him the confidence to hail a jeep-type vehicle that was coming along the tunnel towards him. It had been moving very slowly with its headlights blazing and a spotlight on the roof that moved back and forth along the walls. It was one of the engineers making a final inspection and dictating his report into a hand-held tape recorder. He had had no difficulty in persuading the man to turn round at the next passing point and take him back the full length of the tunnel.

There was a little miniature compass on the vehicle's dashboard, and with that in his hand and his eyes on the speedometer's kilometre reading, plus a running commentary from the engineer, he got all the information he needed for his later transfer to Intelligence.

'How did you persuade the engineer to talk?' I asked.

'No problem. There's hardly a man doing a job he enjoys that isn't prepared to shoot his mouth off about it to anybody really interested. And since I was an officer, and pretending to be checking the possibilities of the place as a hard-case prison, he regarded it as part of his duties to show me round.' After a moment's pause, he added, 'Ever been in the boiler room of a big coal-fired steam-turbine driven vessel? You know, deep in the bowels of a ship, a thousand steel rungs to climb if she hits a rock, or an iceberg.'

I shook my head. 'Before my time.'

'Well, there you are, then. No way you can know what it was like as we approached the point where they had stopped tunnelling.'

With the air getting increasingly humid, and the heat building, they had put on plastic overalls the engineer produced from the back of the car and continued on foot. The overalls kept the moisture out, but in no time at all the build-up of sweat inside them made for extreme discomfort. 'It would have been better if we had stripped off and gone naked up to the viewing platform. And the roar of that underground river. In such a confined space it was deafening, man.' I sensed a shake of his head. 'The *Mauritania*, now. The one that broke the transatlantic record and captured the Blue Riband for the Cunard Line. They're gone now, those wonderful great liners. Just scrap. Four funnels she had and an army of stokers working shifts, shovelling the coal that kept the twenty-four boilers so full of steam that her average speed was that of a Dreadnought. It must have been a hell-hole down there with those coal-black stokers working and looking like demons, their long shovels going back and forth, the furnace doors clanging as they opened and shut their greedy, flaming mouths, like rows of dragons demanding to be fed.' This was the Welsh bard in him enjoying the sound of his own voice, and of the words he was using.

'It was the river, of course,' he went on, 'that provided the sound effects. A great roaring rush of noise, and from where we stood, on a railed-in platform, it went foaming past us, carrying great slabs of ice, occasionally part of a tree, even bits and pieces of shrubbery scoured from the land by an avalanche. I saw a sturgeon go by, turning itself this way and that in an effort to escape the plughole that we could just see away to our right in the mouth of a cavelike aperture, the foaming water smoothing itself out as it gathered speed near the lip of the sill that marked the big, noisy drop to God knows what at the bottom. The engineer told me it was virtually a straight drop for close on a thousand feet.'

Above them, to their left, the river appeared, 'smooth like black silk' and steaming gently as it spewed out from another gaping rock hole. The engineer had then taken him along a probe tunnel drilled through the rock to a point where a stone staircase climbed a hundred feet or more alongside a thundering waterfall, spray and steam mingling in the air and clouding the walls of the gut. The stone of the steps was wet with the spray, slimy with algae, and only a rope handline to save a man if his feet slipped from under him.

Halfway up the fall the steps stopped abruptly. A black hole of a passage ran off to the left. They hadn't gone down that, the engineer merely saying that it was an old watercourse that led out to the north side of the mountain and that it had probably been the original outlet for the river.

At this point an observation platform had been cut in the rock and there were old, somewhat rusty, steel scaffolding poles railing it off from the water rushing past some three metres below. The river was then about five metres across and on the opposite side there was a platform similar to the one they were standing on, except that there was no protective railing. 'Instead, there was a semicircular wall of carefully cut stone, so perfectly fitted together that it was like a part of those Inca ruins you see in pictures of Machu Picchu.'

And then he corrected himself: 'No, the remains of a revetment in a Vauban fortress. The platform on which we were standing was the broken arch of what had once been a stone bridge. This was repeated on the far side, and as the existing means of crossing the river there was the frame of a temporary bridge, rather like those Bailey bridges that littered Europe after World War Two, only this was of forest timber, full-grown conifers providing the supporting arms. And as far as I could see the contraption was in working order.'

He paused, then went on in a sudden rush of words: 'That was strange enough, you would think. But stranger still, far stranger, was the man standing facing us across the river. Still as a statue, he was. A short man, but immensely broad at the shoulders, and he had long flaxen hair, and a beard. He wore what looked like a goatskin cape over one shoulder as though it were a toga and under it a leather jerkin. His right arm and shoulder were bare, the skin very white and glistening with sweat and steam, so that there was a ghostlike quality about him.

'But I tell you this' – his hand gripped my shoulder – 'there was nothing ghostly about his equipment. I could see the snout of a machine-gun pointing out from the embrasure to his left, and laid out on the top of the parapet was a longbow and a selection of steel-tipped arrows. The eyes of this statuesque Viking of a man were bright blue, wide open and staring, but they closed abruptly as the beam of the engineer's torch fastened on him, and in a sudden, quick movement, he ducked into the redoubt, signalling to us to switch the torch off. This we did, and then he came out again, a hand-mike to his mouth. The sweat shone on him as though the pores of his skin were full of phosphorus and he called to us to know what we wanted.'

'In what language?' I asked. And remembering the story of the tribe descended from a lost long ship of the river-borne invasion of Asia by the Rus, I asked him whether it was Swedish.

'God knows what language it was. Nothing I could understand. But I can tell you this much, it wasn't any of the Mediterranean languages, and it wasn't either Russian or Chinese, or even one of the Slav languages. Why? You said you spoke Swedish – right?'

'Yes.' And I told him about the time I was in Canada mapping out a route for the railway the mine owners planned to build to connect up with the CPR. 'We had a gang of loggers clearing the tote-road and a good half of them were Swedes. That's how I learned the essentials. I had to. They were a tough lot and they had a somewhat basic sense of humour.'

'Then we'll just hope these people really are descended from that lost tribe of long-ship survivors.' Laun grinned, then left it at that, explaining to me that they had had to shout to make themselves heard above the rumble of the river, first in Russian, then in a smattering of other languages. But it was no good. Finally the man on the far bank of the torrent had been joined by another, older man, who spoke a little Russian, and after Laun's engineer guide had explained that they were only doing a last check before sealing up the northern end of the tunnel, the guards had seemed satisfied.

'There you are, then,' Laun finished. 'That's all I can tell you.'

'What about the continuation of that old water-course? You said there was a passageway in the rock that went off to the left. In other words, if the wooden walkway had been thrust out across the river they could have gone straight on down the old watercourse. Pity you didn't go down there.'

'I felt I had taken up enough of the Russian engineer's time by then. Doubtless we'll find out where it leads when we make our number to the sultan of the troglodytes and his sultana.'

'When will that be?'

'How the hell do I know? When this cloud-mist lifts and we can see where we're going. Okay?' And before I could think of anything more to say, I heard his regular breathing close against my ear. He was asleep, just like that. He'd closed his eyes and gone, leaving me awake in the dark and suddenly conscious of the damp cold and the fact that my breath was freezing on the outer covering of my sleeping bag.

Time passed slowly. The wind had got up, hammering at the fabric of the tent. We were as high as we had been, except when making it across the Shandur Pass to travel the northern part of Chitral. Was it yesterday, or the day before we had reached the high Pamir plateau? The Roof of the World! I had been keeping a note of our progress by dictating into my pocket tape recorder, but the last few days were all merged in my mind and I hadn't bothered. Too tired, too bloody tired, and the wind, that endless wind.

One thing was very clear in my mind as I lay there trying to recreate the sequence of events – yesterday, at about 1620, we had managed to get a glimpse of our first objective, the deep valley which that ancient traveller had called Nirvana.

We were in thick mist at the time, the wind fortunately swirling it about, otherwise I might not be alive to record the extraordinary events that were to take place before our eyes in the days that followed. The last of the daylight had almost gone, the grey gloom of it fading almost to darkness. Then, suddenly, the dark curtain of the mist was swept aside and I had stopped so abruptly that Laun cannoned into me and my feet began to slip on a smooth slope of rock covered with ice. The ground ahead of me just disappeared. Laun caught hold of me, otherwise I would have gone, for we were standing on the lip of a sheer cliff, and, away to our right, we heard the loud continuous noise of an avalanche. It went on and on, then suddenly stopped, the world instantly silent. Even the wind made no sound. With no trees, no growth of any kind, only the rock of the valley side, the snow and the ice, there was nothing to hinder its passage. We might have been in a balloon.

High above us banks of cloud began to thin and drift away until finally all the sky was revealed, a pale, pastel blue, and in the last of the slanting sunlight we had caught a glimpse of a lake, far away to the north, and deep down, an emerald crescent mounted on the velvet black of deep shade, its backcloth a sheer white slope of virgin snow. Straight ahead of us, on the bearing we had been floundering along, a massive rock pinnacle reared up out of a white sheet of snow, the contrast of the white of the snow and the black of the naked rock, sheathed in a film of ice, seemed to shout aloud its name. And halfway up this incredible needle of a peak there was the dark line of a crack running down to a shadowed cavity.

'There it is!' my companion had said. 'The entrance. Now all we've got to do is get to it.'

'And then what?'

He had looked at me, a quizzical glance, half teeth that showed yellow against the white of the frozen breath on his moustache. 'That we shall discover in due course.' And he had started to plod on again. 'Better put our goggles on.' The sunlight on the snow had become quite blinding.

Though we were tramping along the edge of the valley, we saw virtually nothing of it, for the bottom was deep in shadow. The Himalayan peaks behind us gradually taking on a beautiful, roseate glow, and then the mist had come down, quite suddenly and for no apparent reason, the wind still blowing from the same direction about force 6, maybe 7.

That was our introduction to the Valley of Nirvana and the Black Mountain. We had taken very careful bearings, of course, but once the mist enclosed us we had nothing but our visual memories of the terrain to guide our floundering feet as we trudged steadily on, one step after another, on a bearing of 296° through a grey, wet world that had suddenly become much less cold. Here and there we found ourselves stumbling on patches of melted snow. I took one of my mitts off at a particularly large bald patch and put my hand down to touch a crack in the rock. It was warm.

Remembering that, I wished to God we could have erected our tent where the thermal heat was seeping up from below, but by then we had begun to climb the base of the Black Mountain itself and there were no more bald patches. In places we were up to our waists in drifts as we had been on the Shandur. If only the wind had stopped blowing. But it hadn't. It had increased to gale force, and then it had begun to snow.

That was when Laun had decided enough was enough. We pitched our tent on the only flat place we could find in the vicinity and turned in, exhausted and not bothering about hot food, eating chocolate and biscuits in our sleeping bags. And the wind went on and on, hammering away at our flimsy covering. I lay there, wide awake, haunted by the thought that we might be lying on the very edge of a sheer drop to the valley below. Gradually I became conscious of my companion shivering. His breathing was still regular, so I knew he was asleep, but he was obviously cold, and so was I. But I was at least twenty years younger, and though he had shown himself extremely tough, age must make a difference.

My mind began drifting. At times I felt almost disembodied, floating free in a strange world, no longer conscious of the man lying close up against me and breathing so steadily, so calmly. It was as though I were in limbo, the world all round me a black void. Only that hellish wind to remind me I was not dead.

I tried to concentrate on the next stage of our journey. Tomorrow, or the day after – some time soon – we would be inside the mountain. Then what? Would Vikki be there, waiting for me? I tried fantasizing about her, but it was no good. I couldn't even be sure she really would be the sultana, and the devil of it was I couldn't remember what she looked like.

My need of feminine companionship at that moment was very great. I had to have something to hold on to, thinking of Charon and the river we had to face, steaming like the Styx. Or was limbo a cold emptiness of ice? It frightened me that I couldn't conjure up in my mind's eye the features of the girl I had danced with, couldn't even recall the dances – only how we had lain on the floor in Ana Kikinda's parlour and copulated. No feeling, no emotion, no love – just the tearing off of clothes and a hot, steamy lay.

The only features I could remember were those of Anamaria – the harelip, the odd, distorted sucking of that mouth, and the breasts, so beautifully shaped, the lovely, warm, passionate body. Her need of me, and mine of her – in that comfortable hotel bedroom with a staggering view over Istanbul and the Golden Horn . . . God! How I wished it was Anamaria, not Vikki, waiting for me inside that mountain.

Had she made it? Had there been money waiting for her at Alma-Ata? My mind drifted away to Alex Goodbody, imagining his face when I presented him with the bill for Anamaria's ticket to Alma-Ata. I could of course pretend she was a whore I had to get rid of. He would probably understand that. She wasn't a whore in the true sense. If either of them was a whore, it was Vikki. A man-hungry little dancer, lonely, lost and seeking a *raison d'être* for life, seeking it in her dancing and her sexuality, and in the cold, electronic operation of her computer.

Was that why she had left Kazakhstan? Yes, perhaps she really was this wretched sultana we were tramping across the Roof of the World to meet. But it couldn't be. It was too ridiculous. To think of my having to negotiate a deal with little Vikki, who had come rushing out on to that restaurant dance floor . . .

I must have gone to sleep then, for I woke to a world in which there was no wind, only a grey, opaque nothingness, quite white with the brightness of the sun behind it. The cold was gone. It was just damp, and

Laun was sitting up boiling a tin of self-heating soup he had pulled in from his sledge.

We were lucky. The planned march that day was a short one, so that for once we were able to linger over breakfast, even brewing mugs of instant coffee on our little spirit stove. Then, as we began to pack up for the trek ahead, the weather suddenly changed. In an instant the wind was back, hitting us with terrifying force, the tent straining at its fastenings, the snow blotting everything out, driving in an almost solid mass of ice crystals – a real Pamir storm was how he described it.

CHAPTER TWO

We were two more nights, huddled, cold and exhausted, in that little tent, expecting our flimsy shelter to take off at any moment. Then, some time during that second night, the wind died. I think it was the unexpected silence that woke us. We were on our way just as the surrounding peaks showed up in the coming dawn, and when the sun lifted high enough to limn them in light we found ourselves skiing across a field of fresh snow that was no longer white, but flushed with pink. By then we had been on the march for over two hours. Soon we were climbing again, the going difficult. We were following what looked like a track which revealed itself in snow-bald patches, and in these patches the air steamed gently. It was these patches of warmth that kept us going. But we could never linger, for the air that exuded from them was stale, in some cases quite foetid, so that we knew they were ventilation holes. What they were ventilating we could only imagine – it could be animals byred for the winter or the lost tribe pumping out their foul air. It was at this point that the mist came creeping up on us again. By then we had strapped our skis back on the sledges for we were now clambering over jumbled rock or slipping into crevices deep in snow, the climb getting steeper and steeper.

Once the sledge Laun was pulling dropped off a rock ledge into what I thought was some sort of a crevasse. He was leading it at the time, and if I hadn't managed to catch hold of his ice axe he would have gone too, for it wasn't a gully between rocks, it was a cliff edge. God knows how far he would have fallen. The cloud-mist had been thickening all day, and at this point the limit of visibility was barely a dozen metres.

After that we pitched the tent on the first level patch of snow we came to. It was a long rock ledge with about a two-foot layer of snow and ice on it. It was there, digging down to get to solid ice into which we could drive one of our steel pegs, that I uncovered a footprint. It was close to a small fissure and the ice there was mushy. It was a large, rather shapeless print, so that we presumed it was a man wearing some sort of moccasin.

At any rate, it was human, and it was substantive. Something we were glad to know when, at 0327, the early hours of the morning, we were woken by strange guttural sounds outside the tent.

At first I thought it was some animal, a bear, perhaps a stray yak or one of the big-horned mountain goats. But then I realized the sounds were human voices whispering to each other. My companion pushed himself up on one elbow and spoke to them in Pashtu.

The whispering ceased abruptly. The night was suddenly very still, only Laun asking them to return in the morning and take us to the Sultan. Silence. He tried again, this time in Dari. A shuffling sound as one of them moved round the tent. 'Or to the Sultana.' Then, taking a chance that it really was Vikki, he added that he had with him a young Englishman – 'who has known her for many years'.

Still no answer.

'Try them in Swedish,' he said to me.

When I had spoken a few words there was a sudden jabber of talk from outside. Laun grabbed my arm. 'You're through to them, boy. Try them again. Say you know their Sultana.'

A long silence followed, and then one of them said, speaking slowly in a bastard form of Swedish that sounded very like Russian, that they would return in the morning when the sun was above the mountain. *After we have reported to the Sultan. You wait here. You do not move. Understood?*

'*Ja.*' I realized then that I could understand their language, but could not speak it. Even my Swedish was too rusty. '*Underforsta.*' That was the Norsk for *understand* and it seemed to ring a bell with my unknown friend. He consulted his companions, and then to my surprise, he said, 'Okay,' repeating the word I had used – *underforsta* and adding that they would report now to their guard commander. Then, if the Sultan agreed, they would send somebody to guide us.

I told him, would he please report to the Sultana also, and I tried to tell him that I had been her dancing partner when we were in Constantza. But that was too difficult. However, I was able to make him understand I was a personal friend of the Sultana and he seemed to accept that. I gave him my name and made him repeat it.

They left shortly after that, instructing us again not to move. '*Stille.*' He repeated it twice, and then he was gone.

'Nothing to do but wait now,' Laun said, insisting I tell him the whole story of my relationship with the young woman I knew as Vikki. 'I need to know, so that I can assess the situation.' He gave that quick bark of a laugh. 'We're going into something we can't understand, something that is ages old, if what your friend Caminade has told us is true. Just think for a moment: if that manuscript he found in the loft of his parents' home in Domme is correct – and I don't think we can regard it as anything else – then these people we have just been talking to are descended from the crew of a Viking long ship that lost its way in the great sweep south of the Swedish Rus about eight hundred and something. That's almost twelve hundred years ago. Just think about it. And all the time cultivating that hidden valley, living a troglodyte existence in the caves and watercourses that run under this mountain. Thermal heat laid on by Providence. Natural defences that keep the rest of the world at bay.'

His hand reached out and gripped my arm. 'My God! Just think of it – a whole millennium and more cut off from the rest of the human race! And tomorrow we're being led down underground passages into their world. And we know nothing about them, do we now? Their religion, for instance. What god, or gods, do they believe in? For all we know they may worship a heart-hungry monster of a god, the way the Aztecs worshipped Huizilopochtli. We may be booked for sacrifice.'

'For God's sake!' He was putting into words thoughts that I had pushed to the back of my mind, thoughts that were too frightful to contemplate. I had been trying to persuade myself that they would prove to be just good, simple people.

'What happens if the Sultana here is not your little dancing girl? Or, worse still, if she doesn't want to know you? Just face up to it, boy. We've got to have some sort of a plan worked out so that we're ready if things go wrong for us.'

To make a dash for it was out of the question. We agreed on that. They knew the country. We would not have a hope of getting away. In the end we decided the only thing we could do was face up to them, behave as though we were special envoys from the outside world on a mission of friendship to their ruler and his consort, the Sultana. Everything therefore depended either on Vikki being the Sultana or the Sultan himself having need of outside contacts.

Thinking back over all I had heard about the difference between her and the other inmates of that orphanage in the Carpathians, her overbearing attitude of superiority, her constant claim that she was the daughter of a sultan, all the little things that seemed to add up and complement the paleness of her skin, the bright, golden halo of her hair, her remoteness from others, the things that the Kikindas had let slip, their acceptance of her domineering, selfish behaviour and of her insistence on being free to do exactly what she wanted, going off on her own, escaping into the screen world of her little computer . . . It all added up, so that I was almost convinced everything would be all right.

But still, at the back of my mind, that niggling doubt.

Laun had talked a lot during our mountain trek about the Victorian players of the Great Game, their bravery, their foolhardiness, the dreadful periods when a cruel despot – khan, emir, sheikh or sultan – had felt it safe to throw British officers into some hell-hole of a prison, even have them murdered. The Emir of Bokhara, for instance, ordering a colonel and a captain dragged out of prison to dig their own graves, then kneeling in the square before his palace, their heads sent rolling in the dust by the executioner's sword, and all because Queen Victoria had not replied to his letter! The massacres, the lies, the double-crosses, and here were we, thrusting our own necks into an under-mountain sultanate – and for what?

I suppose we were talking it over for almost an hour, and at the end of it, no plan of action if it wasn't Vikki. 'Better get some sleep,' Laun said finally, and as usual he dropped off as though he hadn't a care in the world.

Dawn broke with the cloud-mist on fire as the sun rose above the mountain tops. Crawling out of the tent to relieve myself, the stillness was absolute, no wind now and not a sound to break the utter silence of the great plateau and the peak up which we were climbing. Laun joined me, waving his battered cock as he spread his water on the night's virgin fall of snow. He saw me watching and smiled, shaking it vigorously. 'One thing, if they turn nasty, they can't do me much more damage in that direction.'

We had a thermometer among the instruments on the sledge. It showed the air temperature only just below zero. With no wind it seemed relatively warm, only the mist seeping into our bones to give the morning a chill feel. We had an *al fresco* breakfast rather than eating it huddled in the fuggy confines of the tent, and just as we had finished a wind came roaring down from the peak above us.

Suddenly it was bitter cold, and in the same instant the cloud that enveloped us was whirled about, great gaps appeared, glimpses of arctic blue above us, then suddenly the grey miasma was whipped away and flung downwind towards Nirvana. We were looking down into the valley itself then, could see the further shore of the crescent lake, and beyond the eastern side of the valley, layer upon layer of snow-streaked peaks gradually unfolding. And above us the Black Mountain towered into the cold blue, glimpses of the pathway zigzagging up through bare rock outcrops that pushed their dark snouts through the snow.

And Laun was pointing. Pointing to something high above us that had caught my eye in the same instant, a slender, wind-whipped shaft, like the rods they use for beach fishing. I couldn't believe it at first. I thought I was seeing things, something to do with the rarefied atmosphere, my eyes playing tricks. It was there for a moment, and then it retracted itself, as though it was being pulled down from inside the mountain.

'God Almighty!' Laun said. 'Looks like they're not as primitive as I thought.'

'What was it?'

But I think I knew what it was before he said, 'An aerial.' A huge whip aerial that could be raised and lowered from inside a cave or some underground rock cavern. 'Ingenious.' He stood there, not moving and still gazing up at the spot where the whip had been.

We crept back into the relative warmth of the tent, the wind by then blowing so hard I feared the whole thing would take off like a balloon. We were still huddled there, and discussing the implications of that aerial, if it really was an aerial, when they came for us. The time was 0923 and there were four of them, two armed with Kalashnikovs. It came as no surprise to me to find they were armed with modern Russian weapons, but what did surprise me was that they were kitted out in the latest high-altitude clothing, and over their thermal clothing they wore white oilskins.

Our tent and camp gear was packed up and on the

sledge in very quick time, so that we were away just after ten, two of them carrying the loaded sledge between them. This made for much faster movement than if we had been dragging it over the rocks. Here and there steps had been cut and inside half an hour we came to a broad, sloping ledge that had been caused by a fault and was overhung by a cliff of sheer black rock. It was covered in ice and very slippery. One of the sledge carriers produced an ice axe and with this he chipped away at the surface to give our feet a grip. The ledge rose quite steeply to curve round a protruding buttress of rock.

At this point the cloud-mist was below us, a flat cotton-wool plain of dazzling white so that I had the feeling that if I slipped it would be like falling out of an aircraft. The impression was of a cloud-sea stretching to the ends of the earth with innumerable peaks standing out like snow-streaked islands.

We rounded the buttress and immediately came up against a defensive wall. It was almost a metre thick with a passage through it that was in the form of a Z. Beyond the wall was the bottom of the crevice we had seen from below, a broad crack in the rock that extended all the way up an overhanging cliff for a hundred metres and more.

It was into this natural fault-line that our guides led us. There were embrasures cut in the rock face on either side, then a blank wall of rock. Only one way to go at this point – sharp left, straight into the field of fire from the slits that no doubt had been originally designed for defence by the longbow or crossbow. But now, catching a glimpse of the other side in the swing of the torch one of our guards had produced, I saw a heavy machine-gun permanently mounted.

This was the last of the defensive points. The next opening was into a rock room with hand-winding gear, also a heavy-duty electric motor. Slotted into its small cogwheel was a much bigger cog fitted to a metal tube that ran down into the rock below.

Laun, who had been taking in the general layout of the defences with a professional eye, nodded to this contraption. 'The aerial,' he said. 'This is how they managed to raise and lower it so quickly.' And he added, 'They're not backward, these people. They have electricity, and it's powerful enough to drive a heavy steel rod like that up and down. They have power, presumably water power, and since they have sophisticated weapons and clothing, my guess is they're trading with the outside world, but at the same time preserving their independence. I doubt the Russians like that at all.'

Some more steps, going down, fluorescent tubes lighting our way, then into what appeared to be a sort of guardpost, the walls lined with cold-weather clothing and all the equipment necessary for patrolling the outside slopes of the mountain, Kalashnikovs and magazine-loaded handguns, flare pistols, even rocket launchers, and on wooden pallets boxes of ammunition. 'It's a mountain fortress,' I whispered to Laun.

He nodded. 'Vauban would have loved it.'

In addition to walkie-talkies, there was a bank of field telephones. The guard commander was already

talking into one of these. He caught my eye. '*Englez,*
eh?'

I nodded. '*Ja.*'

Listening to him gabbling into the phone's mike I
began to realize how serious our communication problem was going to be. Laun realized it, too. 'I thought
I had a smattering of all the languages of southern
Asia, but this is beyond me. If the Sultana is not your
little dancing partner, then we really do have a linguis-
tic problem.' He glanced round at the equipment
ranged along the rock walls. 'They obviously have
contact with the outside world, but I fear the lingua
franca here is either a bastard form of Swedish or
perhaps a mixture of Tibetan and Mongolian.'

The guardroom was set to one side of a rock staircase leading down into the bowels of the mountain.
This too was lit at intervals by fluorescent tubes and
from the depths below came a steady murmuring
sound. 'Water?'

Laun shook his head. 'Machinery of some kind, I
think. But water powered.'

We had been directed by signs to seat ourselves on
the wooden bench that ran the length of the bare rock
wall opposite the entrance. 'I doubt the dead hand of
Communism ever reached into this mountain fastness.'
He had gripped hold of my arm, but he was talking
to himself rather than to me. 'Nor Genghis Khan and
his Mongol hordes. And Bolshevik collectivization
would not have touched the cave-dwelling people
of that great valley. But I think they must have had
their own form of cooperative farming, their own

government presumably. They were virtually self-sufficient. And because of their remoteness and their natural defences Stalin must have decided it wasn't worth sending the Red Army in.'

He was silent for a moment, and all the while that steady murmur growing louder. 'I think perhaps this is the moment I should tell you; while you were at Pindi and I was up the Malakand road trying to find out what Gingin had discovered that made him a target for those Moscow thugs, I did my best to get a message to these people to tell them we were coming.' He had done this through a Sikh who operated a ham radio from Mardan, a small town on the way up to the pass. 'Maybe that's why they had a patrol out watching for us.'

There was a clanking sound and the murmuring ceased abruptly. The guard commander was on his feet again, motioning for us to pick up our things. Footsteps echoed through the vaulted stairway, the sound of voices, a cackling laugh. There could not surely be anyone else with a laugh like that. And then he was in the guardroom, teeth showing in a big grin. '*Alors, mon ami.* So we meet again, huh?'

'How in God's name did you get here?' All the miles we had struggled through snow, over rocks, climbing, descending, bone-weary and cold, living huddled together in that tiny tent, and here was Antoine Caminade all smiles and camaraderie, looking so fresh and clean, so bloody pleased with himself. 'How—'

'Simple. I come by the front door. You come by

the back. So much more difficult.' Again that cackle of a laugh. 'Come! I take you down to your quarters and then, mebbe, to meet with your girlfriend.' He turned to Laun. 'He is a great one for the ladies, this young man. But per'aps you 'ave not 'ad the opportunity of noticing that on your travels.' He was goading us, but he did it with a wicked gleam in his eye, as though the whole thing was just a bit of fun. 'Come!' He said something to the guard commander, who nodded. 'Okay, so you follow me now.'

We went out into the passage and down the first flight of rock-cut steps to a great slab, two of the guards carrying our loaded sledge, from which I had retrieved my briefcase. The steps continued on, the lit tubes showing them slanting away to the left with a glimpse of several rooms quarried out of the rock and reinforced with what looked like concrete. The slab formed a platform, and on the right-hand side of this a metal cage was poised at the top of a long, slanting shaft. It was somewhat like an Italian *slitovia* and looked as though it dropped virtually the full height of the mountain to finish at the level of the valley's bottom.

There were still several men on the platform, sorting through equipment and stores they were unloading from the cage. They were different from the men in the guardroom, slighter and dark, rather than blond. Their equipment included a generator and the sort of drills used by quarrymen.

'Engineers,' Caminade said.

Laun had moved over to talk to them. He was

asking where they were drilling, but they just stared at him uncomprehendingly. 'You try,' he said, turning to me. But they didn't understand my Swedish either.

'They are Atils,' Caminade said. 'They are part Mongol and they stick to their own language.'

'They're mining engineers, are they?'

'Rock drillers.' And then, without our having to ask him, he said, 'Did you see the aerial they have erected? They are working to make it so that it can be withdrawn deep inside the mountain. Then the line of communication is safe.' A buzzer sounded and he waved us into the cage, adding, 'Now per'aps you begin to understand, eh?'

I never had a chance to time it, but I was told it took approximately twelve and a half minutes to travel up or down the shaft. As the cage slid down the shaft the noise of the underground river increased. Another noise, too, the humming of turbines generating electricity. This hydroelectric plant not only lit the various adit levels with their big male dormitories and numerous family cave dwellings; it also drove the machine tools that, since the Industrial Revolution, had apparently made these people self-sufficient in most of their mechanized requirements.

Their Swedish forebears had developed an iron industry in advance of most other nations, and because of this many of the people here had an inbuilt aptitude for metallurgy, so that when we arrived they were turning out all the cutting and drilling equipment they needed to mine the sapphire and lapis lazuli deposits that enabled them to trade and barter for the things they needed from outside. It was a water-powered industrial complex that produced almost everything the community required. Except, of course, food. This came from the intensive cultivation of the 'Nirvana' valley. The soil there was a rich mixture of degraded limestone and volcanic ash, and with the controlled use of thermal heat they were able to produce three, sometimes four, crops a year.

My knowledge of the working of this self-contained little Nordic state is patchy since I was only there a short time. What they had achieved, *force majeure*, in order to maintain their independence and develop their own individual culture was quite extra-ordinary and merits a properly researched history. But at the moment of my first arrival, descending into the rock depth of the mountain, with the roar of water and the hum of turbines and other machinery coming closer, my feeling was one of intense claustrophobia. I have been down some of the deepest mines in the world and never before suffered any claustrophobic effect, but this was different. What I felt was something close to panic.

I glanced at Laun and saw that he was similarly affected, his teeth gritted and his hands clenched, his whole body tense. As he had already pointed out to me, we were descending into the unknown, forcing our way into the rock kingdom of a people who had isolated themselves from the rest of the world for cen-turies. I wanted to discuss with him what we should do if, when we reached the bottom, they just locked us up and left us there. But instead, I turned to

Antoine, seeking confirmation that the Sultana really was my little dancing partner, but I couldn't get through to him. He was sitting on the bench seat close behind me, his eyes glazed like stone, staring straight through me, lost in some world of his own imagining, and it suddenly struck me that the man was frightened. Frightened of what I didn't know, and I couldn't very well ask him. And then when we reached the bottom, with the roar of the underground river shatteringly loud and the atmosphere damp with the steam that emanated from the thermal nature of its waters, he suddenly gripped my arm. 'A word with you,' he hissed in my ear. 'You come at a bad time. There is a power struggle.' That was all he said then. But later I discovered that Ali Khan, the Sultan, was away, mending his fences and seeking outside support, particularly amongst the Tajiks and the Chechens. With the collapse of the Union (USSR), both these republics had dreams of independence.

There was a rock platform at the bottom of the slideway and here we were met by a bearded man with black hair and a very white skin who had a smattering of French. He wore a cotton tunic rather like a nightshirt. This in complete contrast to the two men behind him, who were fair and stripped to the waist, obviously bodyguards, for they each had a handgun holstered on a broad leather belt and a short sword.

'The Sultan's Secretary,' Antoine whispered to us as we were waved to an electric car, which trundled us smoothly and quite silently along an endless tunnel with many side tunnels branching off it. We didn't talk, but I think that was due to the strangeness of our surroundings, the novelty of it all and the uncertainty of what lay ahead, so many thoughts passing through my mind. And then we had switched off the main artery into a side tunnel where we were stopped at a guardpost. The commander here was a dark, sharp-featured man with a woollen cape thrown over his left shoulder. He looked at the Secretary, then waved us through. No greeting, no vestige of a smile, the thin face set as though carved in stone. I glanced at the Secretary. His eyes met mine for a second and I thought I caught a glimpse of uneasiness in them.

There was no wasted space in those rock chambers, there being apparently just the one for visitors, so that Laun and I were sharing quarters with Antoine. It was a big area with six beds in it, the raw stone of the walls softened by patterned wall hangings, some of which Laun could identify, those from the Swat River district in particular.

At first Antoine would not talk about the internal politics of this very strange community, nor would he elaborate on his warning about a power struggle. 'Politics is nothing to do with me. I am an agent. Nothing more.' And when I questioned him again about the Sultana he said she was not interested in politics. 'Certainly not now. She has the child to keep her occupied.' He gave that cackling laugh of his. 'Before the birth, I tell you she is like a balloon. So big we are betting on it being more than one.'

'When did she give birth?'

'It is just after I arrive here that the waters break.

So, you see, I don't 'ave much time with her.' And he added, 'She is very un'appy, I think. Because when the Sultan return he will have to be told. It is not a boy, you see. An' he is so sure it will be a boy. He needs a boy to safeguard the succession.'

I should have appreciated the significance of this, but my mind had fastened on his admission that he was an agent. A business agent, he said. But Laun leapt to a quite different conclusion and asked what he had meant by 'a power struggle'. We were into a discussion then on the merits of various religions and the ethics of human existence, for the power struggle was apparently between a mixed-up version of the old Viking gods, Communist materialism and the Mafia grab rule of an Iranian despot.

After the First World War and the blood-birth of the USSR the then ruler of this undermountain Pamir community declared it an independent state. At the same time, he turned from Buddhism to Islam. His name was Thorfinn. 'A very pragmatical man,' was Antoine's explanation. He had been succeeded by his son, whose name had been changed to Mohammed. 'Is a strange world. Here is a man who, like all his predecessors, rule the people as a captain rule his crew, demanding of them absolute obedience, total discipline.

'You will not believe this, but every year, when the sun climb above the mountain here and shine on the lake, all the people, all the male people that is, are gathered together in a great cave, and then a young woman, the fairest of course, is ceremonially raped before them all by the winner of the winter games. No other woman there, only men, every man in the community over sixteen years of age. And after, they come forward one by one and kiss the feet of the Sultan and with their hands between his swear ever-lasting service and obedience.'

And when Laun asked him how he knew all this, he said, 'I have been here before. Some years back, as a friend of the Sultan Mohammed III. It was the time of the swearing and he allowed me to attend.' He wouldn't say how he had come to be on such intimate terms with the Sultan, and when I asked him about the present ruler he just shook his head and muttered something about it being a long story. 'Ask Erik Bigblad,' he said. 'He has been on the Outside, to Moscow, Vladivostok, San Francisco, Manchester, Birmingham. He is something like a businessman. He has travelled and he speaks a little English. Ask him. If you can find him, and if they ever let you out of this sealed-off rabbit warren.' And with a wave of the hand and an attempt at a jocular grin, he slipped away.

A meal was brought to us on a trolley by one of the guards. There was a communal lavatory a few metres along the alleyway that led to the Secretariat and the quarters of what we came to regard as the Praetorian Guard. Beyond was the armoury and the treasury, both with iron grilles and heavy metal doors like those in a bank vault.

A few hours, and Laun had recovered sufficiently to go walkabout, exploring the alleyways between our quarters and the guardpost through which we had entered this special section of the underground state. He had the gift of easy contact with men of any race and, having found his way to the main turbine cave, he was there more than two hours, talking, through what he called 'various lingos', to the engineers and technicians. These were the men on whom the whole underground complex depended, and what he discovered, before the guards found him and hauled him back to our quarters, was that the whole place was seething with discontent.

Conditions of work was the main cause. The temperature and atmospheric difference between their workplace and their homes had become much more pronounced since Ali Khan had assumed sole control of the development of the mountain's water power and thermal potential.

'Modernization, that was his term for it,' Laun said. 'And he was not interested in working conditions, only in the efficiency of the workforce.'

He had been recruited to run the Secretariat by the old Sultan, Mohammed III, on the last of his visits to the outside. A mixture of Armenian and Iranian, he was both clever and extremely ambitious. The Sultan was looking for somebody with an industrial and managerial background to form a Secretariat that would administer the production and marketing of the state's goods now that they were becoming increasingly involved with the outside as a result of recent gemstone finds.

Most of this we learned from Antoine the following day. The Sultan had met Ali Khan on a visit to the great Nurek hydroelectric power station. He was then managing a small, specialized machine-tool plant and becoming very conscious of the fact that, with only one outlet, he had reached a point where he had nowhere to go. The fact that Mohammed III was an old man now, and had no legitimate successor, must have influenced him, since his living standards inside the Black Mountain would be drastically reduced.

Barely two years after his appointment to head the Secretariat, Mohammed III had been taken ill and had died very suddenly. By then Ali Khan had the nucleus of a guard, thugs who were mainly recruited from the Mafia with whom he had developed contacts for the marketing of the rubies they were just beginning to mine. With the people puzzled and uneasy at the sudden disappearance of the man who had led them for so long, and divided as to who should be their new ruler, he had seized the opportunity and filled the vacancy.

'There was apparently no immediate opposition,' Antoine told us. 'I suppose it seemed natural. He was the Secretariat. He has the reins of power already in his hands. He has charge of all the finance, and he has his bodyguard.' And he added, 'It was all right when he only run the Secretariat, but I think the quick realization of absolute power go to his head. He become suddenly a man very much in the mode of the old khanates and sultanates of your Great Game era. He begin ruling by fear, a despot, and he has a cruel streak in him.'

'That is what I hear,' Laun said. 'A despot in the

mode of the old khanates and sultanates of the Great Game era, like the worst of the Afghan rulers.'

Antoine nodded. 'Just so, and his temper, never really under control, becoming more and more unpredictable. Do they tell you they sent a deputation to him about the worsening conditions? Do they tell you what he does to them?' And he went straight on, his voice become quite high pitched as his words fleshed out his own fear of the man. 'He has them thrown into a damp dungeon of a cave, where the guard hang them up by their ankles and thrash the soles of their feet so badly that when they finally drop them to the floor they cannot stand. Do they tell you that?'

It was when we were alone again that Laun asked me suddenly, 'What did you do with that handgun I gave you? Way back when we were in the Khyber.'

My mind at that moment was focused on the nature of the man with whom I was supposed to do business. I had forgotten all about it. 'Put it in my briefcase, I suppose.'

'Well, check it. Caminade is scared, you see. He may be exaggerating, but it's more than a power struggle. Of that I am sure. There is a seething undercurrent of fear and revolt. And if it weren't such a feudal set-up, and they weren't so afraid of this man . . .' He shrugged. 'Go on. Check it, man. You may need it.'

The little automatic was still there, lost among a bundle of papers. I held it up for him to see and he nodded. 'Good.' He hesitated, then went on slowly, as though thinking it through as he talked, 'All it needs is a man to lead them. And a figurehead. Somebody rooted in the past, somebody who is representative of their old way of life and their traditional values. This Sultana of yours. They say she is in direct line of descent. I am talking about the peasants, the families living in the outer cave dwellings that lead straight on to the floor of the valley. They are the real people of this underground warren. They are the men and women who tend the irrigation canals and grow the food.'

He was talking about revolution. 'You must be mad,' I said. 'Have you forgotten the Sultan has his own bodyguard? Down the alleyway here, just beyond the armoury.'

'Of course I haven't forgotten.'

But my mind was still on the reason for my being here. I had no experience of dealing with a sultan, and certainly not the sort of man that he and Antoine had described.

'The day after tomorrow,' he said.

'What? What do you mean, the day after tomorrow?'

'That's when he's due to return.' And he went on, still speaking slowly, 'Ali Khan is from the world of Communism and Islamic fundamentalism, and of course the Mafia. And that has been his recruiting source. His bodyguard are imported thugs, nothing to do with the Rus, the people who have been here and formed this community over a period of twelve centuries.' He gave a shrug. 'Well, there you are then.

Praetorian guards change sides. Read your Roman history. The story of the Caesars.'

What exactly Antoine was doing here, neither Laun nor I could discover. He had a great facility for sliding away from any questions he did not wish to answer. He appeared to be waiting for the Sultan's return, but why he would not say. His nerves were on edge. We were both agreed on that, but whether it was because he had made the Sultan an offer he could not deliver and was scared of the man's violent nature, or because he had got himself involved in some secret plot to overthrow him, we could not fathom. It made for an uneasy relationship, particularly in my case, for on two separate days I had approached the Sultan's Secretary through him, requesting an audience with the Sultana. I still did not know for certain it was Vikki, and Laun was adamant that I did not try to approach her direct. On both days my request was met by the statement that the Sultana was still recovering from the birth of her child. Finally I decided I would have to bluff my way into the Secretary's private office and talk to him personally.

By then both Laun and I had come to the conclusion that the Secretary was the key man. He might not hold the power, but he held the vital offices. His name was Basil Van. Laun thought it might be an assumed name, since Van was one of the half dozen *vilayets* bonded together under a Russo-Turkish treaty a few months before the First World War, then disbanded barely two years later by the Young Turks, who caused at least half a million Armenians to be massacred on the deportation march into Syria. And Basil was the name of the Byzantine Emperor at the time the Rus dominated the Black Sea.

I managed to get as far as the opening into Basil Van's office, only to find it guarded and myself barred from entering.

And then, the following morning, just as we had finished breakfast, one of the Secretary's minions appeared and indicated by signs that I was to follow him. The word Sultana was mentioned and I thought I was being taken to her, but instead I finished up in the Secretary's personal office facing the man himself. He was seated at a big stainless-steel desk with several phones on it. He rose with a little nod of the head by way of greeting and waved me to the seat opposite him. He was full of questions. Why did I want to see the Sultana? Why not the Sultan? What was the real purpose of my visit? All this I had explained in a carefully worded letter of intent. Now he wanted it verbally, which was difficult with the interrogation jumping from one language to another. Also he seemed agitated, speaking at times so fast I had to ask him to repeat.

Finally he said, 'Okay. Now I take you to the Sultana.' But instead of getting up he leaned towards me, his hands suddenly pressed flat on the desktop as though to steady them, his voice even more agitated as he said, 'This is confidential, Mr Cartwright. Secret. You understand? It is politics.' He was speaking in English then, slowly and choosing his words with care.

Part of what he told me I already knew, but in

Antoine's version of the situation, and in Laun's, the Sultana's role was passive. The Secretary's view of her was quite different. She claimed, he said, to be a great-great-granddaughter of Thorfinn, whose family origins went back to the lost long ship and the first Pamir settlement.

'Are you sure?'

He shrugged. 'It is what they believe.'

Vikki? That little girl dancing alone on the deserted floor while the band played and the restaurant watched. That hard little body pressed against mine. And later ... It couldn't surely be Vikki. And then the Secretary said, 'She is a very strong-willed young woman. They think of her as the flag of their resistance.' And after a moment's thought, he went on, 'Oh, yes, there is resistance already.'

Now that he had switched to English he seemed gradually to be finding the words he wanted. 'And she is part of it. She is full of intrigue. She has no power. Not yet. But already she is talking to the outside world. She uses people. She uses me. I know because I do the same. She uses the technicians also, and they are descended from the Atils. She is building her own network for information.'

'You say she talks to the outside world. How?'

'Through her computer. And it is me who gets her that computer. It is very new, very powerful. She is talking to Kazakhstan, to Tajikistan, even to Chechnya.' Again that expressive shrug, the hands still flat on the desk. 'I have no way to know for certain, but that is what she says. And not to the politicians.

To the military, I think. Talking direct.' And he added, 'But not during the past week or two, of course. Not while she have this baby. And that' – he was speaking very softly – 'is something that concern me most deeply. It is a girl.'

His almost black eyes were now fastened on mine as he asked whether I really had been a close friend of the Sultana before Ali Khan found her and brought her back as his wife.

I hesitated, not sure what he expected me to say. I was out of my depth, in a world that was so far removed from the reality of my own. Yet was it? I was suddenly looking back in a mental flash at the history of my own century, man behaving to man as he had always behaved since the beginning of time. But now, it seemed, everything moving faster, and everything on a much larger scale, the cruelties to millions rather than to small groups or individuals. 'I can't answer your question, not until I have met her.' And I explained about the little girl who had danced alone on the floor of that restaurant in Constantza. And all the time I was thinking of his reference to the new computer he had acquired for her and how she talked to the world beyond this mountain state.

And then, when he began asking me about a young woman 'with an ugly mouth' she had persuaded him to extract from Kazakhstan, I knew without any doubt it was Vikki, and the ugly mouth a reference to Anamaria's harelip.

'From Alma-Ata?' I said.

He nodded. 'Yes, from Alma-Ata.'

Whether it was because I knew where she had come from I don't know, but he suddenly made up his mind, slapped his hands on the desktop and pushed himself to his feet. 'Come! I take you to the seraglio.'

He paused then, looking at me hard, wondering whether he could trust me. Finally he gave a little shrug and smiled. 'Good!' And then in a whisper, 'The Sultan, you see, he is his own bad enemy. There is a sickness, I think. Here.' And he touched his hand to his forehead. 'And remember please – I *am* the Secretariat. I administer the treasury. I have all the records. You want to do business is best for you to do business with me.'

I stood there, staring at him, momentarily stunned by this blatant attempt to bypass the Sultan. I did not say anything for a moment, staring at him and wondering what his game really was. And nobody to ask, nobody to confide in. There was Laun, of course, but by now I was beginning to wonder whether he, like Antoine, had his own reasons for behaving as he had since I had joined up with him. In the end I said, 'You know why I am here. From what you have told me I think my people can be of help to you.'

There was a moment's silence, then he nodded. 'Come! We talk about this again – but later. Now I take you to the Sultana. She is expecting you.'

He took me out through the Secretariat's main office, I think to give me an idea of the size of the operation he ran, and so impress upon me his own importance. We passed through three huge caves, all of them crowded with desks, two with desk-top computers and word processors, the third with typewriters and calculators, all the electronics required for the storing of records. Each cave was open plan and the operators were predominantly female, some of them quite young and beautiful with pale features and flaxen hair. They reminded me of Vikki, but only because of their colouring and the shape of their heads. They hadn't that hard, determined look, they were just electronic machine operators.

And then we came to a smaller cave with just two machines in it, both of them much larger than those in the main office. I thought I recognized one as an old Reuters news dispenser, but he hurried me past, merely saying, 'There are times when the Sultan has need of update information on the Outside. So many changes, eh? The Communist world falling in pieces.'

I asked him how he managed the servicing and repair of all this electronic equipment. He nodded. 'That is, of course, the big problem. It is simple to buy equipment with the sort of products we extract from the mountain, but to keep it running . . .' He shrugged, his palms spread. 'Is a problem. Ali Khan does not permit expeditions outside, not even for instruction. So everything has to be learned from manuals. And they have to be translated, of course, into the Atil language, so there are at first many mistakes. But now it is okay. We manage.'

We were back in the main tunnelway then. He ignored the parked trolley cars, walking briskly until we came to a solitary guard at the mouth of a right-hand branch turning. Suddenly there was a glimmer of daylight. Four huge double-glazed portholes looked out over the valley floor. 'Good vista, eh?' Right again and a gold-embroidered drape covering a beautifully worked marble portico. 'The Sultan's apartments.' A few metres further and we stopped at a smaller, less ostentatiously marble-panelled entrance. He pressed a bell push and spoke into a wall-mike announcing our arrival.

Was this the moment? Would she come to the entrance herself? I felt my palms suddenly moist, and I was trembling with the excitement of this moment, seeing again that little figure darting out on to that wooden square of a dance floor, the jazz tune beating at the muscles of my feet ... It was ridiculous. The passage of the years was wiped away by the strangeness of my surroundings, the whole nature of the place so alien that anything seemed possible. If I had been in a mine ... But this wasn't a mine. These were the living quarters of a mad despot of a sultan and I was standing at the entrance to his wife's apartments.

The idea that it could be Vikki was wiped from my mind and I was left wondering once again what the hell I had got myself into.

The curtain was drawn smoothly to one side and we were confronted by a steel-barred gate and the face of an elderly woman staring out at us. She acknowledged the Secretary with a brief nod. She didn't smile, but she did turn the lock and swing the gate open. The room we entered was hung with wild abstracts full of the most violent colours. I could have relaxed then if I had known anything about art, for these were unframed oils by a well-known Romanian artist. As it was, the violence of the colours only served to increase my nervous tension, though at the same time I realized how perfectly their stark sunset colours contrasted with the naked rock of the walls.

'I will leave you now,' the Secretary said. 'I expect the Sultan here about twelve thirty in time for lunch.'

I asked him when he would be able to arrange for me to see the Sultan and he gave a little shrug and shook his head, glancing down at his watch. 'Not today, I think. It is already after twelve. They will inform me when he arrives at the tunnel entrance. So I think it best you arrange with the Sultana to lunch here. He has much business to attend to.'

He went out then into the hallway with its rock-cut seats, and I heard the click of the lock as the gate shut, the swish of the heavy drape. The servant woman had also left and I was alone in this chamber of horrors. So much violence in the colouring, and the pictures themselves – I began to look at them more closely.

And then a voice said, very quietly, 'Paul. I am so glad.'

I hadn't heard her enter and I turned.

'I hear you are coming.' And again she said, 'I am so glad. Look! Here is the money, and in dollars.' She was smiling, the harelip stretched in a grimace. But her eyes were shining as she added, 'I tell you I repay you. Remember? In that room in the hotel at Istanbul. I promise I repay you.'

Stupidly all I could think to say was, 'So it is Vikki. She's here.'

I saw the light die out of her eyes, her hand with the money in it stretched out towards me. 'Take it, please.'

I shook my head. 'After all that's happened, it doesn't matter. Keep it.'

'But I promise. So here it is. You must take it, then I am out of your debt.'

And because there seemed nothing else for it, I took the money, and she turned abruptly. 'Now I get Vikki for you.' But at the curtained opening to the inner rooms she paused, looking back over her shoulder. 'I am glad. Glad that you are safe, Paul.'

And then she was gone and I was alone in that room, thinking of all the things I could have said, that I wanted to say – but hadn't. And the gold crucifix – without thinking my hand had strayed up to my neck, just to make sure. It was still there. I hadn't thanked her? And now, waiting alone in that strange rock chamber with its flamboyant pictures, waiting for Vikki – and thinking all the time of Anamaria.

I was waiting there on tenterhooks for what seemed a long time, watching the way through to her apartments, wondering what to say to her, hoping I could manage better than I had with Anamaria. I looked down at the money in my hand, wondering how she had got hold of it, hoping it was Vikki who had given it to her – the exact amount to the last cent of the cost of the ticket I had bought her. How could I make her take it back without causing offence? Perhaps if I did it through Vikki? The dollars had presumably come from her, and it was obvious she wouldn't be worrying about a few hundred dollars. And Alex couldn't complain about the cost of an extra flight ticket, not with the report I would be taking back to him.

The room was empty now, only the distant murmur of turbines and water, the silence otherwise rock hard.

Time passed. I flopped down into one of the big black leather armchairs that reminded me of the Bucureşti Hotel, and feeling the leather damp against my skin I thought there wasn't much difference between the situation here and the turmoil I had left behind in Romania. In front of me, brightly lit by the fluorescent tube just above it, was a painting of Theseus and the Minotaur. It was full of hectic movement, blood-red colours against the brown of the bull's hide and the rock walls of the labyrinth. It was in tune with my thoughts, Theseus, his hands on the wide-spread horns, somersaulting towards the upflung tail, and his dancing troupe all in the process of jumping on or off the broad back of the beast. I thought I heard a child crying and there was the faint sound of music.

I had my eyes half closed, the picture more in my mind than on the wall, so exactly did it match my own situation and the mood I was in. I never heard her enter, only the music getting louder. And then it changed. *Bolero*. And I heard a voice behind me say very softly, 'You like to dance with me.'

It wasn't a question, more an order, the voice the same but more imperious now.

I turned and looked at her, taller than I remembered. Her hair less bright and cut short like a boy, her eyes dark ringed and with none of the sparkle I remembered. She was dressed in a sari, dark gold slashed with crimson.

I could have jumped to my feet, opened my arms to her and whirled her away to the thump-thump-thump of that blood-pounding music. Instead, I rose quite slowly, almost reluctantly. 'So it *is* you!' My voice sounded far away and unfamiliar.

We stood there, facing each other for a moment, neither of us saying anything. She looked tired. But that was understandable. 'How's the baby? Was that her crying just now?'

'You know, then?'

'Know what?'

'That it is a girl.' She seemed to shake herself. 'Yes, of course, I suppose everybody knows. Gossip travels fast in the world I live in now. Have you met my husband yet?'

I shook my head.

'No, of course not. He is away.' She turned, went to the draped entrance and called out to Anamaria in Romanian. The music stopped, *Bolero* cut off in the midst of a thump.

'I look forward to meeting him,' I murmured politely.

'Yes, he will be here soon.' She glanced at the big ruby-ringed watch on her wrist, a nervous flick of the eyes and hand. 'In fact, he should have arrived by now. I hope he has had a good journey.' A pause, and then she said, 'You stay here, please.' She came towards me then. 'You will stay, yes?' She reached out and gripped my hand. 'Is better that you stay. So please. I order some food.' She turned and called out to Anamaria again. And then to me, 'What do you think of Basil Van?'

I wasn't sure how to answer her. And I wasn't at all sure how the Sultan would react to finding a stranger, and a foreigner at that, having lunch with his wife, in her private apartment. 'I think I had better go,' I said.

'No.' She gripped hold of my hand again. 'Stay with me. Please. With you here he may control himself more correctly.' She bent her head and to my astonishment kissed my hand. Her lips were cold, the imprint of her lipstick a mark of how urgently she had pressed her mouth against the back of my hand. I think it was then I began to realize how frightened she was.

She suddenly left me, flitting across the room to the sound of her humming another tune of Ravel's music. 'Ana!' She asked her for more of *Bolero*, again in Romanian, and then she was coming back to me, her hands weaving above her head as the drum-pulse filled the room once more. She seized hold of my arm, thrust it round her waist, humming all the time with the music.

God! What a bloody fool I was. I should have put her arm away from me and fled. But the music, that damned music, and her body pressed to mine. Her urgency. I could feel it in every pulse of her being. I couldn't leave her. And *Bolero* throbbing through us, my mind going back. But her body wasn't hard now. It was softer than I remembered on that first dancing occasion. She was a woman now, a mother figure with breasts grown large with the suckling demands of her daughter's mouth.

Her hand reached down and she suddenly drew back. 'What is that?'

Her fingers, probing my thigh, fastened on the hardness there, her eyes glazing for a moment. And then she drew back and her voice was hard above the music as she said, 'You fool! You stupid bloody fool!'

It was the little handgun Laun had given me. I had taken it from my briefcase and stuffed it into my trouser pocket.

'I thought . . .' She was suddenly giggling.

'What?' I asked, feeling my blood stir. 'What did you think it was?'

'Never you mind.' She was still giggling, giggling uncontrollably. Embarrassment? Women always giggle when they are embarrassed. Or was it nerves?

The music stopped abruptly and she was out of my arms. Anamaria came in with a tray of food, and from beyond the iron-grilled entrance came the sound of a different instrument, a bagpipe playing a very different tune.

I caught Anamaria's eye. 'The Sultan,' she said. 'He always has a piper greet him – every morning, every evening, whenever he moves about his sultanate. He is from the highlands, an Iranian mountain village, and it remind him of where he come from. Also, of course, to greet him when he return from the Outside.' And then I saw the hat, that battered imitation of the floppy, tug-into-any-shape Paddington Bear headgear.

She had hung it on the back of an upright chair close beside the rock archway that apparently led to the kitchen.

The skirl of the pipes was coming nearer. Anamaria had put the tray down on the centre table. She was standing very still, her eyes on Vikki, as though waiting for some sign. The female attendant – I think she was the nurse – hovered by the marble entranceway, her head on one side, listening intently. A young woman came in with a jug and some glasses on a silver tray and stopped, her mouth hanging open. The piping was suddenly much louder.

'He is coming.' This from the female attendant. She pushed her hand up through her greying hair, her eyes darting round the room.

The piping stopped abruptly and I heard Anamaria whisper, *'Dumnezeu!'* Our eyes met. 'He is not going to his apartment. He is coming straight here.' Her dark skin had gone quite white.

I turned to Vikki. She was standing tall and rigid, her features frozen into a mask of fear. Or was it hatred? Her hands plucked at the sari as a voice called through the entrance intercom for the gate to be opened – *in the name of the Sultan*.

My hand reached into the pocket of my trousers. I didn't realize it at the time, the movement entirely involuntary. There was menace in the formality of that announcement. The woman by the gate turned her head and looked at Vikki, her eyes wide like a startled animal. 'In the name of the Sultan – open!' The repetition, and the hard-voiced order, sent a shiver through the room. I suddenly realized that, apart from myself, they were all women. I was the only man present and their fear filled the room like a charge of electricity, enveloping my own nerves, so that I felt as though lightning had struck.

I saw Vikki give a slight nod, heard the sound of the locks turning, the iron-bound gate opening, and then he was striding in, hollow eyed and bearded, his skin white, his hair black. He was taller than I had expected, the same height and something of the same appearance as his Secretary, moustache and beard making an almost round frame to the red of the lips. His eyes, jet black in contrast to the pallor of his dark skin, stared straight at Vikki, gleaming with a strange sparkle in the fluorescent lighting.

'Is it true?' His voice was soft as silk.

She didn't answer, just stood there, staring at him, a sort of fascinated horror in her gaze.

Did she know what was coming? I think she did. Anamaria certainly knew.

'Where is the child?' And when nobody answered, he turned to the elderly attendant and ordered her to fetch it.

'No!' It was Vikki, a sudden cry torn from the depths of her motherhood. 'No – please, Ali.'

But the nurse had already scuttled into the inner apartment. Nobody moved. Nobody spoke. Behind the Sultan stood Basil Van. The piper was there, several of the guards, and there was Antoine lurking in the background. The cry of a child cut into the silence. The nurse was back, the baby in her arms.

There was a moment when nobody moved. It was as though we were all of us holding our breath. Then Ali Khan darted forward, his long white robe swirling around his ankles. He seized the wrinkled little creature from the nurse's arms and dumped it on the table, sweeping the luncheon things onto the floor with a crash of broken china and earthenware.

He turned then, his eyes fastened on Vikki. 'Well?' He was holding the little bundle down with his hand and he was trembling, literally trembling. And he was speaking in English, I think so that the guards and others would not understand. 'Well?' he said again. 'Which is it? A boy? Or is it a girl?'

The only answer he got was the baby's cries. It was struggling now as though the tension of the room had struck a chord in its tiny being.

'Have you lost your tongue? Speak! Boy, or girl?' And the way he said *or girl*, it was obvious he had already decided. 'If you don't tell me, then I discover the truth for myself.'

He bent down, seized the child's loose clothing with both his hands and ripped the material apart with such ferocity that the baby's female nakedness was instantly revealed in its entirety.

'So!' He stood there, like a conjuror who has just brought off a new and difficult trick. But his face was not the face of a conjuror. It was suffused with a deep, consuming rage. 'You stupid little fool! I tell you what to do if it is a female. And look!' He pointed, almost dramatically, to the deep crease between the loins where the tiny penis should have been. 'Why don't

413

you do what I say, change this thing for a boy child? Anybody's child. So long as it is a boy. I told you. But you don't do it.' And with a lightning movement of his hands he struck her across the face first on one side then the other – several times.

'Now I must do what you don't do.' He leaned forward, turning at the same time, and picking up the tiny mite by one leg, he dashed it against the rock wall. But he was so wrought up that it was the baby's shoulder that took the blow. There was a soft crunch of bone breaking, screams of shock and pain, and then he was whirling the bleeding rag round his head and this time he smashed the skull with a sound like the cracking of an egg.

It was all over and nobody seemed to have moved, all of us in a state of shock.

But one of us had moved. It was Anamaria, and whilst Vikki was still rooted to the spot, appalled whimperings issuing from her open mouth, Anamaria had drawn one of her deadly hatpins from her Paddington Bear hat, and while Ali Khan was still staring down at the bloody little mess on the floor where he had flung the dead infant like a discarded rag doll, she had sprung across the few feet that separated her from the Sultan and rammed the slender steel blade deep into his guts.

Her action triggered an instant response in me, a totally automatic reaction. My hand came out of my pocket, the little pistol gripped tight. A few paces and my fingers squeezed the trigger. I don't know what I intended. I think my purpose was to pump bullets into

414

the area of the hatpin wound so that Anamaria could not be accused of killing the bloody man. I say I think that was my purpose, but I didn't think. There was no time. I just did what in that instant I felt I had to do.

It was like Kas all over again. I saw Ali Khan's mad eyes begin to glaze, and he opened his mouth just like Kasim had opened his as the waves swept over him and he sank from sight. Does that make me a killer? Was I born with some deep instinct to kill? And Anamaria's voice in my ear saying, 'Why did you do it?' And I think she added something like, 'Oh, Paul. There was no need.'

How now! A rat? Dead for a ducat, dead! The Danish prince's words flashed into my mind as the man who had ruled this little undermountain sultanate folded slowly at the knees, then fell quite suddenly into the crockery he had swept off the table. The clatter of the broken china acted like the crack of a starter's pistol. Where most of those in the room had been frozen into shocked immobility, suddenly there was movement and the quiet hiss of expelled breath. Then somebody cried, 'Erik!' and gave instructions, a quick gabble in the native tongue. It was Antoine Caminade, moving quickly to a big, fair-haired man who had come in with Laun.

'*Guides ki-jai!*' That cry again and Laun shaking the big man's arm, the urgency in his voice transferred to the physical action. 'Come on, man! What are you waiting for?'

But the man they all knew as Erik Bigblad just stood there, staring down at that rag doll of a baby with its brains seeping out of its tiny smashed-up skull, and at the man who had killed it and was now himself an empty shell. Bigblad's eyes were wide in his broad face, wide and very blue, his stare one of disbelief.

The shock of what had happened must have been much greater for him than for the rest of us. He had only just returned from Kiev, the latest of several visits to the Soviet Union, and was totally unprepared for the scene that suddenly confronted him.

I didn't know this at the time, nor I think did Laun. 'For God's sake, man!' He was still shaking Bigblad by the arm. 'Now's your chance.' He drew back his hand and I thought for a moment he was going to slap the man's face to bring him out of his trance. But then the great shoulders heaved and he looked slowly round the room, everybody silent, watching him.

Suddenly he seemed to shake himself and in that instant he came alive, turning on his heels, quick as a flash, and shouting something incomprehensible as he dived for the entrance.

Laun was close behind him, Antoine too, and I followed them as the big fellow began to bellow out orders that rattled and boomed in the rock corridor. And away in the distance voices answering, the clash of steel, the sudden stutter of a machine-pistol, shouts and cries. We passed the entrance to the Sultan's apartment. Daylight glimmered through the four great portholes, two of the Sultan's guards lying in pools of their own blood. We turned right into the main tunnel and there was a tight-packed mass of fair-haired men outside the armoury, Kalashnikovs and hand grenades being passed out to them.

But it was all over. Black market thugs don't make good fighters. Word of what had happened had reached the Praetorian Guard and they were already busy trying to negotiate terms.

Erik Bigblad turned to us and in thick, guttural English said, 'Stop now. I command here. You go back. Tell Sultana all is gud. No problem now.'

'What are you going to do with them?' Laun asked.

The big man grinned. 'Some I think we send down the river. Others not so bad we send out by the old road tunnel.' He leaned his head down. 'You have some better plan?'

I saw Laun hesitate. But then he gave a little shrug. 'No.'

'Gud! I command now. For the Sultana. Tell her that, please. Also that I and my lieutenants will come to swear when we have bring order to her state.' And he added, 'You tell me what we shall call this new state. Or perhaps you ask the Secretary that. Ask Basil Van. He has gud brains, and we will need him. Okay?'

We left him then, and as we walked back past the four great portholes, now with a glimmer of sun on snow, back to Vikki's quarters, Laun said, 'That man is brighter than I thought.'

PART FIVE

THE LITTLE SULTANA

CHAPTER ONE

'**Why did** you do it?' He sounded more puzzled than angry. 'To go and throw everything away like that and to the top-selling broadsheet—'

'Not everything,' I murmured.

'No. Not everything, I agree. But the gaps can easily be filled in by any competent geologist, and there are plenty of those in the pay of the big mining houses.'

'Possibly,' I said. 'But to enlarge and develop what is at the moment a fairly primitive operation would require the cooperation of key personnel.'

'Basil Van.' He nodded. 'Of course. But I see no problem there. In essence he's a small-time business-man. You made that perfectly clear. So he will go where the money is. Unless of course they have killed him by the time you get back there.'

I didn't argue. I didn't tell him I hadn't yet made up my mind whether I would go back there or not. And I didn't, of course, tell him that it was Vikki, not Basil Van, who was the key – and I had had the sense to keep her out of it as far as possible when writing the article.

'But why? That's what I can't understand.' Alex Goodbody was leaning across the desk. 'Why didn't you keep your mouth shut? At least until you had talked it over with me. The people I had in mind would have paid handsomely.' And he added quickly, 'And of course we would have paid you accordingly. Or on a percentage basis if you wanted it that way.'

'That's the trouble,' I said. 'The payment would have been to your people, not to me.' I had had almost three weeks to think this thing through. All the difficulties and delays of travelling back through Dushanbe and Samarkand, by ferry across the Caspian from Krasnovodsk to Baku, and then by tanker from Batum on the Black Sea to Constantza, finally a delayed flight out of Otopeni, the Bucharest airport, to London's Stansted Airport. And I had been on my own, nobody to talk to – all the time in the world to consider my options.

'I suppose you'll be writing a book about your experiences?' He was feeling me out now, wondering doubtless how much he would have to pay me to get his hands on my contacts.

'Maybe.' That was what the agency through which I had sold the article had advised, and I was still thinking about it. It would not be for the money, though that would be an important factor if I did decide to form my own company, but to build up a reputation for myself.

'If you'll excuse me . . .' I was scrambling to my

feet, in a hurry now to get out of that office where he was the boss and, viewed from where he sat, I was just a raw recruit to the Potentials operation, a relative new boy who, because I had been in the right place at the right moment, had fallen on his feet and got himself involved in a very peculiar set-up that might or might not prove to be a winner.

'I need more time,' I murmured.

'You've had plenty of time.' His voice had changed. It was harder, much harder, a warning, I realized, that I was now going to have to face up to quite a different man. This was the Alex Goodbody – AG to his staff – who faced up in his turn to the high-powered negotiators of some of the world's largest international conglomerates, struggling for a slice of the action that would at least cover Resource Potentials' costs, and preferably ensure a profit for the organization commensurate with the size of the deal he had been able to arrange.

I suddenly felt quite scared of him. I knew it was irrational, but his face was set now in chiselled lines, his eyes gone hard and staring into mine across the desk. This wasn't an ordinary man. He was more than just a mining engineer turned businessman, his contacts extending into some very dark corners. Nothing I could prove. Just something sensed. I was suddenly remembering again the scene in the cutting on the Khyber, the engine and the brakes showering sparks, Gingin in Laun's arms, and Laun himself – the Great Game, modern version – and Z, his sudden death . . . If I formed my own company, operating it as a learner, on my own – I'd be out of my depth and alone, facing men like Goodbody, and others probably, much more ruthless.

A moment's hesitation and then I said, 'I'm sorry. I need time. Please understand. It's a big decision I have to make.'

The silence that had descended on that large office held for a moment longer, the eyes staring at me out of that rock-hard face, and myself standing there, rooted to the spot, like a rabbit transfixed by a snake.

'Of course.' He was suddenly giving me the kindly smile routine. 'Once, when I was a kid' – his voice no longer grated, the lines of his face smoothed out – 'I had a similar decision to make. You go away and think about it. I know how you feel. Take your time. But not too much.' He was also on his feet now and he held out his hand, and with the other he pulled his desk diary towards him. 'Let's see now. Today's Tuesday. Shall we say Thursday? I've a lunch appointment, but the evening's free. The Savoy Grill, seven thirty. That suit you?' And when I nodded, he slapped me on the shoulder. 'Have a good rest, my boy. You're tired now, probably a little confused, finding yourself back in London again after the places and situations you've been in.'

He saw me to the door, then paused. 'My secretary has booked you into a nice little service flat we have just off St James's Street. You'll be quiet there and able to think.' He opened the door. 'Just one other thing. I told you I had had a similar decision to make. I was about your age then, a little younger. Very naïve. I had

424

just pulled off a good contract, the world at my feet, and I thought all of life would be as simple as that. As I say, I was very naïve.'

He nodded, smiling. And that was that.

I had two whole days, all on my own – the key to a flat in the very centre of London, the freedom to use my credit card for anything I wanted. His secretary had smiled at me a little sadly as she said that, adding, 'You'll find Bessie is used to looking after men who've been running a hard project.'

Bessie was the resident housekeeper at what turned out to be an apartment, rather than a flat. It took up the whole of the third floor of an old Georgian building. And Bessie was quite a girl. However, I went straight to bed on my own and lay there in the dark, thinking, just thinking. But it didn't help me to make a decision. It didn't even send me to sleep. My mind went over and over the pros and cons, all the possibilities.

And then it was Wednesday morning, pale grey and wintry. Did I flip a coin? But I hadn't got a coin, only a lot of foreign notes and that credit card. And then I suddenly remembered that poor, wretched girl, the way she had said no, it was impossible, she couldn't leave Vikki when everything was in a 'flux'. Such an odd word for her to use. I wondered where she had got it from, whether there was some significance in her use of it. Recalling the scene in that cave room full of violently coloured pictures, with Erik Bigblad's men wrapping Ali Khan's corpse in the cloth that had been set for our lunch and carrying it out, and her eyes fixed on mine, big and almost luminous. She had wanted to come, and yet, with barely a moment's hesitation, she had rejected my offer.

And I was glad. That was what really hit me now. My reaction had been one of relief. If she had said yes, she would come with me, then I would have been responsible for her and have landed myself with an open-ended commitment, the cost of which would make any decision to leave Resource Potentials and go it alone out of the question.

I had said goodbye to Vikki, even kissed her. But it meant nothing. Anamaria was waiting to see me out, standing by the barred gate in the rock alcove of the entrance. She had held out her hand to me and wished me luck and a safe journey. It had been a tentative gesture and I was conscious of the fact that she was trembling slightly. I was tempted to kiss the hand, a gesture of contrition for having accepted her decision to stay with such alacrity, but I was afraid if I did so she would immediately think I hadn't kissed her properly because of her mouth. So we just shook hands and without a backward glance I had followed Laun to our quarters and packed the things I needed for the journey. When that was done, and I had checked out with the Secretariat, I had proceeded straight to the steel doors that sealed the abandoned tunnel off from the outside world.

I was longer than I expected at the Secretariat. It wasn't just the passes and the visas that had had to be prepared for me, there was also Basil Van to see and the need to explain the role I could play in the market-

426

ing and the mining of the recently located corundums, particularly the rubies. And all, of course, without committing myself, particularly as Laun Said had been present part of the time.

We could have talked for much longer, but the Secretary had more immediate problems to deal with. Erik Bigblad's lieutenants kept on interrupting us. A lot of decisions had to be made, and quickly. The speed with which the Secretariat dealt with them was proof that Van had been preparing for this moment over a long period, and from what he had already told me, that Vikki was the 'flag of their resistance', I realized that it was almost certainly he who had decided Vikki should succeed Ali Khan, ruling the state as the Sultana.

I must have gone to sleep again, for I woke with a start to a knock on the door and the grate of a key turning. It was eight thirty and the maidservant came in with a tray and a wonderful smell of coffee.

Breakfast in bed, an English breakfast – bacon, eggs, kidneys, mushrooms and fried bread – real coffee and an English newspaper. Outside, the sounds of London winding itself up for the day reached me distantly, all those millions coming to work, keeping the great city's business cogs turning, and I was lying here, luxuriating in the knowledge that I was back in my own country and I didn't have to travel anywhere, not today, or tomorrow. No tickets to worry about, no visas, no travel connections to keep, no climbing impossible mountain tracks; I was back in my own country, and for this day at any rate I was a man of leisure with nothing to worry about.

And then the bedside phone rang. It was AG. 'Everything all right, Paul?' Only once before had he used my Christian name, that was when he had phoned me at the Bucureşti to tell me I would be taking over from Z.

'Yes, everything's fine,' I said. 'Very comfortable.'

'Good, good. Now, a man has just phoned the office here, from Schipol Airport. He wants to see you and can be in London by 1300 hours. Says it's urgent. I suggested you meet in the bar of the Café Royal. Okay?' And he added, 'For obvious reasons we don't like anybody outside of the organization to know where our people hole up in London.'

'Who is he?'

'Wouldn't give his name, but he's French and said you'd know who it was if he said his family came from Domme.'

'Caminade!' I said. 'Antoine Caminade.'

There was a grunt of agreement. 'The man who tailed you from Bucharest right across to India's North-West Frontier. We've checked on him. He has some sort of vague connection with DC Minérales de Toulouse.' There was a pause, as though he was thinking about that. Then he said, 'I have told my secretary to have a table booked for you at 1330. I shall be most interested to know why he wants to see you so urgently. And remember, as of this moment you are still in our employ. You understand, Paul?' And he rang off, not waiting for my reply.

I put the phone down, trying to remember whether I had referred to Antoine by name in that article.

So much for the leisurely day in which to sort myself out and decide whether or not to take the plunge and go it alone as a mining consultant. It meant an office, a secretary and an accountant to cope with the Inland Revenue, and there would be VAT – all the boring financial details that I knew existed, but which I had never had to handle myself. To start with I would have to form a company, arrange a bank account, lodge shares and there would have to be a company secretary. Oh, my God! The ramifications were endless. And I would still have to earn the money to keep the thing going.

Antoine was punctual to the minute and his usual ebullient self, despite having come through from Samarkand, disposing of all the western Communist republics and East European countries in two days. He was wearing a Russian fur hat with earflaps tucked up on each side of his head like the ears of a teddy bear and an overcoat with padded shoulders and what he assured me was a genuine markhor goatskin collar. It looked very odd and I was glad when he took it off and handed hat and coat to the waiter.

He didn't want an aperitif. I was having a Virgin Mary and he said that would suit him fine, adding that he never took hard liquor in the middle of the day.

There was something oddly exciting about the brasserie at the Café Royal. The association with

Oscar Wilde perhaps, and the brash decor, as it was then, seemed the perfect background for Antoine's ridiculous flamboyance. Also, it was just right for the mood I was in, which was one of expectation, almost of elation, as though my whole being was poised for take-off into the flight of fantasy that had filled my head ever since my interview with AG.

I don't remember what we ate, but with the Potentials credit card still in my pocket, I ordered the best claret they could produce, which was good enough for Antoine to say he would stick with it when we came to the coffee. And it was then, over that second bottle, that he said something that made up my mind for me.

He was telling me about his last day at what Laun and I had come to regard as the State of Nirvana, the lake being the *raison d'être* and the driving force of the whole underground complex. It was a fascinating and very graphic description of the ceremony of Swearing, the great horns of bone blown as each man came forward to pledge his allegiance to Vikki. And the men themselves, all the most important members of the community, with long, straight-bladed swords, some with helmets, brightly burnished and emblazoned. He was floating his hands in the air to emphasize the individual characteristics of each chieftain. They were all male.

And then, suddenly, he mentioned the name Ibn Khazar. 'Strange, is it not? No women present in that grand cavern with the great open archway looking out on to the lake. Just the one, of course, sitting alone on a bearskin stretched over her rock "throne". All men

– *tous hommes*. And they are swearing loyalty to her, loyalty to the death. Why? Because she claims Thorfinn among her forebears. Nothing more. They don't know that she has hacked her way into the upper circles of at least one of the Red Army units that were in the Afghan War. And if they did, they would not understand.'

'They are following the lead of Erik Bigblad,' I said.

'I know, I know – *d'accord*. But not all.' And that is when I heard the name Ibn Khazar for the first time. The Khazars of Atil, he explained, had controlled the long-ship route south down the Volga in the ninth century. That was how the Khazar descendants in Nirvana had got their position and why they had such influence in the *Thing*, the political gathering that had apparently not met since Ali Khan had seized power. 'Ibn Khazar did not move when his name was called. You did not know this, did you?'

'No,' I said.

He nodded. 'It is important, Paul, because he is a schemer, and a dangerous man. He has connections with the Moscow Mafia and, with his followers, he represents a significant opposition. He refuses to swear, and so do all the others who are standing in a little group round him. And they are armed.'

He paused there, leaning across the table, his eyes catching the light of a candelabra, so that with those round, metal-framed glasses he had the appearance once again of an owl.

'I thought for a moment there would be trouble,'

he went on. 'Erik and some of his people were also reaching for their weapons. But then that young woman, sitting quite upright on her fur-cushioned rock seat, called them to order. She was speaking in the vernacular of the cave people and her voice, perhaps because it was the only feminine voice there and of a higher timbre, cut across the growling of the men like the flash of a sword. She was demanding a refer-endum, the vote to be taken there and then, and she ordered that the number of those willing to swear the oath and the number of those refusing be entered in the records. And then, when the vote had been taken, she ordered those who had refused to withdraw, since they could no longer be regarded as part of the Swear-ing ceremony.'

He stopped there, his sense of the dramatic overrid-ing his compulsion to exploit me as his sole audience.

'So what happened?' I asked, supplying the neces-sary prompt.

He leaned back, smiling. 'Ibn Khazar is not a tall man. In fact, he is quite small. As I say, a schemer, very Slav in appearance, and Erik, squat and fair, is pushing towards him through the packed cave. Ibn Khazar stands there for a moment – stands his ground, I think you would say. Then his supporters become unnerved. There are fifty-two of them. But gathering around Erik are the long-ship descendants, all thickset, fair-haired men. At the counting they had numbered a thousand and thirty-one, all of them growling out their willingness to take the oath.'

'And the Khazars?' I asked.

He waved his hands in a gesture of dismissal. 'They begin to melt away. I see Ibn Khazar standing there until he is alone, staring with, I think, some hostility at that little Sultana of yours. Then he is gone.'

'So what happened then? Were they attacked?'

'No. Nothing happen. They just melt away, and the Swearing is continuing without them.'

'Hardly surprising,' I murmured, 'the odds against them being so great.' But I did not like it, the whole stability of the project put in jeopardy. And the man facing me across the table, a Frenchman, and for all I knew a man who also had contacts with the Mafia.

The coffee came and the second bottle, carefully decanted at the table. My mind was running back over the times Antoine had infiltrated himself into my life, back to that first meeting in the Bucureşti. And now, coming post-haste from the Pamirs and somehow managing to contact AG by phone immediately on his arrival in Holland, and then to persuade him that it was worth his while to fix up this meeting with me. There had to be a reason, something he had not told me.

I refilled his glass, watching him out of the corners of my eyes. 'Why are you here?' I said quietly as though it was an afterthought.

I saw the hesitation as he considered how to answer me. Finally, with a little shrug, he said, 'To arrange something. What else?'

'Did Goodbody authorize you to deal with me direct?'

'No, he don't authorize me nothing.'

'Then why did he arrange for you to meet me? Is he planning a tie-up between your people and his?'

He drew in his breath, the intake of the air making a little sucking sound between his teeth. 'Per'aps.' He didn't look at me, his long fingers playing with the pepperpot, shifting it about as though it was a Dalek. 'It depends,' he added. 'I don't know for sure who your people are, do I?'

So he had leapt to that possibility. I tried another direct question. 'Have you talked to DC Minérales de Toulouse about it?'

A pause, and then he shook his head. 'Not yet.'

'Why not? Is there some other organization you have to consult?'

He picked up his glass. '*C'est bon, ça,*' he murmured, avoiding my question, and drinking slowly, reflectively. Then suddenly he put the glass down again, his mind made up. 'I don't work for them. I work for myself. But I have an arrangement with them, so that if your people don't pay for this luncheon I charge it to them.' A flash of those very white teeth and a wink. 'They are very rich. Most disgustingly rich. And they pay nothing, except for results. You understand what I mean? That is why I say I work for myself. I am a consultant, like your Monsieur Goodbody and his Resource Potentials.'

He hesitated for a while, then leaning suddenly forward in a very conspiratorial manner he asked me straight out whether I had considered going it alone. 'You have all the qualifications, a degree in mining, even a course in business efficiency and some experi-

ence of merchant banking.' He gave a little laugh. 'You
see, it is all there in the little dossier on you my people
prepare. Now' – his voice dropped almost to a whisper
– 'in the Nirvana . . . That is what you call it, eh?'

I nodded, waiting, wondering what was coming,
but pretty certain I knew. 'Well?'

'You and I,' he went on. 'We are sitting on something that is maybe very big. Do you agree?'

I didn't say anything, leaving it to him to make the
running.

'Okay. We are agreed. All the time – I have to
admit it – you have been ahead of me. And now I will
be very frank, all my cards, as you say, on the table. I
cannot move without you.'

'Why?'

His eyes were fixed on me, but not with hostility.
I thought I detected something of a pleading look as
he went on, 'Before I leave to come here I have a long
talk with Basil Van.' He paused, and I could see he
was thinking out exactly what he was going to say.
And then, choosing his words very carefully: 'What he
tell me is this – and these are his actual words – he said
he was not in a position to reach any sort of agreement
or contract with me or with Minérales de Toulouse.
That was a matter for the Sultana. But he warned me
he thought she would not make any agreement without
consulting you. In brief, *mon ami*, you are the key to
any outside contract. How you get to that position I
do not ask, but I have my suspicions.' That with a
flicker of his left eye. 'And there is that young woman
with the split lip and the limp.'

He stopped there, a long, reflective silence. 'I saw what happen, of course, when the girl baby is killed by the Sultan, and then what that woman does, and what you do. I don't know whether you realize this, *mon ami*' – and he patted my hand – 'but you are lucky to be alive, vair lucky. I know all that, what I don't know, of course, is what go on before – why you are in such a privilege position.'

He looked at me, staring hopefully, and when he realized I wasn't going to enlighten him, he returned to that last interview he had had with Secretary Van. It was then that he told me something I did not know. 'Ibn Khazar himself is expendable,' he said. 'Like I say, he is a schemer. I think per'aps Erik, who is a born leader, but has not too much up here.' He tapped his forehead. 'I think per'aps Erik would have liked to take him up in the hoist and put him out onto the Black Mountain to fend for himself. But he cannot do that without the Khazar people agree. And the Khazar people are very important. Neither he, nor the Sultana, nor any of us – we cannot afford to lose them.'

'Why on earth not?'

'They are most of the brains of the community. They are the engineers, the electric experts, the mechanics. They have drawn the charts of the water channels and the electric cables. They service the hoist, the electric cars, the turbines, the air conditioning and ventilation system, and it is they who construct and install that retracting mountain-top aerial. In fact, those fifty-two Khazars virtually keep the place running. That is why those underground people cannot afford to lose them. So . . .' He picked up the wine carafe, refilled his glass, then passed it to me. '*Santé!*' A flash of those white teeth again. '*Et bonne fortune! I think we need it, yes?*'

'You're going back?'

'But of course. And you? You will go back, surely?'

I didn't say anything for a moment, drinking my wine and considering. Was I going back? Why did he think I would? And then I realized, seeing it from his point of view: those two women, of course, the fascination of the place, the challenge and the promise of a future stretching before me.

My return to Nirvana seemed suddenly inevitable.